The Ottoman Secret

RAYMOND KHOURY

PENGUIN BOOKS

PENGUIN BOOKS

UK | USA | Canada | Ireland | Australia
India | New Zealand | South Africa

Penguin Books is part of the Penguin Random House group of companies
whose addresses can be found at global.penguinrandomhouse.com

First published in the United States as *Caliphate* by Forge 2019
First published in Great Britain as *The Ottoman Secret* by Michael Joseph 2019
This edition published by Penguin Books 2019

002

Copyright © Raymond Khoury, 2019

The moral right of the author has been asserted

This is a work of fiction. All of the characters, organizations and events portrayed in this novel are
either products of the author's imagination or are used fictitiously

Set in 11.88/14.2 pt Garamond MT Std
by Integra Software Services Pvt. Ltd, Pondicherry
Printed and bound in Great Britain by Clays Ltd, Elcograf S.p.A.

A CIP catalogue record for this book is available from the British Library

ISBN: 978-1-405-93961-4

History is nothing but the lies that
are no longer disputed

Napoleon Bonaparte

The Players

Jon II **Sobieski**	King of Poland and commander of the Pope's relief army
Count von **Starhemberg**	Commander of Vienna during the siege of 1683
Georg **Kolschitzky**	Polish translator and trader, hero of the siege of 1683

Prologue

The sultan wasn't sure what woke him up.

A ruffle of air, a barely detectable flutter of movement, a disturbance at the edge of his consciousness. Whatever it was, it was enough to cause him to stir within the lush expanse of his bedding and crack open his eyes, slightly at first as they adjusted to the faint light of the glowing embers in the fireplace, then jolting wide once they focused to reveal the tall figure standing by the side of his bed.

'*Salamu alaykum,* padishah,' the man said, his voice calm and low.

The sultan bolted off his pillow, his pulse rocketing with fear as he tried to process what he was seeing: an intruder— an assassin?—here, in his sumptuous chamber, deep in the palace, past an army of guards and eunuchs.

Not just an intruder: the man was, the sultan now realized, naked.

'What the—who are y—'

'Shhh,' the man ordered him, bending down with lightning speed to press one hand firmly against the sultan's mouth while raising his own index finger to his lips. 'Be calm and stay quiet, Your Sublimity. I'm not here to cause you any harm.'

Confusion now flooded in alongside the fear. The sultan struggled to breathe evenly and fought to regain some kind of control over his senses, but the barrage of inexplicable stimuli wasn't giving him any respite, for now that his eyes were finally focused, he could also see that the man's chest was covered with strange markings. Tattoos of words and numbers and drawings and diagrams, all over his torso.

'I need you to listen,' the man said.

He wasn't speaking Ottoman Turkish, the official language of the empire since its inception. It wasn't Persian either, a language the educated upper echelon of society could speak and read, mostly used for literature and poetry. No, the man was using an unusual dialect of Arabic, a language the sultan only used when reading and discussing religious verse.

'But before you do,' he continued, 'I need you to believe.'

The man held the sultan's gaze, then dropped his chin and shut his eyes. He mumbled some words the sultan couldn't make out. Then he vanished.

He simply disappeared.

The sultan's head snapped left, right, scanning the vast room in utter panic. What kind of magic was this? Then, a few seconds later, the man reappeared without any warning, standing at the far side of the chamber by the two-tiered marble fountain.

'I'm here to help you, Your Eminence' the man told the sultan. 'But in order for that to happen, I need you to believe what I say.'

Another mumble, then he disappeared again.

The sultan was now sitting up, rigid with paralysis. His breathing was frantic, his heart galloping furiously inside his chest. He thought of calling out for his guards. One scream and a dozen of his most trusted janissaries would come charging through the door, sabres drawn. But he hesitated. In part, he was too shocked, too terrified to react. He also thought they might take him for a fool if the intruder wasn't there.

Before he could ponder things too much, the man was

back, where he'd first appeared, right by the sultan's bed, mere inches from him. Only this time, the intruder reached down to the floor and raised a *yataghan,* a short sabre with a curved blade that was so sharp it could lop off a man's head with a single flick. The sultan recognized it as one he kept in a display cabinet by the divan, only it wasn't there any more. It was now pressed against his neck.

'If I wanted to kill you, you would have already died a thousand deaths,' the man said. 'But as I said, I'm here to be of service. More importantly, I'm here to save you and Kara Mustafa Pasha from a catastrophic defeat.'

Then he disappeared again, and the dagger fell to the ground and clattered against the marble flooring.

Almost instantly, the man appeared again, at the foot of the bed.

The sultan lurched back and slammed against the bed's gilded headboard. His breath was coming short and fast, and he was overcome with violent shivers.

What was this creature, and how did it know about his plans?

He studied the intruder. 'Who are you?' he asked. 'What are you? Are you'—he hesitated, then asked—'a *djinn*?'

The stranger's face cracked under the hint of a smile.

Unlike his father, Mehmed wasn't mentally unstable or degenerate. He was a quiet and melancholy man, but he had one obsession: the legacy of his conquering ancestors. He was immersed in the mystique of the dynasty to which he belonged, and hungered to mimic his ancestors' exploits. Lately, he had thrown himself into research to prepare for the coming summer's offensive, carefully studying the chronicles of past military campaigns that lined the shelves of the imperial archives. But Mehmed was also a pious man, and, as such, was very familiar with the *djinns*, the supernatural creatures of Islamic mythology romanticized as 'genies'. They enjoyed free will and could be agents of good and evil.

Without flinching, the intruder watched him in silence. 'I am a friend who wants to help you achieve success beyond anything you've dreamed of,' he finally told him. 'And if you heed my words and allow me to assist you, I can promise you that the Golden Apple will only be the beginning of your great and most glorious legacy.'

His words caught the sultan's breath.

How could this intruder know what they were planning?

Two months earlier, the sultan's gardeners had planted the imperial tug outside the palace gates—out in the open, for all to see. The meaning of the ancient war banners—tall, elaborately carved crimson poles topped by a flurry of horses' tails—was well known, as it was a ritual that dated back to the days of the sultan's steppe warrior ancestors: the Commander of the Faithful would be going to war.

The objective of the campaign, however, was a closely guarded secret.

'Oh, yes, your eminence. I know all about your meeting with Kara Mustafa last week,' the tattooed man continued, referring to the sultan's grand vizier. 'I know that once the winter snows melt, your army will be marching west. I also know its target won't be the piddling fortified towns that pepper the lands west of Belgrade. No, your army will be marching on Vienna itself and on Leopold, the usurper who dares call himself Holy Roman Emperor.'

Leopold. The mere mention of the man's name made Mehmed's blood boil.

The sultan nursed a hatred for Leopold I that was far more severe than that for his other enemies in Russia or Poland. Mehmed, as the occupier of the old imperial Byzantine throne in Constantinople, considered himself the rightful

Kayser-i-Rum—the Caesar of the Roman Empire. To him, the Habsburg monarch was a false claimant to the throne, one who ruled from a distant city that had no historical significance to the old empire. Stripping him of his capital and converting his people to the one true faith would be a most fitting end to his brazen delusions.

'Listen to me,' the intruder continued, 'and you'll fly the flag of Islam over the Golden Apple and turn its great cathedral into a mosque. And that'll only be the beginning. Listen to me, and you won't be known as *avci* any more. Even *fatih* won't be enough. They'll need a stronger word to describe your conquests.'

Avci. Oh, how he hated that word.

It was as if the strange, naked man was peering into his very soul.

Under previous sultans, the Ottomans had reached the gates of Vienna twice. Both times, they had failed to take the city. And although the empire's territorial expansion in Africa and Europe during Mehmed's reign had reached its peak, he couldn't really claim credit for these triumphs. Those conquests were the work of his grand viziers. Mehmed himself was more renowned for his abilities at hunting down stags and bears in the forests around his palace at Edirne—a far cry from the exploits of his legendary uncle, the sultan Murad IV, who had taken Erivan and Baghdad, and his namesake and illustrious ancestor Mehmed II, who had conquered Constantinople and toppled the Byzantine Empire at the ripe old age of twenty-one. Both sultans had fully earned their epithets of *fatih*—the conqueror. Mehmed IV, however, had to content himself with *avci*—the hunter.

Taking Vienna would change all that.

A barrage of questions assaulted the sultan's mind. He was scared, beyond any fear he'd ever known. But he was also intrigued.

He calmed his breathing and, after one final internal debate, nodded.

'Tell me more.'

One year later, almost to the day, in early September of 1683, the army of Christendom was finally within striking distance of Vienna and the Ottoman army that had laid siege to it since the beginning of summer.

Sixty thousand warriors were now gathered on open ground outside the small town of Tulln, lined up in front of its wooden defensive palisade for the grand ceremonial review that would precede their heroic march into battle.

The beleaguered capital was only twenty miles away.

Facing them from outside the large ceremonial tent were their leaders, the princes and dukes that Pope Innocent XI had summoned and financed, all of them illustrious and battle-hardened professional soldiers of the highest order. They were all here to halt the advance of the largest army ever seen in Europe, a Muslim army that threatened not just Vienna but their own states.

At the centre of this pre-eminent line-up was the most senior of them all, the army of liberation's main commander: John III Sobieski, King of Poland and Grand Duke of Lithuania.

Sobieski—an ox of a man and a formidable military leader—had ridden in a week earlier at the head of an army of fifteen thousand horsemen. His force included two thousand *husaria,* the fierce 'winged' hussars; with their sixteen-foot lances, spear-like swords, and plumed helmets, they were the most fearsome heavy cavalry of their time.

It had been a long, hard march, and the Polish king was exhausted. Still, as he surveyed his troops, he felt a surge of pride and anticipation. He knew that the hopes of a deeply worried Europe rested most heavily on his shoulders, and he would not disappoint its people. He couldn't. God had tasked him with saving the Christian states from the heathens. It was, he was certain, his destiny. His eternal place at Saint Peter's side was assured.

He stood in muted appreciation as the troops, musketeers, dragoons and cuirassiers, their cannon and mortars proudly on display, were paraded before him and the rest of the commanders. As the final regiment took up its position, he turned and glanced at the man to his right, Charles, Duke of Lorraine.

He didn't need to say anything. His look of utter confidence said it all.

It was a look Lorraine knew well. The duke, who still walked with a limp from a broken leg sustained in battle seven years earlier, was the brother-in-law of the Habsburg emperor. Leopold had appointed him field commander of his forces earlier that year. An affable, unpretentious man, the duke was, like Sobieski, a fierce, courageous soldier who bore his battle scars proudly and commanded great respect and trust from his men.

His presence by Sobieski's side only heightened the Polish king's confidence.

With all the troops now in place, the king and the duke led the rest of the commanders in kneeling before their men while the Archbishop of Gran prepared to celebrate Mass and bless the valiant soldiers of Christ. The emperor himself was not there. The cowardly Leopold and his court had fled the capital one week before the arrival of the Ottoman army earlier that summer, and he had no intention of joining the men who were here to save it. He wasn't alone; more than fifty thousand Viennese had followed their monarch in abandoning the city for safer ground further west. Their places were taken over by an equal number of country folk who fled the neighbouring villages and sought refuge behind the city's fortified walls—a refuge that was on the verge of collapse.

Sobieski knew how desperate things were. For weeks, the Ottomans had rained cannon fire on the besieged city. At the same time, Ottoman sappers had dug tunnels under its defensive walls and exploded mines to wreck them. The Viennese defenders had so far managed to repel each assault, but they were bloodied, starved and exhausted. From messages sneaked out of the city by intrepid couriers, Sobieski knew it would only take one final well-placed charge to cleave an opening through the fortifications and allow the Turks to stream into the city. He also knew that when that happened, no one would be spared.

The sultan had already sent two missives to Leopold in which he'd laid out his intentions in startlingly clear terms. Ottoman rules of engagement prescribed that any city that did not accede to the sultan's demand of surrender and open its gates, and whose people did not forsake their religion and convert to Islam, would not be spared. Flayed skins and sacks of severed heads would be gifted to the victorious pasha, and those who were not put under the blade would be enslaved.

Sobieski and the rest of the gathered commanders had also heard first-hand reports of how Kara Mustafa Pasha, the grand vizier at the head of the sultan's army, had demonstrated that his master would be taken at his word: en route to Vienna, a few miles outside the city, Kara Mustafa had his men slaughter all four thousand citizens of the small town of Perchtoldsdorf—after its garrison had surrendered. They also burned down its church, which was packed with women and children. The people of Vienna had taken note. Kara Mustafa's bloodthirst ensured that they would fight to the death.

As far away as England and Spain, terrified prayers were given in churches asking for salvation from the heathen invasion.

It would all hinge on the men gathered here, at Tulln.

With the court choristers in mid-hymn, something caught Sobieski's eye. It came from the far right of the plain, at the very edge of the gathered force: a cloud of dust, topped by several fluttering flags.

The profound solemnity of the moment made the disturbance all the more egregious.

Even from this great distance, he immediately realized what he was looking at: intricately woven silk flags carrying Koranic verses, ones that served to remind soldiers of their faith while invoking a sense of divinely protected victory.

Ottoman flags.

Sobieski stiffened and he glanced at Lorraine. The duke's face mirrored his own angry scowl. Lorraine had evidently also recognized the sultan's banners.

The procession caused a ripple of commotion across the gathered troops as it advanced slowly, unhindered. The hot, still air was choked with portent and malice, and yet, the small convoy was allowed to progress. As it drew nearer, Sobieski could now make out three horsemen, each of them carrying a banner and trailing a camel.

They made their way across the ground until they were within fifty yards of the ceremonial tent. A wall of guards moved to block their advance, swords raised. The lead horseman calmly raised his arm and brought the convoy to a halt just before them. Then the three riders dismounted, took a few steps toward the guards and the royal enclosure, and, with the edges of the guards' swords hovering a hair's breadth from their necks, bowed.

Sobieski and Lorraine exchanged a confused look. They didn't know what to make of this. Envoys of the Ottoman host, clearly—but for what reason? Within days, if not hours, they would be engaged in a fight to the death. What did this signify? They could see that the riders were dressed in ceremonial costume and didn't seem to be armed. More intriguing were the camels, which were huge, adorned with exquisitely embroidered fabrics and precious metal trimmings, and carried large carved-leather packs hung across their backs.

Sobieski studied the lead horseman, who now straightened and slowly pulled his coat wide open, as did his companions, to show that they were unarmed. Indeed, no muskets, pistols or sabres were strapped across their chests. The lead Ottoman turned to show the guards as much, then turned back to face the king and made a gesture asking for permission to approach the enclosure.

The Polish king was a hard and naturally suspicious man, but he was also a pragmatist. If this was another formal demand for surrender, he would have two of the envoys executed before the third, who would be allowed to return to his master to relay its rejection. But a summons for surrender didn't require three loaded camels. Was there something else on the sultan's mind? A call to negotiate a truce, perhaps? Something that might spare the inevitable deaths that were to come, even with victory?

The commander of the guards looked to Sobieski for instructions. The king motioned for the riders to be let through.

Shadowed very closely by the guards whose swords were still drawn and ready, the three men moved as one, advancing in triangular formation with measured pace until they were standing no more than fifteen feet from the gathered commanders. There, they bowed again.

The leader said, 'I carry greetings from His Eminence my lord padishah Mehmed the fourth, the Sultan of Sultans, Khan of Khans, Commander of the Faithful and ruler of the black and white seas and of Rumeli, and from his most valiant serasker in this holiest of campaigns, the grand vizier Kara Mustafa Pasha.'

Sobieski studied the Ottoman as an interpreter translated his words. The envoy, a tall man who was not out of his twenties, was sweating profusely, but the king saw no fear in his eyes. It was clearly more from the long ride under the harsh summer sun while dressed in full ceremonial regalia: baggy *shalwar* trousers, long boots, turban and a flowing red coat.

'My greetings to your eminent master, soldier. And what is the purpose of your venture?'

The envoy bowed again. The two men with him did the same. Then he straightened and looked the king straight in the eye.

'I have been sent to convey a message from my master.'

Sobieski frowned. 'And what would that be?'

The man didn't react at first. Then a wry, curiously serene smile seeped across his face and he said, 'He wishes you a peaceful journey,' before adding, *'Allahu akbar.'*

And with that, he slipped his hands in his pockets, and before the king, the guards or any of the commanders could even react, he blew up.

As did the two other envoys and the camels—a massive explosion that ripped through the royal enclosure and reduced it and everything around it to flaming debris.

Confusion and panic streaked across the gathered troops as they watched their leaders disappear in a raging fireball. The real horror, however, was yet to descend on them, the one that was now being heralded by the piercing war cries and the deep, ominous thuds of Ottoman kettledrums echoing out from behind the nearby hills.

In that instant, in a blink of an eye, everything changed.

History changed.

Sobieski wouldn't lead his winged hussars to a crushing defeat of the Ottoman army in the fields outside Vienna. He wouldn't save the city, nor would he stand before the grand vizier's ravaged camp in victory and proclaim '*Venimus, vidimus, deus vicit*' ('We came, We saw, God conquered'). The grand vizier wouldn't flee to Belgrade, where, on the sultan's orders, three months later—on Christmas Day, as church bells were ringing across Europe—he would be strangled, decapitated, have his head skinned and stuffed and presented to the sultan at his hunting palace in Edirne. Three years later, the Duke of Lorraine wouldn't retake Buda from the weakened Ottomans. Max Emmanuel wouldn't liberate Belgrade two years after that. Prince Eugene of Savoy wouldn't deal a crushing blow to the sultan at Senta in 1697.

There would be no miraculous victories, no 'Age of Heroes'. They were all dead, blown to bits in the meadow outside Tulln, with no one to fill their illustrious boots.

Nothing like this had ever been done before.

The Ottoman envoy had used explosives that were twenty times more powerful than gunpowder. In fact, up until that day, the sticks strapped under his coat and stowed in the camels' pouches had never been seen. And they wouldn't be, not for another two hundred years. Not until 1867, in fact, when Alfred Nobel, the Swedish chemist, would invent his *Extradynamit* blasting powder.

The sheer audacity of the method of attack was also unheard of. Until that day, the concept of a suicide bomber had not existed. It would only rear its ugly head for the first time much later, in Russia in the late 1800s, when Nobel's invention would become the method of choice for suicidal revolutionary assassins.

Which is how it all should have been.

But wasn't.

And all because of a man who stumbled on to a great secret in an underground crypt in Palmyra.

I

Paris
Present Day
Shawwal, AH 1438 (July, AD 2017)*

The dizzy, light-headed feeling was vaguely familiar.

Although Ayman Rasheed had done it before, the last time had been years ago. And the sensation was so bizarre, so intense, so overwhelming that after each trip he'd wondered if anyone ever got used to it. Not that he imagined many others knew about it, let alone had experienced it. There had to be some others, though, surely—after all, it had been out there for centuries, millennia even—but if so, where were they?

Or, rather, *when*?

He had no way of knowing, and he'd long since learned to avoid speculating about it. It only led down a bottomless rabbit hole of questions and infinite possibilities.

This time, though, the sensations were far more intense for the simple reason that Ayman Rasheed wasn't in good shape. In fact, he knew he was barely clinging to life, which was why he'd had to make the jump as quickly as possible.

* AH: *Anno Hegirae* ('in the year of the hejira'), referring to the lunar-based Islamic calendar, which begins its count from the Islamic New Year in AD 622, the time of the hegira, the migration of the prophet Muhammad and his followers from Mecca to Medina to escape an assassination plot. The Islamic calendar was used across the Ottoman Empire for religious matters alongside the Rumi calendar ('the Roman calendar'), which was based on the Julian calendar but also adjusted to begin in AD 622.

As his eyes struggled to adjust to the faint light of the streetlamps on the bridge looming over him, he felt the dizziness return. He muttered a curse and spat out some blood before huddling down and scanning his surroundings, alert to any potential threat, the cool air floating up from the river cutting a bone-deep chill into his naked body.

For that was how he always arrived after a jump: bare-skinned, stripped of any clothing or possessions.

The Paris he'd arrived in was very different, of course. Beyond what he could see, it was smelly, the air thick with pollutants, a stench that felt more disagreeable, poisonous even, compared with the stink from the lack of modern sewage that he'd grown accustomed to over the last couple of decades. It was noisy, too—that was the one thing that always hit hardest, even at this time of night, when the city was mostly asleep. An ambient buzz, a thrum, distant gears and pistons from cars, buses, generators and all kinds of mechanical contraptions burrowing almost surreptitiously into one's consciousness from everywhere and nowhere.

He'd forgotten how noisy that world was.

He coughed up more blood and felt a renewed onslaught of dizziness and nausea. This wasn't good. He needed his strength and all of his guile to pull this off and save himself. He shut his eyes for a moment, concentrating on calming his racing heartbeat, willing his senses to fall into step and guard him from any potential threat. He just needed to get to the hospital. Just that. The rest would take care of itself. Any other outcome was inconceivable to him. After everything he'd been through, after everything he'd achieved, he couldn't allow it all to come to a pathetic end here, alone and anonymous, a naked, tattooed corpse curled up in a dark corner on the banks of the Seine.

He slunk back to the dark cover of a stairwell that led

down from the bridge and waited. He knew exactly where he was, of course. He'd been careful to arrive in a place that would minimize the risk of discovery and, worse, obliteration. Like appearing in the middle of a busy road and getting hit by a bus, for example. Or somewhere that was now occupied by something solid, like a concrete wall or a parked car. Or in a crowded building, and causing a stir. Parks were a good option: open spaces, sparsely populated, although there was always the risk that, over time, they would be developed or that trees with thick trunks would have grown there in the intervening years. Another option was to choose a historic monument: an ancient, classic building, one that was most likely to be protected and maintained in its original form, one that stood a good chance of surviving the vagaries of time with little change.

Rasheed's first trip to this new world had been the most dangerous. He'd been curious to see the result of his work, but he'd be travelling blind. He'd never been to Paris in his time—before this had all begun, before he had ever done a time jump—and he hadn't thought of researching it either back then. Going for extreme caution on that first jump, he'd decided to use the river as his port of arrival, thinking that in all of Paris it was the one thing he was reasonably certain would remain unchanged over time. It had been a hot summer's day in the middle of August, so he assumed the water temperature would be bearable. And he wouldn't have clothes to weigh him down. The only thing he had to worry about was being run over by one of the many commercial barges plying its waters, but on a Friday and close to the riverbank, it was a reasonable risk.

It had worked out fine. And preferring not to get soaked on future visits, he'd sought out other safe landing spots. He was currently at one of those: a cobblestone quay on the right bank of the Seine, tucked away from the glare of the city's surveillance cameras, under the old Pont Royal bridge, facing the side of the Palais des Tuileries, at the westernmost end of the Louvre courtyard.

He had no way of knowing that the palace itself should not have been there. It had been burned down by the Paris Commune in 1871. Except, in the Paris he had just arrived in, there had been no Paris Commune. There had been no French Revolution either. Only an Ottoman conquest that had—as he had seen first hand on his previous visits—survived and thrived for more than three hundred years.

Thanks to him.

Only this was no curiosity trip—it was not a victory tour. It was a matter of life and death.

His own.

He scanned his surroundings and saw no one. It was Friday, the holy day of rest and congregation. The busy docks that lined the riverbanks would be shut. People would rise late, have breakfast with their families, and then, shortly before noon, they would head off to the mosques for the big *Salat el Jumu'ah* prayers. But that was later. It was still barely dawn. The city had yet to awaken, and the quays were quiet.

After a spell, Rasheed sensed something off to his far left. Some movement. He crept deeper into the shadows, hugging the wall, and his chest tightened as he stifled a cough.

He waited, then peered out, slowly, cautiously.

A figure was approaching. A man out on a walk, smoking a cigarette.

There was no one else around.

Rasheed risked another look and sized him up. Height, broad size—he would do.

He slid back against the wall and tensed up, waiting. From deep inside him, another geyser of blood threatened to explode, but he suppressed it, causing a burn to tear through his lungs. He tried to still his breathing, which was rising alarmingly, not out of fear but due to involuntary cardiac exertion. He would rather have waited a bit longer before striking, to allow the after-effects of his trip to settle, but the opportunity was here, now, and to wait longer was to invite more risk.

A charge of adrenaline fought back his dizziness as the man's footfalls drew closer. When he judged them to indicate the man was within striking distance, he emerged, fast, blocking his target's path.

The man froze in place, thrown by the sight of a powerful nude man covered in markings standing before him. And before the man could react, before his brain had even processed the strange sight, Rasheed dredged up the force to lash out. A quick side kick to the groin caused the man to falter back, his face crumpled from debilitating pain. Rasheed moved in instantly and followed the first strike with a savage haymaker to the man's left ear that almost made him lose consciousness. His legs buckled, and by the time he fell to his knees, Rasheed was already behind him, hooking one arm around the man's neck, his other pressing against the back of his head.

Then Rasheed squeezed.

The man struggled to free himself, but Rasheed held him in place despite the burning sensation searing through his own biceps and forearm. He could smell the stink of tobacco, which mixed badly with the dizziness that suddenly roared back into his skull. He dredged up all the strength he could muster to keep the man in his grip. Seconds dragged into torturous minutes until the lack of oxygen caused the man's resistance to wane and his body went slack.

Rasheed stayed clamped around the man's neck. He wasn't after unconsciousness. He needed something more permanent.

Moments later, he achieved his goal. He dropped the limp corpse to the ground just as the feeling of choking on his own blood surged within him, making him cough out violently. He wiped his mouth with his hand and steadied himself against the wall, struggling to stay upright from the dizziness. He couldn't let it overcome him again. He had to move fast.

He pulled the man's clothes off—robe, shirt, sash, baggy trousers—and he grabbed the loose turban that had fallen off during the scuffle and slipped them on. In a small pocket in the man's trousers, he found an ID card, a couple of bank-notes, and a set of keys. He studied the card. The address meant nothing to him, but he memorized the name on it. He didn't intend to use it, but details were important, and he knew it could come in handy.

His head still throbbing, he dragged the man's naked body to the edge of the water. He was about to roll him in when a scream shattered the peaceful night air.

'Stop! What are you doing? Somebody stop him,' a woman cried out.

He froze and glanced across the river. A man and woman were at the base of the bridge's stairs directly across from him. The man was now edging closer to the water, pointing at him and shouting, too.

Rasheed ignored them.

He just flipped the body into the river, turned, and made for the stairs, dredging up another gob of blood as he stumbled off into the darkness.

2

By noon, the heavy sun had the city firmly in its grip, an oppressive presence over an auspicious Friday at the overcrowded Mehmediyye Mosque.

Across Paris, the unrelenting heatwave was suffocating. In the shade of a coffee house by the banks of the Seine, it might have been slightly more tolerable, but under the towering dome of the prayer hall, with the midday sun at its most potent and the massive hall filled to capacity, it felt like being in a hammam. Or perhaps Kamal Arslan Agha of the counterterrorism directorate of the sultan's *Tashkeelat-i Hafiye*—the secret police—was feeling it more acutely than any of the other supplicants around him. He was in full uniform, which didn't help. He was also a key player in the events that were scheduled to follow today's noon prayer. A lot of eyes would be on him.

With the last *rak'at* finished, the horde of men rose to their feet and moved to collect their footwear. All around him, the hall reverberated with portent, the shuffling noise amplified by the heat. Kamal caught the eye of his partner, Taymoor Erkun Agha, who had arrived earlier and had been a few rows closer to the pulpit. By the time the slow wave of worshippers reached the main doors, Taymoor had caught up with Kamal.

'That was painful,' Taymoor said. 'This new imam—the man's a human sleeping pill.'

'Another late night?' Kamal asked, instantly regretting it.

Taymoor recoiled slightly with mock indignation. 'Not here, brother. Where's your respect?'

Kamal gave him a slight roll of the eyes. 'Spare me.'

'All I can say is, thank God for text messaging. How did our parents ever manage to hook up with anyone without it?'

'I'm pretty sure they didn't,' Kamal replied.

'That's just sad.'

'But thanks for the inspiring imagery.'

Taymoor's boasts about his nocturnal pursuits had become tiresome to Kamal. He'd suffered them ever since the beginning of their partnership within the Hafiye, a partnership that began three years ago, when they were both fresh out of the military academy. But now, with the two young agents' newly growing notoriety within the service, the boasts had got worse. Both men were unmarried, despite being thirty years old, naturally blessed with handsome physiques that had been further enhanced by years of hard training, and, as officers of the state, highly eligible—a fact that Taymoor was certainly exploiting to the fullest, oblivious to the more conservative, repressive tide that the new sultan had ushered in. Kamal couldn't conceive of him ever entering into a marriage contract, which was probably a blessing for the aspiring brides of the city. As for Kamal, marriage was something he did aspire to, but it wasn't likely to happen any time soon.

The one woman he wanted above all others was one he could never have.

Taymoor gave him a slap on the shoulder and ushered him out. 'Come on. Our legions of admirers are waiting.'

In the large vestibule, the two agents retrieved their boots and their *börk* headgear—tall tubes of white felt that rose at the front before folding back like a sleeve to below the neck. Even though it was the day of communal prayer and rest, the formal proceedings that were to follow the prayer meant Kamal and his partner had to be in uniform: baggy *shalwar* trousers, a long-sleeved tunic and a short-sleeved kaftan with elaborate frogging all the way up the chest, all of it in ominous blacks and greys. On the right collar of the kaftan was the emblem of the Hafiye: three interlocked crescents, each with a small five-pointed star cradled between its sharp tips. The left collar displayed rank—in Kamal and Taymoor's case, *chaouch komiser,* or sergeant inspector—which was confirmed in tattoos on the right arm and leg of each agent, a tradition that dated back several centuries to the earliest days of the janissaries, when it was both a symbol of brotherhood and an aide to identifying corpses after battle. The two men weren't likely to be caught up in battle any time soon, but the war they were engaged in, a war of suicide bombers and car bombs, did carry a real risk of putting their tattoos to use.

They also wore wide belts that held holsters for their standard-issue Galip automatic handguns and loops that housed their *khanjar* daggers.

The two men followed the crowd out to the vast rectangular courtyard fronting the mosque. Two floors of semicircular vaulted arcades lined all four sides of the monumental space, which had managed to retain its original name of *cour d'honneur* in common parlance, even though Ottoman Turkish had, after three hundred years of foreign rule, long since replaced French as the city's main language.

The vast compound's original name, Les Invalides, was of course long gone. Its renaming had posed a dilemma for Mehmed IV, the sultan whose army had conquered the French capital in the summer of 1100.* Besides the magnificent domed chapel at Les Invalides, Paris also boasted the sublime cathedral of Notre-Dame. Mehmed couldn't put his name to both. In his infinite wisdom, he decided to bestow his name on the

* 1100 in the Islamic hijri calendar, or AD 1689.

former, which became the Mehmediyye—as had Saint Peter's Basilica in Rome after the Papal States had fallen and the pope had been beheaded, but that was acceptable since they were in different cities. Notre-Dame, on the other hand, would have to settle for basking in the splendour of the sultan's nickname: the conqueror. Shorn of its stained-glass windows and other Christian iconography, dressed in domes, and flanked by minarets, it had become the Fatih Mosque.

The sun, close to its zenith, wasn't sparing any corner of the courtyard from its merciless pounding. Its ferocity blasted Kamal and Taymoor the instant they stepped outside. Their uniforms, though of the linen and cotton summer variant, were still way too heavy for the conditions. With sweat running down the length of his spine, Kamal would have much preferred to be in his lighter, off-duty attire, but today he wasn't there as a civilian. He and Taymoor were being fêted. Which didn't sit all that comfortably with Kamal. They'd worked hard, to be sure. They'd put in the hours and the legwork. They'd been focused. But they'd also had a lucky break. A break that, admittedly, had saved many lives.

Of that, Kamal was very proud.

The courtyard was heaving with people. Kamal took in the scene, one he'd witnessed many times before. It was an impressive setting. The viewing areas were laid out on either side of the length of the courtyard. Along the east arcade were eight public grandstands, stepped but devoid of any seating. Facing them along the opposite side were two official tribunes. Those did have seating and rose more steeply, which was useful given the more substantial turbans and headgear most of those seated there would be wearing. As guests of honour, Kamal and Taymoor would watch from there, along with their superiors from the Hafiye and a number of state officials. At the far end of the courtyard, facing the Seine, two of the mosque complex's six minarets rose proudly, the tallest landmarks in the sprawling city.

In one corner, Kamal spotted the state television crew filming the proceedings. Armed ceremonial guards stood by the pillars around the arcade. As with all public spaces in the empire, the grandstands and the tribunes had separate male and female sections. On both sides of the huge courtyard, attendees would be corralled in segregated areas.

Kamal and Taymoor made their way to their designated area through a stream of congratulations and pats on the back from officers of the Hafiye.

'*Tebrikler, mulasim komiser,*' one of the officers congratulated Kamal. 'The youngest in the department, eh? Just don't let the expectations become too much of a burden on you.' He squeezed Kamal's shoulder a bit too tightly.

Kamal responded to the backhanded praise with a curt nod and moved on. He had already heard the murmurs: promotions to lieutenant inspector for both partners were in the offing. Still, Kamal couldn't find the peace of mind to savour the moment. He kept glancing across the courtyard, scanning the faces in the women's public stands, looking for her.

It was almost impossible to distinguish individual faces, of course—the headscarves and veils, some less opaque than others, were intended to block that kind of scrutiny. Still, once or twice his eyes fell on a figure that, for the briefest of instants, he thought might be her. But then something about the body language, the height, an almost imperceptible detail told him he was mistaken.

It didn't relieve his discomfort.

As he caught up with Taymoor, he glanced up at the upper-level arcade and saw Mumtaz Sikander Pasha, the beylerbey of the Paris *eyalet,* a province that included not just the great metropolis itself but the entire ancient kingdom of

23

France. Dressed in his ceremonial robe, his head wrapped in a bulbous turban that was only dwarfed by the girth of his waist, the governor was making his way to his box, which was already crowded with senior officials, including, Kamal now saw, the overall commander of the Paris division of the Hafiye, Huseyin Celaleddin Pasha.

Celaleddin was tall and, given his position in Ottoman society, unusually slim. His jutting chin, always tilted slightly upwards, and his sloped-back brow made it hard to tell what was going on behind the discerning eyes that now caught sight of Kamal. The commander surprised Kamal by acknowledging him with a subtle congratulatory nod. Kamal responded with a slight bow before his superior turned away to greet the beylerbey.

Taymoor led him to their places. After pausing to bask in the attention a bit longer, he took his seat and, with beaming satisfaction, patted the one next to him. 'Front row, brother. It's our day.'

'*Mashallah*,' Kamal replied half-heartedly as he did another quick scan of the female tribune before sitting down.

His distant attitude wasn't lost on Taymoor. 'Why the sour face?' he asked. Then his face cracked with a bawdy grin. 'You got somewhere else you'd rather be?'

Kamal shrugged. 'Of course not.'

Taymoor let out a small snort, then studied him for a moment. 'You know something? We're partners. We face danger, death maybe, on a daily basis—together. We're supposed to share. I tell you everything—'

'Yeah, too much maybe,' Kamal griped.

'Protest all you want. I know you love it.' He dropped his voice. 'You're as much of a depraved *luti* as I am. You just don't like talking about it. So go on, tell me, who is she? Who's turning your balls blue?'

Kamal had to play the game. He knew they were both lying to each other, but it suited him fine. He didn't want Taymoor to know what strings were tugging at his heart. It was enough of a burden to keep it locked away deep inside of him; he'd never live it down if his licentious partner found out.

So he chose to keep up the act and not answer while an ominous silence descended on the courtyard. All attention turned to its far end, where five men appeared from a portal in the arcade. They were dressed in ceremonial uniforms. The middle man, though, stood out because of his black robes and turban and his hulking, heavyset frame. Even under the robes, it was clearly more muscle than fat.

He was also striking because of the long sword he carried.

Kamal and Taymoor watched as the procession made its way solemnly to the centre of the courtyard.

'To be continued,' Taymoor warned jokingly, wagging a finger at his partner. 'You know better than to mess with my bloodhound nose, right, brother?'

Kamal forced an enigmatic smile—the fact was, Taymoor did have great investigative instincts. In terms of their work, this was an undeniable asset. But in terms of Kamal's personal life, he could have done without it.

He turned his attention to the centre of the far portal, where four officers now appeared, two on either side of a fifth man, who was dressed in a simple white robe. He was blindfolded, and his hands were tied behind his back.

The arena went quiet as the officers escorted the man to the centre of the courtyard and handed him over to the first group before marching back the way they came.

The large man with the sword stepped forward and, facing the prisoner, took hold of the man's shoulder, guiding him to the ground until he was kneeling. Then the large man stepped back, took a sheet of paper from one of his assistants, and began to read out the execution order in a loud voice that echoed across the stillness of the enclosed space.

Kamal had heard those same charges read out many times before—'enemy of the state,' 'high treason'—as well as the verdict. He had heard them most recently a week earlier, in that same spot, proclaimed by the same executioner, the state's executioner corps being a small, exclusive club. But this time, the words carried far more resonance for him. This time, the condemned man kneeling on the parched cobblestones of the *cour d'honneur* was put there by Kamal and Taymoor.

It should have been an untainted day of great pride for him. When it came to terrorists, to barbarians who were plotting to murder innocent citizens, he never questioned whether the punishment fitted the crime. Case in point: the condemned man currently before them in the courtyard, an Algerian extremist who, along with his brother and a few others, had made his way to Paris with the intention of attacking the festival celebrating the impending marriage of the beylerbey's youngest daughter to one of the sultan's favourite sons. A lot of dignitaries would have been in attendance, including the bey himself. A major catastrophe had been averted, and Kamal and Taymoor had become heroes overnight.

The executioner finished reading out the order, then started to recite some verses from the Koran. Kamal's scowl was fixated on the condemned man, who remained impassive and wasn't pulling against his restraints or pleading for his life. Kamal knew that by the time the day of execution arrived, any strength the man had left would have been sapped away by the terror of what awaited him. He also knew that the rumours about sedatives being slipped into the final meals of the condemned were true.

The executioner finished his recitation. Then he straightened up and looked to the governor's box.

Kamal, and everyone else in the courtyard, followed his gaze.

The beylerbey stared down in silence, then gave him a small, impassive nod.

The executioner bowed his head in acknowledgment, and then he turned to the condemned man. He bent down and used his free hand to adjust the position of the man's head, exposing his bare neck more fully. Then he bent down further and spoke some words to him, instructing the man to recite the *shahada,* the declaration of absolute faith.

The executioner then took a step back, planted his feet firmly, and, holding the sword in both hands, swung it around slowly to the prisoner's neck, which he nicked with its blade. The prisoner, surprised, flinched instinctively, tensing up and straightening his neck—exactly what his executioner wanted; he had already raised the sword high above the prisoner's head, and, in a fluid, lightning-quick move, he brought it down full force.

The blade went right through the prisoner's neck in one clean cut. One single, brutally efficient, fatal blow. The man's head didn't just drop: it sprang off, hit the ground and rolled through a full turn before coming to a stop. The executioner took a swift step back to avoid getting his robes soiled as blood instantly squirted out of the headless body, which remained immobile in its kneeling position.

Across the courtyard, shouts of *'Allahu akbar'*—God is the greatest—rang out. Taymoor hissed it, too, as he pumped the air with his fist before glancing over at Kamal with a fierce glow in his eyes and clenched teeth.

'That'll teach those sons of whores,' he rasped.

Kamal nodded, even though he knew it wouldn't. Death, after all, was no deterrent to those fanatics. If anything, it was the opposite.

As the blood flow slowed, the executioner surveyed his handiwork with no visible emotion. One of his assistants handed him a small bottle of water and a cloth, which he casually took without looking away from his victim. He poured water over his blade and wiped it with the cloth, which he then discarded on to the rigid corpse.

A four-man crew of attendants pulling a steel cart appeared from a far alcove. Moving with well-practised efficiency, they unfurled a white plastic sheet and placed it on the ground next to the lifeless, headless body. Three of them rolled the corpse on to the sheet and lifted it on to the cart while the fourth retrieved the head and placed it in a bag made of the same white plastic. Moments later, they were wheeling it all away.

The courtyard could now welcome its next victim.

Today's ceremony would feature seven beheadings. The next three, co-conspirators of the Algerian, didn't trouble Kamal. After all, it was he and Taymoor who had uncovered the plot, identified the terrorists and led the team that had tracked them down and brought them in after an intense, frantic manhunt.

The final two didn't bother him either. He had played no part in their arrest, but they were tried and convicted murderers who, high on *khat,* had killed an elderly couple while robbing their mansion in Saint-Germain.

The fifth prisoner, however, did.

His name was Halil Azmi, and he was a *muderis*—a teacher, in this case a university law professor. Agents from the Hafiye's Z Directorate, the ever-expanding internal security force tasked with protecting the imperial order, had arrested him along with two others, a prominent journalist and a lawyer. The three men were accused of belonging to the White Rose, an underground subversive organization that the Z agents had recently uncovered, and a closed court had deemed them to be 'colluding to instigate revolt'.

He was also *her* friend.

Which was why Kamal was now scouring the female grandstands again, looking for Nisreen, his brother's wife, hoping she wouldn't be there as the professor was paraded into a chorus of suppressed gasps from the public stands.

Part of him begrudged Nisreen the unease that was needling him. He felt irritated by her ill-judged friendship, one that was spoiling his moment of glory. At the same time, he couldn't help but empathize with what she must be feeling, knowing her friend would soon lose his life. He hoped she wouldn't witness what was about to come, hoped it wouldn't cement an indelible link between him, an agent of the Hafiye, and Azmi's fate.

His heart seized as his eyes snagged something, a pair of eyes that were looking his way, and for a second he felt her there, watching him, loathing him from across the courtyard, the last vestiges of a friendship that had started when they were children about to be obliterated forever under the scorching sun. For a moment, he froze—then the woman turned, and, despite her light headscarf that also veiled the lower half of her face, he knew it wasn't her.

He looked away. And with the high sun pummelling the courtyard, Azmi was positioned so that, like the others before him, he was kneeling no more than twenty *kadems* from Kamal.

The professor wasn't cowering. He held his head high and seemed oblivious to everyone in the crowd. Instead, he was staring stoically at the official tribune.

Kamal couldn't help but meet his gaze, couldn't tear himself away from the man's eyes, which seemed to have zeroed in on him, a silent, accusing glare that triggered a pounding inside the agent's ears that drowned out the executioner's voice along with the sound of his blade as it cleaved the air before slicing through the professor's neck.

Which was when Kamal's mobile phone buzzed in his pocket.

As did Taymoor's.

3

For Sayyid Ramazan Hekim, being summoned away from the family that Friday wasn't hugely unwelcome. The week had been a dark one, and he knew it would only get worse once Nisreen heard the inevitable confirmation that the execution of her friend Halil Azmi had been carried out.

He would have liked to be with her at that moment. But, at the same time, he knew there was nothing he could do to comfort her. They'd already said all that needed to be said. Better to leave her with the kids. They would distract her.

Ramazan wasn't as strongly affected by Azmi's fate as his wife was. He hadn't even met the man. He didn't know many of his wife's law colleagues, and recently he'd purposely avoided them. But Nisreen had on several occasions related their dissenting views on what the state had become, and he knew they would attract trouble, trouble he was fully determined to steer clear of. He and Nisreen had argued about that, of course. It was one thing to disagree with what the sultan and his cronies were doing; it was quite another to be publicly vocal about it. Ramazan felt his primary duty was to his wife, his children and the patients under his care. Sometimes, late at night, he would wonder if that meant he was reasonable and cautious or a coward. He stoically pushed back against the latter and prided himself on the former. It would all eventually pass—such periods of political strife always did. And when they did, he would have kept his family safe.

Under normal circumstances, this would have been the

end of another week of routine, and the next day would have ushered in a new one. Ramazan knew routine all too well. He liked routine. Routine was order. Routine promoted peace of mind. It was the life he'd chosen. After all, being an anaesthetist wasn't particularly exciting. It wasn't particularly glamorous either. In fact, it was quite the opposite: an invisible career. For even though he held his patients' lives in his hands when they were in the operating theatre, even though they voluntarily relinquished all control of their bodies and minds to him, he'd long since got used to the fact that, afterwards, they always remembered the names of their surgeon, never their anaesthetist.

In the current climate, being anonymous was probably a good thing.

Today, however, as he walked down the halls of the cardio-thoracic wing at the hospital that was part of the Hurrem Sultan Külliye on the Île de la Cité, Ramazan sensed something far from routine was brewing.

'You say he walked in early this morning, alone, in bad shape and coughing blood—but we don't know anything about him?' he asked, moving briskly alongside Moshe Fonseca, a surgeon he'd worked with frequently.

'Nothing beyond the fact that he needs surgery rather urgently,' Fonseca replied.

The sprawling complex, the largest *külliye* in Paris, had more humble origins as the Hôtel-Dieu Hospital, which dated back to the seventh century. It had grown a lot since the Ottomans had taken over the city. Like all *külliyes,* it was funded by a voluntary charitable endowment, known as a *waqf.* Charity was highly encouraged by Islam, and large *waqf* complexes became a key part of the Ottomans' colonization of foreign lands. These pious bequests by the imperial family and the ruling class ranged from hostels, mills, factories and caravanserais to entire villages and included all the revenue that these properties generated.

The Hurrem Sultan had been founded by the wife of a sultan and was named after her. Like the largest *külliyes,* it also housed a mosque, school, bathhouse, hospice, inn and public soup kitchen. Its hospital was one of the most advanced in Paris, and Ramazan had a solid reputation as its star anaesthetist.

'We don't even know his name?' he asked.

'He hasn't said a word,' the surgeon replied. 'But that's hardly the most unusual thing about him.'

'What then?'

Fonseca gave him a loaded sideways glance. 'You'll see.'

The surgeon's reply didn't just feed Ramazan's confusion—it worried him. 'Has he been reported to the Zaptiye?'

Fonseca stopped. After a quick glance to make sure no one was within earshot, he dropped his voice and said, 'There's no need for the police at this stage. Let's save the man's life first. He's going to be here for a while and he's going to be pretty helpless. Let's not make things worse for him before we know what his story is.'

Ramazan held his gaze and considered his words, then nodded. Neither he nor Fonseca were huge fans of the Zaptiye—the city's police force. Not nowadays.

They rounded a corner and entered the ward, where they made their way past several other patients to reach the man in question.

He was lying in a bed in a far corner by a window, hooked up to several monitors that beeped softly. A nurse by the name of Anbara was checking the drips that snaked into the intravenous cannula attached to his right arm. When she saw the doctors, she bowed slightly and retreated from the bed. The surgeon gave her a small nod back before turning to the patient.

33

Ramazan couldn't tell much about the man, given that he was covered by a bedsheet and had a transparent plastic oxygen mask strapped to his face. From what he could see, Ramazan thought the man might be in his late sixties. He had a full head of grey, slicked-back hair.

He couldn't see much else.

'My name is Moshe Fonseca, *effendi*,' Fonseca told the man in his customary upbeat, confidence-inspiring tone. 'I'm in charge of the hospital's cardiothoracic unit. How are you feeling today?'

The man's eyes narrowed as he seemed to study the surgeon for a brief moment. Then he replied with a slow, gentle nod, closing his eyes as he did.

'Good. Well, you'll be relieved to know your case doesn't present anything we can't fix,' Fonseca continued. 'Basically, you've got what we call mitral valve stenosis. We all have four valves in our heart. The mitral is one of them, and sometimes, for any number of reasons—age maybe, or you might have been born with it, or maybe you had a bad case of rheumatic fever at some point—this valve gets narrower, and it stops opening properly. Which means there's less blood flowing into your left ventricle, which is the main pumping chamber of your heart. I imagine you've been feeling very tired and short of breath lately, yes?'

The man nodded.

'All these symptoms—coughing blood, the heart arrhythmia—they're all because of this. Your lungs are severely congested; your heart has clearly been strained for quite some time. Frankly, I'm surprised you haven't had this treated before now. It can easily cause clots that lead to a transient ischemic attack, which is a kind of mini stroke, or even a full stroke and—well, that's not something we want, is it?'

Fonseca studied the man, but the patient said nothing.

34

After a moment, Fonseca just nodded and said, 'The main thing: you're here now, and we're going to fix this. The way we do this is by replacing your valve with a bioprosthetic one that will do the job your valve hasn't been doing. That's going to be my job.' He gestured at Ramazan. 'And this here is Sayyid Ramazan Hekim, one of our finest anaesthetist. He'll be the one putting you to sleep. As your condition is rather urgent, I'd rather not wait any more than we have to before doing this, so we've scheduled you in this afternoon. I trust you have no problems with that?'

The man shook his head.

'Ramazan Hekim will answer any questions you might have,' Fonseca continued, 'and he also has some pre-op questions to ask you, although I'm not sure how fruitful that's going to be given your'—he hesitated—'condition.'

The man didn't react.

'Very well then,' Fonseca said. 'All you need to do now is relax. You're in good hands and you have nothing to worry about. I'll see you in the recovery room.' He turned to Ramazan. 'He's all yours.'

Ramazan looked a question at him, still wondering about what the surgeon had meant by his earlier comment.

'It might be a good idea for you to examine his breathing again,' the surgeon told him. 'The fluid level in his lungs is quite high.'

Fonseca lingered for a second with a telling look, as if to make sure his message had sunk in, then wandered off.

Ramazan stood there, confused. He glanced at Anbara, who didn't react. Then he looked at the patient, wondering what Fonseca was talking about. Examine his breathing? The man was connected to monitors that gave far more information than anything he could glean from a simple stethoscope. Still, the surgeon had been noticeably pointed about it.

He reached into the tray unit by the bed, picked up a stethoscope, and moved in closer.

'All right, let's see how your lungs are doing, shall we?'

The man's eyes tightened, visibly uncomfortable about this, which Ramazan noticed as he folded down the sheet covering him. Then he pulled the man's hospital gown up to expose his chest.

And froze.

The man's chest was covered in tattoos. All of it, all the way down to his waist. Ramazan had never seen anything like it. He couldn't see them as clearly as he would have liked, since some of them were obscured under the man's chest hair, but from what he could see, they didn't seem ornamental or symbolic. Rather, they were words and numbers written in the same Arabic-Persian alphabet that Ramazan used, only they were written the wrong way, from left to right. The letters were small, the technique intricate. He thought some looked like they might be names and dates, but it was hard to tell. They were difficult to read, given that they were mirror images of normal writing.

There were also several drawings and diagrams, images that looked technical that Ramazan didn't recognize at all.

Still rigid with surprise, he glanced up at the patient. The man was watching him, his cold, impassive eyes clearly probing him. Ramazan felt a deep-seated unease—and, oddly, he felt scared. He wasn't sure why, but something about the man's unwavering gaze, coupled with the tattoos and the strong torso they covered, made him very uncomfortable.

He glanced furtively at the tattoos again, then forced his attention away from them and did his best to sound casual and seem unperturbed by what he'd seen.

'This might feel a bit cold,' he said as he placed the stethoscope's resonator on the man's chest. 'Take a deep breath, please.'

4

Lying in his hospital bed, Ayman Rasheed eyed the anaesthetist intently, looking for a reaction.

As the man pulled back his gown, Rasheed saw surprise and confusion along with the reaction he liked most of all: fear. Which was good. The doctor wasn't just unsettled by what he'd seen. He was scared.

And fear, as Rasheed knew, made people clam up and keep their mouths shut.

The tattoos were always going to be a problem. He'd known that all along, but he had no choice. In all these years, he'd been very careful about who he'd allowed to see them. He'd stopped shaving his torso long ago, since he no longer needed them, but they were still visible. The surgeon, the anaesthetist, others potentially—they would be wondering about them, asking themselves questions. And the Hafiye— his brainchild, the agency he had created after the dust of conquest had settled, to help ensure the empire's survival— had its tentacles everywhere.

The good news was that it was unlikely any of them would understand their relevance. He hoped that they would think it curious but not much more. That they would think he was some kind of freak, someone on the fringes of society, an eccentric. Tattoos had been a common sight in the world he'd left behind, more and more so with each generation, but he didn't know if they were as popular in this new world, in the one he'd helped create.

Either way, he didn't intend to stick around too long or

answer any questions they had. Once he was fixed, once the operation was done and he'd recovered enough strength, he'd go back and leave them even more confused than they now were.

The crisis had struck him the day before, at his summer palace at Versailles. It had happened at the tail end of a long, formal lunch with some visiting British dignitaries.

He'd felt increasingly dizzy for days, exhausted after the most trivial effort. For a tough, solid man like him, it was far from the norm. The fatigue and shortness of breath had got worse until, two days before the Versailles event, he'd started coughing up blood. Then at the lunch, just as the servants were bringing out great platters of fruit and pistachio and honey desserts, he felt his heart race suddenly and uncontrollably and saw his own panic reflected in the horrified faces around the table. He turned pale and tried to rise out of his chair, only to collapse to the floor amid screams of alarm from his staff and guests.

He was rushed to his chambers. He tried asking for them to hurry with fetching the *hekimbaşı,* his chief physician, but his speech was slurry and he could barely remember the man's name. The right side of his face felt numb, and his right arm had virtually no strength in it. Once at his bedside, the assembled physicians seemed stumped and could do little to make him feel better as his vision grew blurrier and the room darkened around him.

Miraculously, though, Ayman Rasheed had started to feel a bit better a few hours later. But he knew something was very, very wrong. He also knew he couldn't count on his physicians to take care of it. They were, by his modern standards, clueless.

It wasn't through a lack of will or effort: medicine and science, built on a foundation of ancient Greek texts, had taken pride of place since the earliest days of the empire. The Otto-mans had been the first to inoculate their children against smallpox, a practice they began in the late 1600s, long before anyone else. It was simply a question of progress. They just weren't there yet. Eighteenth-century Islamic medicine wasn't yet aware of viruses and bacteria. It was still based on Galenism, a tradition that considered illness to be an imbal-ance in the four elemental humours that governed the human body: blood, phlegm, yellow bile and black bile. And although Rasheed had brought a lot of advanced knowledge back from his world, most of it had been in the art of war, not in medicine.

He knew it was going to take more than the herbs and distillations in their pharmacopoeias to cure him. There was no time to waste.

He needed modern medicine. But he had to play it safe.

He got his janissary corps to rush him back to his Paris palace, where he locked himself in his chambers after issuing strict instructions that he was not to be disturbed. He spent a fretful night waiting. He also calculated the exact number of days he needed to factor in to arrive there one day after his last visit. Then, just before dawn, he slipped out of the Lou-vre through a hidden passage and made his way to the banks of the Seine, as he had done more than once before.

There, by the edge of the river, he had uttered the long sequence of Palmyrene words—the ones he'd had decades to memorize—and jumped.

He was relieved to hear that his condition was treatable. He'd made the right decision, no doubt. He would have died had he not made the jump. The surgeon had confirmed it.

Despite his great discomfort, it felt good to be there again. It had been years since he'd been back, and seeing it again gave him a boost. After all that time, the empire was still there.

Under strain, perhaps, but still there. It had endured, against the odds, resisting the vagaries of time and despite powerful foreign enemies at its borders and a vast array of religious and ethnic groups within them—even if those groups had shrunk over the centuries because of conversions.

He could proudly claim to have had a lot to do with that endurance.

He'd avoided coming back for—how long had it been? Almost a decade. He'd seen how the empire was going through tough times—due to the Americans, Rasheed had discovered, a fact that greatly displeased him. They were wrecking his world again, although this time it was more of an indirect consequence, made worse by the hot-headed tyrant currently occupying the throne in Istanbul.

Perhaps he needed to do something about that.

It had been on his mind since his last couple of visits, but he'd ultimately chosen to turn his back on his legacy, retreat to the comforts of his cosseted life as governor, and leave fate to run its course.

The truth was, he'd achieved so much, and he was tired. He was enjoying the fruits of his work, payback for the harsh times that had rained down on him before that fateful discovery in Palmyra a lifetime ago. It also hadn't helped that in 2017—*this* 2017, now referred to throughout the empire as 1438, following the Islamic calendar—he was nobody. An anonymous man by deed and by choice, needing to be cautious at all times, fearful of discovery, and, even before his health had deteriorated, unsure he had the energy or the will to try to affect the course of events and help steer the empire back to better days. Whereas back in the eighteenth century, he had it all. He was powerful, he was feared, he was revered. He was considered a visionary, a genius. He enjoyed a spectacular life, ruling over the Paris *eyalet,* one of the jewels of the empire, second only to Istanbul itself. Even the sultan held him in utmost respect. It was a far more satisfying and enjoyable place and time to inhabit.

But now he was back. Not by choice. And, with a bit of luck, not for long.

He knew they would treat him, of course, regardless of the tattoos, regardless of his silence, regardless of their not knowing the first thing about him.

Hospitals in the Ottoman Empire—known as *darusshifas,* which meant 'houses of cures'—were charitable institutions that followed the Islamic moral imperative to treat everyone, regardless of their status or even their religion. Rasheed had no reason to think this practice had changed over the centuries, and on a previous visit, anticipating a need just like the one that had brought him to this hospital, he had checked out the Hurrem Sultan and had been pleased to be proved right.

Watching the anaesthetist examine him, Rasheed didn't think he would be a problem. Rasheed knew how to read men, and the look of fear in the man's eyes told him all he needed to know about him. He was weak. A lamb, a follower, a man without much of a spine.

The surgeon, however, was different. He seemed to be more sharply observant than his colleague. Rasheed knew he'd need to remain alert to any nuanced shifts in his behaviour.

When the man had introduced himself, Rasheed had been surprised to realize he was obviously a Jew. He'd met quite a few since landing in the sultan's chamber all those years ago. The Ottomans had welcomed them with open arms after the Spaniards had expelled them during the Inquisition, and Rasheed had grown to appreciate or disdain them as he would any other person, according to their individual merits and regardless of their religion. But he also knew their numbers in the empire had dwindled over the centuries. Although

41

the empire was tolerant of other faiths and allowed them to worship freely, this tolerance was based on a precept of order that assumed the superiority of Muslims over non-Muslims. Conversion to Islam was not forced, but over the centuries the Ottomans had put in place burdens—taxes, being ineligible for any government post, even limitations on what colours of clothing could be worn—directed at non-Muslims as powerful enticements to convert.

At first, Christians and Jews had resisted the notion, even if it meant they would be second-class citizens. But after Vienna, Rome and Paris fell, their resolve to hang on to their birth religions weakened, then collapsed. The cohabitation and interdependence of the different faiths gave way to mass conversions.

Faith was the primary organizing principle of Ottoman society, and with time there was no ethnic consciousness left. That was very much part of Rasheed's grand design. He knew it was the greatest threat to stability; he had experienced it first-hand back in his original homeland, a lifetime ago. He'd seen its blood-soaked effect across the entire region.

Yes, the endurance of the empire owed him a great deal indeed, he thought, as he considered the two men who would help settle that debt and enable him to go back and live out the rest of his days in splendour.

Nothing—*nothing*—was going to interfere with that.

5

On a quay by the Bayezid Bridge, Kamal and Taymoor flashed their badges and cut through the Zaptiye cordon to reach the small huddle of police officers.

One of them frowned as he saw them approach.

'Here we go,' he chortled to his buddies, knowing that Kamal and Taymoor were well within earshot. 'We can rest easy. The "experts" are here.' No air quotes were necessary. His tone didn't leave much room for a misreading.

'*Salamu alaykum* too, *mulasim komiser*,' Kamal returned with a sardonic smile. 'Mind if we take a look?'

'A look I don't mind. Assuming you can swoop in here and take over, I do. What is it with you guys anyway? Is there anything you don't butt into these days?'

'Not my call.' Kamal shrugged as he moved in close to the dead body. 'Just following orders.'

'Honestly, we had better things to do today than barge in on you like this,' Taymoor added, his grin and the raised eyebrows that accompanied 'barge' confirming how pleased with himself he was.

'Orders.' The lieutenant inspector virtually spat the word out. 'Well, who knows? Maybe this poor *effendi* and his dastardly friends were plotting to use the river to flood the whole city, and your being here will save us all.'

'It's happened before. The saving part, anyway,' Taymoor said as he brushed past him to join Kamal.

A year ago, Kamal would have also questioned the order for him and Taymoor to look into such a situation. A dead

43

body had been fished out of the Seine. At this stage, there was nothing that cried out terrorism or internal security. Accident, murder or suicide—it was clearly a police matter. But things had changed. The charged situation across the empire meant the bosses at the Hafiye felt a need to be on top of any suspect event. Which meant that Kamal and Taymoor were often getting dispatched to check out cases that, at first look anyway, fell outside their operational purview.

Which often didn't sit well with the cops whose toes were being trampled.

Kamal pulled back the sheet to expose the body.

It was male, middle-aged. Unusually, the man was naked.

'What do we know?' Kamal asked.

'Seriously?' the lieutenant inspector scoffed. 'You mean you haven't divined it already?'

Kamal gave him an impatient, withering look. 'The sooner we can establish that this doesn't concern us, the sooner we can get out of your hair.'

'Although I, for one, will forever savour the memory of this delightful rendezvous,' Taymoor added.

Kamal shifted his withering look to his partner.

The lieutenant inspector nodded grudgingly. 'Well, in that case ...' He pointed at a man who was sitting on a bench closer to the bridge. A couple of cops were shadowing him. 'That guy over there? He was fishing from the Osman Bridge. Saw the body floating by, half submerged. Called it in. River patrol set up some nets by this bridge and snagged him.'

Kamal got down on his haunches for a closer look. He noticed it immediately. The heavy bruising around the neck. There was no sign of cadaveric spasm either, not that it was always there. But this was no swimming accident. It wasn't a suicide either.

'I assume he wasn't carrying any ID?' Taymoor said. 'I

mean, you checked everywhere, right?' A raised eyebrow accompanied the 'everywhere'.

Kamal ignored him and asked, 'What's the coroner saying for time of death?'

'Fresh,' the lieutenant inspector replied. 'He hadn't been in the water long.'

Kamal nodded and glanced at the water. The current wasn't strong at that time of year. The body hadn't travelled far.

'We need to find where he went in,' he said. 'And what happened to his clothes.'

'Genius,' the lieutenant inspector said. 'Praise God that you're here.'

Kamal got up but didn't rise to the jibe. Instead, he looked up, checking for cameras, then reached into his pocket, pulled out a card and held it out to the cop with two fingers. 'Let me know what your men find. We'll hold off on filing our report until you do.' He gave him a pointed glance.

The cop understood and snatched the card.

Kamal nodded to Taymoor, and they walked away.

'Can you believe that dickhead?' Taymoor complained as he drove east on the boulevard that ran alongside the river. 'As if we don't have bigger fish to fry'—said with the smirk.

Kamal slid him a sideways scowl. 'Are you done? 'Cause I'm happy to walk back.'

Taymoor laughed.

In truth, Kamal hadn't been any happier about being summoned out there than the cops were about seeing him. He and Taymoor did have, to use Taymoor's cheesy words, bigger fish to fry. Terrorist whales, not civilian-homicide goldfish. He also empathized with the cops' frustration at having him and Taymoor show up. If this was a murder, it would be something they'd be loath to share for the simple reason that, in Ottoman Paris, murders were rare. The capital penalty for it under *shari'a* law was a major deterrent. There were crimes of passion, as well as honour killings—women murdered by male relatives who considered them to have dishonoured the family, typically for eloping or getting pregnant out of wedlock. They had become a rarity in the big cities, where attitudes had changed after the previous sultan, the progressive Murad V, introduced legislation making them a crime. But honour killings were now on the rise again after his successor, Abdülhamid III, had given the imams more power and turned back the clock on many of Murad's reforms. Far from the cities, though, it was as if the reforms had never happened. The commonly held credo of 'my horse, my gun, and my woman are sacred' may have been updated to include a car instead of a horse, but the belief was still deeply entrenched in the patriarchal and tribal system of many of the empire's provinces.

But this was no honour killing.

In terms of the recovered body, there wasn't much more to be done. No one had filed a missing person report. Kamal had already called the Hafiye's surveillance centre and told a senior analyst he knew there to go through all the CCTV footage of the riverbank since that day's first light, going back one *fersah* from where they'd fished the man out. He knew it wasn't a long shot. With the security services installing more cameras every day, there was hardly a corner left in the city that wasn't under constant watch.

It was still the holy day of rest, which was why Kamal and Taymoor were soon seated across from each other on the pavement terrace of a *kahvehane* on the left bank. Separating them was a table with a backgammon set and an empty jug of mint lemonade. Two *narguileh* water pipes stood proudly on either side of the table.

Clattering dice, gurgling water and boisterous conversation reverberated all around them as men of all ages filled the curved bamboo chairs of the coffee house while indulging in their age-old love of all three pastimes. Around them, waiters in dirty white aprons flitted among the tables, precariously balancing tiny cups of strong coffee, glasses of heavily sweetened Arab tea and tongs holding the heated tobacco coals for the water pipes. There were no women around: this *kahvehane* didn't have a separate 'family area' where women could sit with other women or with their husbands, brothers and fathers. Most coffee houses in Paris didn't have such sections either.

'Come on,' Taymoor hissed, '*Du shesh*'—two sixes. Holding the small ivory dice with three fingers, he kissed them, then flicked them on to the elaborately carved game board.

The dice tumbled, spun and finally settled. Sure enough, two sixes showed up.

'*Allez,*' Taymoor rasped as he pumped the air with his fist.

Oddly, people across the empire still called out the dice rolls using Persian numbers, a tradition that was as old as the game itself. Taymoor's last outburst was another linguistic anomaly, this one a leftover from the *eyalet*'s French history.

Taymoor didn't have to move any of his checkers. His victory was now numerically unavoidable. He took a celebratory pull from his mouthpiece, causing the water pipe to gurgle so loudly it seemed to be heckling his opponent, then sat back with a big, smug grin on his face. 'Had enough? Or are you feeling particularly masochistic tonight?'

Kamal frowned at him—then he flicked both sides of the board upward, slamming it shut like a vertical clamshell. '*Hasiktir,*' he cursed. 'Your dice are impossible today.'

The outburst startled everyone around them. Bad sportsmanship at backgammon was a major faux pas in Ottoman circles, but no one was going to scowl at them tonight.

'Go easy on him, Taymoor Agha,' a man sitting on the next table laughed. 'Today, you are both champions.' He raised his glass to him. A wave of others joined in his toast.

Taymoor raised his own glass, smiled and bowed his head in thanks.

'For our heroes,' the jovial coffee house's owner bellowed as he wobbled over with a tray of fresh drinks. 'You've never tasted anything like it, trust me,' he said as he laid down the two tall glasses of pomegranate and plum *khoshâb*. 'I've made it for you with a touch of amber, musk and my secret ingredient.' He paused, then leaned in with a wink and whispered, 'wisteria.'

Taymoor nodded his thanks as the man retreated from the table. Then he turned to his partner. 'Would you stop already?'

'What?'

'Look at you. All glum on one of the biggest days in our— hell, in anyone's—life. Come on, brother. Live it up.' He leaned in and gave Kamal a big slap on the shoulder.

Kamal raised his glass half-heartedly. 'You're right.' He took a sip.

Taymoor frowned. 'Your sister-in-law chose to be friends with an enemy of the state, all right? That's her problem, not yours. She's an adult. There's only so much you can do.'

Kamal nodded. 'I know, I know.'

'You need to talk to Ramazan,' Taymoor told him. 'He needs to set her straight before she gets caught up in a bad situation.'

Kamal scoffed. 'Set her straight? Are you kidding me? No one sets Nisreen straight. No one ever has. Except her father.'

'So talk to her father.'

'It's a bit complicated, given that he passed away two years ago.'

Taymoor took another long pull. 'Well, someone's got to

48

talk to her.' He edged in, lowering his voice. 'I don't want to see you get into trouble because of her.'

'Me, or us?'

Taymoor looked at him askance. 'That's not fair, brother.'

Kamal's face scrunched with remorse. 'I'm sorry. It's just . . . the way things are going, it feels like we're all going to get sucked into some kind of trouble, doesn't it?'

Which threw Taymoor. 'What are you talking about?'

'The psychos hoping to get their seventy-two virgins by blowing themselves to smithereens? I'm all in. Find them, take them out, every last one of them—absolutely. That's what I signed up for. White Rose subversives and anarchists like Azmi plotting to topple the Divan? They need to be stopped, no question. But the rest of it? They've got a radio DJ in the dock for insulting the beylerbey's son by questioning his real estate dealings. A university professor was fired for giving a seminar about the merits of solar power. They even locked up two puppeteers for "incitement to anarchy"'—using air quotes around the words—'just because their puppet show linked the sultan's ripping up of environmental controls and the grand vizier's factories to poisoning a town.'

'It's not conclusive. The Environment Department's still looking into that.'

'It's a puppet show, brother.'

Taymoor shrugged. 'That's not us. That's Z Directorate. It's their business.'

'We're on the same team.'

'Our job is to get the killers. That's what we do. It's not complicated.'

'Yeah, but . . . you don't think this is going overboard? Everyone seems to be guilty of something these days. It's getting so that people are scared to think.'

'Maybe they should be.' He edged closer. 'Some thoughts

can be more dangerous than explosive vests. We're at war, brother. It might not be a war in the old sense of the word, but it's a war. We're under attack from all sides, and we're vulnerable. And if we let some cracks set in, then everything could fall apart.'

Just then, Taymoor's phone beeped with an incoming text. He picked it up with a grin. 'Saved by the bell. That's way too heavy a conversation for today, brother.' He glanced at the screen, and then his grin widened.

'Hot date?' Kamal asked.

'Care to rephrase that without limiting yourself to the singular?'

Kamal played the game, kept up the pretence, and rolled his eyes as Taymoor got up.

'I'm out of here,' Taymoor said. 'Take a breath and kick back a little, brother. Or I just might have to find myself a new partner.' He gave him a playful, pointed look.

Kamal gave him a nod. 'New me. Tomorrow. Promise.'

'Good. See you at the castle, bright and early.' Taymoor wagged a finger as he stepped away through a wave of congratulatory pats. 'No rest for the vigilant: remember, bad guys are waiting.'

6

By sunset, once the *maghrib* prayers were done, enough time had passed since the mystery patient had walked into the hospital for him to be operated on safely.

There were still a lot of unknowns, especially for Ramazan, who would be administering the anaesthetic. The man's medical history was an empty file. This was far from ideal, dangerous even, but he had no choice. The surgery—open heart, not exactly a minor procedure—was unavoidable. He would just have to be overly cautious and monitor the man's vitals like a hawk during the operation, which would last several hours.

But that was easier said than done, given the questions swirling through Ramazan's mind concerning the man's bizarre tattoos. He'd never seen anything like them, and the few words he'd managed to read had awakened an unusually clingy curiosity inside him.

They were in the pre-op room, preparing the man for surgery. A nurse was standing by the bed jotting down the readings from the monitors on to a chart while Ramazan prepared the drugs that he would feed into the man's IV drip.

As he worked, Ramazan couldn't help but glance at him, and each time he did, the man was staring back at him with that same inscrutable, hard look. Which was unusual—and disturbing. Normally, while waiting to go under the knife, patients were nervous. They were about to put their lives in someone else's hands and cede control over their bodies and minds to a total stranger. Worse, the anaesthetist could be the last person they ever spoke to. This usually made them overly talkative, and they mostly discussed their fears: what if they didn't ever wake up? Or, worse, what if they woke during surgery? They were usually desperate for reassurance, of which Ramazan would offer plenty. Then he'd distract them with small talk.

This patient didn't need reassurance or seem nervous. If anything, he seemed coiled up, on edge, watching, studying. Confrontational. And all of it in that unsettling silence.

What's his story? Ramazan kept wondering, although he wasn't sure he really wanted to find out.

Anbara came in and said, 'They're ready for you.'

Ramazan nodded to the nurse and turned to the patient, noticing from the monitor that the man's heart rate spiked up at her words—which was not uncommon. But it was unusual in that the man had appeared to be totally undaunted until then.

'I'm going to give you a short-acting sedative now,' Ramazan told him. 'Then we'll wheel you in.'

He was about to squeeze the plunger into the intravenous feed when the man's arm suddenly lashed out and grabbed Ramazan's wrist. He held it firmly in place, his grip so tight it hurt Ramazan. His eyes narrowed with menace as, with his other hand, he moved his oxygen mask off to one side, exposing his mouth. Then he spoke for the first time.

'Make sure you don't screw this up, *hakim*,' he said in a low hiss. 'Make sure. Because you and all the rest of you, all of you—you owe me.' He pointed a threatening finger at Ramazan's face. 'None of you would be here if it wasn't for me. None of this—none of you would even exist if I hadn't done what I did. So get it right. You understand me?'

Ramazan couldn't breathe. He just stood there, nailed to the spot, paralysed. Then his free hand came to life and he squeezed the plunger, sending the sedative on its way—the whole lot, in one go. The drug was fast-acting, and within seconds Ramazan felt the man's grip loosen. He pulled his hand free and, trying to recover his poise, placed it by the patient's side. He glanced nervously at Anbara and saw his mystified, rattled look reflected in her face.

She didn't say anything. He didn't either. He just held her gaze for a second, then dropped his eyes back to his patient.

The man's gaze was still fixed on him, but it had softened.

'You've got nothing to worry about,' Ramazan told him, trying to sound unfazed by what had just happened. 'I'm going to give you a painkiller along with the anaesthetic, and *inshallah*'—if God wills it—'this will all be over before you know it.'

The man's eyelids had drooped down, and he was having trouble keeping his eyes open. His mouth was bent in a disturbing half-smile. 'Make sure, *hakim*,' he muttered, the words coming out slurred. 'You owe me. All of you. Even the sultan. He knows.'

Even in this half-gone state, his scowl was still unsettling. Then his words faded into a low mumble, and he drifted off into a stupor.

Anbara replaced the breathing mask over the man's mouth as his eyelids shuttered. She looked up at Ramazan, her expression one of confusion tinged with fear.

'Let's wheel him in,' he said.

Throughout the surgery, Ramazan was in a cloud.

Fonseca carried out the valve replacement calmly and expertly, as he had countless times before. Ramazan, however, had to struggle to stay focused. He was still unsettled by the stranger's weird outburst.

He hadn't mentioned it to Fonseca. He would, of course— but he didn't want to do it just before the surgery. He needed some time to process it himself.

Ramazan had enough experience to know that people's true natures generally did come out under heavy sedation and, to an even greater extent, anaesthesia. He'd seen it before surgery, as they spiralled into unconsciousness, and even more strongly after, when it took hours for the drugs to get out of their systems. In that twilight zone between consciousness and unconsciousness, natural tendencies and true temperament were unmasked. Kind, relaxed people were often giggly; aggressive people, hostile. Kids woke up crying for their mothers. Truths were also sometimes revealed, but they were often nothing more than truths that had left their mark on their victims' bodies as well as their psyches: unwanted pregnancies, cancers, physical abuse. Outwardly brave-faced people confessed their terror at the prospect of never waking up; others shared secrets as if they were in a confession booth, perhaps seeking absolution before possible death.

After the drugs wore off completely, patients generally forgot what they had said.

Somehow, and regardless of how absurd or senseless the stranger's words had sounded, he'd sensed a puzzling honesty in them. He had a nagging sense that the patient thoroughly believed what he'd said. Which could mean nothing more than that the man was mentally unstable. A nut.

But it wasn't just what he'd said. Far more perplexing was how he'd said it.

The man spoke in a very strange dialect. Ramazan couldn't place it. It wasn't the vernacular Turkish he was used to, the language that had supplanted French as the lingua franca of the region but that, over the centuries, had become infused with an abundance of French words. Instead, it was Ottoman Turkish, the complex imperial language whose use was nowadays limited to bureaucratic documents, scholarly works and the pretentious conversations of the highly educated elite. Ramazan had rarely heard it spoken in casual conversation. And it wasn't even the normal Ottoman-Turkish Ramazan knew: the man's syntax and vocabulary were highly unusual; his manner of speech, formal and rigid. Ramazan considered himself a well-travelled man and had ventured as far as Istanbul and Cairo, but he'd never heard it spoken that way before. It was thoroughly bewildering, and reminded Ramazan of some of the old classical texts he'd read as a student.

Then there were the mirror-image tattoos.

Ramazan couldn't help but be intrigued. He'd often been told that he had obsessive traits—by Nisreen, who ribbed him about it often; by his father; and by his brother, back when they were close—and, given the precision involved in his work, such traits weren't uncommon. His colleagues at the hospital often teased him about the ten-minute ritual he followed each time he put in an intravenous cannula. Whether or not he was obsessive, his eyes kept getting drawn to the tattoos throughout the procedure, which ended up taking almost five hours. Although the man's chest had been freshly shaved by the nurses, Ramazan couldn't really see much at all. The man's chest area was open, and what skin was visible was folded and obscured by the retractor, antiseptic solution and surgical drape.

After watching Fonseca stitch the man up, Ramazan started weaning him off the main anaesthetic. Ramazan would keep him intubated and heavily drugged, of course. The feeling of having a breathing tube down his throat, the discomfort, and the very nature of being a patient in intensive care would be as unpleasant as the operation itself. It would be hours before he would wake the man up—how long, exactly, he couldn't tell, since each situation was unique. Although there hadn't been any complications during the surgery, given the mystery patient's age and condition Ramazan didn't expect him to be conscious soon, not before at least five or six hours had passed.

Fonseca left the operating theatre, leaving the stranger and his recovery in Ramazan's hands. By the time they wheeled him into the male patients' intensive care unit, it was late, and Ramazan was exhausted. It was time to go home.

But he couldn't leave. Not just yet.

He couldn't resist wanting to know more, despite the voice deep inside him that was warning him to stay away.

He needed to have one last look.

Ramazan watched calmly as the cardiothoracic nurses hooked the patient up to various monitors and IV drips and looped restraints around his hands so he wouldn't pull his breathing tube out. Nisreen needed to know that Ramazan would be home even later than he'd earlier assumed. He didn't want to risk waking her up, so he pulled out his mobile phone and sent her a text message. She replied promptly and said she was going to bed. He replied with a 'good night,' and the response was a solitary ب—the texting shorthand for *bawsa,* meaning a kiss, common across the Ottoman Empire, as opposed to the *x* symbol used in the Americas, which had a Christian, religious origin. Not the most passionate exchange, but then again he didn't expect her to be in the best of moods, not after the day's events. And their marriage had long lost what little passion it used to have. At least they were still together.

He left the ICU and got himself a strong cup of coffee. By the time he came back to the patient's room, the last of the nurses was leaving. He nodded to her as she passed him, then edged closer to the bed, riding a swell of trepidation.

The stranger was still unconscious.

Ramazan just stood there for a long moment, weary and woolly-headed, uncertain about what he was even doing there, the low beeps of the monitors and the gurgle of the breathing pump adding to his trance. Then he snapped out of it and, with hesitant fingers, reached over and pulled down the blanket and the hospital gown to uncover the man's chest.

The man had a wide dressing across the middle of his chest where the vertical incision had been made, but some tattoos were visible now on either side and below it.

Ramazan stared at them, mesmerized. Then he looked over his shoulder, made sure no one was coming in, and pulled out his mobile phone. He took a series of quick pictures of the tattoos. He also took one of the man's face, for no conscious reason. Then he put away his phone and covered the man up.

He hovered there a bit longer, studying him, unsure about the hold this stranger had over him. Then he tore himself away, left the room and made his way home.

7

After Taymoor left, Kamal ended up at home, a small top-floor studio three blocks east of the Halles Bazaar that was currently swirling in a haze of apple-and-honey-flavoured tobacco smoke from a *narguileh* water pipe, cold *raki*, take-away pizza—a recent craze imported from the Naples *eyalet* that was sweeping the city—and bland escapist television.

While he was never much of a social animal, Kamal hadn't always been that much of a loner. He lived alone, which was normal, given that he wasn't married. Mixed cohabitation was, of course, out of the question in Ottoman society, given the strict limitations that tradition imposed on how men and women could interact. Dating wasn't allowed; unmarried men and women could meet openly only for brief encounters in the company of chaperones and strictly as a prelude to marriage. Not even Murad and his reforms had been able to do much to loosen that. But, of course, human desire was impossible to cage entirely. Men and women found ways to see each other in secret, despite the risks involved. And in those instances, women often found the veil to be a useful ally in helping shroud their movements.

Beyond the confines of his single lifestyle, things had become more complicated lately, making it harder for Kamal to be around some people. Across the various strata of society, people were becoming edgier, more fearful and more polarized. Now his job was even making some of his closest friends and family palpably less comfortable around him. To many, he was a hero and a protector—more than ever, after the recent arrests—but to others, he was a pariah, even though he was part of the anti-terrorist unit and not the fearsome Z Directorate that handled internal security. More often than not, it didn't bother him too much; he viewed their apprehension about him as misguided paranoia. What did bother him—what was causing him more anguish than he'd ever known—was the fact that the apprehensive group included his brother Ramazan and Ramazan's wife, Nisreen.

What did all the adulation in the world matter if those he loved most held him in such contempt?

They'd stopped inviting him over or even speaking with him weeks ago, after yet another argument had degenerated into hurtful words. He hadn't seen them or his beloved little nephew and niece for—how long had it been? He couldn't remember. It was . . . insane. After all, he was putting his life on the line to protect them, to keep their way of life safe. How could they not see that?

Taymoor was right. They were in the wrong. Nisreen had chosen her friends poorly. Azmi was a traitor, after all—a member of the White Rose. She ought to have known better. That's all there was to it.

They'd come round. They had to.

And yet . . . Ramazan and Nisreen—they weren't fools. Not by any stretch of the imagination. How could they be getting this so wrong?

As if to taunt him, the evening news came on, and the first image was of the beheadings ceremony that morning. Kamal reached for the remote and switched channels, only to come upon an almost identical report. A third channel yielded the same result. He turned off the television, took a deep pull of his water pipe, and stared out the open French windows. The late-evening sky was awash with swathes of purples and pinks, bathed with a tranquillity that seemed oblivious to his malaise.

It hadn't always been this way.

As a child, Kamal had known a gentler world. Of course, the cold war with the CRA—the Christian Republic of America—had always been there, but it hadn't threatened to boil over as it now did. And the great war against Russia had simmered back to a tense stalemate, even though the tsar never missed an opportunity to rattle his tongue about the constant encroachment of Islam on to Orthodox lands, no matter how well Murad V had treated the Slavic people living under his rule in the Balkans.

But there was peace, and there was prosperity: having long since subjugated their Persian adversaries and conquered Arabia, the Ottomans controlled the largest oil reserves on the planet. And with a virtual monopoly on the global supply of oil—which was also cheap to produce—they had, for almost a century, maintained a firm lid on the ambitions of their enemies.

Under the previous sultan's inspired leadership, the empire had thrived. Murad had been ambitiously progressive. A tireless reformer, he championed the social, economic, cultural and even religious transformation of his empire and only stopped short of political reform. He made cautious but marked progress in spreading education, improving the rights of women and the conditions of the poor, and encouraging the arts. Murad had also overseen the launch of the Internet across the empire, an invention that had originated in an Istanbul university lab—something that the staunchly Puritan Americans were still unwilling to embrace.

He had set the empire on course for a fairer, brighter future. But it was a tightrope to walk. Relaxing the limitations of free speech, combined with the networking effect of the Internet, had allowed radical new ideas to blossom; Murad had let the genie out of the bottle, and he needed to make sure it didn't overwhelm him and his rule. He also had to make sure any public debate of these reforms didn't escalate into civil unrest, since facing off against the reforms and their supporters was an entrenched religious establishment that wasn't easy to tame.

For a while, Murad managed to maintain order and stability and safeguard his empire's *hayba*—its stature and prestige—without having to resort to excessive coercion. But the reform tightrope proved to be trickier far from the capital, in a remote corner of the empire: the Diriyah *eyalet* of the Arabian peninsula.

There, long-simmering Islamist resentment boiled over into outright rebellion.

The resentment had its roots three centuries earlier, when Saud ibn Muhammad ibn Muqrin, the local emir of Al Diriyah, became a vocal critic of the Ottomans who had conquered his lands. He considered Mehmed IV, who was sultan at the time, unworthy of his position as caliph—the leader of the world's Muslims and defender of the faith. After all, most Ottomans didn't even speak Arabic, the language of the holy Koran, and many elements of their culture and daily life were at odds with the strict teachings of orthodox Islam. Furthermore, no sultan had ever made the hajj pilgrimage, which was every Muslim's sacred duty. Saud set about to liberate his homeland from Ottoman control and wipe out what he perceived as Ottomans' heretical practices. The sultan, who considered himself the shadow of God on earth, was infuriated. Fresh from his conquest of Vienna, Rome and the rest of western Europe, he sent his Egyptian vassals in, took control of the peninsula, and had Saud and several of his Salafi scholars, most notably a preacher by the name of Abd al-Wahhab, publicly berated and humiliated before they were put to the sword.

Three hundred years later, Saud's ideas resurfaced with a vengeance. Abd al-Wahhab's descendants rose up against Murad's reforms, angrily believing they distanced the empire from its Islamic roots, only this time their tactics were different. Armed attackers and suicide bombers began to strike random targets across the empire. Then they hit Istanbul itself, hijacking a commercial airliner and crashing it into the Topkapi Palace.

The sultan had been out on an unannounced hunting trip that morning, but over two hundred of his subjects were killed.

Murad responded ferociously. As his ancestor had done, he sent in another Egyptian force, this time supported by air strikes and aerial drones, to subjugate the rebels. The troops met stiff resistance, countless civilians were killed, and the campaign was trumpeted as a success, even though the fanatics' scattershot attacks never stopped.

The plane strike also had a ripple effect in a quiet home in Paris. It was there that Kamal, fresh out of school at eighteen, decided to enrol at the military academy at Poitiers and not, following his older brother, the university.

He'd never been particularly academic. His interest in life was more visceral, and the idea of defending his family and fellow countrymen was too strong to resist. But by the time he graduated and joined the Hafiye's counterterrorism directorate, everything had changed.

After forty years of dignified rule, Murad V succumbed to a brain aneurysm at the age of seventy-one.

Abdülhamid III, the petulant tyrant who grabbed the throne as his successor, turned out to be everything his father was not.

And in an unfortunate synchronicity of terrible luck for the empire, the Americans' energy revolution took hold, choking the life out of the Ottomans' golden goose and gutting their economy almost overnight.

It galled Kamal that a people the Ottomans had long derided for being backwardly racist—the CRA was exclusively Christian and exclusively white; no one else was allowed in—had pulled the economic rug right from under them. But the truth was that the Americans' alternative to oil shouldn't have hit the Ottomans as hard as it did. After all, their elected monarch, Elijah Huntington, had announced his intentions publicly long before they actually managed to make it happen.

A decade earlier, Huntington had decided that his people couldn't, and wouldn't, remain reliant on a foreign empire—much less a Muslim one—for their energy needs. He proclaimed that America had to come up with an alternative, one they could produce themselves. He also decreed that it shouldn't harm the environment. His vision wasn't just shaped by his strategic foresight; it was also driven by his faith. As a devout servant of Christ and a passionate follower of the longstanding Puritan tradition that guided his rule, he fervently believed that doing everything in his power to protect the planet—God's creation—was his sacred duty.

Huntington's fiery speeches galvanized public opinion; public officials and big business, despite fierce lobbying by the coal and auto industries, had no choice but to follow suit. The best minds up and down the Americas went to work, and in less than a decade they turned his vision of clean energy into reality: wind farms, ocean-wave generators and solar power became the primary sources of energy across the Christian nation. While the Ottoman Empire obstinately clung to its reliance on fossil fuels, the Americans, with an eye on weakening their Muslim rivals, aggressively pushed the spread of their new technologies in the Far East and Africa, whose inhabitants happily joined in the revolution.

The price of oil—the empire's main source of revenue—collapsed, dropping from a high of well over a hundred kurush to its present level of ten.

As a consequence, the empire started to hurt. Badly.

In such a time of crisis, the Ottomans would have benefited from the stewardship of a wise and noble leader, someone with a calm temperament and a reasoned mind. Someone like Murad V. But he was now gone, and Abdülhamid III was anything but calm and reasoned.

The new sultan was forty-six when he seized power after his father's death. He had not been chosen for rule, nor was he the sultan's eldest son. Ottoman imperial succession still followed a centuries-old tradition of having no appointed heir to the throne. The many sons of the sultan, brothers and half-brothers born and raised in the harem, sons of a multitude of Christian slaves who were never wed to the monarch, would have to fight for the throne. Whoever emerged victorious would then have his rivals killed—siblings, cousins, uncles, any male with a potential claim to the throne. This 'law of fratricide' ensured that only the most ruthless of princes acceded to power.

Unfortunately for the empire, Abdülhamid had little to offer beyond a narcissistic craving for power. Guided by a monstrous ego, a fiery temper and a rigid, incurious mind, he was far from qualified to deal with the economic tsunami caused by Huntington's vision.

With the empire's currency collapsing and its economy buckling under severe strain, Abdülhamid and his cabinet of self-serving sycophants put into place a series of measures that hit hard. Taxes were raised, although, much to the distaste of the populace, the *askeri*—the privileged ruling class of clergy, military and state officials—were still exempt. Social services, particularly for schooling and medical care, were caught in a spiral of cuts. Inflation rose. Imperial public spending shrank, and the little that remained was earmarked for Istanbul, seat of the sultan, and its surroundings, where it was eaten away by the inflated price-rigging of the sultan's cronies.

Unrest, inevitably, began to stir.

Some of it manifested physically: demonstrations and riots, which were swiftly shut down by the authorities using violence and mass arrests.

A different reaction to the economic crisis was far more insidious and harder to stifle: the questioning of absolute rule.

Galvanized by the widespread discontent, intellectuals across the empire—and nowhere more so than at the far reaches of the empire, in the ancient capital of arts and culture of Paris—began to explore alternatives to the centuries-old status quo. The whispers got louder. Radical ideas weren't just being aired in private discussions any more; previously unthinkable questions were finding their way into print and even into radio and television broadcasts.

The state hit back.

Mass surveillance, aided and abetted by the state's mandatory 'Social Credit System', was expanded indiscriminately. Television and radio stations were nationalized and placed under the control of the Supreme Council for Radio and Television. Newspapers that questioned the state's actions were vilified and purged of their best reporters before ending up under the stewardship of government insiders. Countless university professors and lawyers lost their jobs.

Back when Kamal was enrolled at the academy in Poitiers, those who were brave enough to risk criticizing the Divan or the ruling elite could expect a hefty fine, a set of lashings or a short prison sentence. Those days were long gone. The prisons were filled with 'enemies of the state' whose families were offered no information since all charges under statute 275 of the Ottoman Criminal Code, the one dealing with treason, were classified.

Kamal was right in the thick of it. As a patriotic, faithful subject of the sultan, his duty was to protect the state from all threats, and the state was certainly under threat. He knew that extreme measures were called for. But a growing number of people whose opinions he valued—Nisreen and his brother at their forefront—were claiming otherwise. For them, these extreme measures were nothing more than a cynical ploy; Abdülhamid and his corrupt viziers were using the spectre of Islamic terrorism to blur the lines between extremism and dissent, allowing them to brand anything that threatened their rule as 'ideological subversion' and treason.

Kamal took a deep drag from his *narguileh,* and, as its soothing effect wormed its way into the darkest recesses of his mind, he thought back to when he'd last discussed it all with his father, during a phone call a few weeks back. A veterinary surgeon who'd decamped from Paris to the Périgord and become a poultry farmer after losing his wife to a galloping cancer seven years ago, Kamal and Ramazan's father was an earnest man, part of an older, more conservative generation that tended to support its sultan's policies more blindly. He'd reminded Kamal of his responsibilities to keep his fellow imperial subjects safe and of his duty to his sultan and to his God. Beyond the echoes of that conversation, Kamal also drew solace from the doctrine he'd been taught at the academy, the one his superiors had been trumpeting loudly since the unrest had begun: citizens had no right to revolt against their rulers because civilization was the result of social and political consensus, and continually challenging its traditions would inevitably lead to anarchy.

And nothing was worse than anarchy.

The knock at Kamal's front door took a moment to register.

It wasn't loud—more of a furtive, brief double tap. A familiar one. He checked his watch. It was well past ten. He thought briefly about whether to answer, and then, when it came again, he raised himself off the large floor cushion, trudged over, and opened the door.

Leyla slipped in, shut the door behind her quietly, and stood there, her back against the wall, her eyes and mouth gleaming with excitement.

Kamal studied her uncertainly. 'Leyla, tonight's not—'

She quickly quieted him by pressing a firm, perfectly manicured finger to his mouth. 'Don't be silly. I'm here now. My *hero*.' She beamed at him.

'Don't—' he started to say, but she leaned towards him and kissed him.

'They're all asleep. Very, very soundly.' She lived with her parents and one younger brother in an apartment two floors below him.

In a society that was still bound by the restrictive limitations of *shari'a* law, her presence in his apartment was highly dangerous for them both—but also highly tantalizing.

It was hard to say which was more provocative: her face or her body. Kamal had explored both in many snatched opportunities, ones that were almost always instigated by her. She was young—barely twenty—and she had an untamed spirit along with a nerve and audacity that knew little bounds. Like many other young women of her world, Leyla knew how to get around the severe boundaries that dictated what she could do, where she could go and who she could see, and she was determined to make the most of it while she could. She would soon be married off to an older man, a moneyed jeweller she'd met twice while chaperoned and veiled. It had been enough to give her an unshakeable feeling that the man was more interested in men than in women, but she also knew he would provide her with everything her parents could never afford. Hers would be a lush, comfortable life, and, although she would have preferred to spend it with Kamal, he'd made clear from the beginning of their liaison that marriage wasn't an option.

He gave her a slow shake of his head and let out a small chuckle, but she stilled it as she pressed her finger back against his lips, moving it tantalizingly left and right both as a scolding 'no' gesture and a tease, her head slightly tilted down, her dark eyes angled alluringly upwards and hooked into his, her mouth slightly open, her plump lips moist and beckoning. And in a stampede of heartbeats, an unwelcome intrusion turned into an irresistible, ravenous hunger.

Kamal grabbed her hand and pushed it aside as he planted his mouth on hers and kissed her, hard. Her whole body arched forward to welcome him as her mouth feasted hungrily on his tongue while he pressed against her, pinning her against the wall, his hands now tight around her jaw, keeping her in place for him to feed off like a starved beast at a trough. Then he released her face from his grip and moved his hands down, exploring and cupping the curves of her body, kneading its sensitive spots, the sudden spikes in her breathing guiding his fingers like strings on a puppet; then in a fury of movement, he had pushed their robes aside, grabbed her from under her thighs, lifted her so she was straddling him, and pushed inside her.

They dropped to the floor, where Kamal lost himself in a frenzy of urgent desire, her gasps egging him on, one hand now braced against her mouth to muffle her moans, his eyes locked on her rapturous face but not registering it, each desperate thrust like the lash of a whip to tame the accusing eyes that were stalking him.

But they wouldn't let go—neither Nisreen's stare, which Kamal now saw on every woman in the stands, nor her friend Azmi's unflinching glare as it burned into him in the moments leading up to his death.

They were still there, long after Leyla had gone. Another tall glass of *raki* hadn't helped. Worse, his mind was luring him down a previously unthinkable abyss: it was making him question his career choice.

Gazing out across the skyline of sleepy domes and minarets, he found himself wondering if he wouldn't have been better off following a more benign path like that of his brother, an uncomplicated family man who went about his work quietly and built model train sets on Fridays. Ramazan also saved lives, but he did it without anyone looking at him as if he were a monster.

And he did it with Nisreen by his side.

As far as Kamal was concerned, that, more than anything, would have justified any career choice.

But it was too late to do anything about that, and he knew it.

8

Seven blocks north of Kamal's studio, Ramazan did his best to unlock the front door to his home quietly before stepping inside.

The family apartment was on the fifth floor of a nineteenth-century stone building in the Mahmud Pasha *mahalle*—one of the residential neighbourhoods that formed the city—and conveniently located only a stone's throw from Bekri Mustapha Avenue and its bustling markets.

It was late, and the only light came from a lone dim lamp that shone from a small side table in the entrance hall.

He set his satchel down, slipped off his shoes, and then took off his robe and unrolled his turban. As he always did when he came home late, his first port of call was the children's room. They were both fast asleep, in their customary positions: Tarek, his eight-year-old son, sprawled across his bed with the sheets kicked off, one arm curled around Firas, the stuffed toy dinosaur that was his inseparable companion; and Noor, just short of her sixth birthday, rolled up and cocooned under her blanket, her tousled curls barely visible. A small night light projected stars and a crescent moon on to the ceiling. No matter what life was slinging at him, no matter what stresses were buffeting him, seeing them was like a honey and aniseed infusion on a cold wintry night.

He stood there for a minute, just watching them, serenaded by the sound of their gentle breaths. Then he pulled away and padded over to the master bedroom.

He peered in from the doorway. His eyes had adjusted to

the faint light from the hallway, and, although the room was dark, he was relieved to find that Nisreen was fast asleep as well. It was good that she'd been able to fall asleep; Ramazan had little doubt of the torment she must have felt all day because of Azmi's execution. Her face was facing his way and he stood there, contemplating her.

Even in torment, she was gorgeous; there was no doubt about that. Even asleep, when her face was sunken into the pillow and her mesmeric almond eyes weren't on display, when the aura she radiated was at rest, she was still bewitching.

Gorgeous, clever, capable and a great mother: he was a lucky man, and he knew it. Too lucky maybe—he often wondered about how he'd lucked out when, ten years ago, their parents had arranged their marriage. He was twenty-four and she was just shy of twenty. He hadn't worried so much during those first few years, when he was still in that optimistic, upbeat bliss of a new marriage, babies, young children, a career on the rise. But with time he couldn't escape the notion that he was punching above his weight. Way above. It was painfully evident at dinner parties and at other social encounters: she more than held her ground, she was accomplished, and charismatic men were irresistibly drawn to her. To her credit, she never played games, never led any of them on, never gave them the slightest opening. She was unfailingly respectful and loyal towards her husband. But he could sense the malaise growing inside her, the apathy, the dissatisfaction. He could feel her slipping away. They hadn't discussed it outright, only tiptoed politely around it, and when they had, she'd always assured him that things were fine. But he still saw it in her face every morning and every night before he turned out the lights.

The situation around them wasn't helping; in fact, it was accentuating their divide. Nisreen's friends were courting disaster. As a lawyer at the vanguard of reform for women's rights, Nisreen had already been skirting the periphery of trouble, and that was before she'd started defending journalists and academics who had been yanked out of their homes or protesters who had been hauled off the streets. This worried Ramazan; at times, he tried to find some comfort in the fact that his brother was in the secret police, but he wasn't sure how much that would help if things ever got ugly.

She was getting sucked into the spiralling unrest, and he feared for her safety, but he also knew there wasn't much he could do about it. Nisreen was a conscientious wife and mother, to be sure. But she was also a woman of strong convictions and a fighter. She was animated by a flame that he could never fully grasp, let alone match. And the more he played it safe and stayed out of the troubles swirling around them, the more he excused himself from any invitations to join in any form of protest, the more he could see the chagrin darken her face.

As he stood there, the serenity he'd felt from seeing his children drained away, supplanted by a roiling anxiety about what the future held for him and Nisreen.

He wasn't ready for bed. He made his way back to the front of the apartment, past the family living room and the *sala,* the more elegant, formal sitting room that was used for entertaining guests, and entered his study at the front of the apartment. This was his sanctuary. Given the work he did, Ramazan needed to have other interests to distract him from the strain, stress and even the occasional boredom of his job. Several of the anaesthetists he knew felt the same way. One of his closest colleagues was a volunteer doctor for the ambulance service in his spare time. Some were avid sportsmen; others were real polymaths: musicians, authors, painters. Ramazan was a train buff, as attested not only by the large table that stood proudly in the middle of the room housing his model railway, an elaborate set that he had spent years building, but also by the model trains lining his bookshelves.

He padded around the table and opened a corner cabinet, from which he dug out a bottle of *yeni raki,* the more distinctively bitter *raki* that was distilled from sugar-beet alcohol, and poured himself a tall glass.

Alcohol was still, of course, banned for Muslims across the empire, but its prohibition had ebbed and flowed over the centuries, depending on who was in power. Some sultans, like Suleiman the Magnificent, were excessively puritanical. He had decreed that drunks were to be punished by having molten lead poured down their throats. His son Selim II, however, was an unrepentant hedonist who repealed his father's ban, claiming that while the prohibition on alcohol was righteous and wise, it was only meant for the common folk and not for the more refined upper tiers of society who knew how to drink in moderation.

In the palaces and across the empire, water, coffee, tea, and fruit juice were the only approved drinks for Muslims and the only ones consumed publicly. Privately, things were different. The Zaptiye turned a blind eye to what took place in the privacy of people's homes; they only swooped in and arrested offenders when things got out of hand or when political winds required a face-saving display.

Drink in hand, Ramazan edged over to the balcony doors and looked out. Illuminated minarets, taller than any building across the cityscape by decree, poked the dark sky, the slow blinking of the lights at the top of their finials hypnotic and soothing. In the distance, the dome of the Mehmediyye Mosque, exquisitely lit up, slumbered in splendour. On that warm summer night and under an unusually luminous crescent moon, one could be forgiven for imagining the city as a beacon of tranquillity. The menace that loomed over its citizens was nowhere in sight, but Ramazan, like anyone else who was up this late, knew it was there. It had merely slunk back into the shadows, waiting for the next opportunity to strike.

He finished his drink and poured himself a second glass. He was tired, but he wasn't sleepy. A strange current was rippling through him. His mind was too fired up, captive to both the concern over his wife and the curiosity about his mysterious patient.

He checked his watch. It was twenty past two.

He wasn't ready for bed. He retrieved his mobile phone and, ignoring a silent scream of warning deep within him, pulled up the pictures he'd taken of the stranger's tattoos.

9

One by one, Ramazan enlarged the pictures for a closer look.

Written that way, back to front, the words tattooed on his patient were hard to read. He wondered about that. The obvious answer was that they'd been done that way so the stranger could read them while looking at himself in a mirror. Ramazan thought of a further reason: it made them harder for a casual observer to read. Which was useful if one had something to hide.

He stepped out to the hall and held the phone so it faced the mirror above the side table. He studied the photograph. The words were easily readable now. There were several names and dates—'Dorde Petrovic, Visevac, 16/11/1762'; 'Alexander Ypsilantis, Istanbul, 12/12/1792', and others—but he didn't recognize any of them. He pulled up another photograph. More names, plenty of them—'François-Marie Arouet / Voltaire', 'Rousseau', 'Napoleon', and others—alongside places and numbers that looked like more dates from some distant, centuries-far future, all of which meant nothing to him either. He flicked to the next shot. More unintelligible gibberish with lines like '3NG / 1diatomite / min sod carb'.

He went through a few more photographs that showed the tattooed drawings. They also seemed random. One was a diagram showing the inner workings of some kind of box that had a long handle coming out of it and coiled cylinders inside it. Another was a diagram of a mechanical contraption that had a crank handle, what looked like a rotating barrel made up of several cylinders, and various springs and pins linking them. A few others showed schematics that involved vats, cylinders, tubes and valves linking them, and fire—and these registered with him. Sizzling with curiosity now, he kept going until, a couple of images later, he came across something else that triggered a burst of recognition.

At first, it looked like just another list of names and places. 'Thomas Savery / Salisbury Court / London', 'Denis Papin / Paris 75 / London 87 / Marburg', and a few others. In his haste, he was about to flick to the next photo when he made the association and realized what he was looking at. He swiped back to the drawing of the vats and the tubes.

Savery, Papin and some of the other listed names, like Huygens and Newcomen, were centuries-old inventors who had pioneered the steam engine.

The tattooed schematics depicted early versions of it.

The inventors—English, French, Dutch—had all moved to Vienna not long after its fall to the empire in 1094.* Like many scientists, they had been attracted by the sultan's offers of unlimited funding and resources. They were all part of the Ottoman industrial revolution, a golden era for the empire that had begun during its victorious sweep across Europe in the late seventeenth century and had changed the world.

The inventors in question had collaborated on creating the first steam-powered trains, which had a dramatic effect on shortening travel times between Istanbul and the far reaches of the empire, allowing the efficient shuttling of troops and military supplies. This had played a huge role in the conquest of Europe after the fall of Vienna.

Why did the stranger have those names and schematics tattooed across his torso?

* 1094 in the Islamic hijri calendar, or AD 1683.

Ramazan mulled it over in the darkness, deciding he needed to investigate further. On tired feet, he padded to the family living room, where he sat at the low desk and switched on the computer. He scrolled through the pictures he'd taken of the tattoos again, still wondering about them. He was having second thoughts about running queries through the government-controlled *Hafiza* Internet search engine, which was the only one available in the empire. Abdülhamid's tight controls meant that only government-approved websites and content were authorized to be online. Anything else was blocked. Even so, Ramazan knew that he still needed to be careful about what he typed into the search box. Everything accessed online would go through the authorities' filters. Websites, email—every keystroke would be suspect and analysed by algorithms, and there was no way to evade them. The Internet was heavily censored and monitored—goals easily achieved, since the state was also the only Internet provider across the empire and everything passed through its servers. A small group of rebellious coders had tried to spread a VPN by putting it on discs distributed on the sly, but that soon ended after the authorities caught them and had them publicly flogged and locked up. The VPN discs that were still in circulation were highly prized until the government's coders figured out a way to flag anyone using them. Arrests followed. No one was using the discs any more.

Ramazan hesitated, pondering his next move. It was very late, he'd had a long day, and he was exhausted and weary. But there was a stubborn curiosity flickering deep inside him that he couldn't extinguish. He shrugged and decided that his queries shouldn't raise any red flags, then started typing the words into *Hafiza* methodically and cautiously. Most of what he inputted yielded nothing. Many of the names gave no result; it was as if those people had never existed. A few, like Baruch Spinoza, were obscure writers and political thinkers whose work had been officially discredited centuries ago. But then the result from one of the queries he entered shot a spike of dread through him: '3NG / 1diatomite / min sod carb' turned out to be an abbreviated formula for manufacturing dynamite. Which triggered a sudden, unexpected association in Ramazan's mind regarding one of the schematic diagram tattoos he hadn't recognized before that moment: he was now sure that it depicted an ancient, plunger-type blasting detonator.

In a panic, he killed the browser window and jabbed the computer's power button. He watched the screen die out, then shut his eyes, furious at himself. Researching dynamite couldn't be good. Not good at all. He might have some explaining to do. Which was not something anyone looked forward to. His heart was now kickboxing its way out of his chest, his mind ruing his overzealous curiosity—and yet he still couldn't ignore the question gnawing at him: What did this all mean?

Ramazan couldn't make sense of what he had uncovered—he wasn't even sure he wanted to any more—but it only added to the portentous feeling he had about the man. The tattoos could point to a dangerous psychotic, someone who should be reported to the authorities. An enemy of the state. If they asked, he could always excuse it that way. He was being a patriot. Then again, the tattoos could be dismissed as no more than the eccentric markings of an original or deranged mind, his odd outburst further proof of his imbalance. That was what a rational, calm mind would have concluded, and Ramazan was a rational, calm man. Too rational and too calm, perhaps. But he was also an intelligent man and an instinctive one, and, faced with what he had seen, he was finding it hard to dismiss it. Something didn't feel right. And in some strange, unfamiliar way, it didn't just scare him.

It excited him.

Sayyid Ramazan Hekim didn't get excited too often.

There was a hidden story locked away inside that man. Ramazan thought about the dynamite again and wondered if the man wasn't a threat to the people, to the city, to the empire. He had to find out more. He needed to investigate. And if the man did turn out to be an enemy of the state, one intent on causing death to the innocent, and if Ramazan were to be the one to flush him out and get him locked away before he could strike, it would be a massive coup. It would be life-changing, especially when it came to his marriage. He'd reap the praise and the high esteem that his brother Kamal had been basking in since the arrests. Even more important, he might even get to savour the kind of admiration Nisreen once held for his brother. He'd be the hero, without any of his brother's taint.

The prospect was electrifying.

He checked his watch. It was almost five. Dawn wasn't far off.

'What are you doing up this late? It's the middle of the night.'

Her voice snapped him out of his reverie, and he looked up.

Nisreen was there, leaning against the doorjamb, looking half asleep with her tousled hair and eyelids that were struggling to stay open.

'I—I couldn't sleep. The surgery was—it took for ever,' he said, trying to smother any hint of deceit from his voice.

'Oh. Is your patient all right?'

'Yes. Well—yes, I think so. He is.'

She seemed momentarily confused. Then her features relaxed somewhat. 'Good.' She studied him, then asked, 'Are you going to stay up?'

'No. I mean—I don't know. It's . . .' He made a show of checking his watch again. 'Actually, I should head back soon.

79

He'll be coming out of sleep, and I really ought to be there when he does.'

There was a lag in Nisreen's reaction. He wondered if he should stay, be with her on this troubled night, comfort her. But he didn't want to talk about Azmi's death, which the conversation would inevitably drift to. And he needed to find out more about his mysterious patient. If there was something sinister to uncover, something that might turn him into a hero, his window of opportunity wasn't unlimited.

Nisreen nodded slowly and asked, 'You want me to make you a cup of coffee?'

'No, thank you. I'll get one at the hospital.' He smiled, then regretted it instantly. She knew him too well not to notice that it was forced.

She nodded again. 'I'll see you later then.' She was about to turn, then said, 'You should probably get out of those clothes. Why don't you have a shower? It'll wake you up.'

'I didn't want to wake you.'

She gave him a sheepish look. 'I already am.'

'Okay.'

He followed her to the bedroom. She got back into bed while he headed to the bathroom and washed. By the time he came out to get dressed, she was asleep again.

He said his *fajr* prayers, though they didn't provide him with any of the clarity he was hoping for or give him any respite from the apprehension he felt about what he was doing. Then he slipped out of the apartment and headed back to the hospital.

He wanted to be there when the mystery man regained consciousness.

Nisreen heard the front door click shut and sat up.

She'd woken up when Ramazan came home, but she'd stayed in bed and acted asleep when she felt him approach the bedroom. She didn't like doing that, and it wasn't something she did on a regular basis. But she'd had a tough day and neither wanted to discuss it with her husband, risking one of their tense debates, nor felt like engaging in small talk about anything else.

It had surprised her that he hadn't come to bed, which was his normal routine, especially that late, which was also unusual. Instead, she heard him walk off to the front of the apartment; heard the soft clink of ice cubes against glass, once and then again; felt the minutes turn into hours—and still he wasn't back—all of which was highly unusual. And when she finally decided to get out of bed and investigate, just as she was about to reach the doorway to the family room, she heard his sharp intake of breath, his hissed, muttered curse, and the violent stab of his finger on the computer's keyboard.

She'd stopped in her tracks, wondering whether to intrude on whatever was going on. Then she thought that he might have already heard her approach and maybe that was why he'd rushed to shut down the computer. When she did make an appearance, it was clear that he was being evasive. Being so principled and honest also made him a very bad liar, especially to someone who knew him as well as she did.

Lies were not part of their life together. She didn't think so—at least, nothing more than the trivial white lies that were often necessary among all couples. But she was absolutely certain that Ramazan was hiding something, and this was beyond unusual. It was unheard of in their relationship. Her husband had always been unimpeachably scrupulous— a good man, even boringly so, she now thought, a feeling she wasn't proud of, although that didn't make it untrue.

She was still hurting from Azmi's death, and wasn't sure she was thinking clearly. But she couldn't get back to sleep, not after what had just happened. The idea of Ramazan hiding something from her was so puzzling that she couldn't stop herself from getting out of bed, making her way to the family room, and turning on the computer.

And pulling up its web search history.

She should have known better, but her tired mind got the best of her, because her husband's web searches, which took her by complete surprise, weren't just destined to feed her curiosity.

They also landed four *fersahs* away, the equivalent of around fourteen miles, to the east of their apartment, at a highly guarded compound no civilian had ever been allowed to enter.

The vast complex covered over ten *dunams* and comprised power stations with chiller plants and cooling towers to keep them running and a central windowless structure that housed endless banks of computers capable of storing and processing the communications taking place within the empire's borders: Internet searches, emails, landline and mobile phone calls and texts, as well as all kinds of personal data—purchases, coffeehouse bills, parking receipts, travel itineraries, and other kinds of digital 'pocket litter'.

For the favoured few who knew about it, the compound was called the Comprehensive Imperial Cybersecurity Initiative Data Centre, and the exabytes of data on its servers were destined for two programs. The first was the Social Credit System, which rated all citizens and was accessible to the state's officials and bureaucrats, allowing them to know at a glance who was late in paying bills, who had plagiarized schoolwork, who had health issues, or who had made inappropriate comments online. A parallel set of data was destined for the Insider Threat Program, which was run by the Hafiye and was far more sinister. Running foul of that program inevitably led to far more serious consequences than being refused an insurance policy or turned down for a job.

The programs sucked in data in ways that were known, assumed, rumoured—and unsuspected. More often than not, they were effective in catching their subjects unawares.

As they already had that night.

The wards of the Hurrem Sultan were quiet, a fitting end to the day of rest.

Tomorrow, a new week would begin, and the halls would be heaving with activity.

Not tonight, though. And not in room 7 of the intensive care unit, where a tattooed man was blissfully adrift in an ocean of sedatives and painkillers.

His untethered mind had a lot of territory it could explore, for Ayman Rasheed had lived a life that was arguably fuller than any man had managed. That night, however, it had chosen to revisit the catalyst to everything that was to come, the fuse that exploded any barriers to the possible and sent him on his journey into the unknown, and the man who had provided him with that fuse.

It happened in Palmyra, Syria, in October 2015. Which wasn't just a different place and time.

It was a different world altogether.

The prisoner held up his emaciated, filthy hands and stared at them. They still twitched uncontrollably. They hadn't really stopped, not since that first beating from—how long ago had it been? Days? Weeks?

He wasn't sure.

Any notion of time wasn't really relevant any more. Not to him. Or, he knew, to any of the other men he could hear getting beaten and tortured beyond the confines of the cold, filthy room he was being held in.

His hands, though, were an odd fascination for him simply because they were still there. And given that the rest of him was also still there, given that he was still a living, breathing mass of cells, given that he still existed, he wondered if his inner torment about what he'd done, about the great secret he'd been forced to divulge—and his fear about the forces his disclosure could unleash—was misjudged.

He'd held out reasonably well after the initial beating. He was, after all, seventy-three years old. In good shape, for sure, fit and youthful after all those years in the field, working the digs in the heat and the dust, running the show as the old city's director of antiquities and the curator of its museum, excavating the treasures of its glorious past. Still, seventy-three and hosepipe lashings don't mix well.

The next level of interrogation and suffering, however, was enough to break him.

He didn't last half an hour when they put him through the shabah*— the Ghost—which consisted of tying his hands behind his back before hoisting him off the ground from his cuffs. Simple, but ferociously effective. The first shoulder had popped out of its socket almost immediately, the second no more than ten agonizing minutes later. The pain had been excruciating and, in his experience, beyond compare. It was only after he'd lost consciousness that they'd brought him down. At least he'd been spared the more vicious of their torture techniques, the ones he and his fellow Syrians knew all too well, the ones the Assad regime had used on its people for decades, the same ones that their ISIS nemeses, the Islamists who'd grabbed him, were now using on countless others. The sadistic contraptions with other disturbingly whimsical names like the Flying Carpet, the German Chair or the Black Slave.*

They weren't necessary.

No, after the Ghost, he talked. He gave them what they wanted.

After watching the Islamists loot and destroy dozens of Syria's most prized archaeological heritage sites and converge on Palmyra, he and his colleagues from the museum had spirited away hundreds of statues and ancient artefacts, Roman and Byzantine treasures that the barbarians wanted to plunder and sell to help finance their murderous rampage.

And now that he was no longer of any use to them, he knew they'd soon kill him.

It was a fate he could have avoided if he'd wanted to. He could have joined those who'd left before the ISIS militants had overrun the city. Many had. But Palmyra was his home. He'd devoted his whole life to it. Ancient Greek, Roman, Palmyrene, Byzantine, Umayyad, Mamluk, Ottoman—the city, first settled over ten thousand years ago, had flourished under a multitude of empires. He'd been instrumental in uncovering and preserving its epic heritage, and there was a lot here to protect: temples and shrines and statues and carvings that couldn't be moved to safety or hidden. Palmyra had been his life, a city that had entrusted him with many of its secrets. He'd always assumed he would die there, although not like this. Not at the hands of these savages.

Perhaps his revelations would spare him the monstrous pain of a slow beheading, one that, he grimly imagined, would inevitably be plastered all over their YouTube and Facebook accounts. But death would be a small mercy at this point. He would welcome it, especially after hearing about what was to come from the demon now facing him in his grubby cell, sitting cross-legged on the floor.

His tormentor.

The man who, while questioning him, had read his expression perfectly. The inquisitor who had sensed that the old director of antiquities was hiding something else, something greater than the artefacts he'd helped bury, who'd known that he hadn't given up his biggest secret. The brute who'd dragged the director's nine-year-old niece into this hellhole, held a blade to her throat, and described every sordid act he and his men would do to her if the old man didn't speak up.

He'd had no choice but to give the beast what he wanted. And now the beast was back, with a curious look in his dispassionate, calculating eyes. A look that presaged disaster.

The prisoner felt utterly helpless and at his mercy, a pathetic, crushed supplicant. How he wished he had memorized the incantation. It was complicated, a strange sequence of words from a long-lost language, and it wouldn't have been easy, especially since the slightest mistake might stop it from working and could leave him stranded. Still, how he wished he could have used it to escape. He would have taken the risk of being stranded; he would have preferred to be anywhere but here. But it was too late for that now.

He was too scared to ask, but he couldn't hold it back.

'You . . . you tried it, didn't you?'

His captor responded only with a couple of slow, thoughtful nods.

The prisoner's breath caught. 'And . . . ?'

The man remained silent for a moment, considering his reply, before his face widened in an unsettling, leery satisfaction. 'It was . . . exhilarating. Beyond words, really. But then, you know that. You've tried it, too.'

The prisoner had only ever dared try his great discovery once, and very briefly at that. He'd been mystified, a couple of years earlier, when he'd first found the ancient writings that were carved into the walls of a small, hidden chamber at the edge of the Temple of Baalshamin, a second-century edifice dedicated to the Canaanite sky god. He'd spent long hours trying to decipher their message, and, once he had, he'd checked his work over and over to make sure he'd got it right. What they told was impossible, he'd thought. Surely, impossible. And yet there it was, reaching out from the distant past, bewitching him, beckoning him with its tantalizing lure, and he couldn't resist trying it.

No one could have resisted that.

And so, after much thought about how far back to travel, he'd done it. It had worked, but it had also scared the hell out of him. He'd never had the guts to try it again. Perhaps that was how any sane man would react.

The question was, Was his captor sane? Were any of them?

He wasn't too sure they were.

In his more lucid, calmer moments, he tried not to be overly harsh on himself. He hadn't given up his secret easily. No one could accuse him of that. Not after what they'd done to him.

'Where did you . . . ?' he asked his captor. 'How far back did you—'

The man stilled him with a tut-tut from his mouth and a lightning-quick, small wag of his finger. But he said nothing.

The prisoner froze.

The man studied him, his mind clearly running through some kind of internal deliberation. 'You've given me something with limitless potential. For that I should be immensely grateful to you. But at the same time something with this much potential needs to be handled with care. Extreme care. And extreme discretion. I'm going to need time to think about it. A lot of time. As you can imagine, there are so many possible choices, so many possibilities. Which means I have a lot of work to do. A lot of reading, thinking, planning. And I can't risk having anyone else know about this.'

He reached under his jacket and pulled out a knife. It was matt black, military spec, its blade ending in an upturned arc.

The director of antiquities went rigid at the sight.

'Besides,' the man said as he tapped the blade casually against his open palm, 'killing you now won't really change much in terms of your future. You won't have one, not after I'm done. You won't be around to witness it—at least, I don't think you will. It wouldn't make sense, would it?'

The director was unable to focus on what the man was saying. Every neuron inside him was focused on the blade. He tried to formulate some kind of plea, to prod his mouth to eke out something that might change his captor's mind, but his senses were too jumbled to react. All he could manage was a meek, mumbled 'Please', but even as he said it, he knew it wouldn't change anything.

'It's actually a shame you won't be around to see it,' the man said as he set the knife down on the floor beside him and pulled a handgun out from his belt, 'because I really do believe it's going to be glorious.'

And with that, he raised the gun to the director's head and pulled the trigger.

So many possibilities, Ayman Rasheed thought, as he sat in the trashed office of the director of antiquities.

So many possibilities and such a huge decision to make . . . but also so much to look forward to if he got it right.

As he stared out the window at the destruction and chaos outside the gates of the museum, Rasheed contemplated how much his world had changed. How outside factors, ones way beyond his control, had ended up with him here, in Palmyra, surrounded by strangers, fighting an enemy with many faces in a land that was not his own.

A week had passed since the fateful moment when he saw the hesitation and fear in the museum director's eyes, and he could think of nothing else. He could barely sleep. Ever since he'd done it, ever since he'd tried it out for himself, his mind was drunk with excitement. The director's secret had opened up a whole universe of possibilities, quite literally. Which meant Rasheed had to think hard and choose from his staggering array of options very, very carefully. The future of hundreds of millions of people—billions, even—rested on his shoulders.

Their future . . . or their past?

He was still having a hard time getting his head around it.

An incredible choice to have to make for any man, to be sure. A monstrous responsibility, and a gift that could, in the wrong hands, be easily squandered.

Rasheed wasn't about to let that happen.

This prodigious gift, after all, hadn't fallen into the hands of some illiterate, impulsive fool. It had found its way to him: an erudite, thoughtful man. A man whose career was built on intellect as well as instinct, a calculating strategist who appreciated the long view and never rushed into things, unlike so many of his peers.

And, most crucially, in the light of what he'd stumbled upon, an inquisitive man who also had a long-standing passion for a subject that would now serve him well: history.

Allah worked in mysterious ways, indeed.

11

Paris
Present Day

'When are we going to the beach, *anneh*?'

Tarek, Noor and Nisreen were in the kitchen having breakfast. The sun poking through the slats was still low. Even this early, it was hinting at the blaze that was coming.

Nisreen hadn't gone back to bed after her troubling discovery on the computer. She'd barely managed a couple hours' snooze on the sofa before Noor had wandered in and tugged her arm to wake her before giving up and snuggling up next to her.

'In two weeks' time,' Nisreen replied with a smile.

Tarek beamed and held up Firas, his stuffed dinosaur. 'Two weeks. You hear that?' He turned back to his mum. 'I promised to build him a castle. A huuuge one,' he added excitedly, with arms stretched wide open and an even wider grin.

Nisreen chuckled. She and Ramazan had planned to take the kids to the south coast for the annual week of celebrations that marked the accession of the sultan to the throne. They tried to get away at least three times a year, either to the mountains or to the sea. Nisreen couldn't wait, and the prospect managed to push some light into a small corner of her heart.

'*Baba* promised he would teach me how to swim,' Noor said in between focused bites of her cheese *borek*.

'You're too young to swim,' Tarek countered.

'Tarek,' Nisreen said with a raised finger—then her phone rang.

'I only learned last year. She's still five,' he protested. 'Besides,' he grinned at his sister, 'she looks so cute in her little pink armbands.'

Noor stuck her tongue out at him as Nisreen glanced at her phone and took the call.

Her face darkened almost immediately.

A few words were all it took to snuff out the light that Tarek's question had sparked.

The Hafiye was a half hour's brisk walk from Kamal's home.

It was based in the old Grand Châtelet on the right bank of the Seine, across the river from the Île de la Cité. He often walked to work, opting for the lazy comfort of a taxi or the tram only on the harshest, darkest mornings of winter. Today, however, he'd ridden his motorbike in after waking up heavy-headed and running late. Cutting through the snarls of traffic made the heat and humidity a bit more bearable.

No one would be rebuking him for any tardiness today. Not after the ceremony the day before, which he was gleefully reminded of by almost every person he encountered while making his way through the labyrinthine compound to reach his desk. No, today Kamal could glide by on the kudos afforded him by his colleagues, from the security guards in the entrance lobby, who almost apologized for having to scan his ID, to the senior officers who gave him acknowledging nods as he walked past their glass-fronted offices. It should have felt great, but somehow it didn't. He decided the best thing he could do was bury himself in his work and hope that he could soon ferret out another real enemy of the state, someone with lethal intent whose comeuppance could help shore up Kamal's faith in what he was doing.

Even with the modern additions, the *ancien régime* stronghold was a grim place. It had been entirely rebuilt by Louis XIV in AD 1684, a decade before the Ottomans had swept into Paris and beheaded him. They were greatly aided by the fact that fourteen years earlier, in an act of unfortunate recklessness, Louis had declared Paris safe from foreign attack and ordered its ring of defensive walls to be torn down in order to expand the spread of the city, replacing the walls with grand boulevards. During his reign, the Grand Châtelet was a sprawling fortress with forbidding walls and a clutch of squat, turreted towers that housed the police headquarters, courts and several prisons. Its dank subterranean dungeons had enjoyed a fearsome notoriety, far worse than that of the Bastille, which was a mile to the east. The Ottomans saw no reason to undermine that reputation. Under their rule, the prison was just as full, its reputation just as sinister. It had grown over the centuries, with newer buildings seamlessly blended into the ancient fortress and its stone towers. The Ottomans preferred to keep historically significant structures, only altering them so that they became unquestionably Ottoman and Islamic in appearance, totemic reminders of the conquered past.

The Hafiye initially shared the compound, nicknamed the Citadel, with the Zaptiye, the police force that handled basic tasks like traffic violations, domestic altercations, alcohol and drug use, robbery and the occasional homicide. Given that penalties under *shari'a* law were harsh and could easily lead to the loss of a limb or worse, crime rates were low. But with the ever-present dual threats of terrorism and civil unrest, the Hafiye had expanded and taken over the entire compound. Kamal and his brethren now ruled the streets, and the Zaptiye had to relocate to a building nearby, close to the old Hôtel de Ville.

Kamal's and Taymoor's workstations faced each other on the fourth floor of one of the new additions, in a low-ceilinged open-plan space that they shared with a dozen of their colleagues. There were several other areas of similar size, one per section, all of them buzzing with agents who were busy sifting through surveillance logs, recordings and transcripts, and informants' reports. Runners hurried along the hallways, ferrying coffee and paperwork. There were no women around. The small department of female agents, which handled cases involving women, was housed in a small, separate building that had its own entrance. Male and female agents were only allowed to work together when it was deemed crucial to a case. Under Abdülhamid's conservative agenda, fraternizing between the two was not only discouraged. It was banned.

Taymoor's desk was a mess, of course—it always was—and he still hadn't come in. Clearly, Kamal's partner was milking the previous day's limelight for all its worth. Which suited Kamal fine. He wasn't sure he could handle Taymoor's gung-ho fervour just yet.

He spent half an hour trawling through the overnight surveillance reports but didn't find anything noteworthy. Once he was done, he picked up his phone and rang the analyst he'd tasked with going over the CCTV footage from the riverbank.

'*Chaouch komiser,*' the man replied, 'I was about to call you.'

'Tell me,' Kamal said.

'There's something you should see. It might not be anything, but—'

'I'll come down,' Kamal told him.

He was getting up to leave when he saw Taymoor making his way in. Their eyes met, and Taymoor's expression tightened with a sudden tinge of seriousness.

'Do I even dare ask why you're late?' Kamal asked when he reached him.

Taymoor brushed off his comment. 'Forget that, brother. Did you know Nisreen is here?'

'What? Where?'

'Downstairs, at reception. She's causing a scene. I think you'd better get down there.'

Kamal was already moving.

Two colleagues and a runner were waiting by the elevators. Kamal nodded to them curtly as he tapped the down button impatiently, glaring at the digital display that showed both elevators to be stuck on higher floors. He gave up and darted for the stairs, flying down three steps at a time, and burst on to the ground floor. He blew across the busy foyer, and, as he approached the duty officer's station, he could see a small gaggle of men crowding it, with two lone women among them.

One of them was Nisreen. He spotted her from across the huge hall.

He wasn't sure at first. Being married, she didn't have to cover her face completely when she wasn't home or with other women behind closed doors, and she generally left most of her face unveiled, like non-Muslim women, only bothering with a thin veil around her hair that got progressively lower with each passing year. Today, however, she was wrapped under a more opaque veil and was harder to recognize—another shift in the city's social dynamic under the new regime. Her body, however, had to be covered up. That had never changed much, and that morning she was in a summer *ferace,* a loose coat that had room in its sleeves for her to conceal her hands.

Her companion was even more shrouded than her, her face concealed behind a thicker grey muslin veil. Kamal couldn't tell if he knew her.

94

Police officers were watching from the sidelines, while at the core of the disturbance Nisreen was arguing forcefully with the official and two of his men.

'What do you mean, you don't have to explain anything?' her furious voice echoed around the stone chamber as Kamal made his way through the small crowd to reach her. 'The man is missing and all we want to know is whether or not you have him.'

The duty officer was unmoved. 'You know very well that there's nothing to discuss in cases of state security. End of story.'

'End of story? The man has a wife,' she insisted, pointing at her companion, a woman who, Kamal now saw, was in her mid-thirties and was standing beside Nisreen quietly, her head slumped. Then Nisreen spotted him. He felt her stab of recognition, a cold, hard glare that was loaded with hurt and sadness and rage and defiance—then she continued, as if he didn't exist. 'He's got four children. Don't they deserve to know something more than "end of story"? What kind of a barbarian have you turned into?' She turned to the others, incensed. 'All of you? How can you do this?' Her eyes snared him again, their almond charm replaced by fierce anger.

Kamal was about to intercede when the duty officer slapped his hand hard against the desk. 'Nisreen *hatun,* I would respectfully suggest you leave here now while you still have that option.'

'What are you going to do?' Nisreen shot back angrily. 'Lock us up, too? Are you going to put all of Paris in your cages?'

Kamal stepped in and waved a calming gesture at the duty officer. '*Başçavuş*—'

The duty officer ignored him. 'I don't know about that, but I could certainly be happy to start with—'

Kamal interrupted him, louder and more forcefully this time. '*Başçavuş* Ahmet Effendi, please. There's no need to aggravate an already inflamed situation. I'm sure she doesn't mean any disrespect—'

'Oh, I mean it,' Nisreen interjected, her tone soaked with contempt. 'I absolutely mean it, every damn—'

Kamal raised an open palm to still her. 'Nisreen, please. You need to calm down.' He glanced over at the duty officer, gave him an 'I'll handle this' look and gesture, and turned back to face Nisreen. 'What's this about?'

'You don't know?' Delivered with as much sarcasm as scorn.

'No, I don't.'

Nisreen studied him for a tight intake of breath, then said, 'This woman is the wife of Ibrahim Sinasi. Her husband didn't come home from work last night. A shopkeeper who knows him saw three men lead him into a black SUV and drive away. She's worried sick. His children are worried sick. The man's a playwright, for God's sake.' She paused, then waved him off. 'Why the hell am I bothering telling you this? You're worse than they are.' She turned to her companion. 'Let's get out of here.'

'Nisreen, please, wait. I'm just—'

She turned abruptly. 'What? What are you going to say?' She jabbed an accusing finger at the duty officer. 'We know you have him. We know he's here.' The man remained stone-faced. She spun her gaze on to Kamal. 'Are you going to get him to tell us what's going on? Are you going to help me get to the bottom of this so I can get this woman's husband back home where he belongs?'

'It's not that simple. You know that.'

'It should be,' she spat out. 'It used to be. Back when we were civilized. Back when you and the rest of these thugs

96

had a conscience and a backbone.' She adjusted her veil as she turned to her companion. 'Let's go.'

He reached out and took her by the arm to stop her. 'Nisreen—'

She swung around angrily and swatted his hand off. 'Don't touch me. Don't you dare touch me.'

Kamal froze.

They stood there for a few frenzied heartbeats, facing off, her anger burning through his regret. 'Where does this end, Kamal Agha?' she finally hissed. 'What are you going to do, lock us all up? Or feed us all to your executioners?'

His eyes dropped as he shook his head. He started to say, 'That's not fair,' but she was already storming out.

He watched her disappear and felt his insides shred.

12

Over at the Hurrem Sultan Külliye, Ramazan was bringing his patient back to consciousness.

Enough time had passed since the surgery, and all the signs were positive. The mystery man had a stable heartbeat. The oxygenation level in his blood was good. His renal function was normal. There was no bleeding in the drainage tubes coming out of his sides of his chest. The lung X-rays were fine. Of equal importance to Ramazan, however, was that the cardiothoracic nurses' night shift would be ending soon, and he figured that a tired nurse would make it easier for him to get some time alone with his patient.

He was pleased to find that Anbara wasn't on duty. They hadn't discussed the man's surprising outburst just before the surgery, and Ramazan wasn't keen to bring it up with her yet either. He needed to understand more about what was going on and thought that the more time that passed without discussing it with her, the more he could downplay it, if need be.

With another nurse assisting him, Ramazan initiated the recovery process, gradually reducing the level of drugs passing through the IV line while monitoring the man's reactions, only this time he was doing it slightly differently. His objective wasn't to bring the patient back to full consciousness as fast as possible.

He had something else in mind.

He watched as the man's vitals ticked up, and then he saw the first stirrings of awakening. There was movement behind the tattooed man's eyelids before they fluttered, barely at first, then more noticeably. Patients are groggy and disoriented when they awaken after surgery. For some, it doesn't take too long to become clear-headed, but for others it can take hours. That was what Ramazan was after: he intended to keep his patient in a bleary state as long as possible. A state where he would be unguarded about what he said.

Making sure the nurse was focused elsewhere, Ramazan tweaked the setting on the tattooed man's IV line so it would keep delivering a mild dose of sedative, along with some of the anaesthetic. How much he'd need to achieve the state he was after, though, was a guess. He'd never attempted to prolong a patient's delirium. It went against everything he stood for as a doctor and clearly violated the rules and practices of his profession. Despite the trepidation pulsating inside him, despite the crippling tightness spreading across his body, he kept going.

He wasn't sure why he was doing this, but he didn't stop to think about it too much. He was doing it, regardless of the consequences, driven by a curiosity he couldn't suppress, the excitement of it egging him on, feeding on itself. It wasn't like him. In fact, he'd never done something like this before. It wasn't his style. He could picture his brother Kamal doing it. Kamal was the one with an appetite for risk and a disdain for rules. Ramazan had always been the sensible one. The safe, reasonable, measured one. The boring, methodical anaesthetist. And maybe that was why he was doing it. Maybe he needed to be more adventurous.

Maybe that was what Nisreen also needed him to be.

Less than a minute later, the tattooed man was slowly emerging from unconsciousness.

'How are you doing, sir?' Ramazan asked him. He gave him a moment, then tapped his left arm gently. 'Can you raise this arm?'

The man was clearly groggy. He also couldn't talk, given the breathing tube that was down his throat. Ramazan felt the man move his arm slightly. He checked his breathing, took his hand and squeezed it, looking for a reaction to make sure there was no residual paralysis. Once he was satisfied that all the signs were good, he had the nurse assist him in removing the man's breathing tube and replacing it with a nasal cannula.

'You see,' Ramazan told him after it was all done, 'you're as good as new. We didn't screw up, just as you ordered. How could we, with someone as important as you, right?'

He gave the nurse a wry little wink as he said it, but he was more focused on his patient, looking for a reaction. The man's eyes were roaming the ceiling, still fighting his drooping eyelids, but then their eyes connected, and he detected something: a hint of a grin and the smallest, slowest of nods.

Ramazan had got through.

He turned to nurse. 'I've got this. You can finish up with the rest of your roster.'

The nurse seemed surprised. 'Are you sure?'

'Yes. You've had a long night. I can take care of this. You should finish up and head home.'

The nurse hesitated, then nodded. 'Okay. Thank you, that's very kind.' She smiled, threw a last passing glance at the patient, then walked out.

A pregnant silence smothered the room, punctuated by the low beeps from the monitors.

Ramazan checked the tattooed man's drugs, then leaned across so he could see him.

'You were right,' he told him. 'We owe you. All of us. We're all grateful to you.'

The man looked at him, his features shuttered with confusion and tiredness. But then it appeared again. The small, self-congratulatory nod.

Anticipation rushed through Ramazan.

'But I'm sure you'd also like me to convey your thanks to the staff,' he said, coaxing him softly. 'They'd be most honoured. What can I tell them, on your behalf?'

Ramazan watched with a tingle of anticipation as the man's expression clouded. The patient seemed to be mired with confusion and was clearly having trouble ordering his thoughts. Then he seemed to reach some inner peace and spoke, his voice coarse and weak, his words still in that formal, classical dialect. 'Tell them that it is not only I, your governor, but our esteemed padishah, the sultan *muhteşem* Mehmed himself, nay the entire people of the empire, who are thankful for all your efforts in bringing your governor back to good health.'

Ramazan felt the air rush out of his lungs in a flight of dejection.

The governor?

Ramazan scoffed inwardly, trying to suppress his derision while scolding himself for letting things get this far. The governor, every citizen of the Paris *eyalet,* if not of the empire, knew who that was at the time of *muhteşem* Mehmed— Mehmed the Magnificent, the illustrious Mehmed IV, the sultan whose army had conquered Paris and much of Europe. The governor's name was Ayman Rasheed Pasha. He had been the sultan's philosopher-royal and special counsellor, and he was a titan of Ottoman history. He was in all the history books, and the monuments to his legacy could be seen all over the city, testaments to his glory.

So this delusional joker thinks he's Ayman Rasheed Pasha, he thought. He felt deflated with disappointment. This had been a huge waste of time, but then what did he expect? He had allowed his imagination to run away with him, spurred by a deep-seated need for something unexpected, some magic that might inject some vigour into his life—and his marriage.

He needed to bring the man off the drugs and hope his little excursion outside the bounds of hospital regulations would pass unnoticed. Then he'd leave the man in the nurses' care and try to forget any of it had happened.

He was reaching for the IV line when the man said, 'It would please me to take you back with me. You would be my *hekimbaşı*,' he added—his chief physician.

Ramazan paused. Playing along, he said, 'It would be an honour. But back where?'

The man looked at him curiously, as if he were surprised that Ramazan didn't know. 'To Paris, of course.'

More nonsense. 'But we are in Paris, Your Excellency.'

The man shook his head slowly, a sly twinkle in his eyes. 'Not your Paris. Mine.'

'Your Paris?'

'Yes,' the man said. 'You could make sure I remain in good health, and it would save me from having to make the journey back here again, if there were complications. It's quite tiring, you know. And there's always a risk.'

Ramazan studied his patient warily, now wondering how quickly he could shut down this absurd conversation and get back to reality. 'A risk?' he asked, deciding he might as well bring the man back to full consciousness now and be done with this mockery. 'How so?'

'It's not so easy to travel three hundred years across time. You have to be careful.'

Ramazan suppressed a snort. 'So you've done this before?'

'Oh, yes.'

'When did this all start?'

And then Rasheed began to explain.

Slowly, at first. Then, with Ramazan realizing he needed to hear more and managing the drugs to keep him on the edge of delirium while maintaining a coherence to his words, he spoke more, with Ramazan coaxing him on with carefully worded questions and prompts.

Keeping the nurses at bay, Ramazan kept the man talking for a long time. And the story that he heard didn't seem to him to be that of delusional nutcase or an enemy of the state.

Far from it.

In his own wishful delusion, Ramazan had come to the hospital hoping for a revelation that might change his life.

What he got instead was a story that went beyond anything he could have ever imagined.

13

Ayman Rasheed's story began in the small town of Qayyarah, in the Nineveh Governorate of Iraq. The youngest of three boys, he grew up in a modest home on the west bank of the Tigris River, a home in which tradition, rather than religion, exerted the strongest pull.

Rasheed's father was a conservative, stern, moderately devout man who prayed daily but only took one wife and didn't spurn the occasional cigarette or glass of arak. He owned a small workshop where he made cinder blocks and sold decorative and paving stones to local builders. He put food on the table and a roof over his family's head, and though he never missed a day's work, he still managed the occasional idle evening of fishing or swimming in the river with his sons.

Outside school hours, the boys worked alongside their father from a young age. School was a mixed blessing for Rasheed. He loved reading and excelled in class, his brain compensating for his lack of brawn, but he also got ribbed a lot for it, by his classmates as well as by his more thuggish brothers. Working in his father's small factory was less interesting to him, but it was physically demanding, even more so after the boys' father came back from fighting in the Iraq–Iran War with a leg and three fingers missing along with a bitterness that manifested itself in vicious belt whippings.

As sanctions against Iraq bit and work dried out in the years following Saddam's invasion of Kuwait in 1990, Rasheed's elder brothers were drafted into the dictator's military machine. Rasheed soon followed in their steps. Once there, he quickly outperformed them, even though he lacked their brutal instincts and machismo. His intellect was spotted early, and his work ethic served him well. He was promoted to the rank of major in the Directorate of General Military Intelligence just weeks before the planes hit the Twin Towers.

In the months after 9/11, Rasheed could see the writing on the wall. He knew an invasion was coming, but he was still too junior and his influence inside the DGMI was stifled by Saddam's cocky and arrogant inner circle. The warnings he managed to air were ignored. He lost both brothers to cruise missiles that first week. The onslaught that followed destroyed everything else about his life. The regime was scattered to the wind, the army disbanded, and Rasheed soon found himself back in Qayyarah, unemployed and demeaned in his own land.

Like many other young officers, rudderless and angry following the invasion, he was galvanized into militancy. The death and destruction all around him and the sight of American soldiers strutting around in their wrap-around sunglasses and high-tech weaponry infuriated him. Worse still, and like many of his Sunni brethren, Rasheed was convinced that the invaders were trying to impose a power shift in his country, favouring the country's Shia majority at the Sunnis' expense.

The thinker turned into a soldier. Despite his father's objections, Rasheed soon joined the burgeoning militancy around Mosul, not far from his home town. He and his brigade of insurgents tasted some early success with IED attacks on American military convoys and hit-and-run assaults against private contractors and Kurdish units, but it wasn't long before he was taken prisoner. After a vicious firefight with a marines unit near Kirkuk in the summer of 2004, he was shackled and chained and then quickly escorted to Camp Bucca in southern Iraq.

It was in Bucca's sprawling compounds, safe from the bloody mayhem outside its walls, that ISIS would first take root.

Day in, day out, with his brothers dead and his country destroyed, everything Rasheed saw and heard around him fuelled his rage. Mistreatment, humiliation and abuse were rampant. Husbands, fathers, and sons were rounded up in neighbourhood raids and locked up, even though many of them were not even combatants. Others imprisoned there, however, were not as benign, and it was towards them that Rasheed gravitated, especially after receiving news that his parents had died in a Shi'ite militia attack on his home town.

Rasheed changed. He was trapped in a painful spiral of grief, anger and hopelessness. At first, he plodded through the long, solitary hours by pumping iron, channelling his rage to sharpen his physical prowess. More crucially, he also began conversing with people he'd always vilified: the radical Islamists.

Most of those who would become the leaders of ISIS spent time in US prisons during the American occupation of Iraq, whether at Bucca, Camp Cropper, or, more infamously, Abu Ghraib—time that had a radicalizing and incendiary effect on them. But it was Bucca that became the main incubator for the movement. It was there that Saddam Baathists like Rasheed, who were for the most part only mildly devout, and fundamentalist Islamists, two groups who were previously enemies, found themselves thrown together for the first time. Incarceration gave them the opportunity to talk, air their grievances and discover a common cause: they were both Sunni, and they both hated the Americans and the Shi'ites, their ancient sectarian foes. In those prisons, they plotted what they would do once freed, and freed they were—either by their captors, as in Rasheed's case during autumn 2007, or in armed prison breaks after the Americans had handed the prisons over to their new Shi'ite allies.

For Rasheed, going home was no longer an option. It had been superseded by a burning desire for retribution and war.

Not just any war. A holy war. Jihad.

There would be no shortage of foot soldiers to wage it, not after the Americans disbanded the Iraqi army and left its four hundred thousand men stripped of their jobs and their pensions—but not their guns.

In Baghdad, Rasheed sought out the men he'd met at Bucca and rejoined the fight—a fight that began in Iraq and soon spread to Syria. Thousands of local fighters were joined by hordes of foreign jihadists, fanatics who dreamed of establishing an Islamic caliphate where the rules of the seventh century still applied or of finding martyrdom while trying. And while the gruesome public face of the growing uprising featured a garish collection of religious extremists, its hidden leadership was almost entirely composed of highly trained former Iraqi officers like Rasheed who had served under Saddam and for whom the Islamists were no more than useful idiots—convenient, if expendable, allies.

Rasheed's expertise in military intelligence, his strategic guile and his tactical ruthlessness rapidly pushed him up the ladder of ISIS's command structure. With each passing week, more bodies piled up and more land fell under their control. Huge swathes of Iraq and Syria—an area the size of Britain—were in its dishevelled fighters' hands, and over twelve million people lived under their tyranny. But it didn't last long, and Rasheed was clever enough to see what was coming.

It wasn't going to end well. Not for the struggle against the Syrian regime and their Shi'ite rivals, and not for him. Attacking Europe and cheerleading other attacks as far away as Boston and San Bernardino had created a tidal wave of enmity against ISIS. Russia and America were now fully engaged, and while they had conflicting agendas, their objective was the same: to wipe ISIS out, even at the cost of keeping the Syrian regime, its butchers and its chemical weapons, in power.

Aerial raids on Raqqa and other ISIS strongholds killed hundreds of its fighters and destroyed many of its oil refineries and tanker convoys. American warplanes destroyed one of its vaults in Mosul, turning hundreds of millions of dollar bills into ash. The world's richest terrorist group was on the ropes. Fighters were abandoning the sinking ship in droves, shaving off their beards and melting into the chaos.

Their caliphate wasn't going to happen.

Long before the tide of battle had turned, Rasheed had been out of step with the obscurantist dystopia the jihadists were trying to forge. Closing down schools, making all shops close at prayer times, outlawing cigarettes and music. Forcing women to cover up from head to toe in black, whippings for even showing an eyebrow. Sadistic public stonings and executions, including crucifixions. This was as bad as life under the Taliban, if not worse. No one in their right mind would want to live that way.

Rasheed certainly didn't.

He considered himself a good Muslim, but this wasn't the world he aspired to create. With each passing week, he watched with increased irritation as the movement's cretinous leaders made new blunders and announced even more asinine edicts. He'd hitched his wagon to them out of anger and desperation, but the whole caliphate train had derailed and it was about to go hurtling over a cliff.

It was time to bail.

Capturing the museum director and getting his hands on the man's phenomenal discovery couldn't have happened at a more opportune time. And Rasheed knew enough about history to know how radically different the great caliphates were from the crass version these barbarians were aiming for.

A thousand years before ISIS, Arab intellectual achievement and culture led the world while Christendom languished in the gloom of the Dark Ages. Back then, Muslim societies were open and curious, while Christian Europe was insular and fearful of blasphemy. Education was valued and scientific knowledge was prized. Aristotle's writings were translated and studied in Baghdad and Cordoba, but they were banned in Rome and Paris.

Rasheed knew all about those heady days, when his ancestors were propelled by a self-confident openness to new ideas and a desire to appropriate, learn, and expand. A world view that was based on a unique mix of theology and rational thinking had produced groundbreaking advances in medicine, astronomy, cartography and mathematics. Art, poetry and music flourished. Muslim thinkers were also at the vanguard of developing sophisticated arguments in philosophy, theology, law and literature. Ancient Greek, Indian and Persian texts were translated into Arabic, studied by Muslim scholars working alongside Christian and Jewish colleagues, and used to inspire further discovery by the likes of Thomas Aquinas. For seven hundred years, the international language of science was Arabic. Baghdad, home to Bayt al-Hikma, the House of Wisdom founded by the caliph Harun al-Rashid in the late eighth century, was the epicentre of the intellectual world.

Rasheed also knew all about the glorious era when Islamic empires

*stretched from Spain to China. The Moors had ruled as far as the Ibe-
rian Peninsula and the South of France; the Ottomans overran the
Balkans and Hungary and were at the gates of Vienna. These were
truly the days of empire and caliphate. The Christian world had trembled before the armies of Islam, armies Rasheed would have been proud
to serve in, armies led by men who were driven by a thirst for conquest
and glory but who were also animated by an expansive spirit, a hunger
for knowledge, art, wisdom and conversation. But those exalted days
were long gone. It had been centuries, Rasheed felt, since his people had
achieved anything they could be proud of.*

Avicenna, Averroës, Rhazes.

Abd al-Rahman III, Saladin, Suleiman the Magnificent.

*Names that, to this day, many centuries later, still inspire awe,
admiration and respect.*

*When was the last time anyone from Rasheed's part of the world had
been held in such high esteem——not just by his own people, but by the
whole world?*

*Rasheed knew that his jihadist comrades and their aspirations were
a far, far cry from all that. But thanks to the museum director's secret,
he now had an alternative.*

There definitely was a caliphate to strive for.

It just wasn't the one ISIS had in mind.

14

As she and the playwright's wife stood in the stifling heat outside the central tram station of the Hôtel de Ville, Nisreen was still shaking, her mind trapped in a feedback loop of the confrontation with Kamal.

How had he become like that?

'I'm sorry,' she muttered, trying to compose herself. 'I shouldn't have lost my calm.'

The woman looked as distraught as she was. 'What do we do now? Where does this leave us?'

'I'll go see one of the judges I know well. I'm hoping he can help.' She reached out and placed a hand on the woman's forearm supportively. 'Please stay positive, and be strong. I'm going to do everything I can to get him out of there as soon as possible.'

The woman nodded uncertainly. She hesitated, then asked, 'That man. The one you had the . . . He's your brother-in-law, isn't he?'

Nisreen looked at her, then nodded, her expression drowning somewhere between apology, regret and embarrassment. Kamal was currently a shining star of the Hafiye, and in the gossipy circles of Ottoman society such things got noticed. Nisreen was never sure if that drove people who needed help to seek her out or caused them to steer clear of her.

'He looked like he wanted to help,' the woman added. 'But you didn't give him a chance.'

Nisreen shook her head ruefully. 'I'm sorry,' she told her. 'It's just . . .'

'He wanted to help,' the woman insisted, her voice catching with desperation. 'Perhaps you could talk to him, apologize . . . ?'

Nisreen looked at her and nodded slowly, consciously calming herself down. Nowadays, the mere mention of his name was enough to ignite a blaze of anger inside her.

The woman sensed Nisreen's unease and added, 'Or maybe your husband could talk to him?'

'I wish he could,' Nisreen told her. 'They're not exactly on best terms these days.'

The feedback loop in her mind took on a second track: how could two brothers end up being so different from one another?

She'd known Kamal and Ramazan since they were kids. They'd all played together. Kamal was Tarek's and Noor's uncle, for God's sake. But he and his brother had always been different.

Perhaps that was the wrong question. Perhaps the right question was, How could Kamal not see what he had become? How could he face himself in the mirror every day, knowing what he was part of?

She hated the feeling. But beyond the revulsion at seeing him in there, in that uniform, among those people, she hated something else. An old, unspoken emotion that was still there, a remnant from her youth. Despite everything, there was something about him she could never fully extinguish.

She hated that it had to be this way.

Nisreen was born in a poor household on the outskirts of Greater Paris. She wasn't there for too long. When she was eight, her parents had no choice but to sell her to an affluent family.

Although that technically made her a slave, the reality in Ottoman society was far different. The slave trade, a major feature of the empire's military and society for centuries, had been suppressed decades earlier. One of its few surviving forms was the private sale of children by their parents, and the strict rules that governed it were still in place. Nisreen would be treated as a fostered family member, with all the protection and support that entailed. She would be one of the family's servants and would carry out her duties in their household, but she would also share the same food and clothing as the family she was living with. They would bring her up and support her, giving her the same education and training as a 'free' Ottoman girl—or their daughter, if they had one. The term of her servitude was also limited; she would receive a pension for life, and when she was of age to get married, her employers would provide her dowry and, depending on what had been originally agreed on with her parents, select her husband. Courts were available to her if she needed to redress any wrongdoing by her owners.

She had been blessed with a particularly noble and generous master, a legal counsel who belonged to a learned circle of scholars and lawyers and who, after having three sons, had never stopped yearning for a daughter. He was well rewarded with Nisreen. It didn't take long for him to recognize her intelligence, her inquisitive mind and her strength of character. He encouraged her desire to broaden her mind, despite widespread and deeply ingrained attitudes that frowned on such pursuits. In most Ottoman households, despite the progress from Murad's reforms, education of girls was still limited to matters of religion. Traditionally, women had not been allowed to study subjects that could undermine the patriarchal dominance, particularly law. Even literature hadn't been considered an appropriate avenue of study for women. The focus was on forming them into good Muslim wives and mothers, armed with the appropriately refined social graces, rather than on achieving a career; those who did work were paid significantly less than men. Many girls still had to fight their families—particularly their fathers and brothers—to venture beyond these norms.

In Nisreen's case, listening to endless recitations of religious texts wasn't enough to quell her thirst for knowledge. Her master had embraced Murad's reforms and allowed her to put his library to good use. She roamed through the classics of Near Eastern literature and lyric poetry and taught herself French and Persian before eventually exploring his legal texts. When she began to put her thoughts on paper, his support didn't waver, particularly when she pushed back against the conservative denigration of women while promoting girls' education and women's rights. He later helped her obtain a law degree and establish her own legal firm, a small, progressive practice where men and women worked alongside each other, and one that didn't shy away from handling sensitive matters, of which there were plenty, particularly for a woman with Nisreen's beliefs.

The thrust of her work had concerned women's rights, which were still limited, even if attitudes were more progressive than in many other parts of the world, especially when compared with the Christian Republic of America and its Puritan ways, or with Russia, which was staunchly Orthodox. Ottoman women could own property; they could inherit and bequeath wealth; they could establish and run endowments; they could take men to court—even their husbands or male relatives—to defend their interests and plead their cases in front of the judges; they retained their own individual legal status, in accordance with Islamic law, and could retain their own surnames after marriage. Most of this was still unheard of in Christian lands.

Furthermore, Ottoman women could end unwanted marriages in ways women in those countries could only dream of. Divorces among Ottoman couples were frequent and as easily initiated by a woman as by a man. Non-Muslim women living in the empire were even known to convert to Islam in order to be liberated from an unhappy marriage.

The CRA's women, however, did fare better on another front: they could vote. Towards the end of the last century, suffrage had been granted to propertied widows and unmarried women over thirty.

For Nisreen, it all boiled down to two simple principles: rights shouldn't be based on tradition but should be conferred because they were just and reasonable, regardless of their basis in tradition; and women, as human beings, deserved the same fundamental rights as men. She had successfully fought against a proposed law that would have overturned the conviction of men who raped a minor if the aggressor married his victim. She had led the appeal for the release of a female surgeon who had been convicted of sewing up the hymens of young girls. She had defended a trader who had been smuggling in virginity kits from the Far East. But since Abdülhamid had taken the throne, Nisreen's work had brought her into more frequent public conflict with religious leaders as well as with conservative pillars of society, and it wasn't just women whose rights now needed vigorous defending.

A comedian was lashed for defaming the beylerbey after a meme he posted, which showed a popular cartoon hippo juxtaposed with a picture of the beylerbey in which they looked strikingly similar, went viral. The editor of one of the *eyalet*'s most respected newspapers, the outspoken *Tasvir-i efkâr*—its name meant 'imagining ideas'—was jailed for publishing what the state called 'fabricated news', a term they were using with alarming frequency.

It was now far more serious than a matter of principle.

Lives were at stake.

'Try,' the playwright's wife pleaded as a tram pulled in, its bell clanging to alert a couple of careless pedestrians to get out of its way. 'He's on the inside. And he's your family. We need all the help we can get.'

'I will. I promise,' Nisreen reassured her. 'I'd better get back to the office and make those calls.'

'You'll let me know as soon as you hear something?'

'Of course.'

The woman studied her for a moment, great worry radiating out of her eyes. Then she nodded and climbed on to the women's carriage of the tram.

Nisreen stood there with a heavy heart and watched the tram pull away before it disappeared into the late-morning chaos.

She walked away, still reeling from the emotional hurricane she'd whipped up. She needed to calm down and get back to the office, where she would call the judges, starting with one who had been a close friend of her master.

As for Kamal . . . she'd need to talk to Ramazan about that.

She decided to walk to her office, to give her mind a chance to settle. She crossed the crowded street and took the embankment, by the water's edge, where the air was marginally cooler. She liked walking along the river. The water—murky and dark, but flowing by with unbothered continuity—was like a sedative to her rattled senses.

As she stared ahead, she thought back fondly to her master, lamenting that he was not around, wistfully wishing he were still alive to support and guide her through these troubled times. At the same time, however, a small part of her was glad he wasn't around to see what the empire had become, although, even then, she wondered if he wouldn't have relished the idea of diving into the fight for its soul. He had never shied away from a battle. And that part of him still animated her and gave her the strength to continue, despite the fear and the threats. In a way, she felt she owed it to his memory. Without her master's support, she would never have become a respected advocate of women's rights or such a distinctive voice in the Paris press, well regarded and widely read by an expanding audience of literate women. He had made it possible, and she had stepped up and embraced the opportunity. She had loved him and came to consider him as her true father, even after she had left his household—that is, when his wife and her coterie of women had deemed that it was time for Nisreen to get married.

Nisreen's foster parents were friends with Kamal and Ramazan's parents, which was how she'd met the two brothers. Along with her brothers, they'd all been childhood friends. They were allowed to play and go on outings together until Nisreen reached puberty—which was around the time that she had felt the first stirrings of desire for Kamal, feelings that she strongly suspected were reciprocated. But that was when custom dictated that she don the veil and drop out of the brothers' lives, only to reappear when her marriage to Ramazan was arranged by their parents. Of the two, Ramazan had been the obvious choice: older than Kamal, if only by four years, more grounded, a solid earner with respectable prospects for a lifelong career in medicine. Neither she nor Kamal had got a chance to put a word in before it was a fait accompli, and out of respect for her master and his wife and all they had done for her, she never challenged their decision, even though she could see the same unspoken dejection that she felt reflected in Kamal's eyes. But that was all in the distant past, and perhaps her parents had been right all along.

Ramazan had become a reliable husband and father for their two children and was a respectful, kind man and a generous provider, even if the flame of passion between them had never really grown into the bonfire she'd heard about in whispered conversation or read about in contraband literature. Kamal, on the other hand, had followed through on the promise of his rambunctious youth and turned into . . . *that*.

And yet . . .

She fought to push all thought of him away and tried to focus instead on what really mattered: getting the playwright back to his family.

Family was everything, after all.

She firmly believed it, even if it came at a price.

15

In the windowless basement of one of the old castle's modern extensions, Kamal was finding it hard to dodge the aftershocks of his encounter with Nisreen.

He and Taymoor were with the analyst who'd been going over the CCTV footage of the riverbank.

The huge space was one of several data-analysis chambers that were collectively known as the Caves. Each station in the video-surveillance chamber was the same: a desk of controls under a big flat screen and an array of four smaller ones around it. The entire place hummed with an ominous silence. The walls and ceiling were bare and clad with a sound-absorbing, matte charcoal-grey finish, and the air-conditioning was cranked up high. The analysts wore special glasses to protect their eyes from the glare of the screens. Their identical dark-grey uniforms sapped what little humanity there seemed to be in the austere, oppressive space.

'Here, look at this couple,' the analyst told them as he hit the play button and pointed at the big screen with his other hand.

The surveillance-camera footage showed the quay that ran alongside the Seine. And although it was night, the image was surprisingly well lit, courtesy of ever-evolving filters that made snooping at night almost as effective as it was during the day.

It showed a man and a woman coming down the stairs from the bridge. Upon reaching the quay, they're visibly surprised by something—then the surprise quickly turns to shock. The woman starts pointing and screaming. Then the man edges closer to the water, doing the same, his stance confrontational. It isn't long before the man gives up on whatever he was shouting at and turns to comfort his companion. They seem to argue about something, but that also doesn't last long. They then go back up the stairs and disappear from view, clearly moving with purpose.

The analyst paused the frame. 'That's it. Nothing noteworthy before or after.'

'They saw something,' Taymoor said.

Kamal glanced at the time stamp. It showed 5:34 A.M. Predawn. 'Do we have a camera on the opposite quay?'

'We've got one on either side of the bridge, but there's nothing on them.'

'Is there a dead spot?'

'Yes, right under the bridge. The coverage isn't one hundred per cent.'

Kamal frowned.

'We need to find them,' Taymoor said. 'Find out what they saw.'

'We'll track them down,' the analyst said.

'What do we have up on ground level?' Kamal asked. 'At the entrance of the bridge. The top of the stairs.'

'Hang on.' The analyst worked the controls and pulled up the relevant footage. He put in the matching time stamp and hit PLAY.

The screen showed cars and buses driving past, early-morning traffic. Then a man appears from the stairwell.

'There.' Kamal pointed.

They watched as the man staggers on to the pavement and heads away from the bridge. His movement is visibly strained.

'Is he drunk?' the analyst asked.

'Drunk, or injured,' Kamal replied. 'Maybe in a fight.'

The man stops at a crossing by the entrance to the bridge. He waits, slightly hunched over as he glances left and right. Then he crosses the road without waiting for the lights to change before disappearing down a dark side street that leads away from the river.

'I need you to track him,' Kamal said. 'We need to know where he went.'

'And we need his face,' Taymoor added.

The analyst worked the controls to reel back the footage, then played it again in slow motion.

The man seems to keep his head down, but there's one moment when he's scanning for a clear path across the road and his face is partially exposed.

The analyst froze it, then enlarged it.

It wasn't perfect, since the camera was mounted high above street level. But it was something. It showed a man somewhere in his sixties with a full head of hair and a clean-shaven face.

'Let's see where he went,' Taymoor said as the analyst used his controls to track their target across the surveillance net.

Kamal was itching to leave.

Just then, Taymoor's phone rang. As he checked its screen, Kamal said, 'Do you mind doing this alone? I need to take care of something.'

Taymoor didn't question him—not here, not in front of the surveillance analyst. He just gave him a nod of 'okay' and took the call as Kamal headed out.

Taymoor watched his partner walk away as he took the call.

The caller ID just showed A—Taymoor's phone held a lot of contacts that were only listed by an initial, ostensibly for discretion purposes. But A was not what Kamal, or anyone else who happened to see it flash up, would naturally assume.

It was Ali Huseyin, a fellow agent. Only Huseyin wasn't part of the anti-terrorist directorate. He was Z Directorate.

'What's up?'

'Are you alone or with Kamal Agha?'

Taymoor didn't like the sound of that. 'He just left. Why?'

Huseyin paused for a breath, as if to evaluate what to say. 'Someone's been flagged. I thought you should know. But you can't share this with him. I'm telling you as a favour because I owe you, and I don't want you to get any blowback.'

'Who?'

'Sayyid Ramazan Hekim. Kamal's brother.'

Taymoor edged away from the surveillance agent and instinctively glanced towards the doors of the centre, although he knew Kamal wasn't coming back.

'Why?'

'Internet searches. On his home computer.'

Taymoor tensed up. 'You know there's nothing there,' he said, his tone firm and even.

'Maybe. Probably. It's low-level at this point. But you know how it goes, brother. It's not up to me.'

'I know. But it's still bullshit.'

'I hope so. For his sake and yours. Anyway, I'm going out on a limb here, but I thought you should know. Level Three surveillance protocol has been initiated. Maybe it's something; maybe it's nothing. It'll tell us, either way.'

Taymoor took a second to process the news. Level 3— that wasn't good. 'You'll keep me posted. Either way.' Not a request. An instruction.

He knew he could rely on Huseyin.

'Of course.'

'Good,' Taymoor said. Then he hung up, cursing under his breath.

*

It didn't take Kamal long to cut through the Citadel. Minutes after leaving Taymoor, he had reached the huge complex's prison.

He didn't know the desk sergeant who was on duty that morning.

After flashing his creds, Kamal asked, 'You've got someone here I need to see. Ibrahim Sinasi.'

The desk sergeant consulted his screen, and then his face turned sour.

'Is there a problem?' Kamal asked.

The desk sergeant seemed to mull his words carefully before deciding on, 'You don't have the clearance.'

'What?'

'It's a Z Directorate case. Only they can see him, and even that list's restricted.'

Kamal kept his anger in check, but his tone was clear. 'He's a person of interest in a case of ours, too. I need to see him.'

'I told you. I can't allow it,' the prison officer shot back just as firmly. 'You need to take it up with the Z guys.'

Kamal fumed. 'We're on the same side, aren't we?'

'You're not listening, Kamal Agha,' the officer insisted. 'It's not up to me. I don't set the protocol.'

'Who are they? The agents in charge. What are their names? Or is that against protocol, too?'

The desk sergeant glanced at his screen. After a small hesitation, he said, 'Jamal Banna and Onur Goskun.'

Kamal frowned. He didn't know them. The odds were he wouldn't. The Hafiye was a big place, with several hundred agents working out of the Citadel. They didn't all know each other, much less what cases they were working on.

He glared at the desk sergeant. The prison officer's gaze didn't waver. The man just sat there, stone-cold and unmoved. Then, as if with great reluctance, he leaned in, lowered his tone, and added, 'I really shouldn't say this, but . . . I wouldn't push too hard on this.'

'Why not?'

'I hear he's White Rose,' he told Kamal with a shrug. He didn't add anything else. He didn't need to.

Kamal frowned. Another damned plotter. Connections lit up like fuses in Kamal's mind—Azmi, Sinasi, White Rose— all with a connection to Nisreen.

A connection that could put her in grave danger.

'*Bok*,' he cursed, before nodding solemnly and walking away.

He didn't go back to his desk. Instead, he made his way back up and across the large glazed atrium to the Z Directorate's building, oblivious to any familiar faces he crossed in the elevators or down the long corridors.

The two agents, Banna and Goskun, weren't in. He gave his name and number to the directorate's desk sergeant and asked him to get them to call him as soon as possible.

He had to try to fix this. For Nisreen's sake.

But something in the pit of his stomach told him it was already beyond his reach.

16

Sitting quietly at his patient's bedside, Ramazan was trans-
fixed.

He had managed to grab a few more sessions with his
patient, carving out the time in between surgeries, finding a
way to be alone with him, managing the drugs carefully to
make him just conscious enough to continue his story, but
not to realize what was being done to him.

The rest of the time, he kept the man who claimed to be
Ayman Rasheed Pasha under heavy sedation. As his anaesthetist, he was in charge of overseeing his recovery, and there
was no reason for him to be challenged by the nurses, especially since he said there was nothing worrying and told them
he just wanted to give the patient more time to heal before
bringing him back to full consciousness. He knew he
wouldn't be able to get away with it for too long, but one day
was easily within reason.

And that day was now ending. He needed to get the rest of
the story, and fast.

Throughout, Ramazan still wasn't sure what to believe. So
far, the man's tale was so fantastical it defied belief. And yet the
detail throughout lent it such a potent veneer of credibility that
Ramazan couldn't resist coming back, prompting the man and
listening to his mumbled replies. But, then again, how could it
not be true? In addition to having the most prodigious imagination, the man would have to have an uncanny ability to be
lucid and manipulative while heavily drugged and under the
supervision of a highly capable anaesthetist—which Ramazan

knew was highly, highly unlikely—or, well, the alternative was unthinkable. But despite logic, despite the dictates of rational thought, it somehow felt to Ramazan as though what he was hearing was the truth, as if deep inside, the man was secretly delighted to be sharing his tale with someone, as if his ego had held on to it for so long that it needed to burst out and allow him to bask in his glorious achievement.

Ramazan felt as if he had opened a subconscious floodgate, and he wasn't sure what to make of everything that was pouring out.

By early 2016, Ayman Rasheed had left Syria. His days with ISIS were well behind him and he was deep into his research in Istanbul.

It wasn't difficult for him to disappear. Once he had the papers and the money he needed, he arranged for a meeting with his jihadist superiors in Raqqa, the Islamic State's stronghold, which was conveniently north of Palmyra, more than halfway to the Turkish border. On a bleak November morning, he climbed into a Toyota pickup truck—ironically, the dead antiquities director's own vehicle—and set off, alone, leaving the Venice of the sands in his dust.

He never showed up at that meeting in Raqqa. And even though his body wouldn't turn up riddled with bullets and discarded by the side of the road or mangled in the wreckage of a car that had been caught up in an air strike, he knew his commanders wouldn't ask too many questions: Syria had turned into a post-apocalyptic wasteland, and Ayman Rasheed would simply become one more victim sucked up by the war's black hole.

It wasn't too hard for him to get to Istanbul. The border between Syria and Turkey was a porous, 565-mile nonentity. Jihadists travelling to and from the war in Syria had been crossing it with little hindrance for years, and they weren't exactly strapping on their hiking boots and struggling across rough terrain to do so. An extensive transport network, highly regulated and controlled on both sides of the border, had been long established to facilitate the steady stream of people—fighters going in and refugees coming out—along with shipments of guns, money and oil.

Once there, he found a small, inexpensive apartment in Istanbul's bustling, centrally located Beşiktaş neighborhood. Comfortably and anonymously settled in, he could now begin his work.

Most of his waking hours were spent at the Atatürk Library, hours that were long and mentally draining and devoted to one thing and one thing only: acquiring the necessary knowledge to allow him to carry out his world-altering plan. Draining but invigorating beyond anything he'd ever experienced.

At night, when he finally headed home, he would observe and contemplate everything around him as he formulated his vision for the future of Europe. Istanbul was a city that had successfully managed to reconcile its Islamic heritage with its modernity, and this gave him much food for thought. The muezzins' calls to prayer would reverberate across the city like a tranquillizing wave, slowing down its collective pulse and giving the faithful one of five daily moments in which to pause and reflect.

Rasheed loved the peaceful, sedative feeling that came over him whenever he heard the melodious azans, particularly when they were sung by imams who had the right talent for it.

With Allah's help, *he thought*, it won't be long before all of Europe will learn to appreciate this inspiring ritual and kneel before its holy call.

With Allah's help—and his.

It was all he thought about, day and night.

At first, he'd thought he could use it to do something to fix the tragedy that had ended up with him in Palmyra. He could try to rewrite the recent history of his homeland: go back to before the Americans unleashed their attack, warn Saddam about what was to come, try to defuse the crisis before the cruise missiles were launched. But could he, really? How would he have warned Saddam? Would Saddam and his generals have believed him, or would they have thought that he had lost his mind, or more likely and far worse, that he was working for the Americans? Besides, what would it accomplish? He knew the Americans were determined to attack them. History had shown him that with indisputable clarity. Anything he managed to achieve would only be temporary. They'd find another reason to attack, another excuse.

In any case, it was a moot subject. There was the rule, the only rule that accompanied the gift, the crucial rule that shut down that idea: you couldn't travel to any time within your own lifetime. You couldn't land somewhere—some time—where you already existed. It didn't allow it.

There couldn't be two of you at any one moment in time.

No, even if it were possible, using this incredible gift to do that would be too simplistic and wasteful. He needed to think bigger. It deserved that he be more ambitious. And the fact that everyone he cared about was dead ensured that he wouldn't miss any part of his current life.

It also allowed his mind to roam free and explore the more distant past.

He quickly latched on to the three moments in history when Islam had come tantalizingly close to achieving total victory over the Christian West—and failed: 732, when the Moors were a couple of hundred miles from Paris; 1529, at the peak of the Empire, when the Ottoman's failed in their siege of Vienna, the seat of the Habsburg monarchy and unofficial capital of the Holy Roman Empire; and 1683, when the Ottomans staged a second unsuccessful attempt to take the Austrian city.

Failures that he could influence and change.

Failures that could be turned into successes.

All three were possible target dates. He had to choose one.

The first was in 732, when the Umayyad caliphate's warriors had overrun North Africa, crossed the straits of Gibraltar, and taken over Spain, Portugal and southwestern France. The emir, Abd al-Rahman, and his men were only two hundred miles south of Paris when they were finally stopped by Charles Martel and his army of Frankish and Germanic fighters in the fields between Tours and Poitiers. That defeat at the hands of a vastly outnumbered force that, historians believe, had no cavalry or chain mail, resulted in nothing less than the preservation of Christianity in Europe.

From a historical point of view, 732 was interesting. Moorish southwestern Europe was firmly under Islamic control. Armed with the foresight he'd be bringing, along with knowledge of warfare and weaponry, he thought he could easily help the emir defeat Martel and continue to conquer present-day France. Adding to the appeal of 732 was that America had not yet been discovered; that was something he could potentially influence too, and the vision of galleys flying the flag of Islam being the first to claim the great continent on the other side of the Atlantic was hard to resist. He imagined America as a Muslim continent, with mosques and minarets and muezzins' calls echoing across the land the Americans now called home, and the thought amused him greatly. But 732 had other things going against it. The available skills and tools in the eighth century—the technology, if one could call it that—were very far removed from what he would need to make it all happen. There were also far fewer sources of reading he could draw on to familiarize himself with what would probably be, he feared, an environment that was too radically different from anything he could imagine. Finally, he was also pretty sure that the later dates would be much more comfortable and enjoyable to live in.

No, the Ottoman era was surely the way to go.

He knew its history well. The empire had begun humbly in the thirteenth century, when a tribal leader by the name of Osman led his Turkish band of nomadic warriors out of central Asia and started chipping away at Byzantine territory. Two hundred years later, his descendent Mehmed II captured Constantinople, the Byzantine capital, earning him the sobriquet of Kayser-i Rûm: emperor of Rome. The sultan's ambition, and that of those who followed, were thus clearly announced: to reclaim the Roman Empire westward, all the way to Rome.

It was an ambition that fired up Rasheed's imagination.

At its peak, the Ottoman Empire covered over a million square miles across Europe, North Africa and the Middle East, and it was ruled by the same dynasty for over six hundred years. It was staggeringly wealthy and well organized, the undisputed superpower of its era. The sultan was the most powerful man in the world, a figurehead who inspired awe and fear in the West, his cavalry considered literal horsemen of the Apocalypse. But the great prizes of Vienna and the more distant Rome still eluded them.

Their armies reached the gates of Vienna twice. Although both attempts took place at a time when the empire was peaking and Europe was being torn apart by conflict between Protestants and Catholics, fate turned against them at the eleventh hour.

If Rasheed could change the outcome of one of those sieges, everything would be up for grabs. The future of western Europe, and potentially the rest of the world, would be redefined in a radical new way.

The question was, Which of the two campaigns to choose?

In September 1529, Suleiman the Magnificent and his men besieged the Austrian city for a month, shelling it and digging trenches to undermine its fortifications. But by mid-October, just as it seemed as if Vienna was about to fall, the torrential rain that had blighted the siege turned into a highly unseasonable early snow. The Ottoman army had to pull back in haste, retreating through deepening snowdrifts. Vienna and Christian western Europe were saved once more.

In the summer of 1683, the Ottomans were outside Vienna again. The sultan Mehmet IV and his grand vizier, Kara Mustafa, who was leading the charge, had learned the lessons of previous failed attempts to take the city: the imperial army had set off from Istanbul as soon as the spring thaw in the Balkans allowed it and reached the gates of Vienna by mid-July. The siege lasted two months, and the Ottomans came close—very close—to taking their prized 'Golden Apple'. But history was against them yet again, and their defeat in the battlefields outside the city's walls ushered in the long, slow death of the empire.

As days turned into weeks, Ayman Rasheed's thoughts kept zeroing in on that third date: 1683.

The more he thought about it, the more he was convinced that it was *the perfect choice. But to say that it would need a lot of preparation would be the understatement of the millennium.*

He needed to learn everything he could about that time. He needed to read everything he could get his hands on and plan very, very carefully. Only then would he launch his audacious plan.

He would help the Ottomans conquer Vienna in the summer of 1683.

And after Vienna, he would make sure the rest of Europe fell under the sword of Islam.

17

The CCTV footage from the riverbank had allowed the analyst at the surveillance centre to track the target couple from where they'd been filmed shouting and pointing at something all the way back along their walk upriver to where they'd parked their car. A few taps of a keyboard were all it took to tie an address to its licence plate. Which was why Kamal and Taymoor were currently standing outside the service entrance to a restaurant and talking to its sweaty chef.

'The quays? Yes, I was there yesterday morning,' the man was saying a bit too casually. 'My wife and I usually take a walk before work, before it gets too hot. Why?'

'You didn't notice anything out of the ordinary on your walk?' Kamal asked.

He and Taymoor could have handed it to the Zaptiye cops to look into, but they didn't. Kamal had decided he could use the distraction.

He wasn't having one of his best days. The morning altercation with Nisreen had pretty much ruined it from the start. Some data logs from an Arabian bank that he'd hoped would give them an actionable money trail linking one of their executives to a mosque on their watch list turned out to be a dud. He still hadn't heard from the two Z Directorate agents he'd sought out that morning, which was grating on him. Especially now, the day after Friday's executions, when his name should have instilled enough respect in them to spur them to get in touch promptly. And yet silence. And the case of the body in the river wasn't proving to be the distraction he needed right now.

The man was clearly jittery. Nowadays, no one liked talking to the police, secret or otherwise. He feigned a disinterested shrug and said, 'Not really. Why?'

Kamal rolled his eyes and held out his phone to him. It showed the clip of the man and his wife shouting and pointing.

The man visibly stiffened. 'I . . . it's just—'

'You should have reported it,' Kamal pressed. 'You do know it's also a crime to fail to report a crime?'

'Was that really your wife with you? Should we confirm it with her?' Taymoor asked.

'Of course it was my wife. Please'—the man's voice cracked as he nodded—'I know, we should have called someone. But . . .' His words trailed off. He didn't need to explain it. Calling in a crime could get you sucked into a dangerous swamp of inquiries. The presumption of innocence had been badly undermined since Abdülhamid had assumed power.

'So what did you see?' Kamal asked.

He hesitated, then said, 'There was a man there, on the opposite quay. He was bent down over another guy who wasn't moving—I think he was dead. He was undressing him and putting on his clothes.' He was no longer hiding the confusion and fear he was feeling. 'The guy was naked.'

Kamal looked a question at Taymoor.

'At first, we were confused and just shocked, really. It was so . . . weird. Then when he started pulling him to the edge of the quay, we understood what was about to happen. That's when my wife screamed, and he saw us.'

'Then what happened?'

'He looked across the water at us. Scared the hell out of us, too. But he didn't panic. He just dumped the body in the water and ran.'

Kamal and Taymoor were intrigued. And that was before the man added, 'Oh, and one other thing. This guy? He had markings all over his body.'

'Markings?' Kamal asked.

'Yes. Like . . . tattoos. All over his chest.'

This was turning into more than a mere distraction.

'We definitely need to track down this guy,' Taymoor said as they walked back to the car. 'If only to get a look at those tattoos.'

Kamal barely nodded. Of course, he had questions. Why was the man killed? For his clothes? What else was the killer after? And what happened to his own clothes? Did he throw them into the river? The chef hadn't seen him do that. Then there were the tattoos. Still, his mind was elsewhere.

He was feeling antsy and checked his watch. 'I need to make a quick call,' he told Taymoor, before stepping away from him.

He called the Z Directorate switchboard and asked to be put through to one of the agents handling the playwright's case. The call went directly to voicemail. He left a blunt message virtually ordering the guy to return his call.

His face was locked with anger. Taymoor saw it.

'Whoa, you need to get a grip, brother.' Taymoor eyed him curiously. 'What's going on?'

Kamal stared away and didn't reply at first. Then he said, 'I've got something I need to look into. I'll catch up with you later.'

Taymoor started to say something. Kamal paused for a second, but Taymoor seemingly decided against it and shook it away. 'It's nothing. Allah go with you, brother.'

Kamal was happy to leave it at that and walked off.

18

It was a stab in the dark, but it paid off.

He knew Nisreen usually did her best to meet the kids when they got off the school bus around the corner from their apartment building, and today proved no exception. He didn't have to wait there too long.

Her face registered surprise—and not the happy kind—when she spotted him. She hadn't even reached him when she asked, 'What are you doing here?'

'You stormed off before even giving me a chance to—'

'To what? Tell me they just pulled him in for a friendly chat over a cup of rose tea and some baklava? 'Cause that's how you guys do things, right?'

'Would you please take a breath and just give me a chance?'

'A chance for what?'

'I'm not the enemy, Nisreen. I'm trying to help you.'

'Your uniform says otherwise.'

'We stopped five guys who were going to attack the festival, the one for the beylerbey's daughter's wedding. They would have killed God knows how many people. Hell, you and Ramazan might have even been there. And Tarek and Noor, too. So maybe, just maybe, this uniform isn't all bad, no?'

His outburst stilled Nisreen. She looked totally dumbfounded and almost didn't notice the school bus pull up.

Several kids got off, including Tarek and Noor. Their faces lit up when they saw Kamal.

Noor ran toward him with open arms and a huge smile. 'Uncle Kamal.'

He whisked her off her feet in a tight hug. 'How's my favourite little princess? I've missed you so much, *hayatim.*' The endearment meant 'my life,' and nothing could have been more true.

He gave her a big kiss on her forehead before setting her back down and crouching to get level with Tarek's face. Kamal gestured him over. 'And how's my little *şampiyon?*'

His little champion hesitated and glanced at his mother. She gave him a tentative, visibly strained nod that it was okay. Tarek stepped closer, and Kamal gave him a hug, glancing up at Nisreen as he did.

'Are you staying for dinner?' Noor enthused.

Kamal felt a tear through his heart, but he hid it and just gave her a warm smile. 'I don't think so, *hayatim.*'

'I need to speak with Uncle Kamal, children,' Nisreen said. 'Why don't you go up to the apartment? I won't be long.'

The kids glanced uncertainly at them both, then nodded. With parting melancholy glances at Kamal and a small wave from Noor, they walked away.

Kamal watched them go, then turned to Nisreen. 'I'm sorry. I didn't mean for them to see me. But it was the only way to—'

'Why are you here?'

He kept his tone soft. 'I'm worried about you. Tell me what you know about Sinasi.'

'I don't need you to worry about me. Worry about him. He's—'

He cut her off. 'Please, Nisreen, just . . . tell me.'

She sucked in her reluctance. 'He's quite successful. I'm sure you've seen his work, if not in the theatre, then maybe on TV. He was casting his new play, and one of the actors reported him.'

'For what?'

'Incitement to riot—that's what your guy at the Hafiye said.' Nisreen frowned, then added, 'It's the play.'

'What about it?'

'It's the story of a Polish farmer who lives in a small town on the edge of the empire. A place that's ignored by the state. A band of Russian guerrillas are harassing the townspeople. They extort money and food from them. They take women. They kill a couple of farmers who stand up to them. The *ra'ayah* —"the folk"—implore the bey who governs the region for help, but he can't be bothered to lift a finger. They're small and far, and he doesn't want to risk a military conflict that might disturb his lush life and cost money. So the farmer decides to take things into his own hands. He goes around from town to town asking people to speak out. He asks them to stand up and choose who they want for their bey. If he's chosen, he would have control of the local armed regiment—and use it against the guerrillas.'

This got Kamal's attention. 'Which he does, and he saves the day?'

'No,' Nisreen said. 'The bey has him killed. The uprising is put down. The Russians move in unopposed and rape and pillage; then they leave. Order is restored.'

Kamal shook his head.

'It's a play,' Nisreen insisted, her anger back. 'A story. It's people exploring ideas on a stage. Sinasi wasn't plotting to blow anyone up.'

Kamal let out a tense breath. 'You don't know what else he's involved in.'

His words fed Nisreen's anger. 'It's about the play, Kamal.'

He hesitated, then decided to say it. 'They're saying he was White Rose.'

'That's bullshit.' Nisreen snorted, but it was a nervous snort that did little to cover up a clearly deep-seated fear.

'What if he was?' Kamal objected.

'White Rose, White Rose . . . What is this mysterious White Rose that everyone is part of all of a sudden?' Nisreen scoffed. 'What do you really know about it? And why are all the cases involving it dealt with by a closed court?' She shook her head slowly, then stared away, a sunken look in her eyes, before facing Kamal again. 'The attack you stopped . . . of course I'm grateful. Everybody is. Of course I think you're doing the right thing. But that's only part of the fight we're in. And maybe you're too close to it to see what's really happening. The people you work for, the ones you have all this blind faith in? They're the ones who should be in jail, not Sinasi. Abdülhamid and his gang . . . they're robbing us blind and shutting down anyone who speaks up about it. And the rampant corruption, my God, that's bad enough, but then when you throw in the sheer incompetence—can't you see? They're undoing all the progress Murad achieved; they're destroying our faith in government and setting us back a hundred years. Hell, they might even drag us into a war with America if it suits them. You need to wake up, Kamal. If people like you don't, what hope do we have?'

Her words sank in like depth charges detonating deep within him, and he couldn't find the words to answer her. Instead, he just nodded and retreated to the issue at hand. The rest could wait.

'Okay. Give me a chance to look into Sinasi,' he told her. 'If he's not part of anything bad, I'll do everything I can to make sure they release him as quickly as possible.'

Nisreen let out a breath that was drowning in scepticism.

'But if he is, I'm going to need you to be much more careful from here on,' Kamal insisted. 'These people are dangerous.'

'White Rose? Or you and the rest of your people?'

Kamal let it slide. 'Please . . . I'm serious.'

She met his gaze. A couple of seconds, no more. But it was enough to rekindle a whole history of closeness between them.

'I miss you. All of you,' he said.

'We do, too.' She paused, then added, 'All of us.'

He felt the tear rip wider. 'I should let you go. I'll be in touch as soon as I hear anything.'

Nisreen nodded.

He didn't want to go. He wanted to stretch the moment, he wanted to accompany her home, to see his brother, his nephew, his niece. Most of all, he just wanted to be around her longer. But now wasn't the right time.

He caught her wistful look, felt the tear rip open, and walked away.

19

Nisreen had dinner with Tarek and Noor—her special artichoke, lamb and coriander stew, a family favourite and the kind of comfort food she badly needed tonight.

They ate as they always did, at the square table in their kitchen. The French tradition of eating that way, using individual plates and utensils, had survived the conquest and resisted the encroachment of the old Ottoman tradition of sharing food from a central bowl with one's fingers while sitting on cushions on the floor.

Noor was unusually chirpy, which was a welcome deflection from the unease gnawing away at Nisreen. She'd sent a text message to Ramazan earlier, asking when he'd be back, and he'd said that he was working late again, which only added to the distress she felt after seeing Kamal. What she'd seen in his Internet search history was still worrying her, and she even wondered if her husband really was at the hospital after all or if he was involved in something else. Which then gave way to an even more uncomfortable thought: the coincidence of Kamal showing up now. *Surely not*, she thought. She had her misgivings about him, but she knew that she could still read him and still believed in the goodness at his core.

Or did she?

The children put away the plates. Then she gave them their baths, and they were ready for bed.

'Are you okay, *anneh*?' Tarek asked as she tucked him in.

She pulled out as comforting a smile as she could. 'Of course, *hayatim*. Why?'

He hesitated, then asked, 'Why don't we ever see Uncle Kamal any more?'

She struggled for words. 'It's just . . . he's very busy these days. That's all.'

Tarek nodded. 'The guys in class . . . they were saying what a big hero he is. But you and *baba* don't seem to be happy when people mention his name.'

Nisreen let out a ragged breath. 'It's not that simple, *haya-tim*. Maybe when you're older, you'll understand.'

'But he's a hero, isn't he?'

She wasn't sure how to answer that. But there was only one answer she could give him. 'Of course he is.'

Tarek looked at her uncertainly, doubt clouding his face, then nodded.

Nisreen leaned in and kissed his forehead. 'Sleep well, my little *şampiyon*.'

At the ICU's nurse station, Ramazan handed in the last of his paperwork and checked his watch.

It was late. Very late. But he couldn't pull away. Not yet. There was more story to come, and tonight might be the last chance he would have to get the rest of it.

All day, he'd kept wondering if it could really be true, if he'd allowed his desperation and his imagination to push him to such a level of foolhardiness as to have done what he'd done. Wondering if it was all going to backfire on him like a big, bad joke, one that, if it ever came out, might turn him into an object of ridicule, if not cost him his career.

He wasn't sure. Still, he'd come this far. He couldn't leave the rest of it unanswered.

'All done, *hakeem*?' Anbara asked as she emerged from the hallway. She was obviously doing the night shift.

'Yes, pretty much.' He smiled.

'I'll see you tomorrow, then.' She gave him a little wave and headed off.

He waited for her to disappear from view, nodded vaguely at the nurse sitting behind the desk, then walked away in the opposite direction.

Back to room 7, which housed a very special and unusual patient.

20

At first, the idea seemed unimaginably daunting.

An undertaking of this scale, on his own—a Herculean task, to be sure. This would be one of history's boldest projects, perhaps the most ambitious, and Ayman Rasheed was going to try to accomplish it without anyone else's help.

There was arrogance there, certainly, some likely delusion, too, perhaps even lunacy. Imagining it was irresistibly addictive and energizing, like having an adrenaline drip tapped directly into his brain. Rasheed was fully aware of the gargantuan goal he'd given himself, which was why he set himself no target date. He would only launch his plan once he was fully prepared.

Ever methodical and analytical, he chose to divide his work into three parts.

The first was the conquest of Vienna. This involved learning everything he could about the siege of 1683 and why it had failed, then devising a strategy that would work.

This task was the easiest part of the puzzle since it dealt with existing history. He was going to influence a specific event, a past battle. So much had been written about the siege by Ottomanists who had access to numerous first-hand accounts. Entire books were devoted to analysing every detail of the campaign and dissecting its failure. Very quickly, Rasheed felt highly confident that he could easily turn that failure into victory, assuming he could get the sultan to accept his help and follow his advice, which was something else he needed to figure out.

He already had some ideas about that.

The tactical mistakes Kara Mustafa made were clear. Victory would have been his had he not squandered it. Hindsight was truly a wonderful thing, especially when Rasheed had three centuries filled with brilliant and disastrous campaigns to learn from. A few carefully chosen moves would be enough to change everything. A few moves—and some unexpected game changers he had in mind—would make taking Vienna an easy fix.

The second part of his research dealt with a far bigger challenge: taking over the rest of western Europe.

It was one thing to conquer Vienna; it was quite another to hold it, which was necessary well before thinking of conquering territories beyond it. The city was almost a thousand miles from the empire's capital, at a time when travel was slow and arduous. Rivers and chains of mountains stood between it and Istanbul. The Ottoman army that laid siege to Vienna was a mammoth force made up of over a hundred thousand men. When on the move, it formed a convoy six miles long and kicked up a cloud of dust that could be seen for miles. Keeping it there to hold the city and bringing forward its supply lines risked overstretching the empire's resources while making its eastern border vulnerable to its old rival Persia.

Rasheed needed to shrink the landscape and make moving armies and equipment faster and more manageable.

Trains were the answer. The steam engine was in its early stages of development at the time. He needed to dramatically accelerate that. He'd need to lure the brilliant, pioneering inventors from England, France and Holland and have them work for the sultan. Money, or kidnapping, would bring them to him. Bringing forward technological advances that wouldn't have happened for decades, if not centuries, would give the Ottomans a titanic advantage.

With Vienna firmly under Ottoman dominance and well supplied, he could turn to conquering the rest of Europe. Unlike the siege itself, this would be a venture into the unknown, an endless diagram of theoretical actions, reactions and outcomes, since once Vienna fell, history would be changed and everything he was reading about would be altered.

The scope of the exercise facing him was mind-boggling. He immersed himself in studies of those who had attempted something of that scale before him and ended up focusing on Alexander the Great, Napoleon and Hitler. He aimed to be squarely in their league and he found inspiration in their ambition, but he also took heed of their mistakes. This was research that the consummate strategist in Rasheed relished. It was the simulation to end all simulations, and soon it wouldn't be a simulation at all. It would become reality.

He'd need to bring in new weapons and military tactics, of course.

Early in his research, he'd remembered something that had come up in a lecture at the military academy in Iraq, an anecdote that had stamped an indelible impression on his mind. It concerned the Spanish conquest of South America, a notorious day in November 1532, in the highlands of Peru. His instructor had explained how on that day Francisco Pizarro and 168 Spaniards had faced off against the Inca ruler Atahualpa and his entire imperial army. The Spaniards rode horses and had rapier swords and harquebuses, a type of early musket. The Incas, a primitive people who still fought with spears, had never encountered mounted men or firearms. Before the day was out, Pizarro and his men had killed over seven thousand Incas and taken their emperor prisoner—and they'd done it without suffering a single fatality in their own ranks.

Superior weaponry was key, a concept that was not alien to the Ottomans. Not since their first major conquest, when they took Constantinople in 1453. At the time, the Byzantine emperor, Constantine XI, had a Hungarian engineer by the name of Urban working to build him a great cannon. Foolishly, the Byzantines skimped on Urban's payments, leading him to offer his services to the sultan, who was more than delighted to have the brilliant Christian engineer on his side. The result of his work was the Imperial, at the time the largest cannon ever built. It had a bore twenty-nine feet long, fired massive stones that weighed over a thousand pounds, and was so heavy it needed a team of sixty oxen to haul it. It was this cannon that brought down the ancient fortified walls and allowed the Ottomans to take the city.

More than two hundred years later, Rasheed would give the Ottomans an even bigger advantage. His knowledge of what weapons the Ottomans were using in the seventeenth century was pretty basic, but he did know that muzzle-loading flintlock muskets were a far cry from the AK-47s he was used to. He needed a weapon that would completely overwhelm the Ottomans' enemies and bring them to their knees, but one that could realistically be produced at the time. He found his answer in Richard Gatling's American design from 1861, an ingenious weapon that used relatively simple technology.

The Gatling gun looked like a small cannon and was typically fitted on top of a wheeled mount. It had multiple rotating barrels that were fired by turning a hand crank. With two men working the gun, it could achieve two hundred rounds per minute, and it could be easily pulled across a battlefield by two horses.

In a world of muskets and swords, it would be a devastating piece of weaponry. As would military tactics that wouldn't have been dreamed up for centuries and other surprises he would throw into the mix, along with his knowledge of natural events that happened after the summer of 1683, such as bad weather, famines and plagues.

Under his guidance, the Ottomans would be unstoppable.

With King John III Sobieski dead and his hussars decimated, Poland would fall easily. The German states would be next in line. To the south, the Papal States wouldn't present much of a problem militarily. Venice would be followed by Urbino and Genoa before Rome was sacked. Then, after Savoy, Marseilles and Lyons would fall before the sultan's army would reach Louis XIV's palace at Versailles. France was a force to be reckoned with, even though it would be preoccupied with second-guessing the reactions of its other enemies, the British and the Dutch. Rasheed would probably wait until 1694, when a couple of years of catastrophic harvests due to bad weather would lead to a great famine that would kill two million French men and women—more than a thousand dying every day in Paris—and bring the country to its knees.

On the empire's northern border, the power of the tsars in Russia was growing and would need to be checked; the Ottomans' ally, the khan of Crimea and his fearless Tartar horsemen, would doubtless be needed to keep the Russians busy, as would the Swedes, historic allies of the sultan.

Of course, things didn't turn out exactly as he'd planned. But he'd been well prepared, and he was ready.

Europe had fallen. And it remained so, to this day.

One of the fortunate things about Moshe Fonseca was his gregarious personality. The man had a castaway's appetite for small talk and an almost maniacal attention to detail, which meant that Ramazan was lucky to hear him before he walked into Rasheed's room.

He'd barely managed to tweak the IV lines and send Rasheed back to sleep before the surgeon stepped in.

'They told me you were still here,' he told Ramazan in his jovial tone. 'So how's our human notebook doing?'

Ramazan shrugged, trying to appear as nonchalant as he could. 'He seems comfortable.'

Fonseca reached for the patient's chart, which was hanging from the end of the bed, and flicked through its pages. 'His numbers are good. But you're still keeping him under?'

A slight hesitation. 'I brought him out this morning,' Ramazan finally managed. 'But he was in a lot of pain, so I thought I'd keep him sedated a bit longer. Give him a chance to heal some more.'

The surgeon nodded. The answer was plausible. He put the chart back in its place. 'Did you manage to get him to say anything? Do we know anything more about him—well, more than nothing, that is?'

Ramazan stiffened. He still hadn't told Fonseca about the man's pre-op outburst, and evidently the nurse, Anbara, hadn't mentioned it either. He considered bringing it up now, then decided against it. He didn't want to open that door and didn't want to be asked why he hadn't said anything earlier. Most of all, he didn't want to risk Fonseca's finding out about his unofficial sessions with the patient.

'No,' he replied, a knot of dread tightening up inside him. 'He was too weak to talk, especially after I removed the tube.'

'So when do you think? Tomorrow morning?'

'*Inshallah.* He should be in better shape.'

Fonseca looked thoughtful. 'It should be interesting. I'm curious to hear what he has to say. Assuming he decides to talk. Assuming he *can* talk.'

Ramazan stifled the unease that was sweeping through him and let out a small snort of derision. 'We'll see.'

'Has anyone asked about him? The registrar?'

'No.'

'You know we're going to have to file a report soon.'

Even though he brought it up, Fonseca seemed uncomfortable with the notion. Ramazan knew it was because the surgeon wasn't inclined to point a suspicious finger at anyone unless he had a good reason to. They'd spoken about how, as a Jew, Fonseca had experienced a couple of uncomfortable moments since the recent rise of aggressive ultra-imperialist sentiment. He knew what it felt like to be viewed through a distorted lens of suspicion and prejudice.

'Well, let's wait and see what he has to say,' Ramazan offered. 'There might well be nothing to worry about.'

Fonseca nodded his agreement. 'Indeed.' He looked at Ramazan, then nudged his head towards the door. 'How's Khawaja Abdullah doing?' He was referring to a patient who'd gone under his knife earlier that day, with Ramazan assisting. 'Have you checked on him yet?'

Ramazan hesitated, then said, 'No, not yet.'

Fonseca tilted his head towards the door. 'Shall we?'

The anaesthetist stood there awkwardly, fumbling for what to say. He wanted to stay, of course. Desperately. His window was closing, and he needed more time with the tattooed man. But caught off guard like that, he was lost for words. He had no credible reason to stay behind, and he took too long to come up with an alternative excuse. He had no choice.

'Right behind you,' he replied, masking his dismay.

He slid one last parting glance at the mystery man, then followed the surgeon out of the room.

Ramazan would have to come back, but he knew it would be difficult to do so as long as Fonseca was lurking in the corridors. Besides, he was eager to do some research, to see what the history books could tell him about the tattooed man's story. Maybe it would debunk the whole thing and he wouldn't need another session with him. Or maybe it would support his tale, in which case he'd want plenty more.

He decided he'd go home and do some reading about the famous governor. Then, if need be, he'd be back at the man's bedside first thing in the morning, as he'd done earlier that day. After that, he'd probably need to bring his patient out of his induced sleep for good.

He needed to make every minute count.

21

Nisreen sensed that Ramazan was preoccupied the moment he walked in.

She knew it concerned what he'd been hiding from her. After all their years together, she could read the smallest hints in his facial expressions and his body language, even if he was never the most emotionally effusive person and had a frustratingly limited spectrum of reactions to most of what their life as a couple threw at them. The signs were there this evening, and her reading was that he probably wanted to continue with the previous night's activities.

Which was hugely troubling.

She could sense danger in what he was doing. She'd been around it enough, through her work, to recognize it.

After clearing away his plates and putting away the left-over stew, she found Ramazan standing by the French windows in the family room, looking out in silence. She pushed back her unease and cosied up to him casually, placing a comforting hand on his shoulder.

'Are you okay?'

He turned, his expression uncertain. It took him a moment to reply. 'Yes, of course. Why?'

She hesitated. She was bursting to confront him about what he was up to. But she knew Ramazan and knew she needed to broach it carefully. If she wanted to, she had a relatively innocuous way of bringing it up. She could say that she'd used the computer earlier, and when she'd brought up its search history looking for a website she'd visited previously, she'd come across his browsing and was curious as to why it was of interest to him. But given his reaction the night before, he'd probably brush it off, and she wouldn't know any more than she did now.

'Are you sure?' she asked. 'You seem a bit distracted.'

He gave her a gentle smile, but it wasn't reflected in his eyes. 'I'm just tired. That's all. I hardly slept last night.'

'I know. You've never been up like that. Is everything okay?'

Again, a slight hesitation. 'Yes, I told you. It's just a complicated case—that's all. I just need to get some rest. I'm sorry.'

'You're sure?'

He ran a hand down her hair, to her neck. 'Yes.'

She held his gaze, restrained herself, then nodded. 'Okay.' She decided to give him some space—or, more accurately, some rope. 'I'm tired myself. I'm going to run a bath and turn in early.'

'Take your time. I've got a bit of work to do here anyway.'

'Don't stay up too late.'

He smiled again. 'I won't.' Then he leaned in and gave her a kiss—more of a sterile peck, really—before she left him in the family room and headed off to their bedroom.

Still hounded by an unshakeable discomfort, she ran her bath, leaving the doors to their bathroom and bedroom open to give him a false sense of security. Once the bath was full, she turned the taps off and, more noisily than was perhaps the norm, got in.

Nisreen did, in fact, love her baths, both at home and out. Public hammams were a fixture in the social life of the city's women, one of the select places outside the home where they could congregate and socialize. Time spent at the baths was an indulgent, centuries-old tradition and a pampering ritual that had spread to each conquered territory, even if, in its present-day evolution, slave girls and eunuchs were no longer a common sight within their meticulously tiled walls. In more insouciant days, Nisreen and her friends would while away the hours at the beautiful eighteenth-century hammam by the Samaritaine water pumps, but it had been a while since she had last enjoyed such an outing. Those carefree days were a distant memory.

Tonight, though, Nisreen's bath was neither a public opportunity to catch up with friends nor a private one to unwind in the sanctity of her home. It was an uncomfortable deception, a tool of entrapment, and it felt deeply disrespectful to her husband, to the father of her children.

But it was also, she was convinced, necessary.

Ramazan heard the taps running at full blast, waited, heard Nisreen turn the taps off, heard her skin squealing against the back of the porcelain tub as she settled into the water.

By the time he'd been interrupted by Fonseca, he'd heard most of the man's story, from his capture in the Baghdad region by American soldiers—a conceit that was outlandish in itself—to his first appearance before the sultan in his bedchamber in the middle of the night, to how he had intervened in the fields outside Vienna. But there was more he needed to know, a lot more. The man hadn't told him much about what his world was like—the world he left behind, before he reset the clock. For Ramazan, that was as intriguing as his story, perhaps even more so. If the man was a fantasist, that part might be harder for him to conjure up. Beyond that was perhaps the most important part of all, and the key to deciding whether the man was delusional or some kind of magician: How did he do it? What was the method that allowed him to move across time?

He knew Nisreen's bath ritual well enough to know that the sound of running water heralded a solid, uninterrupted half hour of privacy, which he could now put to good use.

He switched on the computer, opened the *Hafiza* browser, and typed in 'Ayman Rasheed Pasha'.

As expected, he got thousands of hits. The eighteenth-century governor of the Paris *eyalet,* the huge Ottoman province that covered the territory of Louis XIV's old kingdom of France, was an Ottoman titan. Like most educated people, Ramazan knew a bit about Rasheed Pasha's history from his schooldays, but a long time had passed and his memory needed a refresher. But before he'd even had a chance to read a word, he saw something that tripped his senses, an image that snared his attention and turned him into a breathless, rigid, embalmed version of himself, his mind crashing against all kinds of logic walls in a desperate search for a workable explanation.

It was an image of an old oil painting, one that was done during the heyday of the famous governor, years after Paris had fallen, well into his highly successful reign over the great city, at the time the largest city in Europe after Istanbul, and the vast territories around it. The man in the painting was the epitome of imperial grandeur. He was depicted in three-quarter view looking over his shoulder while reclining on a large, luxurious divan and framed by a cusped arch. He was dressed in a white shirt with a cross-over collar under a sumptuous deep-red kaftan that had bands of elaborate frogging and a broad fur collar. On his head he wore the distinctly Ottoman *tâj*, a turban in which a length of white fabric is wound around a stiff ribbed cap made of red felt. A bejewelled sword hung on his belt while gold-coloured slippers protruded from under his garments. But it wasn't the opulence of the image that hit Ramazan. It was the man's face. It helped that the painting was done in the Venetian style, rendering it lifelike because of the western shading that was more successful at suggesting volume in the face than the flat, unmodelled planes of earlier Ottoman art. The artist was talented, whoever he was—and no doubt he would be credited somewhere if Ramazan cared to look. For the stern, belligerent-looking face staring out from the screen at Ramazan was, without a doubt, the tattooed man.

It was him.

He stared at the portrait for ages, unable to move his mind past its blunt implications. His thoughts bounded into all kinds of directions, looking for an answer to how this was possible. Was the tattooed man at the hospital simply someone who looked very much like Rasheed, someone obsessed by the great man, a psychotic who lived in a delusion about being him and who had gone as far as to tattoo his body to make his story more potent? Was it even someone who'd gone to the trouble of having facial surgery to look like him? But for what reason? And why the tattoos?

He opened another browser window and searched for a mention of the tattoos but couldn't find any. He ran a separate specific search about them, but also came up empty-handed. Were they simply more evidence of the man's unhinged mind? That had to be the logical explanation. Then there was the accent, that ancient manner of speaking that no one used anymore. Where was that coming from? Was it fake? Was it an attempt to give his story authenticity? Would it stand up to analysis by an expert in linguistics? More than anything, though, there was the casual detail, the storytelling that felt so authentic, so honest, so real. But that could be faked, too, he told himself. If the man was obsessed with Rasheed, he'd know everything about his life. He'd be convincing.

But why? Why would someone do that? What possible reason could he have to try to pull off a stunt like that? He wasn't faking his illness—that much was certain. As for the rest . . . that he was an impostor was certainly easier to swallow than the alternative, which was simply that the tattooed man really was Ayman Rasheed Pasha and that he had come across an ancient secret in Palmyra, which was now a popular tourist spot, and used it to change history.

Impossible.

He scrolled through more images of Rasheed, other paintings from the era. There weren't many, and none were as accomplished or as lifelike as the first one he'd seen, but they served to reinforce its stupefying message. Desperate for more information, Ramazan dived ravenously into articles about Rasheed and his life, speed-reading about him while trying to match it to what the man had said.

The details about Rasheed's life before the conquest of Vienna were sketchy and obviously didn't tally with what he'd heard at the hospital. If Rasheed had indeed materialized out of thin air in the sultan's bedchamber as he said he had, his back-story would have needed to be invented: where he was born, who his parents were, his education. He would have been helped by the fact that, at that time, information was scarce. A few key details were all that mattered. Beyond that, the lack of information would have also helped feed his mystique.

Then, of course, after Rasheed's appearance and after the campaign to take Vienna had begun, there would have been plenty to write about. Rasheed had burst into the very highest echelon of Ottoman power and cemented himself as the adviser the sultan could not do without—his philosopher-royal. Beyond his direct influence in military affairs, the real, historical Rasheed Pasha had spoken and written a lot about a wide range of topics: history, military strategy, political theory, sociology. He was even regarded as a technological visionary, given the inventions he introduced and his descriptions and sketches of what the future might bring. Reading about him, Ramazan came across the most telling line about him, one he now remembered from his days at school, about Ayman Rasheed Pasha's being the Ottoman Leonardo da Vinci, his prodigious and inventive mind considered superior to that of the Italian polymath.

'What are you doing?'

Ramazan's head snapped up.

Nisreen was by the door, wrapped in a flowing robe, its hood down. She didn't look happy.

'How long have you been standing there?' He could barely formulate the question.

'A while.' She stepped into the room and approached him. Her tone got more accusing. 'Ramazan, what are you up to?'

His finger went to kill the browser window, but she quickly raised a finger in a halting gesture.

'Don't. Don't shut it down. And don't lie to me.'

He stilled his hand over the keyboard. 'Darling, there's nothing to lie about. I told you. Just work.'

She stopped so she was facing him from in front of the table, the screen between them. 'Don't lie to me,' she said. 'I've seen it. Dynamite? Detonators? Trains? What the hell are you involved in?'

The words were like a slap. 'What?'

'Your search history. Last night. It's all there.'

Panic flooded his face. 'So you're spying on my Internet searches now?'

'I'm not spying on you,' she shot back. 'I'm worried. About you. About us. If I saw that, you think they didn't, too?'

'They?'

'You know they watch everything. Did you forget that I'm on their watch list? You don't think they see every keystroke that's typed on this computer?'

He stumbled for words, but before he could formulate an answer, she pressed on.

'What have you got yourself into?'

He stared at her, a crippling dread nailing him in place. 'I haven't got myself into anything.'

Her anger flared through. 'Don't give me that. And don't be naive. You're putting us at risk. All of us.' She was steaming, her fierce glare unrelenting. 'I need to know. Now.'

He let out a long, weary exhale, and nodded slowly. In a way, it was a relief. A huge, welcome relief. He wasn't sure he could handle something this momentous on his own. It had come out of nowhere to bear down on him like a gargantuan weight, something so big and so unheard of that it would inevitably, he worried, drown him.

'Sit down,' he said, softly. 'You're going to need to sit down.'

And then he told her.

Everything.

Ramazan and Nisreen's words weren't confined to their home.

What they didn't know, and what they wouldn't have suspected, was that the built-in microphone on their home computer, its embedded webcam, and the voice-activated speaker unit in their kitchen had all been remotely activated that morning.

Which was why nothing prevented their words from being snatched up the second they left their mouths and funneled out of the city almost instantly to the Comprehensive Imperial Cybersecurity Initiative Data Centre's server banks, where rapacious algorithms would chew them over in ever-more inventive ways before spitting out their reports.

Reports that, in many cases, could devastate a life within hours.

22

Curled up in bed in his top-floor studio, Kamal was waging another losing battle against insomnia.

He was still heavy-headed from the *raki* and the *narguileh* that had kept him company for hours, both before and after Leyla had paid him another impromptu late-night visit. He wasn't pleased with himself—for allowing her in, for ravaging her with such ferocity, even though he knew she enjoyed it more that way, and for crassly hustling her out of his apartment after they were done.

Two separate conversations from that day were still hounding him, duelling voices pulling him apart.

He could still hear Taymoor's words, spoken in the car park at the Hafiye earlier that evening, after he'd told Taymoor what Nisreen had said about the missing playwright.

'You, me, a lot of the people in this city,' Taymoor had said, 'we can handle new ideas. Our education protects us. But the rest, the simple folk out there in the villages and farmlands, they can be easily seduced by lies. And they're an army. A huge, dormant, volatile army, one that's easily awakened—and easily manipulated. We have to protect them from themselves.'

'With bullying and intimidation?' Kamal had replied.

'We're protecting the system. A system God bequeathed us that is based on wisdom and reason, and that works. You know that and I know that, because we know what the alternative is. Chaos. Or did you forget what we studied at the academy?'

'Of course not.'

'People like your playwright are easily seduced by this delusion that men can be governed and yet be free,' Taymoor had argued. 'But history's shown us repeatedly that that's a fallacy. We're just too selfish and greedy. It's human nature. We need limits. We need fear to protect us from our own instincts, because the kind of freedom they're talking about just allows corruption and decadence to creep in, just like it did in Greece and in Rome. Is that what you want for us? To bring about our downfall?'

Then Nisreen's words would storm back in and smother Taymoor's arguments. He knew she wasn't prone to hyperbole or to being swept up in nonsensical theories. Which was why her words were so hard to ignore, despite Taymoor's rant.

What is this mysterious White Rose that everyone is part of all of a sudden? What do you really know about it?

What did he really know about it, beyond what little the Z Directorate had shared?

You need to wake up, Kamal.

Seeing her again had hit him hard. Twice, in the same day, after the painful self-imposed exile that had lasted forever.

It was brutal. Everything he missed, the memories of being with her, Ramazan and the kids, all those magical moments he yearned for, came hurtling back into view, only to be snatched away again.

God, how he missed them. All of them.

He needed to get them back into his life.

Across the river, on the small island of Île de la Cité, the halls of the intensive care unit at the Hurrem Sultan Külliye were quiet that night.

Nowhere was quieter than room 7, where, aside from occasional gentle beeps from a monitor, nothing stirred.

Ayman Rasheed was heavily sedated and sleeping soundly.

His mind, however, wasn't at rest. Questions and more questions had stoked it into exploring moments he hadn't thought about in years. They were making him relive all kinds of long-lost experiences, from the most visceral to the most contemplative, which is what was currently going through his mind: the months in Istanbul, at the library, immersed in books, and the long walks along the Bosphorus, at dawn or late at night, pondering, strategizing.

Imagining how he'd make the impossible possible.

Rasheed's third area of study was even more of a challenge: identifying and finding ways to neutralize any eventual threats to the empire.

This wasn't about orchestrating the fall and subjugation of Christian Europe. It probably wouldn't even affect events during his lifetime. But he felt a duty to do everything he could to ensure the empire's survival well into the future—a future he would be able to visit at will to enjoy the fruits of his efforts, if he succeeded.

He began by trying to understand what had led to the collapse of the Ottoman Empire. After the failure to take Vienna, the Ottomans were pushed back by the Habsburgs, whose counter-attacks allowed them to retake lands that had been lost for centuries. This dramatically shrank the empire's territory, but that was only the beginning of the bigger problems facing the Ottomans because it was happening at the same time that Europe—Christian Europe—was evolving and innovating in many key ways. Industrialization, progress in education, advances in military weaponry and tactics—these were areas where the Ottomans had fallen behind, clinging stubbornly to their past and held back by religious and intellectual conservatism that resisted novelty, despised original thought and mistrusted science.

An early example of this was the printing press. Denounced as 'the devil's invention' by the Islamic clergy, it arrived in Istanbul more than fifty years after it had been invented by Gutenberg in 1440, and only because the Jews brought it with them after being kicked out of Spain in 1492. The sultan, Bayezid II, sent his navy to evacuate them and invited them to resettle across his empire. Even then, because of the clergy's resistance, Muslims were not allowed to make use of the printing press until the eighteenth century. Such reactionary, regressive attitudes to progress, more than anything, led to the empire's demise. It struggled to keep up and then fell apart as it half-heartedly tried to figure out how to adapt to this rapidly evolving world.

This was something Rasheed would need to fix. In his world, the Ottoman Empire wouldn't be struggling to follow Europe's lead. It would be the leader.

The deeper he dug, the more Rasheed came to realize that, at the core of it all, the single biggest threat to the empire would be the human mind. At the time of his intervention, European thought would be in a crucial state of flux, evolving from a subjugated acceptance of autocratic rule to a yearning for freedom. In that context, he began to focus on the Enlightenment, and—in many ways an extension of it—the revolutions in France and America and, with those uprisings, the spread of liberalist and republican thinking.

The philosophical seeds of the Enlightenment would have already been sown by the time of the siege of Vienna, but the Enlightenment's main thrust would not yet have occurred. He would need to tackle that head-on, since many of the movement's ideals, like individual liberty, constitutional government and the separation of state and church, were at odds with the basis of a caliphate. Bacon, Descartes, Locke, Spinoza, Leibniz—their work would need to be suppressed, and the ones who were still alive by the time he arrived would need to be killed. Other central figures of the Enlightenment would either be infants or would not have been born yet at the time he would arrive. He would need to wipe them out before their dangerous ideas could sprout, even though he realized they might turn out to be harmless, given the entirely different reality *in which they would grow up. Regardless, names like Montesquieu, Voltaire, Rousseau, Beccaria, Hume, Kant and Smith were firmly in his crosshairs. He would have assassins kill them in infancy. He would see to it that books like the* Two Treatises of Government *and the* Encyclopédie, *the most influential publications of the Enlightenment, would never come into being.*

Of course, he knew other thinkers might rise up in their place. The key was to identify them as early as possible and eliminate them, and to create an environment that wasn't conducive to such thoughts in the first place.

By smothering the ideas of the Enlightenment, he would defuse a potential ticking bomb for the empire. Even if the fix wasn't permanent, it would at least buy time for the Ottoman Empire to grow, prosper and settle into its new expanse. Without the spreading of revolutionary ideas, it would be easier to rule a conquered Europe. There would be no French Revolution, no guillotine for the monarch, no questioning of imperial rule and divine right. The ripples of his disruption of history would be felt far beyond the caliphate's shores, precisely because it would happen at the time when ideals of freedom and human rights were just starting to take hold.

Would England's Glorious Revolution of 1688 still take place, or would the Ottoman invasion divert the attention of William of Orange to defending his Dutch territories? With the main thinkers of the Enlightenment snuffed out before they could even pen their revolutionary ideals, would the American Revolution still happen? And if it did happen, would the British be so preoccupied by what the Ottomans were doing in Europe that they would let their colonies go without a fight, or would the revolution make them want to hang on to the colonies even more?

The very notion that his act would be so hugely disruptive and far-reaching supercharged Rasheed's excitement, particularly when it came to America. He obviously couldn't foretell the effects of his intervention on these great historical cataclysms, and he was very conscious of the fact that, at some point in the future, the human instinct for freedom would still inevitably threaten his caliphate. To head it off, he'd need to figure out how to strike a balance between modernity and Islamic rule—which, by definition, couldn't allow the separation of mosque and state—that would ensure the empire's longevity. For that, he delved into the works of groundbreaking Islamic modernists such as Rifaa al-Tahtawi and Al-Afghani and tried to imagine an empire that espoused multi-ethnicity, culture and modernity but, unlike the Baathist movement in the Iraq he grew up in, didn't belittle the importance of religion.

It wasn't an impossible task. Although no one in the twentieth century had managed it, it had happened under several sultans and, long before that, in the days of the Convivencia in Islamic Spain.

Although this part of his work dealt with the empire's distant future, he still needed to research it fully before embarking on his journey. Once he did, he would never be able to come back and do further reading. By then, these sources of knowledge would be gone, since everything would—he hoped—be different.

Weeks stretched into months as he read, mulled, scribbled and plotted, his thoughts filling several notebooks.

There were so many names and dates for him to remember, so many ideas and strategies, so many technical specifications. He would soon be ready, but he'd need to remember all this information, which was possibly the most daunting task of all, given that he couldn't take anything physical back with him: no books, no notes, not even a single sheet of paper.

He would have to rely on his memory—or so he thought, until one night, while sitting at a café near Taksim Square, he noticed a beefed-up man in tight jeans and a crew cut who was chatting a bit too amiably with two similarly well-built men.

It wasn't the fact that he was—in Rasheed's eyes—undoubtedly gay that caught his attention.

It was his arms.

They were strong. Sculpted.

And they had paragraphs of words and all kinds of imagery tattooed across their taut, hairless skin.

The final piece of the puzzle had fallen into place.

It wouldn't be long now. He would soon be ready to go.

He already had that part of his plan mapped out.

Once he was ready, he'd visit the Topkapi Palace, posing as a tourist. He'd find a hiding spot and stay behind after its gates were closed to the public. Then, at the right hour, in the middle of the night, he'd make his way to the imperial bedchamber, where it would all begin.

The sultan, and history, were waiting.

23

It ended up being a sleepless night for Nisreen and Ramazan.

How could it not? There was so much to discuss, to explore, to bat around.

At first, Nisreen couldn't accept it as fact. Her reaction went from anger, to incredulity, to thinking Ramazan was sprouting some wild tale to hide something bad that he was involved in, then back to disbelief, although with a growing undercurrent of fear.

They mulled and debated and pulled it apart for hours. By the end of their discussion, after they had moved into the bedroom, Nisreen with her back against the headboard, Ramazan reclining in an armchair that faced the bed across from her, they were both utterly drained in body and mind.

After a long silence, Ramazan said, 'So where do we go from here?'

'It's like you said. If he's faking it . . . why?'

'I don't know.'

Nisreen steepled her fingers in front of her mouth and shut her eyes, thinking. 'But if it's true . . . if he's not a pathological liar . . .' She reset her fierce gaze on her husband. 'He didn't say how he does it? How he travels through time?'

'I was going to ask him tonight, but Fonseca interrupted me and I couldn't.'

She nodded thoughtfully. 'Can you imagine?'

'What?'

'If it's true . . . can you imagine what one could do with that kind of knowledge? With that power?'

Ramazan gave her a rueful shake of the head. 'It's limitless.' The enormity of what he'd got himself into seemed to suddenly sink in. 'What have I done? If anyone finds out . . .'

'No one needs to find out. And besides, we don't know if he's telling the truth. But if he is . . . it's got to be something he can pass on. To us. Something you and I could try.'

Ramazan snapped forward in surprise. 'You'd want to try it out?'

'Wouldn't you? I mean, if it's safe—who wouldn't? Besides, how else can we be sure he's not faking it?'

Ramazan shook his head. 'This is insane.'

'He says he came from another world, right? Another version of history. Another 1438.'*

'Yes.'

'Well, what was his 1438 like? Don't you want to know? What was the world he left behind like?'

'He didn't say much about it beyond the war he was in.'

'A big war in the east, right?'

'He called them Iraq and Syria, which I think mean Al Jazira and Al Sham.'

'A war that was started by the Americans,' she said, her tone questioning. 'But then he did say one crucial thing. That the empire—our empire—didn't exist any more.'

'Yes,' Ramazan confirmed. 'He said it got weaker after they failed at Vienna; then it broke up, and other powers took its place.'

'Which means that world, his world, had three hundred years of a very different history.' She paused. 'If that's true . . . I want to know what that world was like.'

'Does it matter?'

'Of course,' Nisreen insisted. 'I want to know how it was

* AD 2017.

different. And why he wanted to change it. Don't you see? That's how the world was supposed to be.'

'Assuming no one else had gone back and changed things before he did.'

She thought about it. 'Maybe. But I still want to know if his world was better or worse than ours.'

'He was caught up in a big war.'

'We've had wars. And in case you haven't noticed, we're in the thick of one right now. A worse kind of war. A silent one. A war where anything we say can get us killed by our own people. Don't you want to know if there was a better world out there?'

'Maybe we should leave it alone. This talk of another world is crazy.'

Nisreen studied him. 'Are you happy with the way things are?'

'What do you mean?'

'Are you happy with how our lives have changed these last few years?'

Ramazan shrugged. 'Well, if you're talking about you and me and the kids, and—'

'I'm talking about the world Tarek and Noor are growing up in. A world that corrupts everyone, that turns one brother against another, against family—a world that sucks the sense and decency out of people. If there was a better version of the world out there, wouldn't you want to know about it?'

Ramazan knew full well whom she was referring to, and he felt a tinge of jealousy. As much as he loved his brother, he was always aware of how Nisreen and others like her were drawn to him. Before, of course. Before the world had shifted unexpectedly under them. Before his brother had fallen from grace.

'What difference does it make?' he fired back. 'We live in our world. Nothing's going to change that. And people are what they are. No one's forcing anyone to be anything different from what they want to be.' He shook his head, angry at himself for saying that about Kamal, and forcing himself to resist Nisreen's drive. 'No. It's too dangerous. We should leave it alone.'

'I guess I shouldn't be surprised,' Nisreen said, visibly dejected. 'You've always been more comfortable taking the safe road.'

'Hey, you were the one who gave me a verbal flogging for looking into it in the first place,' he hissed, mindful of waking up the children. 'Remember?'

Nisreen shrank back under the admonition. 'Fine, but now that you've let the *djinn* out of the bottle, it's too late to put it back.'

Ramazan saw the remorse on her face, but he also saw something else. That familiar disappointment—in him. He couldn't stand it. Even when she was dressing him down for his Internet search, he'd enjoyed the feeling of knowing he'd shown her a different side of him. A daring, reckless side.

He wanted that feeling back.

'So what are you saying?' he asked her. 'What do you want us to do?'

'I want to know what it was like. And I want to know how he does it.'

'If it's real.'

'If it's real.'

Ramazan nodded, deep in thought. 'All right,' he finally relented. 'I can ask him.'

Nisreen sat up. 'Not you. Us. We can ask him.'

Ramazan felt a surge of alarm, not liking where this was going. 'Us?'

'Yes. You and me. Together. I want to be there when you talk to him again.'

'No. No way.'

'Why?'

He grasped for any answer. 'He's in intensive care. I can't have you in there for any reason.'

'He's your patient,' she insisted. 'I'm your wife. You'll figure something out. No one's going to question it too much. He's nobody.'

Ramazan scowled. 'What I'm doing is already tricky enough. Your being there might attract more attention.'

'You said yourself you need to bring him out of his sleep this morning. You probably only have one last session with him. You go in first, make sure it's clear, and then I'll join you. We can always say there's an important family situation I needed to see you about. Something urgent. No one's going to care.'

'What about the kids?'

'I'll call Sumayya.' Sumayya was in her late teens and lived across the street from them. She was their children's preferred babysitter.

'This early?'

'She'll be happy to. She could use the money.'

Ramazan closed his eyes and tilted his head back and said nothing. Then he faced Nisreen again. He knew this was a bad idea. But seeing her fired up like this, imagining himself doing something wild and audacious with her, was hard to resist.

Outside the bedroom windows, the first scouts of dawn were repelling the blackness of night. Soon, the calls to prayer would sound out from the city's minarets.

He looked at her wryly, relishing what he was about to say, pushing away the fear to make way for the words that cut through his better judgement. 'Let's get ready then,' he told her. 'It'll be morning soon. And the earlier we get there, the better.'

24

With Nisreen waiting for him in the female visitors' area of the hospital, Ramazan went in first, reprising his earlier-than-usual appearance of the day before. He had two procedures scheduled that morning, so he would need to be quick. He also knew that he'd need to be careful around the more senior staff, especially Fonseca. He'd already spent way more time than normal with his patient. And he'd need to keep his wits about him, despite having just endured a sleepless and mentally exhausting night.

The male ward was relatively quiet and thinly staffed. He went about his business casually, checking on a few patients and sharing a passing comment with a couple of the attendant nurses—then he saw Anbara heading towards him. Given the time, she had to be coming up to the end of her night shift. He bristled at the sight. He liked her, of course, but he didn't want her there, now, a potential spoiler given her familiarity with his unusual patient.

'*Sabahel nour,*' he told her, smiling amiably as she drew near. 'Quiet night for you, I hope?'

'Yes,' she replied. 'For a change.'

'Good. How's our'—he leaned in and lowered his voice with a wink—'special case?'

Anbara showed slight confusion before realizing what he meant. 'Oh, our illustrious guest?' She blew out a small chuckle. 'His excellency is sound asleep.' Her expression turned more serious. 'I thought you might have concerns about him.'

'Why do you say that?'

'I hear you checked in on him several times yesterday.'

Ramazan tensed up but masked his nervousness. 'No, it's . . . I wanted to keep an eye on his drains, but everything looks fine. And, you know,' he added with a knowing, sarcastic look, 'he is a bit special.'

Anbara nodded conspiringly. 'That he is,' she said.

'I'll bring him out and get him out of your way later, once I'm out of theatre. I know you need the beds.' Changing the subject, he asked, 'Are you done with your shift?'

'Yes,' she said. 'I'm looking forward to my bed.'

'You've earned it.'

He watched her walk off and checked his watch. The timing would be tight. He preferred to know Anbara was gone before he sneaked Nisreen in.

He loitered around, trying to remain inconspicuous, until he saw her leave. A few minutes later, with the ward on a quiet pause, he slipped out to find Nisreen and quickly ushered her in. He had already procured her a doctor's white gown and headdress, which would make her look less conspicuous inside the ICU. She slipped it on quickly in the ladies' room before following him into the unit.

They made their way casually to room 7, passing unnoticed. Once inside, Ramazan shut the door behind them quietly.

'We won't have a lot of time,' Ramazan told his wife.

'How long do you think?'

'I've been able to keep him in that half-conscious state for around fifteen minutes at a time, maybe a bit longer. Then I have to put him back to sleep before he becomes too alert. It's a balancing act.'

Nisreen studied the sleeping patient, then looked at her husband intently.

An electric feeling was coursing through them. They'd never done anything like this before, never conspired together to try something that had an element of danger to it—although this wasn't so much dangerous as it was liable to cause an awkward moment, one that Ramazan could surely talk himself out of if they were discovered. It was mainly the potential outcome that had them all abuzz, the possible revelations that the man might unwittingly share with them if he was telling the truth.

'Ready?' Ramazan asked.

She sucked in a deep breath. 'Definitely.' Then her face lit up with an idea. 'Wait,' she hissed, reaching out to stop him.

She reached under her robe and brought out her handbag, a slim black leather tote with a shoulder strap. She dug inside it and pulled out her mobile phone, keyed in her passcode, then accessed its camera and set it to video mode.

'What are you doing?'

'I want to record this,' she replied. 'If he's telling the truth, it would be crazy to let it happen without a record of it. We need proof.'

'Proof? You want proof of what we're doing?'

'Of course. We have to.'

'No,' he insisted. 'Put it away. It's too risky.'

'I know it is, but this isn't just about you and me. It's much bigger than that.'

Ramazan just stood there, frozen for a moment, looking tortured by indecision. 'If it turns out to be true and your recording were ever discovered . . .'

'I realize that,' she interjected. 'But we need to document it. Every word. We can't risk losing any of it either.'

He stared at her, frozen and wide-eyed—then he relented.

'Fine.' He shrugged. 'We might get our necks chopped because of it, but . . . as you wish.'

She nodded the grisly image away, visibly nervous. 'We're wasting time. Come on.'

He turned and got to work. He tweaked the IV lines and

amended the dosages of the anaesthetic and sedatives that were snaking through the man's veins, all while keeping a careful eye on the read-outs of the instruments monitoring his heartbeat and his breathing.

The effect was faster than it had been the day before, as the tattooed man's body was gradually progressing on its journey to recovery. The first sign was a flicker of movement behind his eyelids, then a twitch of his fingers. Then his eyes fluttered open, slowly, a small war clearly being waged to keep them from closing.

'Good to have you back, Your Excellency,' Ramazan said, glancing at Nisreen, who was holding her phone to face the patient and recording. Ramazan leaned in so that his face was hovering over the man and forced a soothing smile. 'How are you feeling?'

There was a lag as the man, perfectly immobile and still with half-dead eyes, seemed to process the question. 'Good,' he mumbled. 'My mouth. It's very dry.'

'Here,' Ramazan said as he picked up a cup of water from the side table and brought its straw to the man's lips. 'Small sips, slowly.'

As the tattooed man drank, Ramazan glanced nervously at Nisreen. She leaned in with her phone to get a closer look at him. His eyes were still drowsy and didn't pan over to take her in.

Ramazan put aside the cup. 'You were just telling me about your world,' he said in a calm, comforting tone. 'About how it was before you changed it. So fascinating.'

The man closed his eyes and breathed out heavily as he responded with a few slow nods. 'Yes, my world,' he mumbled. 'A very different world.'

'And so France in that other world . . . it wasn't Ottoman?'

The question seemed to confuse the man. 'No . . . it was French.'

'And the rest of Europe?'

A partial clarity was slowly bringing light to his eyes. 'Italy, Germany, Greece—they were all independent countries.'

'*Christian* countries?'

'Of course.' His eyes swung left and right, roaming the ceiling, as if his mind were looking for an anchor. 'The Ottoman Empire was gone. What was left of it . . . a small part . . . was called Turkey.'

'I see,' Ramazan said, visibly keeping any amazement and nervousness stifled, acting as if this were the most trivial and casual conversation he'd ever had. 'And what was it like here, in your world? Did you know Paris?'

'No.'

'I wonder if it was as beautiful as it is today,' Ramazan offered.

The man nodded meekly. 'Oh, yes. Paris was famous for its beauty. But it was falling apart. The West . . . it was all falling apart. And it was all their doing.'

'Whose doing?'

The man's expression soured. 'Them. The West.'

Ramazan wasn't sure what he meant. 'How? What happened?'

The man frowned as he took a brief moment to formulate his reply. 'They were obsessed with the wrong enemies— immigrants, Islam, Russia. They couldn't see their real enemy.'

'Which was . . . ?'

'Their arrogance . . . and their greed.' The man's eyes took on a heightened clarity as the screen of his monitors indicated a rise in his pulse. 'The Americans . . . they were the worst of them all.' His words were coming easier now, less slurred. 'If I miss one thing from that world, it was watching them crumble, victims of their own stupidity.'

Which came as a surprise to Nisreen and Ramazan.

'Why were the Americans so bad?' he asked.

The readings on the monitors rose further as the tattooed man's voice took on a clearer, sharper edge. 'They thought they were special. And in many ways, they were. They put a man on the moon, they made phenomenal medical advances, they outlasted communism. They had all the wealth and technology, the most advanced weapons—but then they started believing that everyone should live the way they did. And they couldn't see how wrong their world was, how decadent they'd become, or how sick their society was.'

He licked his lips to moisten them, and Ramazan helped him sip some more water. After he was done, Ramazan asked, 'Sick? In what way?'

'They had this obsession with freedom. All men are created equal, they liked to say—even though the ones who first proclaimed it were proud slave owners, and this deluded, misguided vision kept growing. But this freedom, this untamed democracy—it was a poisoned chalice. It led to a society where almost anything was allowed. Say anything; do anything. There was no shame in anything. Couples lived together without getting married, without asking for their parents' consent. Girls had abortions like they had manicures; they had babies out of wedlock. Women paraded around half-naked. Men married men. They lost all sense of right and wrong.'

He asked for more water. Ramazan helped him with the cup, then checked the IV drips. This time, the man didn't need prodding.

'The only thing that mattered was to make money,' he continued, fuelled by an inner anger that was now pouring out. 'It didn't matter how you made it as long as you got away with it. The more outrageous and corrupt you were, the more they admired you. Everyone in power was a liar or a cheat or bought by big business. Politicians were in it to feed their wallets and their egos. Bankers and industrialists funded them to get even richer while the poor got poorer. They boasted about being the champions of human rights while backing vicious dictators and destroying countries for profit. They bragged about democracy and demonized countries that didn't have it, but they didn't really believe in democracy. They believed in hypocrisy. Their moral compass had spun out of control, from the very top down. One of their presidents sent them into a long, disastrous war that they knew was based on lies, and he was still re-elected. Another president, a married man, was caught getting a blowjob from some girl in his own office, and they still worshipped him. Then his wife tried to become president after him'—he added, his words dripping with mockery—'a woman, to run the most powerful country on the planet. Imagine the cheek of it, after such a scandal.'

Nisreen couldn't help but interject. 'You said tried,' she asked. 'You mean it was actually possible?'

Rasheed turned his head slightly sideways, momentarily confused by the new voice. Nisreen quickly lowered her phone and leaned back, but she couldn't avoid his seeing her.

'You . . . ? Who are you . . . ?'

Ramazan stepped in quickly to divert his attention and keep him on track. 'Your Excellency, please.'

Rasheed turned to him, visibly confused.

'The woman, who wanted to become president. You were saying she tried.'

Rasheed turned his eyes to Nisreen, then back to Ramazan, and for a moment it looked like he was too dazed to reply.

'She didn't succeed?' Ramazan prodded in a soft tone.

Rasheed turned his head slowly so he was looking at the ceiling again, then he scoffed. 'She lost, of course. Even without the scandal, it was too much—a woman, after a black man. That drove them crazy. Deep down, they're racists, you see. They all are.'

Ramazan looked at Nisreen, both equally bewildered by what they were hearing.

'A *black* man was president of America?' Ramazan asked, trying to dampen the incredulity in his tone. 'There are blacks in America? *Free* blacks?'

His mind flashed back to what he knew of the Christian Republic's history. Slavery of black Africans had begun in America long before the Ottomans had taken Vienna. But after the sultan's forces had swept across Europe, a tidal wave of European refugees fleeing the Muslim invasion had landed on America's shores. White indentured servants and workers were plentiful, and the importation of Africans petered out. Religious fervour grew as a reaction to the Islamic conquest of Europe, leading to the branding of anyone who wasn't Christian and white as a threat. A violent rebellion of black slaves in Virginia was put down, after which all blacks were expelled and sent to Africa, even those who were born in America. The Christian Republic, as Ramazan and Nisreen knew it, was exclusively Christian and white.

Ramazan's question visibly confused Rasheed. 'Free blacks?' He seemed to stumble on it for a moment.

'You said they had a black president, then a woman tried to be president, too.' Ramazan reeled him back. 'But she failed?'

Rasheed's brow furrowed as he struggled to formulate his thoughts. 'Yes, that's right . . . But they got even worse. They elected a con man instead, an ignorant crook who craved adoration and did and said whatever it took to win. That tore them apart even more. I would have loved to see how badly that turned out, but I left shortly after it happened. It didn't matter. Their world was crumbling.' His look took on a glaze of deep animosity. 'They called themselves Christians, but there was nothing Christian about them. They just worshipped money, sex and brainless entertainment. A flashier car, bigger breasts and more likes on their Facebook posts: that's what they lived for, and yet they dared look down on us and criticize the way we lived. These fat, lazy, stupid bastards were happily filling their bodies and minds with junk to the point that they became proud and defensive about their ignorance. And that was the ultimate sting of democracy, you see: the insane idea that one man's ignorance was just as worthy as another man's knowledge. The ludicrous idea that the vote of the uninformed is just as valid as that of the educated.'

A pregnant silence smothered the room. It was a lot to digest.

'But what about the rest of the world?' Ramazan finally asked. 'What about France and the rest of Europe? What were they like?'

'Oh, it wasn't just America. The rot had spread across Europe, too. The same decadence was everywhere. The same foolish, stubborn belief in the collective wisdom of individual ignorance that callous, corrupt rabble-rousers were using to grab power. By spreading all kinds of lies and making the mobs believe that their great heritage, their jobs and their future were being stolen from them, the corrupt manipulated the mobs into voting them into power. It was all going to end badly, not just for them but for us, too. Their collapse was going to bring pain and misery to our lands. It always did. We were never more than pawns in their ego games. It had been that way for centuries. Which is why I believe God sent me this gift. Not just for the glory of our people, but for them, too. Much as it was far from my intention, perhaps I saved them from themselves. Europe has been united for centuries, and the Americans—look at them now. Their president serves for life and the destructive squabbles of frequent elections are avoided. They've still got their values, their traditions. They're even challenging our empire,' Rasheed said as his face took on a confused tinge and he lapsed into a distracted silence. 'Which I must do something about,' he then muttered, almost to himself. 'I really should . . .' His eyes took on a faraway stare as his words petered out.

Ramazan turned to his wife, not knowing what to say.

Nisreen looked stupefied, her brain visibly struggling to process every word, every nuance of what she'd just heard. Ramazan had never seen her so profoundly unsettled. He felt the same.

He glanced at his watch and then looked at her. She understood.

He knew what she was thinking. He could have sat there for hours, too, listening to the mystery man, asking him questions about this strange alternative world he claimed to have lived in, but he knew they didn't have that luxury. They were running down the clock on the man's state of consciousness, and, besides, there was the hospital staff and a potential interruption to consider.

It was the moment of truth. It was time to ask the key question.

He checked the IV drips, tweaked them gently, and then turned to the tattooed man.

'Your Excellency,' he asked, 'what you say is fascinating beyond compare. But tell me, how is it that you are able to do these things?' He sucked in a deep breath, then added, 'How are you able to travel across time?'

25

Kamal had been irritable even before setting foot inside the Hafiye compound that morning.

He didn't head up to his desk. Instead, he cut through the atrium and across to the Z Directorate to find the two agents he still hadn't heard back from.

Banna and Goskun weren't at their desks, which only fuelled his irritation.

He left them another message and stormed off, his veins flowing with fire. Today would not be a good day for any of the persons of interest who were on his and Taymoor's radar.

He didn't make it to his desk. The desk sergeant informed him of something more urgent that required his presence.

The *bashafiye* wanted to see him.

Kamal had never had a one-on-one meeting with the commander before. He'd never been to his office. He hadn't even been on that floor of the building. To his knowledge, very few agents had. The *bashafiye* never summoned mere agents to his inner sanctum. This had to be very, very serious.

Kamal could think of two reasons for his being called there: one good, the other not. He hoped it wasn't the latter.

After being ushered through by the commander's private secretary, Kamal poked his head through the tall carved door. 'You asked for me, Huseyin Pasha?'

Huseyin Celaleddin Pasha, the *bashafiye*—the head of the Paris division of the secret police—was studying some paperwork at his desk. He looked up and waved Kamal in.

'Yes, yes, come in. Have a seat.' He gestured vaguely at the armchairs facing him.

The office, as befitting the city's most powerful law enforcement officer, was on the top floor of one of the modern additions to the old fortress. It was large enough to house a plush divan area that could comfortably seat a dozen men and had a commanding view of the ancient turrets and, beyond, the grand domes and minarets of the city's main mosques, visible even through the partially angled blinds that blunted the intrusive morning sun. Celaleddin was tall and lean, which was unusual for a member of the *askeri*. The elite ruling class of clergy, military and state officials was for the most part still dismissive of the staggering body of scientific evidence concerning the health risks of obesity. They still considered bulging bellies and plump limbs to be proud signs of prosperity.

The expansive carved mahogany surface of his desk was as ruthlessly lean and precise as he was, cluttered by nothing more than a computer screen and keyboard, a mobile phone, a pen and the printouts he had been perusing, which he now neatly arranged into a tidy pile and set down before him.

The commander tilted his head upwards, adopting his customary, probing pose and accentuating the unsettling effect of his deep-set, cavernous eyes. 'Busy?' he asked. 'I imagine you're more fired up than ever after Friday's ceremony.'

'No rest for the vigilant, sir,' Kamal replied, channelling Taymoor's expression.

'Good.' The man studied him for a second. 'I looked for you after it concluded, you know. They said you'd been called away.'

'My profuse apologies, pasha. I didn't know.'

'The bey wanted to meet you.'

'The bey?'

'Oh, yes. He's very grateful, as you can imagine. What you did, you and Taymoor. His daughter's wedding . . . you saved us from a major, major disaster.'

'I'm just glad we were able to stop them.'

'There's talk of you two getting the *Nişan-i İftihar*,' he said, referring to the Order of Glory, one of the highest awards an Ottoman officer could get.

Kamal tilted his head in a small bow. 'It would be a huge honour.'

'And fully deserved. As would be your promotion to *mulasim komiser*. You'd be our youngest ever. How does that sound?'

So the rumours were true. Lieutenant inspector. He bowed again. 'I am most humbled, my pasha.'

The tall man paused for a moment, then leaned in. 'Tell me, Kamal. How are things with your family?'

There it was. The question still caught Kamal off guard, but he managed to brush it off. 'Fine. It's very kind of you to ask.' He hesitated, then decided to say it anyway. 'Why do you ask?'

'You've been making inquiries about someone we arrested recently,' the *bashafiye* replied. 'Someone I believe your sister-in-law has taken an interest in?'

So that's what this was really about.

Kamal felt a ripple of concern. 'His wife asked for her help in finding out what happened to him.'

'Indeed. And your sister-in-law—she's quite a strong-willed woman, isn't she? Tenacious, shall we say?'

'That she is.'

The commander steepled his hands and drummed his index fingers against each other as he mulled over his next words. 'Look, I know how it can be with family. What's happening out there, the things we have to do . . . it's not easy.

And it's causing problems for many of us. What you're going through is by no means unique. But at some point, we all have to put our foot down and remind people, even those closest to us, that we're doing this for them. We're protecting their way of life, even if that means we sometimes have to do things we don't enjoy. Or do things that they may not agree with. They need to understand that we're the ones faced with making these tough decisions—not them. And they should be grateful for it.' He paused and watched Kamal, as if waiting to see if his message had got through.

Kamal just said, 'Yes, sir.'

'This one might be particularly difficult for you. Given her interest in him.'

'How so?'

'Sinasi passed away last night. In his jail cell.' The commander's tone was flat, unburdened by the slightest hint of emotion.

His words jolted Kamal. 'He's dead? How?'

'The coroner says it looks like a heart attack. Probably brought about by the stress of his guilt. It sounds like the man couldn't handle what he'd got himself into. He confessed to being part of the White Rose.'

A surge of emotion swept through Kamal. A heart attack while in custody? It wasn't the first time that had happened at the Citadel, although on the occasion he'd heard about it, it was in a case involving a hardened terrorist suspect and had happened after intense interrogation. But his focus shifted quickly back to Nisreen. Her asking about a White Rose conspirator wasn't good. A far deeper fear had him in its grip: could Nisreen herself have joined them?

As if reading into his silent angst, Celaleddin added, 'It's very tragic, of course. But given his guilt, the outcome would have ultimately been the same for him.' The commander waved his hand sideways, dismissively. 'In the long run, any agitation concerning this man's unfortunate death will settle down and pass; we know that. It always does. But over the next few days, once the news gets out, we're going to have to contain any'—he paused—'unpleasantness that might arise.' His cavernous eyes took on a subtle, heightened intensity. 'I trust your sister-in-law won't be a burden to us on this matter. It could be dangerous for her. Especially when her interest in him raises its own questions.'

His heart was now kicking furiously against his ribcage, as if it were trapped in a furnace. He shook his head. 'She won't, sir.'

'Good. Because there's only so much we can be expected to tolerate—and only so much leeway we can bestow, even on the sister-in-law of an illustrious hero. Do we understand each other?'

'Absolutely, sir.'

The tall man studied Kamal for a beat, then nodded. 'That'll be all.'

As he exited the commander's office and headed for the elevators, Kamal could feel his temples throbbing. It was worse than he'd feared. Nisreen was on their radar.

He needed to get to the bottom of it. Which was going to be much more difficult now that Sinasi was dead. Trouble was brewing; he could feel it. He had to do something.

He pulled out his phone; glanced around furtively, more as a reflex than out of any real sense of threat; and dialled his brother's phone. The call rang through until Ramazan's voicemail picked up.

'It's Kamal. We need to talk. Give me a call back, would you?' He hesitated, then added, 'I really do need to speak with you. Please call me.'

*

Two levels underground, not too far from where Kamal was standing, an analyst in the data analysis section of the Caves stared curiously at the report on his screen.

Like all the other reports he and several dozen of his colleagues spent their shifts analysing, it had originated at the Comprehensive Imperial Cybersecurity Initiative Data Centre, where servers conducted extensive data mining and applied advanced analytics to crunch the bulk data that was streaming in from all kinds of sources. Anything deemed suspect or threatening was forwarded on to the Cave for further—human—analysis.

The computers went far beyond keyword scans and pattern-link analysis of known subjects and scattered bits of information. Voice recognition had reached a level of sophistication whereby the centre's algorithms could now cross-check digital data with transcripts of phone calls and wiretaps to seek out suspicious behaviour and anticipate threatening intent. Over ten thousand target packages were forwarded to the analysis centre every month. Some of these resulted in leads to law enforcement authorities such as the Hafiye, while the rest—the majority—was just human metadata that sank into a state of perpetual analysis limbo.

In this case, the analyst was more intrigued than alarmed. The report in question, which had originated in a low-level surveillance order, was unusual. It was a link analysis between a batch of web searches and the transcript of a conversation that had taken place the night before at a residential address in Paris. Dynamite, detonators, Al Jazira and Al Sham, war, Americans, 'Worried about what you've got yourself into'—these words and others had been enough to flag the conversation. Once combined with the stress-analysis result of the voices engaged in the recorded conversation and the fact that one of the subjects was currently a person of interest, the data batch was elevated to an actionable level. Which was why it had landed in the analyst's in-box folder with an orange—medium-level—threat rating.

The analyst was used to dissecting transcripts and data dumps that appeared to be, and ended up being, nothing more than angry domestic rants or harmless nonsensical ramblings about sensitive subjects. On more than one occasion, conversations between people working in publishing or in film and television were red-flagged because of the fictional ideas they were exploring. People were feeling increasingly polarized about the unrest rippling across the empire and being more vocal when they assumed they weren't being monitored. This report, however, felt different. It was hard to dismiss it that easily.

Its overview had snared the analyst's attention enough for him to pull up the transcript of the conversation and read it in its entirety.

The transcript left him perplexed.

Rereading it didn't change that first impression. He decided to listen to the source material. He pulled up the audio file, put on his earphones and hit the play button, scribbling notes as he listened to the two subjects, a married couple.

Their voices didn't sound unbalanced. It didn't sound as if they were messing around and having a laugh or drunk or under the influence of some other banned substance. They sounded level-headed and rational, despite the elevated stress levels in their readings.

He thought about dismissing the report, but something about it just wouldn't let him do that. He'd listened to enough conversations and read enough transcripts to have honed a strong sense of the potential consequence, or lack of one, in the reports that came through his system. This one, he felt, merited further examination.

The anaesthetist and his wife clearly believed it. The

question was whether the source of the story was reliable. Was this tattooed man a creative raconteur who was just having fun and messing with his doctor's mind? Was this nothing more than a very artful deception?

He tapped his keyboard and checked the primary subject's file. He noted the hospital where the man worked. He then peeked into the hospital records and pulled up its operating-theatre scheduling records. Sure enough, the primary subject was a frequent collaborator of the surgeon he had mentioned in the recorded conversation, Fonseca. And one of the procedures they had carried out two days earlier was on a patient who was only listed as an 'unidentified male walk-in'. The man had heart surgery and was still at the hospital, in its intensive care unit. All of which matched what the man had discussed with his wife.

Weird.

He debated what to do about it. On the one hand, it sounded like an elaborate prank, a wild tale, a delusion. Some kind of game, perhaps, or a lie to cover some sordid misdeed— he'd heard some pretty unusual things said between people, even, or perhaps especially, between married couples. On the other hand, it had an ineffable and yet intense ring of candour about it. His gut was telling him that. It was also telling him something else: that sending it upstream would probably usher some hassle into his life.

Hassle or not, he didn't have much of a choice. He couldn't risk not reporting it. If it turned out to be something bad and if they discovered he'd missed it or chosen to disregard it, he'd have more than just hassle to contend with.

He picked up his phone and pressed his supervisor's number.

'My bey,' he told him, 'forgive the intrusion, but I've got something I feel you should look at.'

26

'It's an incantation,' the tattooed man said. 'A spell.'

Standing by the bed in the windowless room at the hospital, Ramazan glanced at his wife, his mouth agape. 'A spell?'

'My prisoner found it, in Palmyra.' He spoke in a slow tone, the semiconscious haze he was under making his words stumble out in a slight slur. 'In an old temple. Carved into the wall. I made him give it to me . . .' His face tightened under a disturbing frown. 'Then I killed him. To make sure. No one else knows.'

Feeling his pulse throbbing inside his ears, Ramazan asked, 'How does it work?'

'It's Palmyrene. Just . . . words.'

'So you just say these words and you . . . you travel across time?'

'There's only one rule. You can't travel to a time when you already exist. It won't work. And it's . . . it's . . .' The man went quiet as his face clouded with discomfort, and his eyes roamed the room in a wider arc than before.

Ramazan's pulse quickened as worry flushed through him. Was the man getting too conscious? Was he having reservations about the information he was divulging? Moving fast, Ramazan's hand reached across to the IV lines and slightly increased the flow of the drugs that were keeping his patient at the edge of full consciousness. He flicked a quick look at Nisreen, whose expression was also gripped with uncertainty and worry, then turned back to the man in the bed.

'Something this remarkable can't be simple, of course,' Ramazan cajoled him. 'And yet you mastered it.'

The man's eyes roamed the ceiling for a moment, then settled back on Ramazan. 'Yes,' he said, his voice lower than before.

'Please explain,' Ramazan prompted him.

'You say the words and put in the number of days—moons, yes, the number of moons—that you want to travel. In a specific place, in the incantation . . . and, *voilà*.' The frown turned into a slanted half-smile. 'Without clothes. Naked.'

Ramazan was struggling to stay focused. Too many questions were crowding his mind—then he noticed the man's eyes turn to him and stare, his brow furrowing with consternation.

'Who are you, again?' he mumbled.

He was gaining consciousness. His gaze sharpened, suffused with more clarity than before, his expression taking on a hint of the menace he had shown before the surgery. 'What day is this? Where am I?'

He turned his head slowly, as if drawn to something he remembered. To Nisreen.

She quickly lowered her phone again as their eyes met, a moment that triggered further confusion in the man's face.

Ramazan's breath caught. The man was crossing a critical threshold of consciousness. There was no time to waste. He had to try to keep him in that semi-alert state just a little bit longer to get that one last answer out of him—the most crucial one—even at the risk of the man waking up completely.

He increased the dosage again, slightly, knowing that it could very soon overwhelm his patient and send him back to sleep, all while trying to come up with a quick reply that wouldn't raise the man's suspicions. He studied the man's reaction, trying to gauge the drugs' effect. 'I'm your *hekimbaşı*, Excellency,' he told him, using the traditional word for chief physician. 'You've got a little fever—that's all. You were telling me all about this miraculous Palmyrene incantation you discovered. You remember it, don't you?'

The man seemed even more glassy-eyed and disorientated. After a few seconds, he muttered, 'The incantation . . . yes.'

Ramazan discreetly reached for a pen and for the patient's medical chart, flipping it to the back to reach a clean sheet of paper. 'So if you now wanted to go back to your time . . . what would you say? What is the incantation?'

And with Nisreen edging in to make sure her phone captured every sound and recorded his lips forming the mystical words, and Ramazan scribbling what he heard with rapt attention, the tattooed man closed his eyes in concentration and mouthed the incantation, slowly, hesitantly. He stopped to explain where the number of moons was to be inserted, clear-minded enough to avoid getting pulled back in time from his hospital bed inadvertently, before concluding with the rest of the spell.

The long sequence of words coming out of his mouth were strange and completely alien to them, a string of syllables in an unrecognizable, long-forgotten language, one that had fallen out of use for centuries. And yet they had a beauty to them, a lyricism, a cadence that seemed at one with their phenomenal power.

Ramazan felt an indescribable sense of awe. He turned to Nisreen, whose face was also beaming with astonishment. The small windowless room, the hospital, Paris itself—it all fell away, sights and sounds disappearing from around them as they stood there, spellbound, momentarily lost in their own flights of fancy, their minds somersaulting through the possibilities now within their grasp if this was indeed all true—a brief, magical moment of profound wonderment, but one that was also rooted in terror. It was short-lived as reality soon tore through their reverie, reminding them of where they were and of the precariousness of their situation.

Ramazan reached over and adjusted the IV feeds. 'Thank you, Your Excellency. Now you should get some rest.'

He watched as the tattooed man's eyelids slid down and the man's breathing settled into a calm repose.

'You need to leave,' Ramazan told his wife.

'We need to talk.'

'I know. I know. But not now. I've got surgeries. I need to get ready. And you need to get out of here.'

'When then? This can't wait until tonight. We need to talk about this. Lunchtime? Can you get out?'

'I don't know.'

'You can take a lunch break.' She pressed.

'All right. I'll call you as soon as I know when.' He then pointed at her phone. 'Did you get it? All of it?'

'Every word.'

He nodded. 'Let's go.'

They were about to step out; she reached for his arm and stopped him.

'Be careful,' she said. 'Make sure no one else finds out about this.'

Ramazan said nothing at first. Then he nodded. 'I know.'

They stood there, the ramifications percolating inside them—then Ramazan opened the door, looked around, and led Nisreen out.

They were approaching the wide door of the intensive care unit when it swung open and Fonseca walked in, one of the nurses alongside him.

Ramazan reacted quickly, moving in front of Nisreen and spreading his arms welcomingly as he exclaimed, 'Moshe, I was coming to find you.'

She understood just as fast. She tilted her head down and

adjusted her veil, veering away from them as Fonseca replied, 'We've got a busy morning, brother.'

Ramazan didn't dare look back to see where Nisreen was, but he sensed her moving off. 'Is there any other kind?' he asked the surgeon gleefully.

'Let's get started then.'

As they walked back into the ward, Fonseca asked, 'How's our illustrated patient doing?'

Ramazan tried his best to keep his tone even. 'I haven't brought him out yet.'

Which surprised the surgeon. 'Still not? Any complications I should know about?'

'No, not really. I just wanted to give his pain a chance to subside some more.'

'You can't keep him asleep for ever,' Fonseca said, slapping Ramazan on the back. 'Let's wake him up when we're done. I've got to admit, I'm curious about the man. All those strange markings . . . He could have an interesting story to tell.'

'Maybe,' Ramazan replied, feeling an uncomfortable twist in his gut.

27

Nisreen drifted away from the Hurrem Sultan complex and wandered aimlessly down the narrow streets of the Île de la Cité, her mind flooded by the torrent of revelations that had begun the night before.

She soon reached the edge of the island and kept going. She crossed the crowded, built-up bridge to the right bank of the Seine. There, she meandered around the avenue that ran alongside the river, oblivious to the city that was springing to life all around her; deaf to the cacophony of clanging trams, irate car horns and shrill bicycle bells; immune to the dogged male street vendors hawking their wares. She paused once or twice to rest and take in the views of the magnificent buildings that lined the riverbanks, a melting pot of neo-classical Greco-Roman architecture and Islamic minarets and domes—much like those in the empire's capital city of Istanbul with its Byzantine roots, which she'd only seen in pictures—but the city quickly receded from view, a bustling metropolis turned into a muted still life, her mind still snared by a kaleidoscope of possibilities.

She took the stairs down to the river's edge. Despite the crush of barges that were churning up the murky water and the chaotic, crowded quays lining its banks, she managed to find a quiet spot where she could listen to the recording she'd made of the tattooed man's tale. Holding the phone close to her ear, making sure no one was around to overhear the slightest word, she replayed it over and over, dissecting every sentence, every syllable.

Shortly before ten, and with the sun's potent blaze already making itself felt, reality charged back in with a phone call from her assistant, reminding her about a meeting at her office that morning. She dipped into a small café that had a family section at the back, downed a quick coffee and a spinach-filled pastry, and remembered to call Sumayya to make sure everything was fine. Sumayya assured Nisreen it had all gone smoothly and asked if she should meet Tarek and Noor after school. Nisreen thought about it quickly; told her that there was no need, thinking she would be able to do it; thanked her; and hung up. Then she hurried back into the street. She scoured the passing cars, looking for a female taxi, the black ones with darkly tinted windows and, crucially, a woman driver. She couldn't find one. Instead, she walked two blocks to a major cross-street and grabbed a tram, settling into its female compartment for the short ride.

Her law practice occupied half a floor of an old building in the Marais district, squatting in the shadows of the glamorous squares of *hôtels particuliers,* the large mansions that the French nobility had built in the seventeenth century before the invasion. They were now mostly occupied by senior members of the ruling *askeri* elite, some of whom were converts from Catholicism, members of the nobility who had long forgotten their French roots and fully embraced their new identity. The practice was almost entirely staffed by women, apart from one male lawyer, whose name was alongside Nisreen's on the placard, and two junior clerks who worked with him. Nisreen had met him through Halil Azmi, the law professor who had just been beheaded. They were both mourning his loss.

Nisreen felt comfortable enough among her staff to be more relaxed than was customary, and once inside she took off her veil, her headdress and her light coat, even though there were men present who were not her immediate relatives. She sat through her meeting without really engaging the others and wound it up as quickly as she could, then sequestered herself in her office, unable to focus on even the most mundane task.

For the rest of the morning, she avoided her colleagues and let incoming phone calls go to voicemail. Before long, she began to flag. The surge of adrenaline that had kept her on her feet after a sleepless night began to ebb, so she got two more cups of thick coffee and some honey-and-pistachio baklava to give herself a boost. She couldn't allow fatigue to take over. There was too much to consider, too much to discuss with Ramazan.

She found herself pulling up articles on Ottoman history from the Internet and reading about the empire's evolution since its glorious conquest of Vienna in 1094.* It had been a long time since she'd studied the subject, and there was a lot she wanted—more than wanted, needed—to read about. With the tattooed man's words still echoing in her mind, she moved on to refresh her memory of the histories of ancient Rome and Greece and their doomed politics, stopping to skim curiously through Plato's and Socrates' theories on democracy, which she had last encountered during her law studies. She then remembered another side of the story and flicked across to articles about Palmyra, perusing a brief overview of the city's history before staring at images of magnificent Greco-Roman ruins like the Temple of Bel and the Tetrapylon, all ever-popular tourist attractions, her mind drifting off to imagine what it must have been like for the man who discovered the mystical carvings in some long-lost corner of that ancient metropolis—a discovery that ended up costing him his life.

* AD 1683.

She then pulled up a detailed biography of Ayman Rasheed, her pulse racing as she stared at the image of his portrait and read about the philosopher-sage's key role in the battle of Vienna. Everything matched what the tattooed man had told Ramazan: that he was responsible for the tactics of that infamous day, the day that had changed history.

She managed to tear herself away from his biography and looked up the Palmyrene language. Palmyra was pagan for thousands of years before the Romans converted to Christianity and spread it among the locals; it survived until Islam emerged in the seventh century and swept up the entire region. Nisreen scoured random translations of texts, looking for words that sounded familiar from the tattooed man's incantation. She pulled out a notebook from her handbag and began to take notes, first jotting down the long incantation itself, then plugging in Palmyrene words that seemed to fit into it. She felt a buzz of excitement as more and more words started to fall into place, but an uncomfortable feeling arose deep inside her, something begging for her attention. Before she could put a finger on it, an incoming call roused her phone.

Caller ID told her it was the playwright's wife, and Nisreen felt instantly guilty about not being on the case. She took the call and informed the woman that there was no news. She told her she would keep pressing the authorities on it and did her best to calm her down and reassure her. Then, gently, she ended the call.

She mopped her face with her hands and ran her fingers through her hair. She needed to get a grip and calm down. For better or worse, the secret—if it was real, which she was now inclined to believe—was in her and Ramazan's hands. Nothing could change that. They now needed to figure out what to do with it—and make sure it didn't end up bringing devastation to their lives.

For the next couple of hours, her thoughts cartwheeled all over the place. The puzzle of translating the incantation was too compelling, and there was too much to read, too much to think about, which was proving to be a frustrating struggle since she was too tired to dig deep. It would have to wait. And by the time she found herself sitting at a quiet corner table deep inside the family section of a *kahvehane* by the Sultan Majid Imperial Library, which was roughly halfway between her office and the hospital, she was exhausted and weary.

By the looks of it, Ramazan wasn't in much better shape.

They quickly ordered some pomegranate juice along with fried lamb patties and a *halawa* dip and waited until the waiter was out of earshot before speaking.

'I can't stop thinking about this,' Nisreen told Ramazan.

'Me neither.'

'I mean, it's just . . . mind-boggling. You, me, the children . . . everything we know. We're all here because of him. Because of what he did.'

'If what he says is true.'

She sighed, more with mental exhaustion than from the physical tiredness she was also feeling. 'The big if.'

'If it is, the man's even more of a hero than we already give him credit for.'

'"More of a hero?"'

Ramazan looked confused. 'Of course. You heard what he said.'

'Of course, but—what do you mean?'

'That world he described—his world. The world he changed. It sounded like a complete disaster.'

'Is that what you thought?'

'What else could I think? You heard him. Greed. Decadence. Moral decay. Corruption. Leaders robbing their people and getting away with it. Wars based on lies. A world falling apart.'

'I heard all that. But I also heard something else.'

'What?'

'Freedom.'

'Freedom? More like chaos, anarchy.'

'No,' she insisted. 'Freedom. Didn't you hear what he said? A world where almost anything is allowed. Where people get to choose who rules over them, where they live the way they want with whoever they like, where they wear what they want. A world where a black man was president. Where a woman can become president. Where people can openly criticize their leaders without getting jailed. Think about it.'

Nisreen's husband frowned. 'We've had women running the empire.'

'They were the mothers of child sultans, Ramazan. Regents, not women who ruled in their own right. Not women who were chosen by their people. He spoke about a world where a woman can reach that level of achievement,' she said wistfully, 'which has to mean a world where anyone can do absolutely anything.'

'Exactly. They can do anything. Everyone can do anything. Which is what led to their collapse. They taught it to us at school, Nisreen. Surely you haven't forgotten? Democracy inevitably degenerates into anarchy.'

'It can't be that simple.'

'Wiser heads than ours say it is. Our empire has been around for seven centuries. Longer than any other in history. There's a reason for that.'

'And the reason might well be your patient and what he did.'

'In which case we should be grateful to him,' Ramazan replied forcefully. 'Our way of life works. It's like he said. People need a strong guiding hand.'

'A guiding hand, not an iron fist,' she shot back pointedly. 'Do you really think human nature is so vile and weak that we can't be trusted to make our own decisions?'

'It's what history has shown us.'

'Well, maybe history hasn't given us enough of a chance. Maybe it's a process that needs more time to mature. It's a journey of discovery, and maybe it's one that we all deserve a chance to make.'

Ramazan shrugged. 'We've seen what happens when people have too much freedom. Just like he said.'

Nisreen was about to reply but went silent as a waiter passed behind her. Once she was sure he was out of earshot, she said, 'Well, I for one would rather live in a world where we're free to live as we like without this constant fear about what we say or think.'

Ramazan looked exhausted and exasperated in equal parts. 'What difference does it make? We're here now. Whatever he's talking about, it's not relevant to our world.'

She shrank back, deflated.

'Besides, we shouldn't even be talking about this. If it's real, it's *haram*,' he said, using the word for what is forbidden by Islamic law. 'It's *suhr*—magic—'isn't it? Which makes him, what, some kind of *djinn*? God forbids it.'

'How can it be forbidden when it's because of this *suhr* that the whole of Europe is under our flag? I mean, we've always been told that our great empire is the embodiment of the will of God. But it's not, is it? It's what it is because of what your tattooed patient did. Why would God use something that's *haram* to achieve His will?'

'I don't know, Nisreen. It's all so crazy.' Ramazan heaved a ponderous sigh and looked away, shaking his head slowly. After a long pause, he said, 'So I guess we're saying we believe him now?'

'There's only one way to find out.'

Ramazan's eyes flared wide. 'No.'

She leaned in, her voice low but impassioned. 'We have to. We have to try it.'

'Nisreen, no. I forbid it.'

'We have to,' she insisted. 'I need to know if it's true or not. It's the only way.'

'No.'

'We'll be careful,' she insisted.

'How can we be careful about something we don't understand?' he blurted loudly before catching himself and visibly regretting his outburst. 'All we know is it doesn't work within our lifetime. But what does that mean exactly? And where would you want to go? To the past? Or to the future?'

And just then, a sudden realization jolted her, a horror that stung every pore of her body. She went ramrod-stiff.

'*Bok,*' she cursed.

'What?'

Nisreen was scouring her memory, trying to remember precisely what the tattooed man had said—and hadn't. She knew she was right, but she had to be sure. She reached into her handbag and pulled out her notebook, flipped to the pages of notes about the incantation, and scoured them intensely. Then, with jittery fingers, she grabbed her phone, turned the media volume right down to make sure no one would hear anything, and played the recording, forwarding to the part that was worrying her and holding the phone up close to her ear.

Ramazan was visibly alarmed, leaning in while darting glances around them to make sure no one was near. 'What are you doing?' he hissed.

'Hang on.'

She found the right spot and listened to it.

She was right.

'Damn it,' she hissed. 'How could we have missed that?'

'What?'

'We forgot to ask a key question.'

'Which is?'

'When he gave us the incantation, the example he used was of how he would travel back to his time, which was what you asked him. But he didn't tell us how to travel forwards.' Her words were tumbling out, having a hard time catching up with her mind, which was frantically looking for a solution. 'We wouldn't know how to get back here if we went back in time. You have to talk to him one last time. You have to get him to tell you how he came here.'

Nisreen's words were like a chainsaw to his already-frayed nerves. She was asking him to go back in and risk more time with Rasheed. 'I can't,' he hissed.

'You have to.'

'I can't. I've got two more surgeries this afternoon. Then Fonseca wants me to wake our guy up. He's insisting.'

'So do it then.'

Her fierce determination was so hard to resist. But he had to. 'He wants to be there. He's really curious about him.'

'Delay him. Do it alone.'

'No,' Ramazan replied. 'We've put ourselves at enough risk already.' He was about to add, 'We should just let it go,' when that familiar feeling swept over him: that Nisreen considered him weak and cowardly. 'Besides,' he said instead, 'Moshe . . . he's a stubborn bastard. And he'll be out of the operating theatre before me. He'll be waiting for me.'

'Find a way.' There was fire in her eyes. 'You have to, Ramazan. Delay him somehow.'

Ramazan's expression darkened further. Fear was assaulting him from all sides. 'This isn't good. Even if I manage it . . . if I bring him out fully just after that, he might remember. Which might trigger him and make him remember everything. Which is the last thing we need. I mean, who knows what he might do if he thinks we know something we shouldn't. And what if he asks me about it in front of Fonseca?'

'I don't know. Just . . . say he's delirious. Say he must have dreamed it. Say it's quite common. You're the expert, not him.'

She was so good at coming up with solutions. 'I don't like it, *hatun*.'

'The incantation is just a one-way ticket without it. It's useless.'

'We can't try this, Nisreen.'

'We can't without the rest of it.'

Ramazan checked his watch. 'I have to get back.'

She reached out and grabbed his arm. 'Find a way, Ramazan. Please. It would be an incredible waste if you didn't.'

He looked at her, searching for a trace of that newfound admiration he'd seen in her eyes the night before, at home, before they'd gone to the hospital. Relenting, he said, 'I'll try.'

As he said it, he thought he glimpsed a flicker of what he'd been hoping for.

She softened her grip, and took his hand instead. 'Whatever happens . . . we're in this together. All the way. And I have faith in you.'

His heart expanded, pushing away the shroud of gloom that was circling him, and he got up, kissed her on the cheek and walked away.

28

Huseyin Celaleddin Pasha stood by the window of his top-floor office with his hands clasped behind his back and stared out while he considered what he'd just heard.

He wasn't alone. Fehmi Kuzey, the man in charge of the Z Directorate, was seated across from his desk. Short and rotund in an almost risible contrast to his boss, Celaleddin's second in command was watching the commander in respectful silence while gently teasing his fluffy trapezoidal goatee.

The briefing had been unusually long. The commander's time was normally sparsely meted out. In this case, however, it had lasted over an hour, during which time they'd listened to the entire recording together.

The silence bore down on Kuzey, but he was used to it. The commander of the Hafiye was a thoughtful, calculating man. Which was only appropriate, given the gravity of the decisions he had to make on an almost daily basis.

'Most curious,' Celaleddin finally said.

'I thought so,' Kuzey agreed.

The tall man turned and edged back to his desk. 'Especially given its source. Kamal Agha's brother. An anaesthetist, of all things.'

'Yes.'

'It's a shame we don't have the whole conversation.'

'They changed rooms. We only had Level Three surveillance on them.'

The commander nodded, then reached out and picked up the file, flipping to the photos of the Insider Threat Program report's two subjects. His ostrich-like features crinkled with concentration as he stared at the face of Nisreen and flashed back to his earlier conversation with Kamal. 'The wife, we know about. She can be a handful. But this doctor? He hasn't popped up on our radar before.'

'No, sir. His file's clean.'

'They're both serious, precise individuals with, from what I can see, a stable marital situation. Not exactly the kind of people one would expect to be prone to delusion.'

'Agreed.'

'Or easily fooled.'

'That's the question.'

He stared at Ramazan's photo again. 'That's the question indeed: is he a gullible fool who's being taken for a ride by some tattooed prankster? Somehow, from what I've heard about her, I don't see Nisreen Hatun marrying someone that naive.'

'It is, however, the most rational explanation,' Kuzey offered. He hesitated, then added, 'But if it were actually true—'

Celaleddin cut him off. 'What is true is that, whether they're being pranked or not, they've chosen to run with it. With something that's *haram*. And that's something the empire can't tolerate.'

Kuzey straightened, evidently chastised. 'Which is why I felt I had to bring it to you, pasha.'

'You did well,' the commander said, extending some relief to his lieutenant. 'But this needs to be shut down quickly, and permanently. We can't allow this kind of thinking to prosper unpunished.'

'No, my bey.'

'The key is obviously the patient. He's the root of it all. It's clear he's having a grand old time pulling the anaesthetist's leg, even while knowing the consequences for himself and for them. He's still at the hospital?'

'Room seven at the ICU.'

'Send someone there. If he can be moved without too much damage to his health, bring him in.'

'And the anaesthetist?'

'Raise him to full eyes and ears. And put Nisreen Hatun on it, too. But no need to bring them in for now, especially her. We can do that once we understand what their mystery man is really up to.'

Kuzey stood up, bowed and left the room.

Celaleddin watched him leave, then stepped across to the window and stared out again.

Ludicrous, he thought. The whole thing was ludicrous. Fascinating, but ludicrous.

He hung on to that thought, even though he couldn't escape the disturbing fissure of doubt that had already begun to crack through his certainty.

Kamal glanced at his phone yet again, willing it to ring.

He and Taymoor, both in plain clothes, were sitting in an unmarked sedan, parked around the corner from the Luxembourg Palace and in sight of the offices of the Bereket Arabian Bank, where the banker who was suspected of funnelling money to an extremist preacher worked.

Electronic surveillance still hadn't yielded any results: the banker and his co-conspirators were clearly making sure they didn't leave a digital trail behind. Which meant old-fashioned legwork was necessary.

Taymoor seemed focused on something on his phone, but Kamal knew that his partner was clearly aware of his own restlessness. He had asked Kamal what the summons to see Celaleddin had been about. Kamal had replied that it was to inform him about the potential medal, which had made his partner question why he hadn't been invited up as well. Kamal hadn't been able to come up with a convincing reply quickly enough and had brushed it off, simply claiming he had no idea.

He checked the reception indicator, even though he already knew that the signal around him was strong. Sure enough, it displayed full bars. But still nothing from Ramazan.

He moved to get out of the car and call him again, then hesitated.

'You okay, brother?' Taymoor asked.

'Yes,' Kamal muttered, his brow knotted in a frown that hadn't left it since the morning.

Then Taymoor's phone rang, a relief from the question as well as a frustration that it wasn't his own phone ringing.

Taymoor knew what the call was about the instant he heard the man's voice.

'It's ramping up.' It was 'A'—Ali Huseyin, the Z agent who had called him about Kamal's brother being put under surveillance.

Taymoor turned slightly and kept a pretence of casual breeziness while he pressed the side button on his phone to lower the volume of the caller's voice. The noise coming off the street through the car's open windows would also help mask the content of what was coming through. 'Tell me more.'

'I'm not sure. It's been quarantined. All I know is some new information came in overnight and they're taking it seriously.'

'How so?'

'It's gone upstairs.'

Taymoor stiffened.

What had Kamal's brother got himself into, and did it have anything to do with Nisreen? It had to, surely. She had dragged her husband into some unsavoury business. And now Kamal was getting dragged into it, too. That had to be why he'd been called up to see Celaleddin earlier—which was what Taymoor had suspected.

He hazarded a side glance at his partner. Kamal seemed focused elsewhere and unconcerned by Taymoor's call.

How much does he know? Taymoor wondered. *Should I tell him?*

He knew he shouldn't. He needed to tread very carefully.

'Find out what you can,' he told his caller, trying to put a lid on the anger that was roiling inside him.

'I told you: it's gone dark.'

'Find out,' he repeated, his tone even but firm. 'And let me know. As soon as you can.'

'Okay, I will, but listen to me, Taymoor. I need you to be careful. For all of us.'

'Don't worry. I'll call you later.'

He clicked off and glanced at Kamal again, unsure about how to handle the information he'd just been given.

Kamal had just dialled someone.

Kamal was oblivious to Taymoor's phone call.

His mind was elsewhere. He was still walking an emotional tightrope. He kept thinking about calling Nisreen himself, but so many reasons pulled him back from making that call, not least of which was the fact that, assuming the best—assuming she had nothing to do with the underground group—he couldn't face having her find out about the playwright's fate from him.

With Taymoor distracted, he picked up his phone and speed-dialled his brother again.

Pick up, damn it, he swore inwardly.

To no avail.

The call just rang through to voicemail as it had before. He killed the call just as Taymoor ended his own.

They looked at each other uncomfortably. Then Kamal noticed something up ahead: a middle-aged, slightly stooped man with round metal spectacles and a pointy waxed moustache was stepping out of the building. He had a leather satchel slung over his shoulder and one arm firmly across it.

'That's our man,' Kamal said, pointing at him.

'I wonder what he's got in that case.'

'The guy's being overly careful. I doubt he'd be walking around with anything incriminating.'

Taymoor seemed more highly strung than usual. 'There's only one way to find out.' And with that, he flung the car door open and climbed out.

Before Kamal could react, Taymoor was taking big strides across the street, straight towards the banker.

As Kamal rushed out of the car himself, he saw Taymoor bring out something that had been hidden from view in his sleeve, an extendable steel baton. He watched as his partner flicked his wrist to expand it to its full size, all while beelining at the oblivious banker like a missile locked on its target.

'Taymoor!' Kamal called out as he sprinted after him— but it was to no avail. His partner had reached his quarry.

The banker turned at Kamal's shout, then froze with alarm as he saw Taymoor bearing down on him.

'Masal kheir, effendi.' Taymoor greeted him with an icy smile, but, before the banker could react, the smile turned into clenched teeth as Taymoor raised the baton and struck the banker viciously hard across the shoulder with it.

The blow was monstrous. The banker lost his footing and stumbled across the pavement, slamming against the side of a parked car. Taymoor was right in his slipstream.

'Be careful, *effendi*. These pavements can be very slippery,' he snarled as he grabbed him by the collar and spun him around so he was facing him.

'Taymoor,' Kamal called out as he rushed over, stopping to avoid a passing car whose driver blared his horn before thundering past.

The banker held a hand against his injured shoulder, his pained face looking at Taymoor in confused terror. 'What are you—'

'Let me help you with this,' Taymoor said, ignoring his plea and yanking the satchel off his shoulder. 'You really shouldn't be carrying anything too heavy in your condition.'

Kamal finally reached him. 'Taymoor, what are you doing?'

'Just helping out a fellow citizen,' he said before he suddenly turned to the banker, grabbed his injured arm, and extended it firmly so it was fully outstretched, holding the man's hand against the roof of the car. Then he brought down his baton in one ferocious swing, striking the banker's forearm full force midway between his wrist and elbow.

The sound of snapping bone was unmistakable.

The banker yelped with pain as his legs gave out from under him and he crumpled to the ground, his back to the car.

Kamal watched in stunned silence as Taymoor scowled at the fallen man, then walked away, toward Kamal, casually, as if nothing had happened. Behind him, terrified pedestrians were cautiously moving closer to help the stricken banker.

Taymoor walked past Kamal, heading back to their car.

'What the hell was that?' Kamal growled at him.

Taymoor held up the case. 'We'll soon find out.'

Kamal grabbed him by the shoulder and flung him around to face him. 'That wasn't our brief. You didn't need to do that.'

'Brother. We've wasted enough time playing cat and mouse with these bastards,' Taymoor shot back. 'What if this one slips through our net? What if we don't stop them in time?'

'We don't know if he's guilty of anything,' Kamal insisted. 'He's just a suspect.'

'When it comes to these fuckers, that's good enough for me,' Taymoor replied. 'Besides, I might have just done him the biggest favour of his life.'

'What are you talking about?'

'Maybe he'll take this as a serious warning. Maybe it'll be a much-needed wake-up call and he'll realize that he needs to stop doing what he's doing before something much more serious happens to him.'

Kamal was infuriated, but he had something more pressing on his mind. He didn't want to escalate the situation. Not now. It would have to wait.

But he couldn't stay there either.

'Fine. You deal with the report. I've got to go.'

He walked off.

'Where the hell do you think you're going?' Taymoor called out after him.

Kamal waved him off without turning. 'I've got to take care of something.'

'Seriously? We're in the middle of—'

'I'll catch up with you as soon as I can,' he shouted back. And without pausing for a follow-up question, he walked away, picking up his step as he pulled out his phone and tried Ramazan again while scouring the street for a taxi.

Ramazan felt the phone in the pocket of his lab coat vibrate but ignored it. It still unsettled him. He'd had a call and a message from his brother earlier, which he hadn't returned. He wondered if that was him calling again. Whatever Kamal was calling about, it couldn't be welcome news. Which was the last thing he needed right now, given that he was in the process of bringing the tattooed man out of his induced sleep.

He'd arranged to meet Fonseca in Rasheed's room but had slipped down to the ICU as quickly as he could, ahead of the agreed time. He figured he had about fifteen minutes before Fonseca showed up. It was tight, but with a bit of luck, it would be enough to get the information he needed.

He watched nervously as Rasheed stirred to life, and checked his watch. Fonseca was maniacally punctual. His window was shutting rapidly.

Rasheed's eyes opened, taking in their surroundings. Ramazan watched as they roamed in ever-widening arcs and finally settled on his face. The man's face was slightly clenched in the familiar confusion Ramazan had seen before.

'Your Excellency,' he said, maintaining the drug flow. 'How are you feeling?'

The man started to form a word through visibly dry lips and was about to answer when Ramazan heard talking outside the room.

It was Fonseca.

29

Ramazan didn't know what to do. Moving on instinct, he quickly turned the IV feed back up. He watched in panic as Rasheed's eyes took on a distant look before they rolled upwards and disappeared behind closed lids just as the door swung open and Fonseca stepped in. The surgeon was accompanied by one of the nurses.

'Ah, Ramazan, you're already here,' the surgeon said. 'Splendid.' He crossed over to the bed and gave the tattooed man a long, curious look. 'I think he's had enough of a rest, don't you?'

Ramazan didn't reply, but Fonseca wasn't exactly waiting for an answer either. He checked out the thin rubber tubes that came out from under the man's covers and ran into a small plastic container hanging from the bed's frame. 'His drains are clear.'

'Yes, there's been no bleeding since the first night,' Ramazan said, calmly.

'Good. I'll take them out in the morning.' He gestured invitingly to Ramazan. 'He's all yours.'

Ramazan managed a smile and, despite the quiver in his hands, started to bring Rasheed to full consciousness.

Again, as he had only minutes before, the tattooed man stirred. His eyes moved around behind his eyelids. Then he opened them, his face clouded by the same bewildered look before his gaze settled on Ramazan's welcoming face.

'Nice to have you back, *effendi*,' Ramazan told him, adroitly opting to use the respectful, but hardly imperial, title. 'How are you feeling?'

Rasheed didn't reply. His eyes were scanning the room, clearly trying to make sense of where he was and what was happening.

Ramazan knew this was different from when he'd been getting Rasheed to discuss the past. Then, he was only semi-conscious and not fully aware of what he was saying. Right now, the drugs would be draining out of him completely, and he'd soon have full awareness. What he remembered from before the surgery, however, was an open question.

Ramazan gave him a moment. Then he tapped his left arm gently, as he had before. 'Can you raise this arm?'

Rasheed, still visibly trying to work things out, raised it.

'Excellent. You must be thirsty. Here.' Ramazan picked up the cup of water from the side table and positioned the straw between the man's dry lips. 'Have some water, *effendi*. Small sips, please.'

He gave him a moment, then took away the cup and turned to Fonseca. 'He's still groggy,' he told him. 'Let's give him a few minutes.'

He watched nervously as Fonseca moved closer, right up to the man's bed. 'I just want to know if he's decided to speak yet,' he told Ramazan without taking his eyes off the tattooed man. 'Or if he's going to keep up the silent treatment. Maybe he'll be more chatty while he's still groggy. What do you say, *effendi*?' he asked the patient. 'Would you care to enlighten us about who you are? You could perhaps start with your name?'

As Rasheed stared at the surgeon with a blank, befuddled expression, Ramazan looked on in silent dread, desperately hoping the man would remember to keep up the mute act he'd come in with.

Who he was came back first.

After that, Rasheed was struggling to remember where he was and what he was doing there.

Confusing bits of information were burgeoning in his dazed mind, random associations of words and visions that he was trying to make sense of. Were they memories or imaginings? He didn't have enough focus to make that distinction. The face looking down on him, though, was unfamiliar. Had he seen him before? The man certainly seemed to think so, but . . . who was he?

He scanned the rest of his surroundings. A hospital room, clearly. A modern one. Yes, a hospital. In Paris. He'd come to Paris, to be treated. That's right. To be cured. He'd come to the hospital he'd scouted before, the . . . He couldn't remember its name.

A woman, a nurse—no recollection of her. Another man—now he seemed somewhat familiar. Why was that? Who was he? He studied him more intently. Yes, there was something about him he remembered. But what? He had to be a doctor, like the other one. Why else would they be there? And what about his condition? He could see a couple of IV lines running down into his arm. Was he cured? Had they fixed what was wrong with him?

What was wrong? He couldn't remember. Sensations came back—coughing violently, spitting out blood, feeling out of breath, exhaustion. He wondered about that. He seemed—better. He sucked in a breath tentatively, felt a pain in his lungs, but even then, it felt better. Like his airways had been cleared and widened.

Yes, he'd come to Paris to be treated. He remembered the darkness, night, by the river. Feeling cold, naked. He remembered someone, a man. Had he killed him? The sensation of the man choking between his arms came rushing back. Yes. He'd taken his clothes. Then the hospital, then . . . what?

The man looking down at him, again. What had he said? 'If he's decided to speak yet?' What did that mean?

One thing he did know. He needed to be cautious. They couldn't know who he really was. And evidently they were curious. How much did they know? Had he told them? Surely not. He couldn't have. That must be what the man meant. Rasheed hadn't said anything. They didn't know who he was.

Good. That was good.

He needed to keep that up as long as he could. It was safer that way.

And yet . . . snippets of conversations were creeping into his thoughts. Conversations about . . . the past. His past. Were they just distant memories or something else? Were they just internal imaginings? They somehow seemed more real, more visceral. And yet he hadn't talked about his past with anyone. Had he? No. He was sure of it. Not back then. No one could know the truth about him.

And yet he could hear these sound bites echoing inside him. Which was worrying.

His mind was feeling clearer with each breath, but he needed more time. And until he was back in control of his senses, he needed to remain silent, or at least say very little. That much was certain. Once he was better, once he knew his health was taken care of, he would wait until he was alone in the room, and he would vanish. They would wonder all they wanted. They'd never know the truth.

He kept staring at the face looming down on him, and said nothing. But his attention was drawn away from him, to the other man again. There was something about him.

Who was he?

He needed to find out. He also needed to find out what condition he was in. He debated it for a moment, then decided to break the façade if only by a crack.

'Am I . . . okay?' he asked, using a frail voice to keep his defences up.

The man looking down on him turned to face the more familiar man, smiling with evident satisfaction.

'Who are you?' Rasheed added weakly.

'You're absolutely fine,' Fonseca told him. 'I'm your surgeon, Moshe Fonseca. You don't remember us meeting before the operation?'

Rasheed feigned studying him, then shook his head once.

Which seemed to surprise Fonseca. 'Ah. Well, you'll be pleased to hear that it all went well, with no complications at all. You've got a lovely new valve in there and I see no reason why you shouldn't be back on your feet in no time.'

Fonseca. Moshe Fonseca. A vague recollection bloomed. The surgeon who fixed him—the Jew. He looked across at the other man. He'd met him with him. He was . . . yes, the anaesthetist. They'd met before the surgery. But there was more to him. Rasheed was sure of it. But what?

A nurse stepped into the room. She seemed distressed. 'Moshe Hekim?' she told Fonseca. 'There are some men here to see you. They're from the Hafiye.' She addressed the other man. 'You too, Ramazan Hekim.'

Ramazan. So that was his name.

The men looked at each other, confusion playing across their faces.

'Where are they?' Fonseca asked her.

'In the waiting area. They insist on seeing you both straightaway.'

Rasheed watched as Fonseca glanced at Ramazan, and something unspoken passed between them. Then the surgeon shrugged with reluctant acceptance. 'Let's see what they want.' He turned to the nurse who'd come in with him. 'This shouldn't take long. Why don't you fill out his chart while we see what they want?' Then he glanced at Ramazan, and they both followed the nurse out.

A murmur of anxiety crept through Rasheed. Agents of the Hafiye, asking to see his doctors? This was no coincidence.

He tensed up and breathed as deeply as he could despite the pain lighting up his chest wall, willing his mind to clear itself, needing to make sure he was lucid enough to deal with the threat he sensed was coming.

Kamal was seething with impatience in his traffic-swamped taxi when an incoming call came in.

He checked the screen. It was his analyst from the Caves. In anger, he hit the receive button, instantly regretting it since the last thing on his mind right now was that insipid body in the Seine.

'*Chaouch komiser*,' the analyst said. 'I know where your suspect went.'

It took a moment to sink in. 'What?'

'Your suspect. The man from the quays. I know where he went. I was able to follow his trail by cross-checking the street cams and matching the time codes with in-taxi cams and—'

It was too much noise for Kamal right now. 'Skip the details. Where did he go?'

'The Hurrem Sultan Külliye. That's where the taxi dropped him off. I checked the hospital logs. They had a walk-in that morning at the same time. And here's the thing, *chaouch komiser*. The man's still there. In intensive care.'

The name of the hospital was like a foghorn in Kamal's ears. The Hurrem Sultan—where his brother worked.

He looked out the taxi's window. The hospital was looming up ahead, across the river. A snarl of traffic was blocking his way.

'All right, thanks. I'll take it from here,' Kamal told him before hanging up.

The hospital. On the face of it, this had nothing to do with Ramazan, surely. It could just be a coincidence. But given everything that was happening with Nisreen, he sensed something there. Another danger. Perhaps a bigger one.

'I'll walk,' he told the driver as he handed him some money.

Then he bolted out of the cab and started running.

30

Ramazan was aware of a growing lump in his throat as he and Fonseca stepped out of the ICU to find the Hafiye agents waiting for them.

There were four men by the double doors that led into the area. All four were in uniform and had that sour, contemptuous edge in their eyes, as if the entire world was teeming with undesirables that they were burdened with weeding out. Two of them stepped forward to meet Ramazan and Fonseca, while the other two stayed put. The shorter of the two who came forward had a sallow face that had been ravaged by acne at some point in the past, while the taller agent had a trio of fresh parallel scabs across his left cheek that looked like they came from someone's nails. It did nothing to brighten the air of malice that surrounded them.

Quick formal introductions were made before Fonseca dived in and asked, 'What's this about?'

'We're interested in a patient of yours,' the acne-scarred agent said. 'An unidentified man who's covered in tattoos. We'd like a word with him.' He turned to Ramazan as he said it.

Ramazan was making a huge effort to keep his fear in check while trying to act unconcerned and leaving the talking to Fonseca.

'He's had major surgery and we've only just brought him out of sedation. He's barely coherent. Whatever it is you want to talk to him about, I'm not sure he's in much of a position to answer.'

'Why don't you leave that for us to decide.' The agent then gave Fonseca a sardonic silent gesture directed at the door of the ICU. 'Lead the way, *hekim*.'

A riot of thoughts was crowding Rasheed's mind as he watched the nurse take readings off the monitors by his bed.

'Your readings are all perfect,' she announced to him as she drew closer and fitted a blood pressure sensor on his arm.

He needed to be ready, needed to be in a position to counter their threat. He'd try going back to the mute act first, see how that played out. It would buy him time to evaluate what was really going on. He also needed to know more about his condition. Fonseca had said he would remove the drains in the morning, which meant he wouldn't be able to go back before then.

'How long do I have to stay in here?' he asked her.

'Oh, not long at all,' she said. 'We'll move you to the ward tomorrow morning and we could send you home in a couple of days.'

'When can I walk?' he asked.

'I'd ask the doctors, but there's no reason why you can't be on your feet,' she replied cheerfully. 'If you feel up to it, they'll be delighted to see you take a few steps. But only a few, mind you. And not alone. With someone to assist you, of course. To carry the drains.' She clicked on the monitor and checked the result. 'You see what I mean? Everything's good. Your blood pressure is just fine. Even a bit higher than I expected.'

'Good,' Rasheed muttered.

'Well, you were in good hands,' she said as she wrote on his chart. 'The best, in fact. And I've got to say, you've been lucky to have Ramazan Hekim keep such a close eye on you throughout your recovery.'

A flush of blood swamped Rasheed's ears. 'What do you mean?'

'He must have come in to check on you half a dozen times since surgery. I've never seen him take such an interest in a patient. Are you related? Or friends maybe?'

Anxious questions were prodding at him from all directions. 'And that's . . . unusual?' he asked.

'Oh, yes. Normally he'd have come in once to check on you and that would be it. You'd be on the ward much sooner, which suits everyone as we need these ICU beds for other patients.'

'But he was here a lot.'

'That he was. You got the royal treatment,' the nurse told him.

'How long have I been in here?'

'Let's see.' She dredged her memory. 'You were admitted Friday morning, and the surgery was that evening. So you've been here for two days.'

The questions gave way to grave concerns as the nurse's words spurred some confusing images in his mind—images and sound bites, fragments of conversations, bouncing around in his head, duelling for his attention. But what were they? Real or imagined? He couldn't tell. Not at first. But by shutting his eyes and concentrating, a few of them started to fall into place, a kind of order appeared, a structure that seemed to revolve around one central image: the doctor, sitting by his bed, and talking.

Talking.

To him.

A two-way conversation. Which Rasheed could barely remember. Two- . . . or three-way? He had a vague flash of another face, a woman, also in his room, by the bed—then it was gone.

What had the doctor done? How much did he know? Was Rasheed compromised? Did they know the truth? Is that why the agents were here? Had the doctor called them? Or was he after something else?

Does he know?

An urgent dread spiked within him. He had to be on high alert. His entire achievement was at risk.

He didn't have too much time to dwell on it. His body was still going through the motions of expunging the drugs that were clouding his thinking when the door to his room opened and the four men—his two doctors and two agents in uniform—walked in.

31

'What is your name, *effendi*?'

Rasheed didn't answer.

The acne-scarred agent stepped closer and bent down to take a closer look at the man. 'I said, what is your name?'

Again, no answer.

The agent swivelled his head to address Fonseca. 'Is there any medical reason for him not to speak?'

Fonseca looked cornered and hesitated before replying. 'Well, he—he's been under heavy sedation, as I told you,' he stammered.

The agent scrutinized Rasheed again. 'Is that so?' He stared at Rasheed's eyes, as if trying to divine what was going on behind them. 'I think he hears me just fine. I think he's just ignoring me. Playing me for a fool. What do you think, Kerim?' he asked his colleague without turning away. 'Do you think he's playing me for a fool?'

'If he is,' the agent with the scratched face replied, 'it's a grave misjudgement on his part.'

The agent stayed in Rasheed's face. Rasheed stayed quiet. Then the agent's eyes moved away, and he noticed the tube coming out from under Rasheed's bedding.

'What is this tube?'

'It's a drain. From his lungs.'

The agent followed it down. It led to a plastic sack that was hung from the side of the bed. 'There's nothing coming out.'

'No.'

'So it's not necessary.'

'Not any more,' Fonseca specified. 'We're going to take it out later today.'

'Any reason you can't do it now?'

Fonseca stumbled for an answer. 'Well, it's—it has to be done under local anaesthetic, and—'

The agent cut him off brusquely. 'So you can do it now, here.'

Fonseca was tripping over his tongue. 'I suppose—I mean, yes, if it's really necessary, but why?'

'Because it'll make him easier to transport.'

'Transport?' Fonseca was alarmed. 'You can't move him. He's just had major surgery.'

'Two days ago,' the agent corrected him. 'He'll be fine. We have medical staff on site at the Citadel if he needs anything.'

'Look, I'm his surgeon. I can't let you—'

The agent glared as he raised a firm, silencing finger at Fonseca. 'Moshe Hekim. Do as you're told.'

Rasheed watched nervously as Fonseca did as he was told.

They injected him with a local anaesthetic, and what followed was quick and painless. A deep inhale, and the tube was pulled out. It was surprisingly long, almost a couple of feet, and the shock of seeing it only added to the heightened paranoia that was gripping him.

They know. They all know. The doctors called them and that's why they want to take me away.

He knew full well what the Citadel was. After all, it was under his rule of the city that it had been taken over and turned into the headquarters of law enforcement. He had overseen the first stages of its expansion.

The fatigue and the drugs were toying with his mind, and worries were pulling him in all kinds of directions. *They're after the incantation. They want it.* He knew what they were capable of, and he knew they'd end up getting it. He also knew he could escape at any time by simply uttering that sequence of words, but he suddenly realized that if they knew what he was capable of, they might gag him so he wouldn't be able to use the spell to escape. Then they might drug him. They might force him to write it down.

Whichever way he looked at it, it was a disaster. His mind was caught in a tempest of panic, and a fierce, stubborn survival instinct was battling to find him a way out. They were going to take him away. They were going to get it out of him, and he couldn't let that happen. At any price. He had to do something, and he had to do it now. He had no choice. He had to make his move, immediately, before it was too late. He had to get the hell out of there while he still could, disappear, and go home and wait until he was fully recovered before coming back to clean up that mess. Starting with the surgeon and the other conniving ferret he was working with. He'd get his revenge on them. But that could wait.

His eyes narrowed and flickered back and forth across the room to take stock of everyone's position while Fonseca sutured the cut from the drain.

When he was finished, the surgeon turned to the agents.

'All done?' the agent with the pockmarked face asked.

Fonseca nodded grudgingly. 'I still think this is a mistake. You're putting his recovery at risk.'

'If anything bad happens, we'll call you.' He turned to the nurse. 'Let's get a wheelchair in here and we'll be on our way.'

Rasheed shut his eyes and concentrated, preparing to make his jump. But his mind was still a jumble of thoughts, and a different plan elbowed its way front and centre.

I can get them, here, now. Take them out. Before this gets out of hand, before they spread whatever it is they know about me. And this way I won't have to risk coming back.

He tilted his head sideways to get a better look at the acne-scarred agent. Then he kicked into gear.

He saw the agent turn to face him, and nodded at him, a small, pathetic nod. And in a weak, barely audible voice, he said, 'Wait. Please. I'll . . . tell you.'

The agent cocked his head with curiosity as he edged closer. 'You want to say something?'

Rasheed nodded again, slowly, and whispered, 'My name. It's . . . Anwar.'

The agent could barely hear him. He flicked a self-satisfied grin at his taller colleague and edged over to the bed, bending down so he could hear him better.

'Speak up, *effendi*. We don't have all day.'

'I . . . my name,' Rasheed repeated, his muscles tensing, his pulse rocketing stealthily inside him.

The agent bent down closer. He was now hovering mere inches over Rasheed.

Rasheed lashed out.

His arm flew out from under the covers and coiled itself around the pockmarked agent's neck, yanking him in and squeezing hard, the man's throat caught in the crook of Rasheed's elbow. Everyone in the room reacted at the same time, but Rasheed's attention was riveted on the taller agent, who was instantly bolting towards the bed while reaching for his handgun. Rasheed was moving just as fast as his other hand reached over to the belt of the agent he had in a chokehold and pulled out the man's weapon. The second agent had his gun out and levelled at the bed in time, but he hesitated at the sight of his partner blocking a clean shot at the bedridden man, which was all the split-second advantage Rasheed needed. He emptied two rounds into the advancing agent— head and chest. The man slammed against the edge of the bed before dropping to the floor.

Rasheed didn't waste a second. His focus was unaffected by the sudden scream of the nurse as he released the first agent from his grip, shoving him away violently before loosing two rounds into him. The man stumbled backwards into the wheeled bedside tray table of monitors and crashed down to the floor with it.

Rasheed yanked the IV catheter out of his arm, swung his feet out from under the covers, and sat up, but a sharp burn ignited in his chest, causing him to flinch from the unexpected pain. He steadied himself against the bed as he swept his gun around the room again, looking for his next target. Fonseca was frozen in place, his arms raised, his feet inching backwards hesitantly, his face twisted with fear. He was mouthing, 'No, please, don't,' but to no avail. Rasheed ended his life with two more well-placed rounds, the headshot sending most of the contents of Fonseca's skull splattering against the pristine white wall behind him.

From the corner of his eye, Rasheed spotted the door of the room, wide open, the other doctor and the nurse rushing out. He fired at them as he pushed himself to his feet, but he wobbled under a surge of dizziness, and the bullets missed their marks, punching into the wall and doorjamb instead.

He steadied himself against the bed for a second, closed his eyes, and inhaled a long breath, wincing at the searing sensation deep in his chest, taking it in the hope that the intake of oxygen was worth the pain.

Then he pushed forward and charged after them.

32

Ramazan's breath seized the instant the man who claimed to be Anwar Rasheed grabbed the Hafiye agent. The next few seconds were a blur of surreal noise and images, like nothing he'd encountered before. The violence rooted him in place, and then he snapped back to life. Just as the tattooed man's gun pivoted toward Fonseca and spat out its rounds, he charged for the door, pushing the screaming nurse out in front of him.

Outside, in the main ICU ward, panic had already spread as nurses and doctors scurried to take cover any way they could.

'Call security!' Ramazan hollered as he sprinted away from the room in a directionless frenzy, straight at the two other Hafiye agents who were already rushing towards him, bodies coiled in low combat crouches, guns drawn.

Without stopping, Ramazan raised one arm while jabbing the air frantically with the other in the direction of the room. 'He's got a gun,' he blurted to them. 'He shot the others.' And as he spun his head to glance back at the room, he saw Rasheed stumble through the door, gun raised.

Ramazan ducked to the side as one of the two agents yelled out, 'Drop your weapon.' A split second later, more gunshots erupted. Ramazan dived to the ground, then twisted around quickly to see what was happening. The agents had taken cover, one behind a wheeled cabinet and the other behind a structural column, and were firing away relentlessly while bullets from Rasheed's gun were flying past, drilling holes in the cabinet and kicking up chips of plaster from the column. He couldn't see Rasheed at first. Then he spotted him, sheltering behind another column.

'Drop your weapon!' an agent yelled again.

Rasheed loosed off three more rounds; then Ramazan heard a quick succession of loud metallic snaps coming from his direction. He was no gun expert, but he knew enough to recognize that sound.

Rasheed's gun was empty.

Rasheed felt debilitated before he even left the room.

He'd moved too soon and hadn't reckoned with how weak he still was and how much his body still needed to recover. Each step was like trudging through quicksand. He felt stabs of pain in multiple areas, with the worst in his chest, like someone was tearing his ribcage open. He was heavy-headed, his vision was woozy, and the gun in his hand felt like it weighed a ton.

He'd misread the situation, misjudged his abilities. Despite the haze, he knew it now. He'd screwed up.

And he was now out of bullets.

But there was still a way out. It was what he should have done in the first place, instead of trying to clear the mess before leaving.

It was time to go.

'Okay, okay, don't shoot,' he yelled back, raising his gun hand while remaining hidden behind the column. 'I'll drop my gun. Don't shoot.'

He bent down and set the gun on the floor, then gave it a good shove in the direction of the agents.

'I'm unarmed. Okay? I'm coming out,' he shouted.

*

Ramazan watched as Rasheed stepped out from behind the column. He had his arms stretched upwards, his palms open, his fingers spread.

Twenty yards across the large room, the two agents also emerged from cover.

'Get down, on the ground. Now!' one of them roared as they advanced carefully towards him, their guns still aimed at him through extended arms and two-handed grips.

Ramazan flicked his gaze back at Rasheed. The tattooed man had stopped moving and was dropping to his knees. He also seemed disconcertingly calm. Which was when it hit Ramazan. He knew what the man was going to do.

He rose up, his eyes laser-focused on his patient, a cocktail of fear, disbelief and anticipation crippling him, even more so when Rasheed levelled his gaze back at him and didn't waver—then the man's lips started moving.

Ramazan wanted to shout out, wanted to warn the agents, wanted to stop Rasheed from doing what he knew he was going to do—but his legs weren't cooperating, nor was his mouth.

The only word it could eke out was a meek, whispered, 'No.'

Dizzy, in pain, his vision blurred and swirling, Rasheed fought hard to concentrate.

Time to go. Time to get the hell out of here.

He could see Ramazan Hekim's face peering out from behind the advancing men, the doctor's eyes wide with horror. Then he shut his eyes and started murmuring the incantation.

It didn't take long.

And when he was done, he felt the familiar icy shiver race through his veins and the sudden prickle of thousands of tiny needles on the inside of his skull—and then he was gone.

*

Ramazan felt his entire body seize up.

Even though he'd heard the man tell him about it, even though he'd discussed it with Nisreen, even though he'd thought about nothing else for the last couple of days, it still shocked the life out of him.

One second, the man was there, in full view, on his knees, his arms outspread—then he was gone. Just like that.

No sound, no wind, no pyrotechnics.

He just vanished.

The agents kept advancing, slower now, scanning the room, sweeping the area for what their brains were still having great difficulty processing.

Then one clear thought burst through Ramazan's daze and slapped him to attention.

He had to run.

He edged backwards, away from them, one cautious, quiet step, then another, then a bit faster, until he was slipping through the double doors and rushing for the hospital's exit.

As he moved, he pulled out his phone, trying to keep it in his grip, trying not to let his jittery fingers lose hold of it, and somehow he managed to hit the right speed-dial key.

Nisreen answered on the second ring.

'Where are you?' he rasped.

33

Right from the very second Rasheed finished saying the spell, the jump felt different to him.

All jumps triggered an instant shock to the senses—the terrifying sense of disembodiment, the dizzying weightlessness, the feeling of being ripped into an infinity of fragments before being instantaneously reassembled as an identical, exact replica a whole universe away. He wasn't really used to it—it was too intense, too overwhelming for anyone to get used to—but he'd done it enough times to know what to expect.

He hadn't expected this.

Visually, he hadn't seen that vista before—a bird's-eye view of the zinc-and-slate-tiled roofs and, beyond, the towering twin spires and minarets of the great Fatih Mosque, its flying buttresses flanking the squatting domes that surrounded it.

Beyond the visual, however, was the sensorial. Specifically, the feeling coming through the soles of his feet, which was no feeling at all. For there was nothing under his feet.

He was in mid-air. And a split-second after materializing, he started falling.

Precipitously.

The entire sensation lasted less than two and a half seconds. That was how long it took for gravity to yank him out of the sky and drop him a hundred feet to the ground.

In his defence, he had no way of knowing that his windowless room in the ICU of the Hurrem Sultan Külliye was on the tenth floor of the building, in a location that, back in 1721, was only occupied by a landscaped garden adjacent to the old Hôtel-Dieu Hospital, the precursor to the Hurrem Sultan. He knew the garden; after all, he'd been to the Ottoman *darusshifa* a few times over the years, most recently to be examined following flare-ups of his illness in the weeks before he had decided to jump to 2017 and get treated. He'd just never seen it from that vantage point: the old hospital was only four storeys high.

His mind also wasn't at its clearest. The heavy, continuous sedation that he'd been subjected to over the last two days was still clogging vital pathways in his mind, heightening his paranoia and clouding his judgement.

In those two and a half seconds, though, a lot did manage to break through the morass in his head. It was still an unresolved mystery of medicine how that actually happened, how our minds could unleash a cascade of images, thoughts and memories in such a brief amount of time. And yet that's what Ayman Rasheed experienced in the last two and half seconds of his illustrious and unique life. He just wouldn't be able to tell anyone about them.

His first thought was one of anger: that it would all come to an end here, now, like this, in a messy, bloody splatter, after all the risks he'd faced and the battles he'd fought. He'd survived the war in Iraq and its barbaric prisons; he'd survived the savage rampage into Syria and fierce firefights against a multitude of enemies there; he'd made it to Turkey unscathed and had survived installing himself by the sultan's side along with the political intrigues, backstabbing and skulduggery that had followed; he'd survived the many battles and campaigns that had begun in the fields outside Vienna in 1683 and culminated with the conquest of Paris a decade later. He's survived all that—and he would die here, now, from nothing more epic or glorious than falling out of a window in time.

And he was naked. That was how they would find him. Sprawled on the ground, limbs undoubtedly broken and bent in a grotesque arrangement, and naked. He pictured the pathetic, revolting sight in his mind's eye. It was not how he had planned to be remembered.

That fierce anger ripped through him as he plummeted, a rage at what he'd done, what he'd had to do, what had led him to have to do it. He cursed the anaesthetist, he cursed the surgeon, but most of all he cursed himself, furious at his own stupidity, his own panic, his own misjudgement, his own failure.

Beyond that, the other main thought that strangled his last breaths was regret. His secret—his world-altering, astounding secret—would die with him. It was how he had wanted it to be, but he now wondered if he had made the right decision.

Right from the beginning, he had contemplated his eventual death and questioned how his knowledge ought to be handled.

He'd initially been worried about how the sultan would react to his revelation. Beyond the fear and the suspicion, there was also the religious ban on what he was bringing. Magic was prohibited by Islam and was only allowed if used to block the evil intentions of a false claimant to prophethood. The hysteria surrounding sorcery was hardly limited to the Ottoman Empire: in America, the Salem witch trials were taking place at the same time. But the sultan had quickly seen the immense benefits of embracing Rasheed's gift and had happily agreed to keep it secret from his viziers and everyone else.

Once he'd achieved his plans and the Ottomans had conquered Europe, once he'd been rewarded with the governorship of France, Rasheed had spent many a moment contemplating how to handle his legacy. He'd mulled over sharing his secret with a chosen acolyte, someone he could mentor before entrusting him with it. It was one way to safeguard what he'd achieved; if, at some point in the future, something catastrophic threatened the empire, his heir could use the secret to travel back in time and prevent it from happening. But then, what if his heir were to die unexpectedly? Did the secret deserve to have more robust safeguards protecting it? That concern had evolved into wondering whether to bestow his knowledge not on one heir but on two, or three; they could be the beginning of a cabal that could extend forever, a secret circle of protectors of the empire who would watch over it and guarantee its permanence. But other concerns challenged his thinking. What if it fell into the wrong hands? What if an enemy of the state or a foreign power like the Americans or the Russians got hold of it? What if they used it against the Ottomans? What if they sent a team back to 1683 to undo everything he'd done?

In the end, it was that fear, the fear that his achievement could be nullified and erased from history, that made him decide to keep it to himself. He wouldn't share it with anyone; he'd use his knowledge of the future to warn those around him as much as he could about the potential dangers to the empire. He'd write, extensively, about different political, societal and technological challenges that might arise. Beyond that, the empire would have to fend for itself. He would have given it a very solid foundation to achieve more longevity that any other civilization in history. If it did fail because of anything other than an act of God, so be it.

He questioned his decision again in those final two and a half seconds of his life, his rush to meet the ground goaded by the regret and the rage. He didn't want it all to be lost. He hadn't told anyone about it. He hadn't married, he'd never shared it with any of his many lovers, he hadn't told any of the children he'd fathered. The only other person who'd known, the sultan, had already died. There was no one around who knew the extent of his extraordinary accomplishment. He would die here, now, a respected, admired leader, a visionary, a pillar of Ottoman history, but no one would speak of how he had single-handedly changed the world.

He would have much preferred to die with a more uplifting, optimistic thought to soften the brutal certainty of his impending demise. Sadly for Ayman Rasheed, no such thought had materialized by the time he hit the ground. In those frantic, breathless two and a half seconds, his story, and his secret, were extinguished for ever.

Or so he thought.

34

'I'm home, why?'

Nisreen tensed up at the breathless and frantic tone of her husband's voice.

After Ramazan had left her at the coffee house, she'd hurried back to the office for a client meeting she couldn't cancel, after which she'd taken a tram back to the bus stop to meet the kids. She was at home, helping the children with their homework, when Ramazan called.

'It's gone bad,' he blurted. 'All of it.'

She turned away from the kids and lowered her voice. 'What are you talking about?'

'Ayman Pasha. They came for him. Agents, from the Hafiye. He shot two of them; then he disappeared. He disappeared, Nisreen.'

His words were like a cattle prod to her brain. 'He what?'

'He disappeared. Vanished, right before my eyes.'

'Aman Tanrım,' she hissed.

'It works, Nisreen. It works. It's all true. But the other agents—they were there. They saw it, too.' His tone had veered from urgency to fear. 'What am I going to do?'

His fear was burning through the airwaves and igniting her own terror. 'You haven't done anything wrong.'

'Two of their men are dead, Nisreen.'

'But it's not your fault. You said he shot them.'

'They're going to want to know why it happened. They're going to want to know how he disappeared. Assuming they don't already know.'

She was scrambling for solutions. 'So you tell them.'

His tone turned even more desperate. 'Are you mad? Tell them? What do you think they'll do after that? You think they're going to say, "*Tashakur, hekim,* we're most grateful to you; now go home and resume your life as if nothing happened?" They're not going to risk leaving me free to run around knowing what I know.'

'So you say you don't know anything. You say you were as shocked as they were.'

'They're not going to buy that. Not one hundred per cent. Which means they won't take the risk of cutting me loose. Just in case I did know.'

He was right. Nisreen knew it. 'Where are you now?'

'I'm heading to the car park.'

'Okay. Okay.' She was struggling to tame the rabid thoughts attacking her. 'We have to get out of here.'

'We? This has nothing to do with you.'

'We have to disappear together, Ramazan. Otherwise, they'll take me and they'll use me to pressure you into giving yourself up.'

'No—'

'Maybe they know about me already,' she suddenly realized. 'Whichever way you look at it, we're in this together.'

'It's hopeless anyway. They're going to find us—you know they will. We're screwed.'

'No,' she insisted firmly. 'We have to disappear, Ramazan. For now, anyway. We have to get away from here.'

'And go where?'

'I don't know. But don't come here. They'll be sending people round. Let's meet somewhere.'

'Where?'

She squeezed her eyes shut, looking for an answer. 'The florist next to Zeynep's place. Pick us up from there.'

'Us?'

'I've got to bring the kids with me. I can't leave them behind.'

'*Istaghfarullah,* Nisreen. The kids? This is crazy.'

'We don't have a choice. We can't leave them behind.' A different thought erupted. 'What about Kamal? Did you call him?'

'No.'

'He can help.'

'No, Nisreen. He's one of them.'

'He's your brother. Call him, I'm sure he—'

'No, Nisreen. And don't call him either. You know he can't be trusted.'

'But he's—'

'Don't call him. Promise me. Not until I see you. Then we'll talk.'

Nisreen forced herself to stop arguing. It could wait. The priority was to get to safety. She needed to get herself and the children out of there, fast.

'Okay,' she told him. 'The florist.'

'Hurry. And be careful.'

'You too.'

Kamal spotted the commotion outside the hospital the second he got across the bridge.

Up ahead, other cops were cordoning off the hospital's entrance. He pulled out his badge as he hurried up to them.

'Kamal Arslan Agha,' he said as he flashed his badge. 'What's going on?'

'There's been a shooting. Three dead,' one of the cops informed him, before adding pointedly, 'I think two of them are yours.'

238

'What?' A spasm of worry shot through him. 'What about the third victim?'

'A doctor.'

The spasm burst wide. 'Who? Do you have a name?'

'No. It's still a mess in there.'

Battling a maelstrom of worry, Kamal cut through the mayhem in the hospital's forecourt while reaching for his phone and speed-dialling his brother's number again, his eyes desperately scanning the gaggle of visibly agitated doctors, nurses and civilians who were streaming out and congregating well clear of the entrance. He couldn't see Ramazan among them. Five police cruisers were scattered haphazardly outside the lobby's portico, and distant sirens were converging.

Ramazan still wasn't picking up his phone. Kamal killed the call as he reached the entrance, where he spotted a balding man in a white hospital coat talking to three police officers.

'Who's in charge here?' He barged in, interrupting them, his badge out.

'I'm the chief of medicine,' the balding man replied.

'What happened?'

The doctor's face crinkled with uncertainty. 'I don't know exactly. It seems four of your men came here to arrest someone—a patient in the ICU. The man shot two of them dead along with one of our surgeons.'

Patient. ICU. The analyst's call. Connections were fusing together in his brain.

He steeled himself for the worst. 'Who was the surgeon?'

'Moshe Fonseca.'

Kamal flinched. Mercifully, it wasn't his brother, but he still recognized the name—it was one he'd heard Ramazan mention, someone he worked with. Back when they still talked.

'My brother works here. Sayyid Ramazan Hekim. Do you know where he is?'

'No, I don't. But the man who killed Moshe—Moshe and your brother operated on him two days ago. He was their patient. They were both with him when it happened.'

'So where's my brother?'

'I don't know. We're looking for him.'

'What about the shooter?'

One of the cops said, 'We don't know. He might still be in there.'

Just then, the crowd cleared enough for Kamal to spot two men in plain clothes that he vaguely recognized in the entrance lobby. They were huddled with four cops and seemed to be giving them instructions. He'd seen them around the Citadel. He didn't know them personally, but he knew they were agents.

Z Directorate ones.

'Excuse me,' he said brusquely as he stepped away and half sprinted over to the two men.

He reached them just as the cops paired up and trotted off in different directions. He had his badge out, but judging by the two agents' reactions, they seemed to already know who he was.

'Kamal Agha,' one of them said.

'You were in there? When the shooting happened?'

The agent looked a question at the other man and hesitated about replying. The other man looked equally uncomfortable; then his expression hardened. 'We've been ordered not to discuss it.'

'What?'

'We can't talk about it.'

'Says who?'

The men said nothing.

'Says who?' Kamal barked.

A hesitation. Then, 'Fehmi Pasha,' from the first one.

Fehmi Kuzey. Celaleddin's top lieutenant and the man in charge of the Z Directorate. For him to be personally involved at this level was beyond ominous.

Kamal frowned, trying to make sense of the colliding bits of narrative. 'We're on the same team. You can talk to me.'

'Our orders were unequivocal. No one.'

Kamal felt an urge to smash something. 'Look, my brother's missing. Ramazan Hekim. You know where he is?'

The exchanged furtive looks again, and then the same agent ventured a nod.

'You saw him?'

Another nod.

'He was there? When the shooting happened?'

More hesitation. No reply this time.

'*Bismillah,* he's my brother. I need to know that he's okay.'

The agent who spoke earlier nodded grudgingly. 'He was there—'

'Enough,' his hard-assed partner interrupted.

'It's his brother,' the first agent countered, then pressed on, words tumbling out quickly. 'He was there when it started. He was in the room with the shooter. But once it was over, he was gone.'

'So where is he?'

'I don't know. We were busy dealing with the shooter.'

'What happened to him?'

This question visibly generated the biggest unease in the two men.

'What? Is he dead?'

Nothing.

'He's not? Is he still in there? Did he get away?'

They were like walls. Concrete, soundproof, immovable

walls. Then the hard-assed agent shook his head. 'You'll have to ask Fehmi Pasha.'

It was all Kamal could do not to grab him and batter a full answer out of him. But he knew he needed to control himself. Now, more than ever.

He had no choice. He needed to find out what happened to his brother.

He dialled Nisreen.

'He disappeared?'

'That's what they're saying,' Fehmi Kuzey told the Hafiye's commander. 'One second he was there; then he wasn't.'

'As in, he gave them the slip.'

'As in, he physically vanished into thin air.'

Celaleddin scowled. 'Fehmi—'

'I know how it sounds, pasha. But that's what they said. These are some of my top guys, and I can tell you they're seriously spooked. You should have heard them describe it.'

'And this happened in their full view? They actually saw it?'

'They had him cornered in the ICU. No windows. One exit, past them. I don't want to believe it either, but unless they're in on it with him, there's no other explanation.'

Most of Huseyin Celaleddin Pasha's finely honed and rigidly rational brain still wasn't buying it. But a small, instinctive cavity within it was rebelling. Yes, people didn't suddenly dematerialize. Sure, it wasn't possible.

And yet . . . he had two men down and a dead surgeon. Whatever really happened, this was no longer some kind of prank. It was dead serious. And his lieutenant had assured him that the agents who'd seen it happen were dependable men. The penalties for lying or for being part of some twisted conspiracy were severe enough to ensure that, almost invariably, any Hafiye agent would be dependable.

He got the rest of the lowdown from Kuzey, fast and efficient. Time was clearly of the essence.

'All right,' he told him. 'We need to contain it. Make sure your men don't speak to anyone about it. And I mean no one. Tell them to round up anyone else who might have seen what happened and put them on ice—discreetly.'

'Yes, pasha.'

'And find Ramazan Hekim and his wife. I want them here before the night is out.'

Kamal listened to the phone ring through for five or six rings and was about to hang up when Nisreen picked up.

'Nisreen, it's me.' He wasn't sure what to say. He didn't want to alarm her and didn't know if she'd heard about the shooting at the hospital. 'I need to talk to Ramazan. Do you know where he is?'

Her reply didn't come easily. 'I don't,' she finally offered, her voice tinged with hesitation. 'Why? What's going on?'

She was lying to him. No doubt. She sounded breathless, and he knew that clipped tone well. She was under duress.

'Is he with you?'

'No, I told you—'

'Nisreen, listen to me. I don't know what's happening, but whatever it is, it's serious. Let me help you.'

More hesitation. This time, he heard footsteps and a passing car horn and realized she was out, on the streets, walking. Fast.

'Nisreen—'

'No. I can't. I'm sorry.'

'Nisreen, listen to me—'

'I can't, Kamal. I promised him.'

'It doesn't matter. Let me—'

'I can't.'

Then he heard Noor's voice say, *'Anneh?'* in a worried, frightened way. Then the line went dead.

Kamal spat out a curse twice, three times. He looked into the distance, his eyes registering nothing, his mind frantically rummaging for a good move. One came fast.

He hit the speed dial again. His phone number was screened and accepted by the system, and one of the trace operators picked up almost instantly. It was a young recruit to the team, one he'd spoken to before.

'I need a location lock on a number,' Kamal told him, and gave him Ramazan's mobile number.

'Coming up,' the operator said.

Kamal heard him tap some keys. Then the operator came back, too soon for him to have initiated the search. 'Hang on, I just gave you guys that location.'

'What?'

'The trace on that number. It's live. I've got it up on my screen as we speak.'

A jolt of alarm. They were already on Ramazan. 'Who has it? Who asked for it?'

'Someone from Z Directorate. Samer Alameddin Agha. So who are we tracking? Must be some target to have you all on his tail.'

'Just ship it to my phone, will you? Quick.'

More tapped keys, then, 'Should be with you—now.'

Kamal opened the link and studied the screen. Ramazan was moving away from the hospital—in a car, judging by the speed. He was headed towards his home.

'Keep me posted,' Kamal told the operator before killing the call and hitting Ramazan's speed dial again. He needed to warn him that he was being tracked. He needed Ramazan to pull the battery out of his phone before they got to him.

The call rang through. As before, his brother didn't pick up. Kamal wasn't waiting. He was already on the move. He cut the call just as it went to voicemail and stepped into the street, right in the path of a slow-moving sedan, his arms up and wide, his open badge in one hand.

The car screeched to a halt. Within seconds, Kamal had yanked the door open, pulled its hapless driver out, and was speeding away, chasing after the moving blip on his phone.

35

With no particular destination in mind, Ramazan steered the family car north, along a wide boulevard, towards the road that circled the city. Nisreen was next to him, Tarek and Noor strapped into the back seats. The evening traffic was heavy but flowing. The evening prayers were done, and the pavements were crowded with people, mostly men, heading home from work.

'Where are we going, *baba*?' Tarek asked in a small, anxious voice.

Ramazan glanced in the rearview mirror. He could just about see the low, anxious eyes of his son peering back at him. He didn't know what to answer and looked over at Nisreen.

She twisted around to face the kids and summoned up a smile and as much chirpiness as she could muster. 'We're— we're just going for a drive, *hayatim*. Maybe we'll get some ice cream. Would you like that?'

The kids both nodded in silence and with a hesitation that was a far cry from the usual delight such an announcement would bring.

Nisreen turned to Ramazan. She dropped her voice. 'Where are we going?'

'I don't know.'

A stifling silence smothered the car.

Nisreen cut through it. 'Kamal called.'

'He's been calling me, too.'

'He was looking for you.'

'*Bok,*' he cursed. 'You spoke to him?'

'I had to, Ramazan. I—'

He interrupted her brusquely. 'What did you say?'

'Nothing. But look at us. Look at what's happening. I don't think we have a choice. I think we need his help.'

'So he can turn us in and be an even bigger hero?'

'He's still your brother,' she countered. 'And I can't see any other option.'

'My brother wouldn't still be one of them,' he shot back bitterly.

'So what are we going to do?'

Ramazan didn't have time to come up with an answer.

The police siren that ripped the air around them took care of that.

Kamal kept one eye on the screen of his phone as he cut through the traffic, weaving between slow-moving cars in fits and spurts and diving into any opening he could fit his car into as he chased after the moving red dot on the live map of the city.

He wasn't in a department vehicle, which meant he didn't have access to a radio and couldn't monitor the progress of whoever else was following the same red dot. He also didn't have a siren or a set of strobe lights to help cleave a path through the sea of cars ahead of him. The horn would have to do, but its effectiveness was limited; Ottoman drivers used their horns so frequently that they had grown immune to them.

He wondered where they were heading. They were about three blocks from the road that led out of the city. Wherever they were intending to go, Kamal had no doubt that they wouldn't reach it. The people tracking them would undoubtedly intercept them before they went too far.

He needed to be there when they did.

The car in front of him slowed as it reached an intersection with a traffic light that turned red. Crushing the horn with his palm, Kamal swerved around it and streaked through the crossing, narrowly avoiding a crowded bus—and, as he did, he heard a siren in the distance, coming from his left, a police car that must have been crossing the next intersection at roughly the same time. That gave him an idea. He pushed ahead, eyes peeled for the next left turning, then dived into it when he spotted it. He blew up the narrow street, emerging on to a parallel avenue to the one he had been on. Up ahead, he could see his target's white strobe lights. Just as the siren was different from that used by the police, so too were the blue and red spinning lights.

It was a Hafiye car, a big matte-black Kartal SUV. It had to be chasing after Ramazan and Nisreen.

The realization lit an even bigger fuse inside Kamal as he pushed ahead more aggressively and muscled his way through the sea of cars until he was right on the Hafiye vehicle's tail.

Then he hit the redial button on his phone, scrolled back one number, and pressed it.

'How did they find us?' Ramazan burst out in a mad panic.

The realization struck Nisreen instantly. 'The phones. The damn phones. They must be tracking them.'

Ramazan floored the accelerator and sped on.

'Ramazan, what are you doing?' Nisreen yelled. 'Stop the car.'

Ramazan didn't reply. His attention was focused on staying ahead of the Zaptiye cruiser two car lengths behind them.

'Ramazan!' Nisreen yelled.

'Let me think,' he shot back, his eyes locked dead ahead, his face and forehead speckled with droplets of sweat.

'Anneh,' Tarek asked meekly from the back.

'Ramazan, please,' Nisreen insisted as she reached back and took hold of the outstretched hands of both children to comfort them—then her phone rang. It showed Kamal. She jabbed the screen to take the call.

'Kamal—'

'Where are you?'

She looked around frantically. 'I don't know, but they're after us. There's a police car right behind us.'

Kamal could hear the siren wailing in the background, behind Nisreen's breathless voice.

It was a police car, not a Hafiye vehicle. Which was maybe better, although he didn't think it would make much of a difference. There were undoubtedly some Hafiye cars converging on them, ones that would reach them before he did.

'I'm almost there,' he told her. 'But you need to stop the car before somebody gets hurt.'

'He won't listen.'

'Tell him I'm saying he should pull over. Tell him,' Kamal insisted.

'Ramazan, please—Kamal says we should stop. He's coming,' he heard her say.

He heard Ramazan rasp, 'Can he guarantee our safety?'

'What?' Kamal said.

'Ask him, can he guarantee we'll be safe?' Ramazan repeated, the visceral desperation in his voice coming through loud and clear.

'What's he talking about?' Kamal blurted as he floored the accelerator to stay in the slipstream of the unmarked department car in front of him. 'Nisreen. What's he talking about? Of course I can keep you safe, but what is going on?'

She didn't answer—then he heard a Hafiye siren barge into earshot, heard her shout, 'No,' heard a deafening metallic crunch, then another, in quick succession, heard muffled thuds that sounded like the phone bouncing around the car's interior, heard the kids shriek, heard a shrill, terrified scream of 'Ramazan!' from Nisreen, heard him yelling back 'Hang on,' with equal terror, then the piercing screech of rubber biting into tarmac right before a crashing sound and all going quiet.

'Nisreen? Nisreen!' he yelled into his phone.

No answer.

Then he heard frenzied, half-muffled sounds—of car doors opening, of movement, of 'Nos' and pleas to be left alone. It all happened very quickly and with brutal intensity. Then all was silent.

'Bok,' he barked as he hammered the steering wheel angrily with his hand.

He darted a look at his screen, flipping it back to the map. The red dot wasn't moving. They were stationary, six or seven blocks away. Not that far—only the traffic ahead of him was now getting heavier and slowing down, possibly because of whatever had happened to Nisreen and Ramazan's car.

Kamal's pulse was thundering in his ears. Every neuron in his body was focused on moving him forwards faster, desperate to get to them, desperate to know that they were okay, that a disaster hadn't happened. But the traffic was definitely getting snarled up, the patchwork of cars getting more dense and filling up every available inch of road, a gradual strangulation of forward momentum until any movement died out altogether and the road turned into a frozen sea of cars, trucks, vans and buses.

Kamal couldn't wait, couldn't sit still, couldn't remain a hostage to pressing down on his horn and shouting out his window. He swore aloud as he flung the car door open and charged ahead, zigzagging through the maze of vehicles, his legs propelling him as fast as they could, his lungs sucking in and burning every molecule of oxygen they could grab hold of, his mind trying to ward off the frightening images being kicked up. Before long, he could see a carnival show of swirling lights up ahead: red and blue and white, flashing out of sync and lighting up the buildings around them. He kept moving as fast as he could until he reached the epicentre of the chaotic scene, which was Ramazan's family car. It appeared to have been squeezed in, rammed and forced to stop between an unmarked sedan to its left and a police cruiser to its right. Kamal could already make out a major dent in its left driver's-side bumper along with nasty scrapes down the sides of both doors. The car that had rammed it had extensive damage to its front right bumper and its side. Ramazan's car's other flank and the police car alongside it had to be as badly damaged, but from where Kamal was standing, he couldn't see how badly they'd come together.

What he could see was that none of them was anywhere near the car: not Ramazan, not Nisreen, not the children. There was a small gaggle of cops at the scene, two of whom were directing traffic down a narrow alley to the far left of the wide boulevard, away from the crashed cars. There were two Hafiye agents, too, along with two others from the car Kamal had been chasing, who had decided to follow him on foot and were now coming up behind him.

Kamal zeroed in on the Hafiye agents, pulling out his badge as he caught up with them. 'The people in that car,' he blurted as he pointed at Ramazan's car. 'The family that was in it. Where are they?'

'They're in custody,' one of them answered, calm and proud. 'We've got them.'

'Who's got them? Where are they?' Kamal rasped.

His fury seemed to take the agent aback. He gave Kamal a confused, dubious look. Then he said, 'They just drove them away. Calm down, will you? We've got them.'

'So they're okay? No one got hurt?'

'They're fine, brother. They're fine.'

Kamal stared at him angrily, still processing it all. Then he nodded and walked away, deep in thought while instinctively drawn to the battered car.

He peered in through the driver's window. There was nothing to see—just the mundane interior of a reasonably tidy family car, one that had undoubtedly hosted many happy occasions but now lay battered and cowed. He glanced at the back seat, at the unbuckled car seats, then at the front passenger seat, where Nisreen would have been sitting, all the while reliving in his mind's eye the scene he had heard: the fear, the desperation, the terror.

Then something snagged his attention. Something small, the edge of something, poking out from under Nisreen's seat. He walked around the car and pulled the passenger door open. It wasn't damaged like the driver's door and opened smoothly. Kamal bent down, reached in, and retrieved what he had seen. It was a mobile phone. Nisreen's phone. He recognized the tan leather protective case she kept it in. Mentally replaying what he'd heard, he realized the phone had fallen out of Nisreen's hand when the authorities had driven into the car.

He glanced around to make sure that no one was looking, then slipped the phone into his pocket, his trained fingers pulling its battery out quickly before he walked away, his entire consciousness focused on one thing and one thing only.

Finding them.

36

The small room was a nightmare in grey: covering the walls, doors, floors and ceilings was the same austere, cruel hue in a shiny vinyl finish that seemed chosen as much for its grimness as for its ease in allowing compromising stains to be wiped away. Even the furniture was grey, only in a dull hue— a large metal table bolted to the floor, a heavily scratched cuff bar running along its centre, and four metal chairs. Apart from the door, the walls were bare, save for a wide mirrored partition that covered most of one wall.

Nisreen and Ramazan were seated at the table. No words were exchanged. They just sat there, equally frightened, equally in shock by all that had happened. But mostly they were equally fearful of where their children were, for they weren't in the room with them. They'd been brought in there almost an hour earlier, alone, and their insistent, desperate queries about their children went unanswered; then they'd been left to stew alone in the grey bunker.

They weren't alone any more. A man was now facing them across the table. He was tall, slim and had deep-set, vivid eyes and a jutting chin that seemed threatening in itself. He'd introduced himself as Huseyin Celaleddin Pasha, the *bashafiye*, even though he needed no introduction. His being there in person hadn't instilled any comfort in Nisreen or in Ramazan. Quite the opposite.

Another man stood by the door. He was squat and round and sported a distinctive ink-black trapezoidal goatee. He wasn't dressed in a guard's uniform; instead, he also projected an air of seniority, although not as chillingly prepossessing as that of the *bashafiye*.

'Where are our children?' Nisreen asked again. Her first attempt had been brushed off and replaced by the introduction.

'They're fine,' Celaleddin answered. 'And I can assure you they're being well looked after.'

'Looked after?' Nisreen fired back angrily. 'They're children, for God's sake. They must be absolutely terrified. You have to let us see them.'

'Why not? Let's have a look, shall we?'

He turned to the man by the door and gave him a nod. The man pulled a small remote control from his pocket and pressed a button on it.

The large mirror turned into a clear glass partition, revealing a similar room to the one Nisreen and Ramazan were in.

The room was also morbidly grey and furnished similarly. Tarek and Noor were sitting at a table with ice-cream bowls and a plate of honey-and-pistachio delicacies. The children seemed calm as they sipped from cups through white plastic straws, their attention spirited away by whatever they were playing or watching on the screens of the tablet computers they each held.

Behind them stood a woman. She was dressed in civilian clothes and was watching over them in silence, her arms folded. Her expression was trying to be neutral, but Nisreen could see the menace simmering behind her eyes.

Nisreen couldn't contain herself. She bolted out of her seat and rushed up to the glass partition, rapping it hard with the flat palms of her hands while failing to hold back a burst of tears.

'Tarek, Noor!' she screamed, but there was no reaction from the other side of the glass. She was now right up against it, her hands stilled, her fingers spread out as she pressed against it in a desperate, futile attempt to get even nearer to them. 'Tarek . . . Noor . . .' she moaned. 'My babies.'

No reaction.

They evidently couldn't hear or see her.

'It's one-way glass and totally soundproof,' Celaleddin informed them. 'But as you can see, they're fine. And they'll stay fine as long as you answer my questions fully and truthfully.'

'What questions?' Ramazan said, his voice quivering. 'Why are we here?'

'You know why you're here. And I want to hear it all, every bit of it. Every detail, every word. Start from the beginning and don't leave anything out. And I beg you to take extra care and make sure you tell me everything. Because if I feel you're holding back, I'll have to instruct my assistant in there to behave less pleasantly.'

He stared at them for a moment, making sure his words implanted themselves firmly. Then he turned to the man by the door and gave him another small nod.

The man raised a small radio to his mouth and mumbled something indecipherable into it.

With Nisreen still standing at the edge of the glass partition, Ramazan turned to face it too, both of them overcome by a crippling dread.

The woman standing behind the children unfolded her arms, reached behind her back and drew out a large knife. It had a smooth, wide blade which shone as it caught a glint of light when she tilted it slightly and held it up, out of view of the children, who were still mesmerized by their screens. Not content with the debilitating effect it already had, she then ran two teasing fingers along the edge of its blade.

A funereal silence suffocated the room.

'She's very skilled,' Celaleddin said. 'Her particular talent is knowing how to make sure things last as long as necessary.'

Nisreen's shoulders hunched, then she turned to face their interrogator. A hatred like she'd never felt before swelled up inside her. 'You're a monster,' she said coldly, her voice trembling.

'Perhaps,' he shrugged with chilling nonchalance. 'But I have to do whatever is necessary to protect the realm, and I need you to believe it. But it doesn't need to come to that. I just need to know what happened in that hospital ward. And the sooner you tell me, the sooner we can all get out of this dreadful place.'

He sat back and spread out his hands. 'Who wants to go first?'

Above ground at the Citadel, Kamal felt like a caged animal in his own way.

Questioning the duty officer at the main reception had yielded nothing: there was no record of Ramazan's or Nisreen's arrest. Over in the operations room, the desk sergeant had claimed he had no record of the team that had been dispatched after them. Kamal had then gone down to the holding cells and interview-room area and asked the duty officer if he knew anything. Again, he got nothing. With no options left, he'd decided to escalate the matter to the Z Directorate boss, but he was told that Fehmi Kuzey had already left the building for the night. Kamal left a message saying he needed to speak with him urgently. After much debate, he decided to take the big step of going to see the *bashafiye,* but he was told in no uncertain terms that the head of the Hafiye wasn't at the Citadel either.

He was being stonewalled—of this he had no doubt.

Celaleddin had been clear in his warning about Nisreen, but something else was at play here, clearly. Something bigger, something that involved Ramazan, too. Something big enough to warrant shutting him out, an act that, Kamal knew, meant his brother and sister-in-law were in serious trouble.

Standing outside the entrance to the fortress, which was now engulfed by the shadows of nightfall, he felt hobbled by equal doses of fury, frustration and worry, but he couldn't give up. He needed to find a crack in the system, a way to find them.

He was racking his brain when his phone rang. Hope sparked, then fizzled just as fast when he saw it was only Taymoor.

'Where are you?' his partner asked. 'What's going on?'

Kamal hesitated. 'I'm—there's something I need to take care of.'

'What?'

'A problem. Family business.'

Taymoor went silent for a couple of seconds. 'Anything I can do?'

Kamal hesitated again. If he was going to ask for Taymoor's help, now was the time to do it. Then again, until he knew what was happening, he thought it might be safer for everyone if he kept things to himself. 'Better you don't get involved,' he finally said.

Taymoor sounded affronted. 'I'm your partner, brother. We're a team.'

'I know. And I appreciate it. Look, it could be nothing,' he lied.

'It doesn't sound like nothing.'

Kamal shrugged—then an idea elbowed its way out of the gloom that had enshrouded him. 'I wish I could disagree with you. I've got to go.'

Before Taymoor could object, he clicked off.

He marched back to the operations room. The desk sergeant frowned as he spotted him, clearly not relishing another stubborn interrogation. Kamal read him and tried to adopt a less belligerent tone.

'I was at the Hurrem Sultan earlier, after the shooting. I spoke to the two agents who were there when it happened, and I need to follow up on something with them, but in the whole mess I didn't note down their names. Could you check on who they were?'

The desk sergeant eyed him guardedly, then relented and tapped a few computer keys. 'Terrible thing that happened.'

'A bad, bad day,' Kamal agreed, laying on the empathy.

'I've got Marwan Jamal and Omar Salamoun,' the sergeant said.

'Do you know where I can find them? I imagine they've got a pretty monstrous debriefing to go through.'

'I haven't seen them all day.'

This surprised Kamal. He feigned a different kind of frustration, a purely professional one. 'Damn it. I really need to talk to them.'

'I can send them an alert to contact you.'

'Great. Would you let me know when they respond to it?'

'Will do, but given the day they've had, I wouldn't hold my breath'—said with a shrug that didn't exactly fill Kamal with hope.

He returned the shrug and walked off, heading for the exit.

There was nothing more he could think of. All avenues of inquiry seemed barred. As much as it killed him to sit on his hands, there was no point sticking around the Citadel. He could only wait for Kuzey or one of the agents from the hospital to call—not that he held out much hope of that. He'd try to come up with some other way to find his brother and

Nisreen, and if all else failed, he'd march up to Celaleddin's office in the morning and demand to see his brother.

He was digging a hand into his pocket to retrieve his motorbike's keys when his fingers fell on something else: Nisreen's phone. He pulled it out and stared at it, debating whether to fire it up, which would activate its tracker. He thought about the risks involved. He was still by the Citadel. If they were aware that they'd missed taking it, if they were looking for it, seeing it light up at the Hafiye headquarters was probably as good a place as any to have it appear. They might conclude that it was sitting innocuously in an agency car or tucked away in an evidence box somewhere in the department, waiting to be claimed by the agents working the case. Firing it up would not necessarily be a great help in discovering what happened to them. The phone was probably locked with a passcode that he had little chance of figuring out.

He decided to try anyway. He put the battery back in and switched the phone on. The screen went through its motions, then lit up with a picture of Tarek and Noor, smiling half mischievously into the camera. He lingered on it for a long moment, staring at their little faces, the picture awakening a painful reminder of all the good times he must have missed out on since he and his brother's family had drifted apart, times he'd never get back. He wondered if things would ever return to the way they were. Right now, he'd more than settle with just knowing they were all safe and well.

He thought about what numbers to key in and felt embarrassed at how much he had to concentrate to remember the children's birthdays. Still, he managed it and made a few attempts using various combinations of the dates, which he knew wouldn't work. Sure enough, they didn't. Nisreen was too clever to use something so easy to crack. He decided to give up for now, pulling out the battery and pocketing it again.

He headed for his bike, trying to rein in his fears and convince himself that nothing disastrous would happen that first night. It might all be cleared up by the morning, and maybe he'd wake up to find out everything was back to normal.

That hopeful notion lasted all of three seconds before his instincts and experience booted it to oblivion.

Something very bad was going down, and right now he was helpless to stop it.

37

Sitting on the edge of the thin mattress in the windowless cell, Nisreen was struggling to stay awake.

She was beyond exhausted. More than her body, it was her mind that was spiralling towards a total shutdown. The events of the last forty-eight hours alone would have depleted the hardiest of souls. The way they'd ended had demolished her. Being locked up in this muggy, desolate cell without her children, not being able to comfort them and not knowing where they were, or who they were with, was like a slow-coursing poison that was killing her off, cell by cell.

Facing her on the other bed in the small room was Ramazan. He was hunched over, cradling his head in his hands, silent and shivering. They'd said all that needed to be said. All they could do now was wait—and hope.

Paralysed by worry and without much else to contemplate, she found herself replaying the last couple days' events over and over in her mind's eye, reliving each step, haunted by regret at having allowed herself to be swept up by that irresistible lure. She chided herself for not resisting. She should have known that digging into Rasheed's secret was terribly dangerous territory, and she should have pulled away before it sucked her and Ramazan in and destroyed them. Because Nisreen was under no illusion what the inevitable outcome of all this was: destruction. Annihilation. She and Ramazan would never be allowed to walk out of there with that secret. Their fate was sealed. As was—she trembled—the fate of the children.

For a few delirious, hopeful seconds, she'd wondered if her disastrous foray into the world of the incantation might have a silver lining, if it might present an escape. She'd spent so much time researching it that she thought she might have memorized it, but she couldn't be sure. It was long, and in a completely foreign language, and her notebook was now in her captors' hands. Still, she imagined them all using it to travel back to a safer time, to a place where no one would know them or threaten them. She thought she would have risked using it, too, if Tarek and Noor were with them, but they weren't, which made any notion of escape impossible. It was also probably why their captors were still keeping them apart.

She would have preferred to keep it from them, to hang on to it as a guarantee of her and Ramazan's continued usefulness, to use it as their life preserver, however temporary. But she hadn't been able to. Not even close. Not when her children were in the hands of those murderous brutes. Not when they were locked in a room with someone who had been proudly introduced as a psychotic butcher.

Another inkling of hope arose from the pit of despair into which she had sunk.

She thought of Kamal.

She imagined him out there searching for them, fighting to get to them. Despite everything, something she sensed in him when he appeared at the children's bus stop the day before made her think he would. And as she slid back against the wall and curled into a ball, her arms tight around her knees in an effort to block the tremors that were rocking her, she held on to that thought for as long as she could.

Alone in his vast office, Huseyin Celaleddin Pasha had some major decisions to make.

He was standing at the picture window, looking out, lost in thought, his mind cosseted by the narcotic array of spotlit turrets, minarets and domes that spread out before him and shimmered in the torrid humidity of the night.

He couldn't remember the last time he'd been as consumed by a troubling situation. There had been crises of late, to be sure. The empire had been enduring some rocky times, and, as the head of the secret police, he had been at the epicentre of most of them. But this crisis had the potential to dwarf them all. If what he'd heard in that interview room was true, it was nothing less than a full-blown existential threat to the empire, one that could, at the whisper of a few words by the wrong person, lead to its being wiped off the pages of history.

The threat had a less monumental, less earth-shattering aspect to it that was no less dangerous. It had to do with the very being of the empire. The empire's core religious tenet was the surrender to the will of God. This submission was the definition of its name, and the sultan, as caliph, was the defender of that faith. But if what Celaleddin had heard was true, it would mean that the empire's glorious conquests weren't due to the will of God. They weren't part of a divine plan. Instead, they were simply the result of the machinations of one man, the ruse of a cunning time traveller, the ploy of a trickster. They were a cheat of history, and that revelation, if it were ever to come out, could cause an upheaval that might be impossible to contain.

Either way, the risks—of someone travelling into the past to undo what had been achieved or of the truth about how the empire had steamrolled its way across Europe coming out—were too great to ignore. This threat needed to be wiped out quickly, absolutely and permanently.

He knew the anaesthetist and his wife had told him the

truth, the whole truth. He'd witnessed their terrorized reaction to the threat facing their children, and he had enough experience with prisoners to know that there was no chance they had held anything back. They had told him everything.

Which made them disposable.

There was no room for anything less than extreme prejudice towards anyone who had been exposed to it, and it had to be done now.

Tonight.

Everything—his entire world—depended on it.

38

Kamal was never the heaviest of sleepers.

And given his state of mind, given the hurricane that was whipping through him tonight, he hadn't even dipped a toe into the shallow end of sleep. Which was why he bolted upright at the barely audible clicks of someone tampering with the lock to his front door the instant they began.

Stark naked, he sprang out of bed, quietly, but he was already too late. He heard the telltale sound of the last pin falling into place and the pained squeal of the door opening before he could make it into the living room. Which posed a problem for two reasons.

One, he would have preferred to benefit from the element of surprise. The intruders—assuming there was more than one—were professionals, to be sure. His lock had way more self-respect than to allow itself to be defiled so easily by anything less. Surprise would have been useful.

Two, his gun was in the front hall, by the door. Which meant he was confined to the bedroom area and naked in both senses of the word. Hardly ideal from a tactical point of view, but there was little use stewing over it.

He slipped back to the bed and quickly arranged his bedding to make it look like he was still curled up under the covers. Then he slinked across to the bedroom door and took up position behind it.

There was nothing within reach that he could use as a weapon. He would have to rely on his bare hands.

He heard stealthy footfalls approaching. More than one

intruder, he was certain, but perhaps no more than two. No words were exchanged. Just a slow, cautious advance into the apartment, with second-long pauses to take stock of their surroundings. Kamal couldn't see any shadows from flashlight beams dancing across the darkened walls either. The pale glow of the city lights was probably enough to guide them. Otherwise they were using night-vision goggles.

Not that it mattered.

They had reached his bedroom door.

His body coiled tight, readying itself to lash out, and he held his breath as he watched intently through the crack between the door and the wall. Blackened silhouettes were gliding forward slowly, in absolute silence, barely discernible from their dark surroundings. He could see two of them. One mere inches away from him, on the other side of the door crack; the other now coming through the door.

Led by the noise suppressor of a handgun.

He went iron-rigid.

He needed them both inside the room before he could act.

One interminable, torturous second after another, waiting, holding back, watching as the lead ghost inched towards the bed and keeping an eye on the position of the second ghost, who finally stepped forward and was now directly on the other side of the door from Kamal.

Perfect.

Kamal unleashed all the pent-up strength in his body at the door, flinging it at the man behind it with all the fury he could muster. It slammed into him like a battering ram, its thunderous punch catching him unawares. He let out a loud grunt as he flew sideways and crashed against the wall.

Kamal knew he had a split-second advantage and didn't even pause to check on the result of his ambush. He was already launching himself on the lead man, whom Kamal reached just as the man spun around and half faced him. Both of Kamal's hands had their individual missions: his left hand rocketed forward at the gun, clasping the intruder's wrist and pushing it away before the man could fire, while his left hand was already balled tight and slicing the air in a beeline for the man's face.

He was partly successful. He managed to push the gun out of contention, but in the darkness and the frenzy, his strike landed slightly off-target and slid off the edge of the intruder's chin. The man recoiled and retaliated with a ferocious knee kick that caught Kamal in the gut. Kamal felt the air explode out of his lungs as he doubled over, and from the edge of perception he heard movement behind him, a hissed curse, a slither of fabric, legs clambering back to life, shoes finding purchase. He needed to move fast—he was a second or two away from having two of them to deal with.

He spun around counter-clockwise and raised his left arm, cocking his elbow as he rammed it backwards and slammed it into the head of the lead intruder, who was now behind him. This time, the strike landed on target and caused the man to falter enough for his grip on his gun to loosen. Kamal grabbed the man's gun hand with both of his, aimed the weapon at the second intruder, who was charging right at him, inches from reach, and pushed against the trigger repeatedly. The gun belched out four silenced rounds that brought the man rag-dolling down to the ground and crumpling messily at Kamal's feet. Not that Kamal was taking note. He was already spinning around again, this time clockwise, pushing the gun away while ramming his balled fist backwards into the centre of the first intruder's face, driving the back of his hand hard into the man's nose. Cartilage, bone and tissue exploded in a bloody mess as the man lost his footing and tumbled to the ground.

Kamal yanked the gun out of his hand, then grabbed the man by the neck and threw him back against the wall by the side of the bed. Without taking his eyes off him, he reached across and hit the bedside light switch.

The man had puffy eyes and was cradling his nose with both hands. Blood streamed through his fingers and down his clothes.

Kamal turned to check on the other intruder. The man evidently wasn't going to pose a threat, not to anyone, ever. Kamal turned back to his captive and yanked his head back by his hair to take a closer look at him. He didn't recognize him.

'Who the hell are you, and what are you doing here?'

Dazed eyes greeted Kamal's question. Then the daze turned into an angry glare. Kamal rebutted it with a hard swing of the gun to the man's left temple, which snapped his head sideways and caused him to grunt heavily from the added pain.

'Answer my questions,' Kamal insisted. 'Who sent you?'

The man spat out some blood as he straightened up, but he remained silent, a scowl of contempt burning the air between them.

Kamal reached out with his left hand and clasped his fingers tightly against the intruder's neck, pinning him in place and partly choking him. Then he moved his gun hand down so that it was now vertical, with the noise suppressor pressed downwards against the man's left knee.

'I won't ask again. And you'll never walk right again. Your choice.'

No answer.

Kamal squeezed the trigger.

The man screamed out and convulsed as the insides of his knee exploded outwards and a volcano of pain erupted across his body.

Kamal held the man firmly in his grip, keeping his head upright, forcing him to maintain eye contact. The man was writhing with pain, shaking his head violently left and right.

Kamal brought the gun back up so it was now inches from the man's mouth.

'I'm not going to kill you. But I'll make sure you won't ever be able to so much as take a piss again without needing someone's help. So I'll ask again. Who are you? Who sent you?'

The man was barely conscious. He was shaking violently, and rivulets of sweat were running down his face and mixing in with the mess of blood and spittle around his mouth.

Kamal moved the gun pointedly away from the man's face and brought it down to his other leg when the man broke.

'Don't,' he muttered. 'Don't.'

Kamal stopped, studied him, then brought the gun back so it rested against the man's gut. 'Talk.'

The man spat out another big glob of blood. 'I'm Z Directorate.' He was glaring at Kamal as he said it, his eyes narrow and hard.

The intruder's words were like a spear through Kamal's gut. 'Why did they send you? Why do they want me dead?'

'We weren't here to kill you. We were ordered to take you away.'

Kamal couldn't make sense of this. 'Why?'

The man cleared his throat. It looked painful. 'I don't know.'

'Let me guess. They think I'm White Rose, too?'

A mocking snort managed to break through the man's tortured face. Which Kamal caught—and didn't understand.

'What?' Kamal barked.

The man didn't respond, but the hint of a taunt was definitely there.

Kamal slapped it off his face. 'What?'

The man swallowed something hard, and then, almost as if gaining strength from Kamal's frustration, he looked at him with clear contempt. 'You have no idea, do you?'

Kamal shoved the gun harder against the man's gut, making him wince. 'I'm about to.'

The contempt turned to a self-satisfied sneer. It looked like what he was holding back was giving him a last, desperate grasp at the upper hand. 'There is no White Rose, you fool.'

Kamal's breath seized. 'What?'

The man eyed him with visible gratification. 'We made it up. The whole thing. And you, all of you . . . you just lapped it up.' He snorted again, a spatter of blood spilling down his lower lip.

Kamal felt his guts cave in as his mind furiously processed what that meant. The immediate avatars that Kamal couldn't duck were names that charged back into his consciousness: the professor, Azmi, and the playwright, Sinasi. And, obviously, Nisreen.

You need to wake up, Kamal.

A sudden urgency about her flooded through him.

'My brother, Ramazan Hekim. His wife, Nisreen. You have them, don't you?'

The man didn't reply. He looked as if he was enjoying the power shift.

Kamal pressed the gun against his surviving knee. 'I won't ask again.'

The power shift evaporated. 'I don't know,' the man blurted grudgingly. 'I don't know anything about them.'

Kamal thought fast. 'Where were you supposed to take me? Back to the Citadel?'

The man shook his head.

'Where then?'

The man went mute. Kamal pressed the gun harder. 'Where?'

'Out of the city. A place in the Chevreuse Forest. The Madeleine Castle.'

Kamal had never heard of it. 'What's out there?'

The man clammed up.

'What's out there?'

'Nothing . . . It's just some old ruins. In the middle of the forest.'

'So why there?'

The man hesitated, then said, 'It's where we take people sometimes.'

Where they take people?

Kamal felt the spear twist deeper.

'So what was the plan? To kill me there?'

'No. Our orders were just to take you there. Nothing else. I swear.'

'So someone was meeting you there?'

The man nodded.

'Who?'

'I don't know.'

Kamal accepted it. The man was under too much duress to be lying to him. Which meant he might even answer the next question without losing another limb.

'Who ordered it?' He had to ask, even though he already knew the answer.

A new level of fear lit up the man's eyes.

Kamal returned a look of cold inevitability as he moved the gun to the man's groin.

He didn't even have to ask again.

'Kuzey Pasha,' the maimed intruder winced.

Kamal felt any remnant of colour drain from his face.

There it was. Confirmation. Fehmi Kuzey. Celaleddin's top lieutenant, the head of the Z Directorate.

Why?

There was one way to find out.

'Where is this place?'

'West of the city. Beyond Versailles. I can show you. It's on my phone.'

Kamal pressed the gun against the man's groin while he rummaged through his pockets. 'Don't try anything.'

He pulled out his phone.

Through badly shaking fingers, the man was able to pull up a map page that showed a forest on the outskirts of Paris, west and slightly south of Versailles. A red pin marked a spot inside its eastern perimeter.

'Okay.'

Kamal took the phone from him. Then he raised the gun and swung it down, hard, across the man's head. The man thudded against the floor and didn't move any more.

Kamal acted fast. He tied the man up, found the intruders' car keys, and relieved both of guns and badges. He then got dressed.

He flew down the stairs, two steps at a time. He was slipping across the landing one floor down when, from the corner of his eye, he noticed that the door to the apartment below his was open a crack, a hint of light from inside breaking out from behind a dark silhouette and a furtive eye that was peeping through the crack. Kamal knew who it belonged to: his neighbour, a successful restaurant owner. Kamal stopped and approached the door.

The restaurateur pulled the door a bit wider. He looked scared.

'I heard noise,' he told Kamal, a shake in his voice. 'I was going to call the—'

'It's all under control,' Kamal said calmly. 'You don't need to worry about it. Go back to bed.'

'Are you sure?'

'Absolutely. Go back to bed. I'm sorry it woke you. We have it under control.' Emphasis on the 'we'. He gave him a firm, reassuring nod.

Time was pressing. He was wasting precious seconds.

His neighbour nodded hesitantly, then slipped back into the darkness.

Kamal didn't wait for him to close the door.

He was soon blasting across the dark, deserted streets in the intruders' unmarked sedan, headed towards the red pin on their map, his heart jackhammering in his chest as he wondered who he would find there and whether he'd manage to get there before it was too late.

39

Dawn was still far off when the medieval castle appeared in the distance, a skulking mass that occupied a small hill and ruled over a sea of blackness. It would have been invisible but for the big, gibbous moon that made its silhouette stand out against the backlit sky and gave it an ethereal shimmer that belied the grim reality of what Kamal had been told it was being used for.

He dimmed the lights of the car as he entered the forest. The smooth asphalt of the main road gave way to a rough, unpaved track that wove its way through dense woodland of beech and oak. The rough, uninhabited landscape didn't seem like it had changed much since the days when it hosted the main pilgrimage and trade route between Paris and Chartres. Then, a couple of *fersahs* later, the ruins of the castle came into view: two squat, round towers, one topped by a turret; a taller, box-like keep that was missing most of its slanted roof; and a fortified wall, big chunks of its crenellated ramparts having long since crumbled away like missing teeth. As Kamal had picked up when running a quick, frantic search of his target, it had been a bustling and highly lucrative tollbooth for pilgrims and traders criss-crossing the land. No one seemed to be beating a path to its gatehouse any more. Those who did, Kamal suspected, never left.

With the car's lights switched off completely, he guided the car by the light of the moon, gliding slowly through the thick forest until he could see the castle walls looming up ahead. Keeping a safe distance away, he stopped, backed the car into a small clearing, and killed the engine.

He opened the glove compartment and took out the standard-issue flashlight, which he checked with a quick flick while covering its lens. Then he drew his handgun, slid the safety off and climbed out.

He advanced towards the castle.

Around him, all was deathly still, but Kamal knew that kind of forest well enough to know it was anything but lifeless. Deer and wild boar would be roaming abundantly. A horrific thought reared up inside him, of bodies left out for the animals to feed on. The forest was huge and remote, an ideal place to get rid of meddlers and troublemakers—one of which he had unwittingly become.

He reached the castle walls. The moat around the fortifications was dry and overgrowing with ferns and shrubbery, but the old wooden bridge that spanned it was still standing. He crossed it cautiously, making sure his footsteps didn't generate any sounds that might alert whoever was inside to his approach.

The inner courtyard was still. No one around, no lights on anywhere. It looked long abandoned, except for the black Kartal SUV—standard issue at the Hafiye—parked outside the entrance to the keep. At least it was on its own. He hoped that meant he wouldn't have too many men to deal with.

Panning his gun left and right in slow sweeps, he was moving cautiously across the courtyard towards the keep's entrance when a scream sliced through the stillness. A woman's angry, pleading scream of 'No!' coming from his left, echoing out from inside a block-like tower that had a single door and no windows.

Nisreen.

He was sure of it.

He had never heard her scream like that, but he was dead certain that it was her.

The sound exploded inside his head, and he bolted towards it instantly, sprinting across the open space as fast as he could.

He burst through the doorway to the tower and immediately spotted a faint light coming from an opening to the right, down a narrow passageway, just as she yelled again. He then heard what sounded like a savage slap, followed by a man's voice cursing loudly and the sound of cloth being ripped apart. Kamal wanted to yell out for her, wanted desperately to shout out to let her know he was there, but he held back as he flew down the passage, his pulse kicking loudly in his ears.

He charged into the room at full pace. His eyes had a split second to register what they saw: Nisreen, on the ground, half naked, straddled across the knees by a man whose face Kamal couldn't see, the whole ghastly scene illuminated by the faint light of a gas lantern. The man had both of Nisreen's wrists clasped in his left hand while his right hand was pulling down his trousers.

'Stop moving, you bitch,' the man raged, 'or I swear I'll—'

He didn't finish his sentence, nor did he even register an intruder before Kamal ploughed into him, hard, shoving him off Nisreen before pummelling his head ferociously with the butt of his gun until the man was still and virtually unrecognizable.

He turned to Nisreen and scampered over to her. She was sobbing in between sharp breaths, her shaky fingers pulling up the edges of shredded clothing to cover her exposed body.

Kamal took her in his arms and hugged her tightly. 'You're okay, Nisreen. You're okay.'

She went limp for no more than a second, then a frantic urgency swept across her, and she pushed him back. Her face was drawn in abject terror.

'Ramazan, the children,' she gasped, a desperate, pained whimper in her voice. 'They're here. They've got them.'

'Where?'

'I don't know. They put hoods over our heads. But they're here. They brought us all here.'

A sudden dread gripped him so fiercely he could barely draw breath.

'Stay here,' he ordered her as he scrambled out of the room.

He ran as fast as he could, down the hallway, out into the courtyard, towards the parked SUV and the entrance to the keep, a short distance that felt endless, his body at full stretch, his mind trying and failing to push away worst-case scenarios, horrific thoughts, pressure mounting in his chest and choking him, hoping against hope that he'd get there in time, that he wasn't too late, and just as he cleared the back of the SUV and reached the door to the keep, a figure appeared in the doorway, moving casually, heading out.

The man froze at the sight of Kamal hurtling towards him. The dim moonlight masked the man's features, but there was enough of it to expose his arm reaching for his weapon.

Kamal didn't hesitate and pumped three rounds into his chest at full stride.

The man thudded to the ground just outside the doorway.

Kamal slowed and moved forwards cautiously, his weapon levelled ahead, his senses on high alert for any other threat.

He heard nothing at first. A portentous stillness crushed the entire hill. Then, at the edge of perception, he heard hesitant, weary footfalls behind him. He turned. Nisreen had followed him out and was now crossing the courtyard, moving slowly.

He swivelled his gaze towards the darkened doorway to the keep in front of him, his senses tingling, then back at her.

'Stop.'

She kept walking.

'Nisreen. Listen to me. Stop.'

Her pace slowed. Then she stopped moving.

He looked at her, his hand half-raised, softly, in a stilling gesture.

'Wait here. Please.'

She stared at him blankly. He met her gaze, tried to telegraph something reassuring, something that more words couldn't convey, but couldn't come up with anything besides another 'Please.'

She returned a small, dazed nod.

He turned away, stepped over the fallen man and entered the keep.

The doorway led to a small low-ceiling foyer that had two door openings leading deeper into the keep, one to the left and the other to the right.

There was some faint light coming from the door to his left.

It drew him in.

The room, vast and high-ceilinged, was lit by another gas lantern. A monumental stone fireplace dominated the far wall, but otherwise the room was devoid of any kind of furnishing; but that wasn't what Kamal first noticed.

It was the barely illuminated human-shaped mounds lying on the floor by the wall to his right.

He felt his insides hollow out, felt his legs about to give, but he managed to remain upright and, inch by inch, crept towards them.

There were three figures. One of them was adult-sized, male judging by his clothing.

The other two were smaller.

Children.

Their heads were shrouded by black hoods.

None of them were moving.

His legs ignored the crippling fear that had engulfed him and kept him advancing, trance-like, until he reached them.

He bent down by one of the smaller bodies. He set the gun down on the floor and watched his arm lengthen, watched his trembling fingers reach out and touch the black hood covering the still figure's head.

Watched them pull it back, gently.

It was Tarek. Staring back at him with wide eyes, a look of eternal fear etched across his small features.

His neck was covered with dark bruises.

Kamal's eyes sheeted over with tears. He felt the inside of his mouth go sickeningly dry, felt his gut rushing up to his throat, but he managed to hold it back as he moved his fingers softly to the boy's neck and, delicately, desperately, searched for a sign of life that he knew he wouldn't find.

There was none.

Then a scream shattered the silence, a scream that Kamal would never forget—a hoarse, piercing wail that rose out of unimaginable pain and shredded the air of the cavernous room.

Kamal spun his gaze around.

Nisreen was by the door, staggering into the room, her hands raised, her fingers splayed wide, her eyes ablaze with horror, her mouth agape in a scream that was now silent.

'No,' Kamal rasped as he sprang to his feet and flew to her.

He caught her mid-step and swept her into his arms, blocking her advance, clasping her tightly against him while she fought him back and swatted him with desperate, weakening arms.

'Let me go,' she screamed, tears flooding her face. 'Let me go to—'

'No,' Kamal whispered, struggling to keep hold of her. 'No.'

'Let me go,' she sobbed.

Her body convulsed in his grip as she fought to free herself, her arms flailing against him, her legs kicking, her eyes drenched in tears, her mouth gasping between frenzied breaths and repeating 'No' over and over and over. Then the last vestiges of strength seeped away, and together they slid down to the cold stone floor, one of his arms still clamped tight around her, the other cradling the back of her head and pressing her into his chest while waves of pain crashed over them both.

They didn't move.

Not for minutes. Not for an hour, perhaps.

All sense of time and place just disappeared, swept away by a tsunami of anguish and sorrow.

Throughout, she kept repeating the same word: 'No'.

An eternity later, when her shaking had slowed and when her sobs had somewhat subsided, he finally, slowly pulled away. Softly, carefully, he released his grip, and without exchanging a word, he watched her rise up and stumble deeper into the room.

There, she knelt before the lifeless bodies and gently, hesitantly, she continued what he had begun.

40

They had been strangled.

All of them.

Ramazan, Tarek and Noor.

In a far corner of the chamber, Kamal found the bodies of two other men, whom he recognized: the two agents he'd spoken to outside the hospital, the ones who were part of the detail that got caught up in the shooting.

That was a question for later.

Right now, neither Kamal nor Nisreen gave a damn about them, about what they were doing there or why they'd been killed.

They had the inconceivable to process.

Interminable minutes stretched endlessly as they sat there, Nisreen cross-legged and hunched over on the cold stone floor, her head bowed as she rocked back and forth gently while hugging her dead children and nuzzling their heads. Kamal, close by on the floor, next to his brother's body, a helpless witness, listening to her barely audible whimpers and her supplications to God, staring at the back of her head, then off into nothingness, then back at her, then away again, numb, speechless, lost in what felt like a surreal out-of-body experience in a temple of pain from which he knew there was no escape.

His brother. His little nephew. His adored niece.

Three out of the handful of people who mattered most to him in the world—perhaps the only ones that mattered to him—were dead, brutally, savagely, barbarically murdered.

And the fourth was, like him, destroyed and suffering a pain without compare.

He was no stranger to death, no novice to people losing their lives to terrorism or to state-sanctioned executions. With each new death, he'd grown more immune to its brutal finality and gained strength and renewed resolve to do his best to stop the loss of innocent lives.

Any strength and immunity were vaporized at the sight of his dead loved ones, his insides obliterated and turned into a cold, barren wasteland.

It was Kamal who finally broke through the silence.

He didn't know how much time had passed, but as far as he could tell, it was still dark outside. Dawn, however, couldn't be too far off. Which meant his fury and his questions would have to wait. More urgent decisions needed to be made.

'We can't stay here,' he said softly. 'It's not safe.'

Nisreen didn't reply at first. She was still on the floor, hunched over while holding her dead children tight against her.

He shuffled over and, slowly, very hesitantly, reached out to place a hand on her shoulder.

She flinched and pulled away the instant it brushed her.

'Don't.' She spoke without turning to face him. 'Don't touch me.'

'Nisreen . . .'

She went silent for a few breaths.

'Did you know about this place?' she finally asked without looking at him. Her tone was calm, but hard and bitter and clearly accusing.

He felt the earth crumble under his feet. 'No. Of course not—'

'Did you ever come here and . . .' She couldn't complete the question.

'Nisreen, listen to me. I swear to you—I never . . . You know me, for God's sake. You think I would ever do something like this?'

'I don't know.'

'You do. Of course you do. You *know* me,' he insisted.

She nodded, barely, but didn't reply. She lowered her head so she was nuzzling Tarek's head and went silent, the only sound a new burst of low sobs.

After a few minutes, she quieted down, then mumbled, 'These bastards . . . the ones who brought us here, the ones you killed . . . did you know them?'

'No.'

'But they were agents. Like you.'

'Nisreen, please—'

'They were following your boss's orders. Your boss.'

'I didn't know them,' he protested, his voice cracking. 'They were Z Directorate. And just so you know . . . the reason I'm here? It's because they sent two others to my place. They wanted to kill me, too. That's what led me here.'

She went silent for a moment. 'Did you kill them?'

'Yes. One of them. The other . . . he's had better days.'

'Good.' She still hadn't looked at him. 'Why would they want you dead?'

'Because I was looking for you. Because they know that if anything happened to you or to Ramazan or to . . . They know I'd never stop until every last one of them was dead.'

She said nothing.

He gave her a moment. 'Nisreen, we have to go. They'll soon know something's wrong. They'll send others.'

She didn't react. After a long moment, she said, 'We can't leave them here. We need to bury them.'

'Of course. But . . . where? We need to keep out of sight. They're going to be looking for us.'

She finally turned to face him. Her eyes were red and swollen, her pupils fully dilated, making them seem hollowed out. As painful as that was to see, it wasn't what pained Kamal the most.

It was the unmistakable accusation in her glare.

'Not here,' she said. 'Anywhere, but not here.'

Kamal understood, and nodded. 'We should get moving then.'

It was the hardest thing he'd ever done.

It was much harder on Nisreen, of course. Hard beyond words, beyond comprehension. But it was also hard on Kamal, and in a different way. On top of the soul-wrenching pain of their deaths, he also had Nisreen and her devastation to contend with.

She was still breathing, still moving, still responding, still *alive* . . . but she wasn't there. Not any more. Life, beyond the strict metabolic sense of the word, had been pounded out of her. Watching her, seeing the utter desolation carved into her face, wondering if this day would ever cease to cast its infernal pall over her every waking moment—it all gutted him. Layered on top of the accusatory undertow he could still feel from her, it was unbearable.

He folded down the back seats of the agency SUV and carried the children over to it. Tarek first, then Noor. He lay them down side by side in the back, leaving enough room for his brother. He brought him over last, all the while shadowed and watched by Nisreen.

It was all done in a deafening silence.

Leaving Nisreen for a moment, he checked the two agents he'd killed. They had their creds on them. He pocketed them and took their weapons.

He suspected he might need them.

He left their phones, and pulled the battery from the phone he'd taken off the killer in his apartment to make sure it wouldn't be used to track them from here on.

There was a lot to process. He'd killed three Hafiye agents tonight and seriously maimed a fourth. He was now a wanted man, an enemy of the state, no question about that—an enemy of a murderous, barbaric state. He'd devoted his life to keeping it safe, but right now all he wanted to do was tear it down with his bare hands. But before he could do that, he needed to know what was going on. He needed to understand what had led to this, why his brother and his family had been targeted, why they'd also come after him. He needed to know what Nisreen knew. But it would have to wait.

He had three burials to take care of.

41

'We have a problem. My men at the castle—they're not responding.'

Celaleddin was home in bed. From behind the edge of the curtains, he could see that dawn hadn't yet broken, which meant that the call, coming at such an early hour, couldn't be about anything good. Kuzey's voice, and his tone, further confirmed that.

His wife had stirred, grumbled, turned over and fallen back asleep. Leaving her there, he climbed out of bed and padded out of their room barefoot in his nightshirt. 'What about the team you sent to Kamal Agha's?'

'The same.'

Celaleddin entered his study, his jaw uncharacteristically dropped low, his gaunt face twisted in a scowl. Maybe they had been careless by only sending two men to take care of him. Kamal had demonstrated his resourcefulness more than once. No one was more aware of that than his superiors at the Hafiye.

'You've sent men out to the castle?'

'They're en route,' Kuzey confirmed, using one of the many old French expressions that had seeped into the Ottoman vernacular. 'I've got the Zaptiye setting up roadblocks around the area.'

'There are a lot of roads to cover. Country lanes and whatnot.'

'I know.'

'I want to know what they find the second they get there.'

'We should know in the next ten minutes.'

Celaleddin pressed the buzzer to summon one of his servants. He needed coffee. A lot of it. It looked as if it was going to be a long, and fraught, day.

He thought about it for a quick second before his servant appeared at the door. 'Coffee,' he said to him abruptly. 'A large pot.'

'Pardon?' Kuzey asked through the phone line.

Celaleddin ignored it, waving his servant off. But he did have something pressing for Kuzey. 'Find me Kamal's partner.'

'Taymoor Agha?' Kuzey asked.

'Yes.' His mind was already putting various permutations of what he imagined was to come through their paces. 'I think we're going to need him.'

With the first glimmer of dawn infusing the horizon, Kamal drove on, the big black SUV powering east along empty country roads. He was avoiding the main highways, maintaining an inconspicuous speed, his eyes alert to any sign of a roadblock or a surveillance drone.

Nisreen sat next to him, staring ahead, both of them observing a funereal silence, an unspoken rage smoldering inside them. Behind them, the three bodies were laid out side by side on their backs, covered by a tarpaulin Kamal had found at the castle.

They needed to be buried, and soon. Islamic tradition called for burials to be carried out as quickly as possible following death. But where?

Paris would have been the normal port of call. It was where Kamal's family hailed from, where the family mosque was, where Kamal and Ramazan's grandparents and great-grandparents were buried. He knew it was where his brother should be laid to rest. He owed him that. But Paris was out of the question. Too many people who knew them, too many law enforcement officers prowling the streets, too many surveillance cameras trawling licence plates and informants looking to ingratiate themselves with the authorities. Right now, Paris had to be avoided at all costs. As did smaller towns, malls—anywhere with lots of people, really.

Which didn't leave many options.

Which was why Kamal was heading east towards Fontainebleau and its great palace, one eye on the road, the other on his rearview mirror, every sensor in his body on high alert.

Not that there weren't lots of people in Fontainebleau. It was home to a spectacular palace of over fifteen hundred rooms that nestled among a vast expanse of gardens and parkland. The old château dated back to the twelfth century, but it had grown spectacularly in the 1500s and had long been a favourite residence and hunting lodge of many of France's kings. After the Ottoman conquest, it had been converted into a sprawling madrasah complex that was home to a community of students, teachers, workers and their families.

It was also surrounded by acres of imperial forest.

Kamal had been there before. As a child, his parents used to take him and Ramazan for picnics by a small lake deep in the forest. They'd often dropped in at the madrasah for a sermon or a late meal before heading back to the city. More recently, it was a place he came to when he wanted to be alone. A place to think, to recharge.

After a little more than an hour's drive, they spotted the tall minarets that surrounded the palace and heard the dawn prayer calls wafting gently from them. A couple of *fersahs* from the madrasah, Kamal turned off the main road and guided the SUV deep into the forest. It was early; with a bit of luck, perhaps they wouldn't come upon any of the madrasah's students making their way to class, or the men and women heading out to work on its citrus groves, olive gardens and dairy farms.

He followed the narrow path until he reached the clearing he knew. It was empty. He killed the engine and stared ahead.

Vertical shafts of light speared the tree cover around them, lighting up scattered ballets of insects and butterflies. A soundtrack of birdsong further enhanced the majestic forest's aura of tranquillity.

It was all wasted on them.

He looked at Nisreen. Her face was locked dead ahead in anger. 'I can't do this. They need a proper burial. This isn't right.'

Kamal suppressed his own anger about that. 'We can't. You know we can't. We can't be around people right now. They'll be looking for us.'

'They.' The word came out like poison.

He felt something cave in inside him. 'I'm sorry. But we don't have a choice.'

He waited until she finally glanced over at him and nodded weakly.

They got out of the car. There was a lot of work to be done. Long-held rituals to be followed.

He carried the bodies down the path from the clearing to the edge of a small lake, one after the other, placing them gently on the soft, dry soil. Nisreen watched, shivering. Her wells of tears still hadn't dried up.

He stepped back, then asked, softly, 'Are you sure you want to do this yourself?'

'Yes.'

He hesitated, then added, 'Can I assist you?'

She stared at him, jaw visibly clenched.

'Let me help you do this. Please.'

She held his gaze. Then she finally relented with a small nod.

It was all done in tense, solemn silence, with only the occasional eye contact between Kamal and Nisreen. He was on edge throughout the ordeal, wondering if she was going to lash out at him or collapse in a heap of tears and cries. He was having a hard time holding in his own sorrow and anger. Remarkably, she held it together while they carried out the preparations, though not without a constant trickle of tears sliding down her cheeks and a tremble in her fingers as she touched her loved one's cold bodies.

They used lake water to wash each body three times, following the prescribed order—upper right side, upper left side, lower right, lower left. Nisreen was visibly at the edge of despair when she washed Noor's hair, stopping several times before managing to complete the task and braiding it three times. Kamal kept having to stop himself from going to her and taking her in his arms, as much for himself as for her, but he held back, restrained by a cavalcade of conflicting emotions.

She stepped back as he cleansed his brother's body, his fingers shivering, his mind lost in a trance of sorrow, branding every pore of his dead brother's face into his memory, taking his time despite the urgency coursing through him.

Throughout, he was hounded by the most awful of thoughts: That he had failed them. That he hadn't kept them safe. That despite being on the inside—the very notion flooded him with a burning, venomous self-hate—he didn't see it coming.

And now they were all dead.

They didn't have any burial shrouds—large, plain white sheets that would have been perfumed by incense five times— nor did they have ropes to secure the sheets once they were folded over them according to the prescribed rituals. Instead, Ramazan, Tarek and Noor would be buried in their long shirts. Their left hands were placed on their chests, their right hands resting on their left hands, as in a position of prayer.

Kamal and Nisreen then stood side by side for the funeral prayers. These would have normally been performed with

Ramazan and Nisreen's friends and with members of their immediate community, but that too was not to be.

Facing the *qiblah*—Mecca—they recited the *Salat al-Janazah*.

Kamal then left Nisreen and chose a clearing at the edge of the great forest. There, using tools he found in the SUV's boot, he dug the graves—gouging the earth angrily, pounding it until his muscles ached, punishing it along with himself, carving wide clefts first, straight down, then narrower ones down the middle in which the dead would be placed. Following tradition, these were perpendicular to the *qiblah*. With Nisreen watching in stricken silence, Kamal placed the bodies in the graves on their right sides, facing the *qiblah*—Ramazan first, then Tarek, then Noor, with Nisreen reciting the supplications as he did so. They had no clay bricks to place over the wrapped bodies to prevent direct contact between them and the soil that would fill the graves. Instead, Kamal just placed as many rocks as he could gather, then he and Nisreen approached each grave and placed three handfuls of soil into it before Kamal added more until each grave was topped by a slightly elevated mound of earth.

No markers were placed over the graves. Islamic tradition allowed small markers or stones but prohibited large monuments or decorations to be placed at grave sites, an anonymity that, given their circumstances, suited Nisreen and Kamal.

They stood by the graves while the whole planet around them seemed to melt into a respectful, eerie silence that was only broken by Nisreen's gentle sobs.

Without looking at her, Kamal said, 'I have no doubt that angels with faces as bright as the sun are already guiding them into the gardens of paradise.'

She wiped her eyes dry and said, 'I can think of none who would be more deserving of that.' Then she couldn't keep it in any more. She dissolved into in a mess of tears and sobs and stumbled away from Kamal, one arm held up to keep him back before she disappeared through the trees.

Much as it killed him to do so, he respected her request and decided to wait for her on an outcrop by the water's edge, channelling his fury to a different vision of the afterlife altogether, with him as the dark-faced angel who would send those responsible for his family's deaths to the gates of hell.

But first they had to survive. He needed to put his rage on hold and think things through. He knew they needed to put as much distance as possible between them and the Chevreuse castle, as fast as possible. The bodies he'd left behind at his apartment and at the castle had probably already been discovered. They'd be hunting Kamal and Nisreen, and he knew how quickly security cordons were put up.

But he needed to give Nisreen any time she needed, even though he could feel the weight of every passing second.

When she finally emerged from the forest, he could see how broken she was, and he knew her suffering wasn't going away any time soon. Still, he couldn't delay asking any longer. He needed to understand what they were facing in order to figure out what their next move should be.

He turned to her. She was facing the lake, her eyes as glassy as its surface.

'Nisreen . . .' He had to wait, then repeat her name, three times. Softly. Patiently. Three words that felt like three deaths.

Slowly, she finally turned to face him.

'I need to know,' he asked. 'What the hell happened? What's going on?'

42

They sat on a large flat outcrop by the water's edge.

Speaking in a dazed, distant tone, Nisreen told Kamal what had happened, right from the beginning.

The tattooed man appearing at the hospital.

Ramazan's suspicions.

His first late-night Internet search session. The words he typed in.

'That would have tripped some alarms,' Kamal said.

Nisreen shrugged. 'They were probably already monitoring our online activity because of me. Because of what I do. He knew that.'

Her words trailed off, as if she felt sudden remorse that what she'd said sounded like she was blaming Ramazan. Kamal didn't press it. He could see how hard it was for her to be reliving every moment of the last few days, putting it under a microscope that wouldn't do her any favours. He also knew people got complacent when they didn't think they were doing anything worthy of being monitored, even when they were aware that every keystroke of theirs was most likely under watch.

He also tried not to dwell on how she probably included him among them when she said 'they'.

She found the strength to tell him about the second night, about confronting Ramazan about his searches. Then she told him what he had told her. About the man. About what he'd told Ramazan.

Kamal, riveted by her every word, didn't interrupt.

She told him about her going to the hospital with Ramazan the next morning, about their conversation with the tattooed man, about him telling them what the incantation was. Then she concluded with what Ramazan had told her on the phone, about the agents showing up at the hospital, the shoot-out, and—crucially—what happened next.

It took Kamal a moment to process this. 'He actually saw him disappear?'

'That's what he told me. He was very clear about that.'

'Like disappear disappear?'

'Yes.'

'Nisreen—'

'Kamal, I'm telling you the man just vanished'—said with a cutting, impatient spike of anger.

Kamal clammed up. He wasn't sure how to continue the conversation. He could see that she was barely holding it together, and he needed to tread softly. Part of him wasn't sure she was thinking clearly at all, given what she had just told him. But he also had too much respect for her and for her intellect to dismiss what she was saying. 'Could it have been a trick? Or something he missed? The guy ducking out and slipping away while he wasn't looking?'

'No. I pressed him on that, too. It happened right in front of him. The others also saw it. That's what shook him so hard. That's why he ran.'

'It's not possible. People don't disappear.'

'They don't travel across time either. But this man did.'

'He claims he did. There has to be another explanation for it.'

'Look where we are, Kamal. Why do you think this is happening? Why do you think they came after us this hard? Why do you think Celaleddin himself interrogated us? Why—'

'Wait, Celaleddin interrogated you?'

Nisreen nodded, visibly pained by the memory.

She told Kamal about their episode at the Citadel.

'Why else would they want us dead? It's because of what we know. What Ramazan saw. You said the two dead men at the castle were agents who were also at the hospital when it happened. That's obviously why they killed them, too. To keep them quiet. To stop any of it from coming out.'

Kamal looked away and acknowledged her words with some thoughtful nods as the impossible started to, if not sink in, then at least slip under the surface. 'And you're saying Rasheed—whoever he was—he gave you the incantation?'

'Yes. Well, sort of. Half of it. He told us how to travel back into the past, but we didn't get the way he came here. To the future.'

'So you know it?'

'Not by heart. I mean, I should. I read and reread it and listened to it so many times while trying to translate it . . . But it's in Palmyrene. It's not related to any language we use.'

'Why were you trying to translate it?'

'I wanted to see if there was any part of it that was specific to going back in time, to the past. I thought that maybe substituting that part with a word that relates to the future or to going forward might be how one travels that way. Like he did. I had it all written down in my notebook along with what I'd managed to translate so far.'

'Which you gave to Celaleddin?'

'Yes. I didn't have a choice. Which is why they don't need us any more.' A haunted, questioning look imbued her face. 'Why did they react so violently? Why the need to . . .' Her breath caught as she stumbled over the words. Then, looking away, she added, in a low voice, 'They're monsters. Just . . . monsters.'

Kamal averted his gaze from her as well and stared down

at his feet. Once again, even though he'd just lost his own brother, even though she had to know how much he loved them all, he couldn't help but feel included in her contempt, but he chose to let it die out rather than give it any oxygen. It helped that he was still trying to understand what had happened.

'This man. The one you're saying was Ayman Rasheed,' he said. 'If everything he said is true . . . he changed history. He went back, and he changed everything. And if he could do that, someone else could do it, too. That kind of knowledge, that kind of power . . . I can't think of a more dangerous weapon. And they knew you and Ramazan had it.'

'But they had no reason to think we would be a threat to the empire. Not in that sense. This is our world. Our whole existence.' She paused, then added, 'Or at least, it was.'

'Even so. For them, the risk is too great. You could go back and change things without meaning to. You could tell someone, and they might decide to use it to destroy all this.' He spread his arms wide. 'Besides, even without acting on it, the knowledge of it alone is dangerous.'

'What do you mean?'

'The empire. The caliphate. We've always believed it to be the will of God. The empire's success, the defeat of the Christians, the fall of Rome before the sword of the sultan. It's all part of a divine plan, right? That's what we hear in the sermons, that's what history tells us. Now imagine if this came out.'

'That it wasn't God's will at all. That it was just the will of one man.'

'Exactly.'

She thought about it for a second, then said, 'Unless you consider him a tool of God, doing His bidding to fix the world. Maybe this is how it was all supposed to be. Maybe

Rasheed brought it back to how it was supposed to be. I mean, how do we know someone else hadn't gone back long before Rasheed did and changed things, perverted history, and turned the world into the one Rasheed knew?'

He was surprised by her clear-headed response and wanted to keep it going. Any distraction he could get her engaged in, no matter how brief, was surely helpful—for them both. 'We don't. But if you're going to open that door, the possibilities become infinite. And it all leads to the same problem: why would God allow so much meddling with His divine plan? Why isn't He in control? That kind of questioning is just as problematic and dangerous.'

She shrugged. 'It doesn't matter anyway. We are where we are.' Her expression retreated into a distant, even more drawn look. 'Nothing's going to change that.'

Kamal said nothing at first. Then he found himself unable to stop pondering something that sounded so incredible he couldn't believe he was about to say it out loud.

'If you had the incantation, if you knew for sure that you had the right wording—and assuming it works—couldn't we use it to go back and fix things? Like go back, I don't know, a week? Before any of this happened?'

'No. He said you can't go back to any time within your life-time. Which makes sense, I suppose. There'd be two of you around, right? Besides, like I said, I'm not sure I remember the exact wording. They have my notebook, and I lost my phone.'

'Your phone? What's that got to do with it?'

'I recorded it. Rasheed, what he told us—I have it on video. All of it. But I lost it when they grabbed us.'

'It's on your phone? Everything Rasheed said?'

'Yes.'

'I have your phone. I found it in your car.'

'Where is it?'

'It's here, in the car.' All kinds of possibilities were now flaring up inside his brain. 'Having the incantation . . . it gives us leverage. We can threaten them. Say we'll go public with it.'

'How? They control everything. And even if they didn't, no one would believe it.'

'They're desperate to keep it under wraps. That's leverage.'

'They'll never let it get that far.' She was shaking her head ruefully. 'They're not going to stop until we're dead.'

'Not if I can help it.'

She shook her head, dejected. 'You won't stand a chance. We both know how effective they are at dealing with anyone they consider a threat.'

He tried not to read anything accusatory in her words. 'Let me worry about that. But I have to get you to safety first.'

'I don't care about that.'

He reached out to grab her by the shoulders, but stopped himself. 'You can't say that.'

Her eyes took on a faraway, chilling tightness. 'If I want to be safe, it's only so I can get back at them. So I can make them pay. Starting with Celaleddin.'

'Let's start by making sure you're safe.'

She turned her gaze on him. 'Where? Wherever I go, nowhere is safe.'

'Wherever *we* go,' Kamal corrected her. 'We're in this together now.'

She gave him a curious, uncomfortable look; then her face softened fractionally.

He was grateful for it. Under the circumstances, he was glad she'd even managed that.

'It would have to be far,' he said. 'Beyond the border. Out of their reach. England, maybe. That's the nearest option. I'll find a way to get you across the Channel.'

'The sultan has agents there, doesn't he?'

Kamal frowned. England wasn't part of the empire, never had been. But the English and the Ottomans had a long history of cooperation, one that went all the way back to 1570, when the pope excommunicated their Protestant queen, Elizabeth I. The rest of Catholic Europe shunned her, too, leading her to forge an alliance with the Ottomans against their mutual enemies. Despite the fact that this alliance was rooted in cold political and economic reasons, Elizabeth eventually came to believe that Protestantism had more in common with Islam than with Catholicism.

'The English would hand me over to them,' Nisreen added, 'assuming they don't find out what's really going on and want me for themselves.'

'Then maybe we use it as a stepping stone to moving on.'

'To where?'

'America?'

Nisreen scoffed. 'Oh, they'd welcome us with open arms, wouldn't they?'

The Christian Republic guarded its religious exclusivity fiercely. There were no mosques, no synagogues, no temples there. Visitors were already Christian, and could prove it under rigorous vetting, or they converted on arrival and agreed to be held in 'Saviour Camps' for months until they were deemed to be fully reborn. Otherwise, they were not allowed in. It was that simple.

'Well . . . I could be useful to them.' As he said it, Kamal couldn't believe the words coming out of his mouth—the mouth of a fêted Hafiye hero, casually discussing betraying his people. But he was more than ready to do that. Right now, he was ready to do whatever it took to bring the whole empire crashing down on its murderous, lying self.

'I'd be the useful one if they ever found out what happened. If anyone would want to change history, it's them.'

She mopped her face with her hands and let out a long, weary breath. 'And maybe they should. Maybe they need to know about this. Maybe they should send someone back to change it to how it was supposed to be.'

'And none of us would be here, right?'

She shrugged and looked at him squarely. 'Would it matter?'

Kamal said nothing. The only person out there that still mattered to him was his father, who was farming his chickens quietly in the Périgord and was likely oblivious to any of this. Perhaps it was better that way, Kamal thought, although he knew he'd need to tell him the truth about how his elder son died, and soon.

After a quiet spell, she said, 'I pushed him.'

'What?'

'Ramazan. I should have told him to stop. I should have made him stop asking questions.' Her voice cracked, and she teared up again. 'Instead, I pushed him to talk to him again, to get the incantation. I insisted on going in with him. Maybe if I hadn't, maybe if I'd—'

'No,' Kamal interjected. 'You can't blame yourself. His curiosity triggered it, and they came after him. They caused this. This is on them, not on him, not on you. They're responsible. And I'm going to make sure they pay for it.'

She calmed her sobs and nodded passively, an internal debate going on.

'I don't want to run,' she finally said.

'I don't think there's much of a—'

'I don't want to run,' she insisted. 'I don't want to live in hiding. I've seen it. I've been around people who've had to do it. It's not a life. It's not for me. Not matter what.'

He let it sink in. 'What then?'

'I don't know.' She fell silent; then her face hardened again. 'I want them dead. I want them all dead. I want them to suffer for what they did.'

He looked at her. She was shivering.

'That makes two of us. But that's my job from here on.'

'No. I want to be part of it. I want to do everything I can to make it happen.'

Her shivering gave her words a steely tinge. She meant every syllable.

'Then that's what we'll do,' he told her. 'We'll make them pay.'

She nodded and looked away.

He sat there for a moment, then got up. 'We'd better get moving.'

'And go where?'

'We don't have money. And we need new papers. IDs to allow us to move around a bit more freely. The only place I know where to get both is in Paris.'

'You want to go back to the city?'

'Yes. It's dangerous, but we might stand a better chance of getting lost in the crowds than out here. We'll need to ditch the car and find another way there. But not yet. We'll wait until it's dark. I think I know a way into the city they won't expect.'

Nisreen didn't comment, but she was visibly uncomfortable with his thinking.

'I want to see that recording,' he added, and got up. 'I'll go get it.'

She pushed herself to her feet. 'I'll come with you.'

They walked through the woods, back to the SUV. She looked like she was about to say something, held back, then said, 'This is so . . . insane.'

'What?'

'Everything. All of it. And now listening to you. Doing the same things that those you normally hunt would do.'

'I don't hunt people, Nisreen.'

She gave him a sceptical shrug.

'Yes, of course, I've hunted people,' he told her. 'But they were terrorists. Nutjobs who were out to kill innocent people.'

'And lawyers and professors who were saying things you didn't like.'

He nodded ruefully. 'I wasn't part of—well, I hope I wasn't. The truth is, I'm not so sure any more.' Anger and regret were duelling inside him. 'Kuzey and his people . . . they were murderers. The White Rose . . . it was all a lie.'

Nisreen looked at him in wide-eyed shock as he filled her in on what the Z Directorate hitman had told him yesterday evening.

'I'm so sorry, Nisreen. I know you can never forgive me for even being—'

'Please.' She raised her hand and cut him off. 'Not now. It's all too much to bear already. Please.'

He said nothing more as all the long weeks and months of distance, anguish and pain came rushing back to the surface, propelled by a far greater pain. One that, he knew, would never let them go.

Then, slowly, they plodded on through the maze of oaks, heading for the car.

They were almost at the clearing when Kamal saw something up ahead through the trunks and foliage, a flash of movement that caught his eye.

Men, moving around the SUV.

They'd found them.

43

Kamal grabbed Nisreen and, with one hand pressed tight against her mouth, whisked her off the path and ducked behind a thick tree trunk.

'Keep quiet,' he whispered, pointing ahead.

She didn't move as he peered out.

He could see a man—then another—by the SUV. One had his back turned to them and was speaking on his phone. The other, to the left of the SUV, was looking away, scanning the forest, waiting. Further back, in the shadows, he spotted another agency Kartal. It had the same predatory matte-black livery as the one they had driven there.

Hafiye agents. But how—

Then he saw him. The man on the phone, turning so his face was visible.

Taymoor.

Kamal stifled a curse. He'd brought him here once, months ago. He'd invited him to accompany him on one of his walks. Allowed him into his sanctuary. A charitable act—a stupid act, he now felt—when his partner had been going through a rough patch of his own.

Had his partner given him up? Or did he just miss something? A surveillance camera, a drone, a tracker? He wasn't sure. Either way, that was quick. Celaleddin was clearly pulling out all the stops to make sure they were found.

Kamal thought fast. The sensible choice was to retreat and slip back into the forest. He knew the woods well, knew the various paths that cut through them, where they led. Knew

303

how to find the river, where they might be able to hop on to a passing barge. Knew where the nearby roads were. Taymoor was probably setting up a cordon around the forest on the assumption that they were still there, but it was huge, and there was too much of a perimeter to cover. But retreating meant abandoning the phone and losing the only piece of leverage they had.

They needed that phone.

There were only two men facing them, for now. Taymoor plus one, whom Kamal now recognized as Kenan Hamza, an agent in their section—a friend, in another life. And Kamal had the element of surprise.

'Don't move,' he mouthed to Nisreen.

Her expression went wide with protest, but he pressed his hand against her mouth and held a finger in front of his own.

'Stay here and keep still,' he whispered. Then he pulled out his gun, bent into a crouch, and headed out.

Waiting until he could see that they weren't looking his way, he crept closer to the clearing, moving from tree to tree, scanning the ground to make sure he didn't step on anything that might rustle or snap and give his presence away, taking his time, his gun drawn and ready. He was halfway to the edge of the clearing when Taymoor and Kenan, their weapons drawn, started moving down the path, the one he and Nisreen had been on, each of them taking up one side of it, keeping as much distance as possible between them.

They were coming after him and Nisreen.

Which actually made things easier.

He stayed behind the tree, listening intently, and waited until they passed his position and had their backs turned to him. Then he emerged, slowly, quietly.

Taymoor must have heard him. His pace slowed and his face swivelled to one side, his attention pricked.

'Don't move,' Kamal called out to them, levelling his gun at their backs. 'Arms up high, where I can see them. Fingers off the triggers.'

Hesitation, for a second.

'Do it, brothers. You know the drill.'

They both raised their arms, slowly, and turned to face him.

'What are you doing?' Taymoor asked. 'Have you lost your mind?'

'Put your guns down on the ground, one at a time. Kenan, you first. And slowly, please. Very, very slowly.'

Kenan started to bend down.

Taymoor said, 'Kamal, come on, this is—'

And just then, just as Kamal's eyes flicked over to Taymoor, Kenan whipped his arm out so his gun was levelled on Kamal and took his shot—only Kamal saw it and reacted just as the agent squeezed the trigger. He dropped to a sideways squat and flicked his gun around—it had less of an arc to cover than Kenan's—and pumped a bullet out a split second before he felt the air to the left of his ear whistle and saw the red mist sprout out of the agent's right thigh.

Kenan's gun flew out of his hand as his leg gave way and he dropped to the ground, lopsided, like a felled tree. Kamal ignored him and pinned his attention back on Taymoor, who had also brought his arms down and was now holding his gun aimed dead straight at his partner.

'What the fuck are you doing?' Taymoor roared, darting a quick glance sideways to check on the fallen man. 'He's one of us.'

'So were the two bastards who came to my house to kill me last night,' Kamal shot back. 'And so were the sons of dogs who killed my brother and his children.'

His words struck Taymoor hard, his expression changing to one of stunned confusion. 'What?'

'You heard me.'

Taymoor was still in shock. 'Ramazan . . . ? And the kids?'

'Yes,' Kamal hissed.

Kenan was writhing on the ground, his hands gripping his thigh as he groaned with pain. Blood was pooling on to the soil under him, but from the amount coming out, Kamal didn't think his shot had severed the femoral artery.

'Help me,' Kenan called out.

Taymoor ignored him. He looked heavily spooked. 'How did this happen? What the hell is going on?' he asked Kamal.

'You wouldn't believe me if I told you.'

'Try me.'

'Not enough time, brother. I doubt we'll be alone here long enough. And Kenan needs your help.'

'Whatever it is, we can work it out.'

'It's too late for that.'

They stared at each other, their gun barrels lined up on each other like two handles tugging at the ends of an invisible rope.

Then a voice cut through the stand-off.

'Is he one of them?'

Kamal and Taymoor both glanced away for an instant to see Nisreen at the edge of the path, across from Taymoor. She was standing by Kenan, who was still squirming with pain. She was holding Kenan's gun in a two-fisted grip and had it aimed right at Taymoor's chest. It was shaking and looked uncomfortable and heavy in her hands.

'Nisreen, stay back,' Kamal yelled.

She didn't flinch. 'Is he one of them?' she asked again, her tone flat and hard as she tightened her grip on the gun.

'No,' Kamal told her. 'Taymoor's my partner. He didn't know about any of this.' The instant he said it, his expression changed. He frowned uncertainly at Taymoor. 'Am I right? Tell me I'm right.'

'Of course, I didn't. *Bismillah,* Kamal. What's got into you?'

'He's still one of them,' Nisreen hissed. 'He's here to kill us, too.'

'No, he's here to bring us in,' Kamal said.

'Same thing.'

'Nisreen, please,' Kamal insisted, then he turned to Taymoor, whose gun was flicking left and right, trying to cover them both, which was hard, given that they were ninety degrees apart. 'Taymoor, listen to me. Put your gun down. Kenan needs help. You need to put a tourniquet around his leg before he bleeds out.'

'You know I can't do tha—'

A shot detonated through the trees, catching both men by surprise, but more so Taymoor, who ducked instinctively, only not before the round had whizzed by him and grazed his scalp. He spun around to face Nisreen, who looked as surprised as he was by the shot she'd just fired.

'You crazy whore,' he raged at her as he dabbed his head with his hand and checked for blood while swinging his gun arm up at her—but in that split second of chaos, Kamal grabbed his opportunity. He charged at Taymoor, reaching him just as Taymoor saw him coming, catching him off balance.

Kamal ploughed into him and pushed his gun arm away while ramming his elbow full force into Taymoor's jaw. Both men fell to the ground heavily, then Kamal followed through with a quick punch to keep up the sensory onslaught, while wrenching the gun out of his partner's hand and flinging it away.

He pulled back and sprang to his feet, covering Taymoor with his gun. Taymoor spat and rose to his feet more slowly. They were both out of breath and grunting heavily.

Taymoor glared at Kamal. 'You've really lost your mind.'

'You didn't leave me any other choice,' Kamal said as he

picked up Taymoor's gun and edged around to join Nisreen. 'I'm going to need your phone, too. Both of you.'

He covered both agents while they grudgingly pulled out their phones and tossed them over to him. He didn't bother to pick them up off the ground. He just put a bullet in each.

He looked over at Nisreen.

Her attention was still nailed on the agents, her gunsight still locked on them.

'Let's go.'

She didn't react at first.

'Nisreen. Time to go,' he called out more forcefully. He gave Taymoor a parting look. Only yesterday the man had been his partner and brother-in-arms. Clearly, the surreal moments were going to keep coming fast. 'I'm sorry, brother,' he told him.

'So am I,' Taymoor shot back angrily.

Kamal nodded ruefully, then turned and walked away.

'I told you she was going to get you into trouble,' Taymoor called out.

Kamal glanced over at Nisreen, who was walking next to him.

He didn't turn back or reply.

He picked up his pace and they reached the clearing. 'Get in,' he told Nisreen, pointing at the SUV they'd arrived in. Then he turned to Taymoor's vehicle and put a bullet in each of its left tyres.

They drove off in a storm of dust, charging down the winding lane that led out of the forest.

'Where do we go now?' she asked.

'I don't know,' he said, leaning over to reach into the glove compartment. 'But we'll be lucky to get out. Others are probably on their way here already.'

He pulled out her phone and showed it to her. 'This is it, right?'

She took it from him. 'Yes.'

'Hang on to it,' he said as the road snaked left. 'It could be our only lifeline—'

His eyes shot wide. Two cars were heading towards them at speed. Police cruisers, given the white bonnets and the light bars on their roofs. No sirens or strobes, though—but they were rushing.

'Hang on,' Kamal rasped as he floored the pedal, charging towards them.

The move was unexpected—and the gap between them shrank so quickly that the police only had a second or two to react before impact.

Kamal didn't waver, streaking straight at them like a missile.

The front car's driver blinked first. He veered away at the last moment, but lost control of the car, which fishtailed as he twisted the wheel and slammed sideways into a big tree, the violence of the impact causing its trunk to punch its way halfway through the car's interior.

The second cruiser stayed the course, but angled away sharply at the last second, narrowly avoiding a frontal collision. It scraped against the SUV as it shot past, metal crunching against metal, but both cars made it past each other without critical damage.

'*Bok!*' Kamal raged as he eyed the mirror angrily and saw the second cruiser's brake lights light up, saw it spin around as its driver pulled a handbrake turn, saw it surging after them, its siren and strobes blaring away furiously.

Nisreen was also twisted around in her seat, eyeing the pursuing car nervously. 'They're coming back.'

'I know.' His mind was already scanning ahead, calculating, assessing, evaluating options. He was trained for this. Only he never expected to be using his training in these circumstances. Not while being chased by his own brethren.

He eased off the accelerator just slightly, not enough to be noticeable, but enough to let his pursuers think they were reeling them in. He watched as the cruiser grew bigger in his mirror, watched as it ate up the gap between them until it was right on their tail. Then he went for it.

He yanked the wheel hard, a quick right-left flick, like he was changing lanes violently, and at the same time, with one eye in the mirror, he slammed the brakes. The cruiser did as expected—it swerved left to avoid ploughing into the SUV's tail, but it didn't brake fast enough and ended up right alongside it. Which was when Kamal hit the accelerator again and flung the steering wheel left.

The heavy SUV rammed the cruiser sideways, and Kamal kept it there, wrestling the police car off its trajectory and sending it flying head-on and full force into another of the big oaks that lined the forest lane. Then he felt something in his hands. A violent shake, a vibration coming from the steering wheel. The collision had caused some damage, twisted something. The front wheels were juddering wildly.

And in the far distance, from the edge of the forest: more sirens.

Far, but closing in.

Converging on them.

'*Bok, bok, bok!*' he roared. Then he saw a turnoff coming up to their right, another lane heading into the forest in another direction.

Without hesitating, he drove the SUV into it.

'Where does this lead?' Nisreen asked as she darted nervous looks behind and ahead.

He glanced at her, his scowl sinking in deeper. 'We'll soon find out.'

44

It only took a minute or two for their SUV to chew up the rest of the winding road and reach a bigger lake deep in the forest.

It swerved to a halt in an angry cloud of dust by the water's edge. Nisreen scanned her surroundings. The remote spot was deserted and quiet, a few park benches languishing empty under the late-morning sun. Which wasn't unusual for a weekday.

Nisreen stared at her phone, thinking hard. Out of desperation, a crazy notion had blasted into her mind. It had latched stubbornly on to her consciousness the second she'd first voiced it back at the clearing, when her mind was in overdrive, and now it was screaming out at her. And maybe it wasn't so crazy after all.

Maybe it was the only way they would live.

She fired up her phone.

'What are you doing?' Kamal asked.

'Find me a pen,' she said, her face locked in concentration, her tone urgent. 'Anything I can write with.'

'Why?'

'Just do it. And switch on your phone.'

Kamal looked at her questioningly.

'Just do it,' she insisted.

The sirens were getting nearer.

He did as she asked, rummaging through the armrest storage box, then the glove compartment, while his phone powered up. He found a black ballpoint pen and handed it to her.

'Okay,' she said as she snatched it from him. 'Open up *Hafiza* on your phone. Put in "Palmyrene language" in quotes, then'—she did a quick mental calculation—'the words for "thirty" and "thousand". Look for the result from the Damascus University website.'

Kamal seemed completely lost.

'Do it,' she ordered him. 'It's the only way.'

His eyes flared with realization. 'Wait, you're not thinking— thirty thousand days?' he blurted.

'We don't have a choice,' she shot back. 'We really don't.'

Precious seconds were ticking away. The sirens, wailing through the dense forest, were getting ever closer.

'You're not seriously saying you want to do this?'

'Do you have a better idea?'

He stared at her blankly but was lost for words. He was just breathing hard, same as her.

'We're wasting time,' she pressed.

'What if—what if it screws up? What if it sends us somewhere wrong?'

'Anywhere's better than here right now.'

'What if we get stuck there? What if we can't get back? You said you don't know how to travel forward in time.'

'You want to come back? To what?' She reached out and grabbed his hands. 'They'll kill us if they grab us, Kamal. You know that. And I don't want to die here. Not at their hands.'

He was still frozen, his jaw visibly clenched.

'I don't want to die,' she repeated.

He sucked in a deep breath and nodded. 'Okay.' And he went to work.

While he did, she scrolled to the video file of the conversation with Rasheed and jumped to the part of it that she knew well, the place where he told them the incantation. She held her phone to her ear and, listening intently and pausing the recording, she used the pen to write the words down on her forearm in large, clear letters.

The sirens were cutting in and out through the trees, an eerie, wailing threat rolling in at them.

'Well?' she asked him as soon as she was done.

He showed her his phone. 'This one?'

She grabbed it from him, and her eyes devoured the words on the screen. 'Perfect,' she said as she wrote them down on her forearm too, then she flung the car door open. 'Let's go.'

He hesitated, but she was already outside.

The sirens were much louder now. Then a black agency SUV burst out of the treeline.

Kamal drew his gun and rushed out after her.

He sprinted around the car and joined Nisreen by the front passenger door. They both ducked down and watched the approaching vehicle from over the car's roof. Another car, a police cruiser, was hot on the Kartal's tail. They were both coming straight at them.

Kamal waited until they were in range, then he sprang up, his handgun clenched tight in a two-fisted grip, and let off a volley of rounds at the lead car. Three of them drilled through the windscreen while the rest punched into the front grille and the bumper.

As expected, the SUV spun sideways and came to a grinding halt. The cruiser chasing it did the same but veered off in the opposite direction before stopping, creating an open V formation.

The cops piled out of their vehicles and scurried for cover behind them. Taymoor wasn't among them. Evidently, they hadn't picked him up yet.

Kamal ducked back down and looked at Nisreen. 'Are we doing this?'

Her face was in full nervous lockdown, too. 'I guess we're about to find out.'

'Kamal Agha,' a man's voice rang out. 'Our orders are to bring you in for questioning. Alive.' He paused, then added, 'That's our preferred outcome. But it's not the only one.'

To make the point, they started firing, peppering the driver's side of Kamal and Nisreen's SUV with bullets.

Kamal waited, then darted up and fired back—then his gun's slide recoiled back and locked. He was out of bullets.

'Damn it.' He glanced at Nisreen.

She was breathing hard.

'No time like the present,' he said.

She nodded, then turned to face him. She set the two phones on the ground beside her and reached out for him. 'Hold my hands,' she told him.

He set his gun down and took her hands in his—then an urgent thought rocked him.

'Wait,' he said.

He pulled the phones closer and hammered them a few times with the grip of his gun, shattering their screens and sending bits of plastic flying. He picked up their cracked carcasses and tossed them into the lake, as far as he could.

'Kamal Agha,' the man's voice bellowed out again. 'This is your final warning.'

Kamal took Nisreen's hands in his. 'Do it.'

She twisted her grip so that her forearms were facing her, allowing her to read the words she'd written on them.

She stared into his eyes.

'Repeat after me. Exactly as I say it. Don't send me back alone.'

'No chance of that,' he assured her.

'Kamal Agha,' the voice echoed. 'Your time's up.'

Nisreen's eyes narrowed—then she started reading out the words of the incantation.

Slowly.

Clearly.

Pausing after every few syllables.

Giving Kamal time to repeat them after her.

Her grip tightening more with every word.

Every syllable.

Then, her eyes signalling that she had almost reached the end, she gave him a final, piercing look, a look that had a lifetime of love and hate and admiration and anguish in it, and shut her eyes and uttered the final words.

For a second, nothing happened.

Kamal shut his eyes.

And then, without notice, without artifice, without any kind of warning, with nothing more than a subtle swish of cloth and air, he felt her grip disappear. He was holding on to nothing.

He hazarded a quick glance.

She was gone.

Only her clothes were there, where she'd been crouched before him, a lifeless, empty clump.

He shut his eyes again.

Tight.

Took a deep breath.

And repeated her final words.

45

Fontainebleau
Muharram, AH 1354 (April, AD 1935)

The instant of travel was just that—instantaneous. But despite its extreme brevity, it hit Kamal like a cosmic slap and tore through him with the most intense and fearsome sensations he'd ever experienced.

He felt as if his body had been hollowed and turned inside out, his eyes crushed into grains of sand, and his brain sucked inwards and compressed to nothingness before suddenly exploding outwards and expanding as if to fill the entire universe. He wanted to scream, needed to yell out his agony, and yet weirdly there was no pain and no time to scream, just a cold, silent nothingness. Every cell in his body had been ripped apart and reassembled in the blink of an eye. The journey was over the very second it began.

He was alive. On the ground, somewhere—some*time*—but alive.

He felt heavy-headed and sweaty, his senses dulled by a high-pitched thrum in his ears, his eyes swimming as they struggled for focus. But he knew he was definitely alive.

Once, just over a year earlier, he'd got caught up in an unexpected explosion in a Paris apartment building. He and Taymoor had gone there to arrest a suspected extremist, and the man had blown himself up inside his apartment just as they entered it. They'd managed to leap back into the hallway a split second before the detonation and had both escaped serious injury. It had been the most debilitating, shattering sensation he'd ever felt, in mind and in body, and yet it paled in comparison to what he'd just experienced. But what he felt right now—confused, numbed, reduced to only the most basic levels of sentience—reminded him of the explosion's after-effects.

This time, though, the fog cleared much faster—and she was there. Crouched on the ground, facing him, just as she had been in what his mind was now reminding him was only a moment ago.

Alive, shaking, glistening with sweat—and naked. Just as, he now realized, he was.

Her face fell further into focus, her expression wild with shock and uncertainty—and the same realization evidently hit her, spurred by the sight of him. She flung her arms around herself to cover her breasts and pulled her thighs together, but her mouth was still ajar, just as Kamal dropped his hands to cover his genitals.

She looked around, her face now alive with wonderment. 'Are we . . . ?' She took in the emptiness surrounding them. 'It worked,' she added, half stating, half questioning, in a breathless, amazed whisper.

They were in the exact same spot, by the edge of the lake, with the same dense forest breaking off and giving way to the secluded clearing that led to the still, green water. The sun was still out, a bit lower and less potent perhaps but unchallenged in a crisp blue sky.

But the cars were all gone. As were their pursuers.

Only they weren't alone.

Alarmed voices and shrieks testified to that.

Kamal and Nisreen turned to where the voices were coming from, further down the lake shore, to see a gaggle of people—adults and children, two or three families maybe, with a few servants attending to them—picnickers enjoying a day out until it had been disrupted by the sudden appearance of a naked couple.

'*Bok,*' Kamal muttered.

The men in the picnic party were already on their feet, gesturing and yelling angrily at Kamal and Nisreen, while the women were moving to shield the children's eyes while turning away themselves.

'Let's get out of here,' Kamal said as he did a quick scan of their surroundings. It was pretty much as he remembered it, except for four cars parked by the edge of the treeline in the shade, closer to his and Nisreen's position than to the picnickers.

Old—*really old*—cars.

Chrome bumpers, spoked wheels, whitewall tyres, fender-mounted spare, flip-out windscreen, black soft-top roof old.

How old, he wasn't sure. He'd never seen any on the road—only in pictures and movies and at the Imperial Science Museum.

'There,' he said as he pointed at them.

He bolted towards them, Nisreen on his tail, the men taking a few seconds before realizing what they were going to do and setting off after them.

Kamal reached the nearest car and yanked its door open.

'Get in the other side,' he blurted to Nisreen as he climbed in himself—only to be greeted by an alien sight. The car's interior looked completely different from anything he was used to. It was literally a museum piece and had a thin, resin steering wheel; a long, spindly gear stick rising from the floor; a thin handbrake stalk rising next to it; two pedals and an unusual smaller third one where the accelerator normally was; and a small trio of dials in the middle of the bare-boned dashboard, next to a single basic key—a key that he now turned urgently.

It clicked into position a quarter turn to the right, but wouldn't go further. It also didn't start the engine. In fact, it didn't generate any reaction under the bonnet.

He clicked it back, then turned it again.

Still nothing.

'What are you doing?' Nisreen asked.

'I don't know how to start this thing,' Kamal shot back, his eyes urgently scanning the plain dash area in front of him, searching for clues.

He spotted a small round knob sticking out from under the edge of the dashboard. It was connected to a long cable that disappeared into the engine compartment, and he realized it might be some kind of choke. He pulled and turned it. And still got nothing.

'There's got to be a starter button somewhere,' he said as he searched for one.

Nisreen was looking out the back of the car. 'Hurry. They're almost here.'

He looked back, saw how close the men were, and decided it wasn't going to work.

'Let's get out of here,' he told her as he pushed his door open. She did the same as he sprinted around the car, took her by the hand, and led her into the woods.

The men chased after them until they reached the edge of the treeline; then they gave up.

Kamal heard their incensed rants and insults fade away as he and Nisreen advanced further into the forest.

When he was finally sure they weren't being followed, he slowed down his pace, then stopped to catch his breath. It was colder than before, especially now they were in the shade. The sun was paler. They'd gone back thirty thousand days, which probably didn't equate to an exact number of years—he'd need to do the maths later. It certainly didn't feel like the height of summer, but it didn't feel like winter either. Spring or autumn, perhaps. But cooler. The air had a biting chill.

He looked back. There was no sign of their pursuers.

He turned to Nisreen. She had one arm across her breasts, the other hand down where her thighs met. He noticed her skin was covered in goosebumps, though he didn't know if that was from the cold or from unease. The sight of her fully naked was a shock to him. He'd never seen her anywhere near that exposed, not given the strict norms of Ottoman society, not given that she was his brother's wife. Over the years, he'd sometimes imagined her in that light, of course, imagined what she might look like if she were his, if they'd been together, but that's just what it had been—his imagination. But here, now, despite everything, despite all that had happened and the dire circumstances they were in, seeing her like that was still unexpected enough to make it hard for him to tear his gaze from her.

A gaze that Nisreen noticed.

'Could you stop looking at me like that?'

He snapped back to full consciousness and turned away, feeling embarrassed. 'I'm sorry. I didn't mean to . . .' His words stumbled over themselves and he went mute.

Hesitantly, he turned back, wanting to catch her eye.

She was half turned away from him but was also looking over her shoulder at him. 'What?'

'We made it,' he told her. 'We're here. Wherever—or whenever here is, anyway.'

She nodded and breathed out with delayed relief, and looked around, taking stock of the quiet forest around them.

'When is here, anyway?' he asked.

'I'm not sure. I had to think fast. We had to jump back to a time before we were alive or it wouldn't work. So I thought, a hundred years, and that's roughly 36,500 days, right? But it would have taken too long to translate. Too complicated. So I picked a round number close to it. Thirty thousand.'

'About twenty per cent less,' Kamal said. 'So we've travelled back around eighty years?'

'I guess so.'

He ran a quick mental calculation. 'So . . . around 1354?* The time of . . .'

'Sultan Bayezid VI,' she told him.

Kamal thought about it. He knew it had been a glorious era for the empire. Oil was pumping out of the Arabian desert and feeding new, hungry technologies. The empire was flush with money and enjoying a prosperous, stable period. Bayezid, Murad V's father, was a dignified, benevolent ruler—just as Murad had turned out to be. He had promoted cultural exchanges between the empire's diverse communities and hosted an annual inter-faith symposium at his palace in Istanbul.

'Could be worse,' Kamal said.

'It's cold, though. It's not summer.'

'Doesn't feel like it, does it?'

He looked around. From his vantage point, out in the middle of Fontainebleau Forest, nothing seemed different. Elsewhere, of course, he knew things would be very, very different. For better or for worse.

But at least they were alive, and they were free. That was what mattered most.

That, and they were together.

He caught himself staring at her again and averted his eyes once more. But he caught a hint of a smile on her face just as he did. 'And this,' he said as he gestured up and down his body, 'this was inevitable, I guess?'

*AD 1935.

321

'That's how it works,' she replied. 'I told you.' Then, suddenly, a look of panic swept over her and she flicked her gaze on to her forearm. Just as quickly, she breathed out a big sigh of relief.

'What?'

She held it up for him to see. 'It's still there.' She stared at it again. 'We have to write it down somewhere. Safeguard it. We can't afford to lose it.'

'We're here now,' he said. 'But yes, you're right. We need to memorize it. Or have it tattooed.'

She looked behind her, her expression darkening with worry. 'We might need it again. They might come after us. They know the incantation.'

'They'd have to know how far back we travelled to follow us.'

Her face lit up with alarm. 'The browser. On your phone. They could find your search history.'

'I busted it up pretty badly. And threw it in the lake. We should be fine.'

'It didn't look that deep,' she countered.

'I doubt they saw me do it.'

'Are you willing to bet our lives on that?'

He frowned, angry with himself. 'I should have saved a bullet for it.' He looked around. It felt too quiet. 'We'd better get moving then.'

'Where shall we go?' She hugged herself more tightly, rubbing her arms with her hands to warm them up. 'We don't have clothes or money or anything.'

'One step at a time.' He looked up at the tree cover. There were several more hours of daylight to come. Then he gathered his bearings, came to a decision, and said, 'Follow me.'

46

The great Fontainebleau madrasah wasn't too far, and getting there would have been an enjoyable afternoon trek had things been different.

Wandering through the forest with no clothes on—Kamal leading, Nisreen following—wasn't initially too uncomfortable. Despite the chill that grew more piercing as the sun drifted downwards, and even though they were totally naked, it went, to them both, from feeling unsettling and uncomfortable to oddly liberating, given the restrictive panoply of clothing they both had to wear whenever they were pretty much anywhere outside the privacy of their own homes.

Their feet, however, didn't quite agree with that rosy outlook.

The ground cover was harsh. Twigs and shards of broken branches, thorns, prickly leaves and pine needles, sharp-edged rocks and chippings—not constant, but all the more irritating for triggering the occasional unexpected jolt of pain. It was far from a smooth, moss-covered carpet. They weren't on a well-travelled path either. They were cutting their own route through virgin ground, subjecting the two hundred thousand nerve endings in their feet to recurring abuse for hours.

Kamal knew he could lead them in roughly the right direction, but it was the afternoon call to prayer from the mosque at Fontainebleau that proved to be their salutary beacon, a call to prayer that was accompanied by a darkening sky that soon became completely overcast. The temperature dropped, and the ambient chill grew more and more uncomfortable. They stopped briefly at a couple of small streams, drinking and using the cold water to nurse the scrapes and cuts on their feet. They had also both grown less shy and more at ease with their nudity, no longer bothering to cover themselves up.

Kamal, walking ahead, wasn't as aware of it as Nisreen was, but he still had to make a conscious effort to avoid staring at her too intently during their breaks.

Nisreen's mind, on the other hand, was grinding over far more important issues, including a disturbingly radical idea that had never really left her since she first voiced it.

An idea she was finding hard to suppress.

By the time the sunset call to prayer resonated across the forest, they knew they were close. The timing was fortunate. The clouds had grown darker and more dense before erupting into an angry thunderstorm. The ground became soggy with mud, and they were now shivering from the cold that was accentuated by their wet skin and hair. Trudging ahead through sheets of rain, with Nisreen covering her arm to protect the words inscribed on it from getting washed away, their advance slowed. They needed to find shelter, a place to dry off and get clothing without being seen. The rapidly encroaching darkness would be a boon in that sense, but the accompanying drop in temperature was a real concern.

In the distance, through the trees and under a sky that was exploring the entire palette of purples and pinks, the first lights of the big madrasah came into view.

A light fog had settled in, hugging the ground leading up to the castle. The rain was now lighter as they crept closer, cautiously, curbing the growing urgency they felt while hoping that the shadows within the dense forest would mask their presence. Coming in from the south, they took cover behind the last line of trees that bordered the grand parterre, the huge formal garden that led to the old palace.

Kamal saw that Nisreen was now shivering badly. He was feeling it, too. His instinct was to pull her closer to warm her up, but he couldn't bring himself to do it, or even suggest it, not while they were naked. Besides, he wasn't sure his cold, clammy skin would provide her with much warmth.

He peered out towards the old castle. He couldn't see any guards. He hadn't expected to see any. This was a religious community, not an imperial palace. The sprawling complex looked placid and non-threatening, the same as he remembered it. Lights were on throughout the windows of its various wings, and Kamal could make out the occasional figure passing into view. It seemed like a normal night at the madrasah. Their prayers done, its occupants would be settling down for supper before retiring to their quarters.

'What do you think?' Nisreen asked, her teeth now chattering from the cold.

'We need to get to the housing wings without being seen.' He pointed ahead and left. 'They used to be over on that side.'

'Used to be,' Nisreen noted pointedly.

'Will be, I guess,' Kamal corrected himself with a slight scoff and a little shake of the head. A long, open pathway, ceremonially lined with elm trees, led in the direction he was pointing at. 'It's too dangerous to take the path. We'd be too exposed.'

'Make it quick. I'm freezing.'

He scanned the area, then decided on an alternative approach. 'Follow me. And stay low.'

He led Nisreen around the soaked parterre, and, hugging the treeline, they looped further west to reach a vast pond that extended up to the palace.

The trees around the pond were wild and had been left to grow right up to the water's edge, which helped make their approach easier. They moved swiftly, with only the occasional splash of a carp darting up to the surface to feed disturbing the stillness around them.

With the old palace now shrouded in near darkness, they slipped across the Garden of the Doves, with Nisreen following in Kamal's footsteps. He stopped and hustled her into cover behind a large boxwood hedge to avoid a couple of strollers from the school, who were out despite the light drizzle. Once clear, they scuttled past a fountain that gurgled gently in its serene surroundings, then through a narrow passage, to reach the oval court that fronted the complex's mosque.

The mosque itself had grown around the old ballroom of Henry II, which had been extended along both sides of its central axis by additions that were topped by a parallel series of domes. Primaticcio and Niccolò dell'Abbate's frescoes were long gone, the pagan imagery of Vulcan, Jupiter and Mercury replaced by tiles of geometric compositions and murals of Koranic calligraphy. Works such as the Nymph of Fontainebleau were also gone, since representations of living beings, human or animal, were banned by Islam. Some figurative imagery had survived, mostly of plants, a few of animals; across the centuries, attitudes had fluctuated depending on who sat on the throne. Some sultans had been unusually tolerant of such art, even going so far as to commission portraits of themselves to hang at the Topkapi in Istanbul. More strictly observant successors were usually quick to erase such trespasses.

Right now, the mosque seemed empty.

Kamal and Nisreen crept around its perimeter to reach the southwesternmost corner of the complex, where Kamal assumed the dormitories would be.

He was right. Behind a low wall, a few items of clothing

hung tantalizingly from long clothes lines, but they were useless to them. They were soaking wet.

Beyond the courtyard, lights shone dimly from the windows.

'Wait here,' he told her. 'I'll go grab what we need.'

He was about to move off when she reached out and grabbed his arm. 'Wait. What if you're captured?'

He put his hand on hers. 'Don't worry.'

'But—'

'Don't worry. I've done this kind of thing before.' Then he shrugged. 'Though maybe not exactly like this.'

'Be careful.'

He knew, from details across her face that he couldn't specifically pinpoint, that she was still trapped in the hellhole of what she'd been through. He smiled warmly back at her. He knew it would be a long time before he'd see a real smile infuse her face—if one ever did.

He wasn't exactly feeling chirpy either. The sadness and the fury were still very much there.

'I'll be right back.'

He left her by the edge of the woods and made his way to the wall.

A small cast-iron gate led into the large courtyard where the clothes were hung. Kamal was careful to swing it open slowly in case it let out a squeal. It didn't.

Now inside the compound, he skulked up to a window that looked on to a well-lit room, and, carefully, he peered inside. A group of young men—students, no doubt—were seated on low cushions, huddled around a large platter of food set on a carpet. It was mealtime. Which meant the rooms might be unoccupied.

He slipped down the building's wall, past a couple more illuminated windows, until he reached one that was dark. He edged up to it and looked in. It was a large dormitory room with two sets of bunk beds, closets, and desks. There was no one inside. He tried the window, but it was closed tight, and he couldn't prise it open. Ravaged by the cold now, he considered shattering the window, then discarded the idea, fearing the noise might alert someone inside. Instead, he kept moving, creeping further along the wall, past several other windows until he found one that was cracked open. It gave on to a similar room, which was also dark and unoccupied.

He climbed in. Once inside, he moved quickly to find what they needed. It wasn't much different from what he was used to back in his time: a pair of baggy black *shalwar* trousers, a white shirt, a tunic, and a kaftan robe, simple pieces made of plain cotton and unadorned by decorative embroidery or buttons, which he pulled on as he found them, relishing the warmth they gave him. Once dressed, he proceeded to collect clothes for Nisreen. He rummaged through the cupboards to see if any of the room's occupants was of a smaller size than the one whose clothes he'd taken. They'd be male clothes, of course, but at that time, even more so than in his, Ottoman men's and women's clothing weren't too dissimilar, especially when it came to the everyday wear of the masses and not the ceremonial outfits of the wealthier classes. He found what he was looking for and grabbed her some trousers, a long-sleeved *gomlek* shirt that would reach her ankles, an *entari* coat that buttoned from the neck to the waist, and a dark-grey *ferace* robe. What he couldn't get her was a veil; instead, he picked up an extra shirt, which she could wrap around her head.

He couldn't find any shoes, but he knew why.

He rolled her clothes up into a large bundle and climbed out the window. He made his way back along the wall until he reached the brightly lit room. He set the bundle down and peered inside. As he expected, the men were wearing soft, mule-like indoor shoes. The outdoor shoes would be by the front door.

Kamal pulled back, saw the door that led into the dormitory, and decided it was worth the risk. Besides, everyone seemed busy with dinner.

He made sure no one was heading back from the paths behind the building, then made his way over to the door, and, slowly, carefully, he pushed it open. He poked his head in for a quick look and saw a row of leather shoes lined up by the door. He hesitated, then heard a woman's voice. She seemed to be getting closer.

He decided to make his move and darted in, grabbed the closest two pairs and slipped out again, not bothering to close the door behind him.

He hugged the building wall and shrank back into the shadows as the light from inside grew wider before the woman stepped outside. She stood there, looking around curiously. He held his breath as she looked left, then right, but didn't see him. She lingered there for a moment longer, looked up at the sky, as if to judge the weather to come, then disappeared back inside, shutting the door behind her.

He scooped up the bundle he'd collected for Nisreen and made a run for it, scampering out the gate before joining her under the trees.

'I got what I could,' he said as he handed her the clothes. 'It might not be your best look, but at least they're dry.'

'I don't care if it's a circus costume. I'd still wear them,' she said as she grabbed them from him. Then she gave him a pointed look and made a twirling gesture with her finger.

Taking the cue, he turned around while she dressed.

The warmth felt better to them, but they were still dazed by the day's events, and they were hungry.

'What now?' she asked. 'Should we stay here? They'd take us in, wouldn't they?'

'In their stolen clothes?'

'It's a big enough place. We can seek shelter in their hospice.'

Kamal shook his head. 'No. It's too close to where we arrived. And it's the first place they'd come looking for us if they decided to come after us. They know I know this place well.'

'What then?'

He'd been thinking about that since they arrived.

'Paris.'

47

At the clearing by the lake, Taymoor stood between the SUV Kamal and Nisreen had escaped in and the water's edge.

A couple of other agents were close by. One of them was inspecting the inside of the vehicle. The others had been sent into the woods to look for the escapees. Taymoor's attention, however, was riveted on the spot behind the SUV, the empty ground between it and the lake.

The ground where Kamal and Nisreen were last seen.

The place where they had been cornered.

The spot, according to the agents and the cops who had chased them there, from which there was no possible escape.

No possible escape. And yet they weren't there. They had done just that—escaped.

How?

He'd sent out men to search the woods, to see if they could find any clue as to the couple's disappearance. And as he stared at the bare, dry earth at the banks of the lake, to his left and to his right, and at the stagnant, shimmering water, he knew he was missing something. Something major. Something he hadn't been deemed worthy to be informed of—neither by his partner nor by his superiors at the Hafiye.

He heard some commotion and turned his attention toward its source. Four cops were coming out of the forest. They had a couple of others with them, civilians, and were shoving them forward, herding them towards Taymoor's position.

'Taymoor Agha,' one of them called out. 'We found these two hiding in the woods.'

They jostled them over to face him. They were both male. The older man looked like he was in his forties and had a craggy, unshaven face. The younger man was somewhere in his twenties and had a handsome, clean face but was a little frail of build. They both looked terrified.

Taymoor knew where the fear was coming from. He knew what they had been doing there.

'They were hiding behind some bushes at the edge of the forest,' one of the cops told Taymoor.

'Hiding in the bushes? Doing what? Having a private little picnic,' he sneered, his anger at being kept in the dark about whatever the hell was going on overcoming his revulsion at having to play the gruff bigot.

'We didn't see anything,' the younger man blurted nervously. 'We just hid because of the shooting.'

'I didn't ask you if you saw something,' Taymoor replied, his tone clinical. 'But I'm now rather convinced that you did.'

He took a step closer to the young man, who dropped his gaze and was now visibly shaking. He remained there for a long moment, giving the fear time to percolate through every pore of the young man. Then, in a lower, almost conspiratorial voice, he added, 'We both know what you two were doing here. And we both know the consequences if I were to take you in for it. But if you tell me what you saw, then I might elect to forget certain things. Maybe a lot of things. What do you say, *habibi*?'

In the Ottoman Empire, beauty had been ungendered for centuries. It was very common for older men to pursue younger, beardless boys romantically as well as for mentoring. Ottoman culture was rife with homoerotic poetry that extolled the virtues of this spiritualization of love. Palace elites and even some sultans engaged openly in pederasty. Things had changed, however, under Abdülhamid's rule.

Intolerance of anyone who didn't fit the state's vision of the ideal citizen became policy. Any form of homosexuality was now deemed a grave moral transgression and was unofficially criminalized, its practice driven underground.

The young man hazarded a glance up at Taymoor, then looked at his friend nervously. The older man's face was stiff with fear and dripping with sweat, but his eyes were clearly signalling for him to keep quiet.

Which Taymoor caught.

He slapped the young man briskly, then used a firm grip to clasp his jaw and force him to face him. 'My memory has a nasty habit of solidifying alarmingly fast,' he told the young man. 'You really don't want to let that happen.'

He fell silent, continuing to scour menacingly. The young man's face rippled with dread before contorting into reluctant, grudging compliance.

'There were two of them,' he told Taymoor. 'A man and a woman.'

'And?'

'It all happened very fast. They rushed out of that car and hid behind it; then the others arrived. Two cars. The man started shooting at them.' He stopped and his eyes narrowed, as if he were studying the result of his revelations and hoping they were having a favourable effect on his inquisitor.

'Then what?'

'They shouted to each other. The officers wanted them to give themselves up. Then there was more shooting. A lot of it.' He paused again.

'Then what? What happened to the man and the woman?'

The young man's eyes flashed wider. Then he dropped his gaze to the ground. And said nothing.

'Where did they go?' Taymoor repeated in a low, harsh hiss.

The young man remained silent.

Taymoor crept closer so he was now looming over the cowering man. 'Where. Did. They. Go?'

The young man peered up at him from the corner of his eyes, then, his lips quivering, he said, 'They disappeared.'

Taymoor's face tightened. 'What do you mean, they disappeared?'

The young man was now shaking uncontrollably and barely able to look at Taymoor. He hazarded a quick glance before he fell to his knees and cupped his face in his hands and started to sob.

'I asked you a question,' Taymoor raged.

'They disappeared,' the young man mumbled through shivering lips, barely daring to glance up at the agent who was towering over him. 'They just vanished into thin air.'

Taymoor flew into a rage. He grabbed the man by the hair and pulled him up with one hand while his other arm swung up and wide, his hand open and ready to deliver another monster slap. The young man yelped and curled into himself defensively. 'It's the truth—I swear it,' he blurted out in a rush to avoid the coming blow. 'They just disappeared. I swear it.'

Taymoor held him there for a moment, then dropped him. The man cowered on the ground by his feet. Taymoor studied him. He didn't know what to make of his answer. What he did know was that it didn't make sense. He'd need a more private session of questioning to get to the truth.

He turned to face the other man. 'What about you? Do you have anything to add?'

The older man looked just as fear-stricken as his younger companion. 'It's like he said,' he managed hesitantly. 'They really vanished. I know it sounds crazy, but that's what happened. I can't explain it.'

Taymoor shrugged in resignation. 'Fine. Have it your way.' He nodded to his men. 'Take them away. We'll try this again later.'

The cops took hold of the men and started pushing them towards their cars. The two men tried to resist, with the younger man pleading, 'It's the truth—I swear it.'

Taymoor just nodded for his men to carry on.

'He's telling the truth,' the older man insisted, his voice breaking. 'That's all we saw. They were just there. Then the man threw something into the lake, and they just disappeared.'

Which froze Taymoor. He snapped his fingers, which made his men stop in their tracks.

He marched closer to the older man and grabbed him by the hair, spinning his face so he was looking him squarely in the eyes.

'He threw something in the lake?'

The man nodded feverishly.

Taymoor's eyes narrowed. 'Show me.'

48

The darkness was a boon, but they didn't need to remain hidden any more. Any observer would simply assume the two humbly dressed figures walking along the edge of the unpaved road were husband and wife or brother and sister. There was nothing remarkable or noteworthy about them as they exchanged polite greetings with those they encountered on their way to the river's edge.

The docks of the town of Fontainebleau weren't far from the old palace. Kamal had a strong feeling they'd find what they needed there. He knew that the Seine, which snaked into the old town before winding its way to Paris and, beyond, to the port of Le Havre and the English Channel, was a busy transport artery, perhaps even more so back then, before lorries were ubiquitous. Barges plied its waters continuously, ferrying goods back and forth across the breadth of the French province. It was a reasonably safe and inconspicuous way to reach Paris.

After a few cautious inquiries, they came across a captain who wasn't overly inquisitive and agreed to give them free passage. They settled on to a small, clear section of deck at the bow of the river barge, their backs resting against a tarpaulin that covered some pallets of roof tiles. The temperature had dropped considerably now that the sun was long gone, with the air on the river much cooler than it was on land. But the skies had cleared, and it didn't look like more rain was on its way.

Kamal and Nisreen huddled close together under a blinking canopy of countless stars as the barge set off into the night.

For a long while, neither of them said a word. They just stared into the distance, lost in their own thoughts.

It was Nisreen who eventually broke the silence. 'What happens now?' she asked. 'What's going to happen to us? What if we can't get back to our time?'

He inhaled deeply and let out a tired sigh. 'I don't know. This wasn't something I saw coming.'

He watched her as her eyes roamed the infinite darkness overhead, as if looking for a sign, a signal, a message from the unknown. 'It's insane, isn't it? We wake up every day, thinking it's just going to be another normal day, oblivious to how lucky we are, unaware about how damn vulnerable we are. And then, in one moment, it's all taken away. Everything falls apart. Everything you hold dear, your whole life, is just cruelly wrenched away from you, and there's nothing you can do about it. It's just gone. Just like that.' She stared deeper into nothingness. 'What kind of a God allows that to happen?'

'I don't have an answer for you, Nisreen. But if I ever do meet him, we're going to have a very unpleasant chat.'

She went silent again.

After a while, she said, 'I feel like I'm in prison. The worst kind of prison. A prison without walls, one that I've put myself in. And I know I'll never be freed.'

Kamal didn't reply. He knew her mind would be prey to a poisonous darkness for some time. He wanted to hug her tightly, to find some way to comfort her, to tell her things would get better, to give her some clichéd line about how time would heal her. But he couldn't bring himself to do that, not with her, not given what had happened.

He was in that same prison himself.

'We're here now,' he finally offered. 'We're here, we're safe, we have each other, and we have this thing, this incredible, scary, horrible ability to go where or when we like. Maybe we need to give ourselves some time to catch our breath and think things through and figure out what's best.'

'I've been thinking about it all day.'

'Me too,' he said.

She went quiet, then said, 'We haven't even been born yet. In this time. We don't exist yet.'

'And yet here we are.'

She shrugged. 'So what if there was a way to leave a message for ourselves—for our future selves?'

'What do you mean?'

'What if we could leave ourselves a message about what happened—about what will happen? A warning for Ramazan to stay away from a tattooed patient who might show up at the hospital, to not go anywhere near him. Then maybe none of this will happen. We wouldn't know anything. They wouldn't come after us.' Her voice cracked as she added, 'Ramazan, Tarek and Noor wouldn't have to die.'

She choked on those last words, her lower lip taking on a small quiver, her damp eyes visibly holding back tears just as they moved off him—then failing and succumbing to the overwhelming sadness.

Kamal felt his heart shatter.

He considered her words as he gave her time for the tears and the sobs to subside.

'Maybe,' he said. 'But if we did that, how would it work in terms of us being here now? What would happen to us?'

She wiped her face with her sleeve. 'I don't know.'

'We wouldn't have a reason to travel back. We wouldn't even know about it. Which means if we saved our future selves, we'd still be there. Another version of us, I suppose. But we can't be in two places at the same time, can we?'

'He said we can't. It's one of the rules. It doesn't allow it.' She went silent for a moment as she wondered about it. 'I suppose we'd need to die here. In this time. To make room for our future selves.' She gave Kamal a weary, uncertain shrug. 'I don't know, Kamal. It all sounds so crazy.'

He nodded. Then he asked, 'But . . . would you?'

'What?'

'Want to die here? In this world?'

'If it meant they could live? If it meant I could be with them again? Of course.'

'But it would be a different you. Not this you.'

'If I can be with them again—this me, or any other me— I'd die here for that.' She paused, studying him. 'Would you?'

He hesitated for the briefest moment, but before he could answer, she added, 'I'm sorry. It's not fair of me to ask you that.'

'There's nothing unfair about it.' He took her hands in his. 'Of course, I would. I'd give anything to undo all that's happened. To give you back your family. Our family. No hesitation. But I want it to be for "this" you. And "this" me.'

'But that's not possible.'

'I know.' He shrugged and looked away. 'Maybe we should do that. Maybe I need to send myself a message, too.'

'What would you tell yourself?'

'To be more aware. To warn myself about getting swept up by the wrong ideas and taken in by the lies, to be awake to what was happening in our world. Maybe I'd try to change things before they went too far.'

This visibly surprised Nisreen. 'You'd want to change things?'

'I could try . . . knowing what we know, having lived through these last few years. I could try.' The thought bloomed across his mind. 'That's what Rasheed did, right? He went back and changed his world. Maybe that's something I could do, too. Maybe there's a way to avoid how it all turned out— not just for us. For everybody. I mean, look at this world, this time we've landed in. We haven't seen much of it, but from what we know about it, it was a better place, wasn't it?'

'Things were different then—now,' she corrected herself, evidently still having a hard time adjusting to the new reality. 'Bayezid was a noble man. Things were good. The Arabians hadn't yet started their attacks, and the Americans hadn't killed our economy. People felt safe and weren't worried about ending up in a jail cell for saying the wrong thing or some nut blowing himself up next to them.' She tilted her head back and stared up at the heavens. 'It was a better time to be alive, to be sure.'

He watched her, studying the lines of her face, every feature that he'd memorized and fallen in love with back in their earlier incarnations—and felt a savage, primal rage at the pain she'd been made to suffer.

'It's just a shame we couldn't all be here together,' she added before turning away. 'I mean, if only we could travel into the future, we could go get them—before any of it happens. Bring them all back here. Start a new life.' She sighed heavily. 'It's all so . . . hopeless.'

Kamal could only watch in muted frustration as she curled into herself, as if defending herself against an unspeakably cruel world, and her silence turned to quiet sobs and shudders.

He hesitated, an epic, gut-wrenching battle going on inside him. Then, carefully, slowly, like he was reaching for something incalculably fragile and precious, he slid his arms around her.

She didn't move at first; then, without raising her head, she melted into his brotherly embrace, her head tucked into his shoulder, her sobs now unleashed into a torrent of agony.

Taymoor felt apprehensive as he entered Celaleddin's office.

He'd never been inside the darkened room before and didn't know what to expect. A lot had happened lately that he didn't understand. He'd been kept in the dark about things and he needed answers.

'Come in, Taymoor Agha, come in.' Celaleddin welcomed him, rising from behind his desk and ushering him to the divan to his right. 'It seems you've had quite a day.'

'*Evet,* my pasha,' he agreed as he angled towards the seating area.

The office's size, location, lighting, furniture, and finishings— everything about it projected power and was designed to intimidate. Through the blinds, Taymoor glimpsed the ancient turrets of the castle and, beyond, the city's lit minarets and domes. Even from that limited perspective, the view was awe-inspiring. He could only guess how impressive it had to be in full view, with the blinds open or from the balcony, perhaps at sunset, when the city was basking in golden glory.

It had been a hell of a day. He'd been awakened in the middle of the night and ordered to lead an emergency manhunt for his partner. He'd discovered the dead bodies of four of his agency brethren in some godforsaken ruins in the middle of nowhere. He'd been shot at by his partner's sister-in-law, who had then, it was claimed, vanished into thin air. Then he'd been summoned to the pasha's inner sanctum. A hell of a day, indeed. And it didn't feel like the onset of night was going to bring any respite.

Celaleddin folded his tall frame into the plush seat across from the agent. He raised his hand and gestured breezily in Taymoor's general direction with two slim fingers. 'I understand you were shot?'

Taymoor reflexively gave his head a gentle rub. 'It's just a graze, pasha. I was lucky. Thank you for asking.'

'It's unfortunate that they were able to escape,' Celaleddin added.

Taymoor thought he detected a tinge of accusation in his

boss's tone. 'He escaped from me. It was a shameful failure on my part. One I'll redress if you were to grace me with the chance to do so.'

'Oh, I intend to do more than give you a chance, Taymoor. I'm going to need you to do something very, very important for us. We need you. The empire needs you. Your sultan needs you. You see, your history with Kamal Agha, your closeness to him, your knowledge about how he thinks—these make you the ideal candidate for this mission. But it's going to require a lot of discretion on your part, and sacrifices. Sacrifices that could well turn out to be . . . permanent.'

Celaleddin went silent, leaving the question implied but not voiced.

Taymoor didn't disappoint him. His brow twitched, but he tried to conceal any sign of confusion—or doubt. 'My life is at the sultan's disposal, for him to do with as he pleases, pasha.'

'I expected nothing less of you, Taymoor,' Celaleddin nodded. 'But this sacrifice also requires you to use extreme prejudice in a way that you might find . . . conflicting.'

'There is no conflict when it comes to my duty to my sultan and to the empire, pasha.'

'Even when it comes to your partner?'

Taymoor's hand instinctively pressed a bit harder against his wound. 'There is no conflict, my pasha.'

Celaleddin studied the young agent.

He'd had a long discussion with Kuzey and with Taymoor's direct superior only moments earlier. The impression he'd been given was clear: yes, they were partners; yes, they were close and had each other's backs when threatened. But there was a growing fault line in their outlook on the security situation facing the empire, one that must have widened after Kamal's sister-in-law took a shot at him. Taymoor's profile was ideal for the task at hand. He had the operational skills, and there was no one else who knew Kamal Agha as well as he did, who could think like him and second-guess his actions. And he was single, with no known emotional ties to anyone. He was the best man for the job. A job that, after much deliberation, Cela-leddin had decided to entrust to a task force of one single man.

The risks of doing otherwise were too great and too uncontrollable.

He'd entrust it to a single man . . . for now. He knew he would always have the option of sending someone else, another task force, back to the same time and place if this approach failed. In fact, if what he believed was correct, he could do that as many times as he liked. Until it worked. At this point, though, it was all guessing. Until he tried it himself, he wasn't sure about anything. But he had to try.

He also realized he might never know if Taymoor succeeded in his task. He'd come up with a way for Taymoor to let him know, to send him a message from the past he would be stuck in, but he wasn't sure it would work. He knew he was still far from fully understanding how this incredible machination worked.

'Let me ask you . . . Kamal Agha. What do you know of what's become of him and of his sister-in-law?'

'Nothing, pasha.'

'Nothing at all?'

'I have no explanation for their escape, for which I accept full responsibility.'

'I'm not looking to assign any blame, Taymoor.'

'Regardless, I should not have let it happen. But I still can't explain it. No one saw anything.'

'No one?'

'No. The men on the scene can't explain it. We have nothing apart from the ridiculous ramblings of a couple of deviants we picked up at the scene, but they don't make any sense. I'll get to the bottom of it though, pasha. I will find them.'

Celaleddin considered him for a moment. Then he rose and crossed over to his desk. 'I know you will, Taymoor. In fact, I'm going to give you the information you need to be able to do that. But we're going to have to move fast. While the trail is still warm.'

He picked up some things off the desk and came back to the divan. As he sat down, he placed them on the large table that separated them.

Taymoor leaned forward for a closer look. There was a small plastic evidence bag, along with a stack of printouts. In the bag were two busted mobile phones.

'You recognize these, of course?' Celaleddin asked, tapping the bag.

The phones were the ones his divers had recovered only hours earlier from the bed of the lake.

He nodded. 'Yes.'

Celaleddin leaned forward and studied him intently. 'This mission needs to be undertaken in the utmost secrecy. No one can know about it. And if you accept it, your life will change irreversibly. There will be no going back.'

Taymoor knew that Celaleddin had left out the flip side to his statement: that if he baulked at carrying out the assignment once he knew what it entailed, he would not be allowed to live.

Taymoor didn't flinch. Instead, he just reiterated his loyalty in the same solemn tone.

'My life is at the sultan's feet, pasha,' he told the commander. 'For him to do with as he pleases.'

49

Shortly before dawn, the barge docked at the busy quay of Bercy.

The largest commercial port in Paris, it owed its name to the small town to which it had originally belonged, a town that had long since been swallowed up by the city.

Even at that hour, it was humming with activity. Barges were jostling in and out, some of them docked five-deep along the wharf while awaiting their turn to load and offload their cargo. On the quay itself, an army of dock workers were busy making sure the voracious city's stockpiles of all kinds of goods, from wheat to orchids to ceramic fixtures, never ran out.

Kamal and Nisreen stayed on board while the pallets and crates were winched off. It was still dark, and the captain had enough empathy not to abandon them to the night. But once day broke and the muezzins' calls to prayer came and went, Kamal began to feel uneasy about staying put longer than necessary and told Nisreen it was time for them to leave. They thanked the captain for his generosity and set off.

After they cleared the bustle of the quay, the change in the city from the time they'd come from was immediately evident. The air was the first thing they noticed; it was no different from the air in the forest and felt cleaner and more pleasant to breathe in than what they remembered of Paris. There were cars, buses and trams around—not many at that time of the morning, when the city was still at rest—but there were far fewer of them. The population of the city was much lower—at three million in its current incarnation, it was barely a third of what it was at the time of their escape.

In fact, everything about it, especially at that hour, was easier on the senses. The pavements were cleaner and easier to navigate, the streets devoid of any form of signage clutter. There weren't even traffic lights. The body language of the people they passed was different, too: more flowing, less jagged. Even the buildings were softer on the eyes: lower, less densely stacked and more ornate. The city was palpably more tranquil in a thousand ways. Perhaps it didn't seem that way to those who hadn't travelled there from Kamal and Nisreen's time—after all, they didn't know any different, and it was still a crowded, bustling metropolis that was doubtless busier and noisier than it had been in years past—but it certainly did to them.

Without money and with hunger now making its displeasure known, they set off for a place where they knew they could get food and a bed: a *waqf* complex, like the one Ramazan had worked at. Kamal had preferred not to ask the barge captain if any of the ones he knew from his time were already around. He knew the Hurrem Sultan was, but he felt it might be too obvious, and hence dangerous, to head there. But he was sure a couple of others were probably old enough to be around. The number of such complexes had grown, and their facilities had expanded in step with the wealth and power of the sultans, and this was a prosperous, peaceful time for the empire.

The nearer of the two was the Haseki Sultan, on the left bank of the Seine, just beyond the Suleiman VI University. Not having any money to take any form of paid transportation, that's where they headed.

Half an hour later, they were walking through its gates.

Like the Hurrem, the Haseki was also a huge complex of

buildings. It housed a mosque, a fifty-room hospice, a medical clinic and the two parts that Kamal and Nisreen needed: an *imaret*—a public kitchen—that led to a small *han,* the inn that welcomed travellers. Like all *waqf* complexes, the Haseki was a strictly run establishment. Imperial generosity didn't stop the careful regulation of the benefits afforded to the guests of its facilities. With close to two thousand people being fed in the vast dining halls of its *imaret* three times a day, rigid rules of seniority had to be followed regarding what was on offer and how it was handed out.

Kamal and Nisreen tried to interact as little as possible as they made their way to the reception office of the *imaret,* where Kamal made the careful introductions. He took on his father's backstory and presented himself as a poultry farmer visiting from the Périgord. Nisreen was his subservient wife, who, true to form, didn't say a word. He sensed some subtle doubting on the part of the clerk, perhaps triggered by their simple clothing. Kamal deflected it by adopting a humble demeanour and feigning to take the official into his confidence, confessing he'd fallen on hard times after his farm had caught fire a few months earlier, destroying his entire flock. He kept a self-effacing and stoic front as he told him he was in Paris to look for other opportunities. The ruse worked, and they were soon issued with an induction document and ushered towards the dining hall, where they handed the document to the marshal overseeing the meal and were invited to join the long queue.

There was no stigma attached to eating at a public kitchen in the empire. Well-to-do families who were going through tough times did it as much as the poor. The rulers regarded the ability to feed vast numbers of people as a necessary, visible symbol of their power, their piety and their legitimacy; the people viewed the food distribution as an enviable privilege.

Those deemed more prestigious—visiting dignitaries, merchants, travellers, and scholars—ate first and better. The needy then followed. Women and children came last.

Kamal and Nisreen ate heartily, polishing off their bowls of honey-and-saffron-sweetened rice and their loaves of bread in no time. Wary of discovery as well as worried about leaving a trail, Kamal tried to keep any conversation with their neighbours at the long table to a minimum. They left as soon as they were done and crossed a colonnaded courtyard that led to the inn. This time, the introduction process went more smoothly, and the innkeeper soon saw fit to grant them a small room, one that overlooked the slanted tile roof of another walled *sahn* courtyard that was flanked by one of the mosque's minarets.

As travellers, they were entitled to three days' hospitality. After that, they would need to fend for themselves. For now, though, they were exhausted, and they collapsed on to the narrow beds, neither of them moving or saying much.

It was a lot to process, for them both.

As Kamal glanced at Nisreen, he couldn't help but feel his own fury rise at what had happened, at what had been done to her. And as much as he tried to engage with her, to comfort her and offer her a supportive ear, he found her distant and reluctant to talk, lost in her own thoughts, as if in a trance.

He had a lot on his mind, too.

They had no money, no papers, no friends or family or any kind of contacts. There was no one they knew at that time, no friendly door to knock on. It was as if they'd landed on a foreign planet. Of course, they could seek out distant relatives, ancestors, great-grandparents possibly, asking for help. But what would they tell them, and why would these people consider them anything other than the strangers they were? More troubling was the question of whether entering their ancestors' lives risked altering their histories and affecting these ancestors' choices from here on, which could then affect Kamal's and Nisreen's own histories in unknown ways.

It was too uncertain and dangerous to consider.

On the other hand, they had some advantages they could put to good use. They knew what the future held—they knew how events would unfold, and they could try to profit from them. In fact, if they were careful and clever, they could carve out a spectacularly successful life for themselves, even though gambling was outlawed and the stock market, back then, was still in its infancy. Still, there had to be plenty of opportunities they could exploit. Which was why part of him just wanted to ask, 'What if we stayed here? What if we lived out the rest of our lives here, in peace?'

He knew it was a pointless question.

The profound sadness, the pain that was still mauling her— it was all there, etched in harsh strokes across her eyes, her mouth, her face. A subtle difference on a beautiful face, but an unmistakable one to someone who knew her as well as he did.

Subtle and entrenched. As it was in him.

Ever since they'd jumped back in time, and even if it was just for a passing, fleeting moment or two—when his mind had been able to wander, when he'd allowed himself to put aside his anger and hunger for revenge and to fall prey to naive hopefulness, when he'd managed to abandon reality and let his imagination roam to an idealized world—he'd caught glimpses of himself imagining staying in this strange new land with Nisreen, creating a new life for themselves. It was a wonderful thing to imagine, and it wasn't something that was unheard of in Ottoman society; far from it.

As the brother-in-law of a widow, it was his duty to look after his surviving family. Marrying her would not have been frowned upon; it would have been celebrated. In normal circumstances, it would help keep the fabric of the family together and keep any inheritance within it. Strictly speaking, they were only breaking with tradition in that widows were expected to observe a mourning period of four months and ten days, during which they were prohibited from interacting with any man they could potentially marry, even with a chaperone present.

In those flights of fancy, Kamal had wondered if, with time, they might not forget about the tragedies that had upended their lives, if their memories might not eventually fade, if he and Nisreen might not, together, be able to forge an alternative existence to settle into. It was a selfish dream, for sure. He was the one who'd always wanted it, and he knew it. But he genuinely felt it would also undoubtedly be good for her, too—to find happiness again, to move past the pain, to enjoy waking up to a new day every morning.

It was just that, though. A dream. An impossible one.

He knew it wouldn't happen, knew it couldn't happen. Every furrow in her face confirmed what he knew, what he realized was the only way anyone in her situation and with her heart could possibly feel. He knew she would never find release from the purgatory that engulfed her. It would never let go. And if it were to ever let go, it would probably be because he wasn't around to remind her of all that had happened.

There could be no happily ever after for them together. Of that he was certain.

He pushed away the thought, deciding it was better not to dwell on it, deciding it was pointless to grind over that dismal notion, telling himself it was better to let the future play itself out and see what it held for them.

And hope it wouldn't be too unkind.

It was a hope that didn't take long to get crushed.

50

Even though the muezzin's call to afternoon prayer was coming from the minaret close to their room, Kamal didn't stir. Instead, its soporific, drawn-out cadences lulled him into an even deeper sleep.

The drum that was struck to signal its associated distribution of food, however, did break through his slumber. They'd already slept through the meal that had followed the midday prayer; this would be the last offering of the day.

He felt woolly-headed, and it took him a moment to process where he was. He pushed himself to his elbows, taking in the strange room, and saw her sitting by the window, staring out.

He asked, 'How long have you been awake?'

'I couldn't sleep.'

He sat up. '*Hatun,* you need rest.'

'I couldn't. I kept thinking about what we were talking about last night. About what I could do to change things. To save them.' She let out a long, exasperated breath. 'It always comes back to the same thing. The impossibility of going back to our own lives. I even thought we could go back to when Rasheed first got sick. In Paris, in his time. Get the forward travel incantation . . . and kill him. So he doesn't ever come to our time.'

Kamal felt saddened. 'It would be safer to leave ourselves a warning.'

'But it might get lost over the years . . . or we might not believe it.'

'The result would be the same. We can't go back.'

'I know . . . but there has to be something we can do.' Her eyes welled up again.

He went to her and hugged her. 'I'm so, so sorry . . .'

They stayed there, in silence, for a long moment. Then she pulled back, slowly.

'You really should get some rest,' he told her. 'Let's go downstairs and eat first. We'll talk about it again later.'

Nisreen crossed over to her bed and sat down. 'I'm not hungry.'

'I don't know when we'll be able to eat next.'

She didn't reply. She just let out an indifferent shrug and got into her bed, pulling the sheet right up to her ears, blocking out the world. 'You go.'

The hollowness that hadn't left his gut for days sank even deeper, but he didn't give it a voice. Instead, he said, 'I'll bring something back for you.'

She didn't reply.

The line for the afternoon meal was longer than it had been in the morning, and a crowd of those waiting for their turn to be called was milling about in the large hall outside the communal dining room. Kamal was cutting through the throng and heading for the marshal who would normally be ushering people at the back of the queue when he spotted him: Taymoor, right there, in the *imaret,* talking to the marshal. A couple of Zaptiye uniformed officers were behind Taymoor, further back in the crowd—not men from his own time but local men, men he must have somehow managed to co-opt, judging by their outdated period uniforms.

Taymoor's face was tight with purpose, his eyes scanning the room as he spoke to the marshal.

The marshal was nodding affirmatively.

Kamal hissed out a curse and pulled back, melting into the

crowd, trying to keep as many unsuspecting bodies between him and Taymoor as possible. A fusillade of questions raked his brain. How was it that Taymoor was here, now? How had he followed them? Had they found his phone in the lake? And, more worryingly, how had he managed to put together a local posse so quickly? How had he persuaded the authorities in this day and age to fall into line and give him their support?

The answers would have to wait. With one wary eye cast in Taymoor's direction, he slipped back until he reached the hallway that branched off towards the inn; then he took off running.

His mind was already processing the geometry of the place and possible escape routes by the time he burst into their room, startling Nisreen.

'We have to go. Now. Taymoor is here.'

Nisreen stared at him with sleepy, confused eyes. 'Taymoor? Here?'

'At the *imaret*. Quick.' Kamal grabbed her hand and yanked her to her feet. 'Let's go.'

He opened the door a crack, peered out.

The corridor was clear.

'Stay close.'

They rushed in the opposite direction, away from the kitchen, towards the entrance to the inn by the mosque. Kamal led Nisreen down a long, narrow passageway, his body taut, every muscle on high alert and ready for any eruption as they slipped past scores of closed doors to other bedrooms.

They were about to climb down the stairs that led to the ground floor of the inn when some bustle coming from below caused him to freeze. He leaned close, pricking his ears, but he already knew what it was. Two police officers, men from the Zaptiye that Taymoor had somehow managed to co-opt, were heading up their way.

'Back, back,' he hissed at Nisreen, hustling her away from the stairs and back in the direction they'd come from.

They flew down the corridor and were just rounding the corner that led to their room when, at the far end of the long passageway, Taymoor appeared.

Taymoor's face crunched into a dark scowl and he took off towards them. Kamal thought he spotted a holstered handgun peeking out from under his overcoat.

Kamal spun on himself and bolted back down the passageway, pulling Nisreen in his wake. He knew they were boxed in, knew there was only one possible way out, which was why he grabbed the first door handle they reached after rounding the corner and charged into a small bedroom that was identical to theirs.

The room was empty, but it wouldn't have mattered to Kamal either way. He didn't plan on being there longer than it took to open its window.

'This way,' he blurted as he clambered over the sill.

'But—'

'Come on,' he insisted, reaching out to her with his hand.

She took it and climbed over to join him on the slanted tile roof of the arcaded courtyard of the big mosque, her eyes vivid with alarm.

'We'll make our way down diagonally,' he hissed. 'Use the lips of the tiles for purchase and watch out for any loose ones.'

She nodded.

They clambered across the roof, Nisreen falling back a bit, struggling through one hesitant step after the other—then a shout from a guest of the inn pointing out of another window told them the time for any caution was gone.

'Hurry,' he rasped.

Kamal saw Taymoor appear from another window and yanked Nisreen closer—but her foot hit a loose tile, which scraped out of its slot and made her slip. Kamal bent down and just managed to grab her as a wave of tiles clattered noisily down the roof before crashing into the courtyard, causing incensed shouts to ring up from below.

Kamal glanced up to see Taymoor at the window.

The two agents' eyes met—two burning glares, years of friendship turned into cold enmity.

'Come on,' he told Nisreen as he pulled her up.

He led her across the rest of the roof, scurrying low and fast until they reached its lip.

In the courtyard below, angry worshippers were cursing up at them with raised fists, their anger at the disrespectful intrusion further inflamed by the realization that one of the culprits was a woman. Kamal tuned them out. Instead, he gripped the edge of the roof and swung over it, hung down from its lip with his fingers, and let go in one fluid move. It was a big drop on to solid paving stones, and he hit the ground heavily, his knees bent to dampen the shock. He threw himself sideways to spread the impact sequentially across five points of body contact, just as he'd been trained, before rolling back on to his feet and running a quick mental check of his body. He was sore but uninjured.

Nisreen popped her head over the edge, further angering the mob and looking unsure about the jump. Kamal ignored the growing swarm of men converging on him and waved her down.

'Hang down and jump!' he shouted up at her. 'I'll catch you. Do it.'

She hesitated for a second, then climbed over the edge, dropped down, and let go. Kamal caught her and they both tumbled to the ground just as the first of the men stepped forward and grabbed him by the shoulder. Kamal sprang to his feet and shoved the man back, hard—only to have another worshipper step in and throw a wild punch at him. Kamal leaned away to avoid it and countered with a clean uppercut to the man's ribcage that dropped him to his knees. A third, younger man stepped into the fray, screaming wild profanities at Nisreen, but a kick to the kidneys followed by a jab that caught him squarely on the ear quickly silenced him.

The crowd was now enraged, their yells intensified, but for a moment they held back, stunned by Kamal's savage reactions.

Kamal knew he had to move quickly.

'Step back, you sons of dogs,' he growled at them, jabbing a forceful finger in Nisreen's direction. 'I'm with the Hafiye and this woman is under the protection of the sultan, you hear me? Step back or suffer the consequences.'

The hard conviction in his tone sent a ripple of hesitation through the mob, long enough to buy them an opening. Kamal had already turned to Nisreen, and, with a quick flick of the hand for her to join him, they were cutting through the crowd, his scowl poisonous, his hand clasped tightly on hers, the men parting grudgingly to let them through.

A couple of doubting younger hotheads stepped forward to confront them, but they were soft and, like the others, lacked Kamal's years of training. He cleaved a path through them with a couple of surgical blows, and before the others could process what was really happening, he and Nisreen were storming out the gates of the mosque and into the street.

Quick scan left, right—a typical Parisian afternoon, only not as they knew it. Fewer people and vehicles, which made Kamal feel more exposed than he would have liked. But at least prayer time meant there was a cluster of worshippers converging on the mosque from all sides, which helped make Kamal and Nisreen's presence less visible to the two Zaptiye officers Kamal spotted outside the entrance to the public kitchen down the street.

Kamal led Nisreen down the pavement in the opposite direction, away from the kitchen and the inn. They kept their heads down and hugged the walls as they scurried away, moving as quickly as was reasonable so as not to attract attention.

Without looking back, Kamal dived into the first side street, Nisreen hot on his heels, then turned into another, zigzagging away from Taymoor and his men, moving deeper into a city that felt as disturbingly foreign as it felt familiar.

51

The past they'd landed in was different from what they knew in so many ways, and, given their predicament, some were proving useful; others, less so. Right now, the lack of surveillance and communication technology that Kamal and his brethren in the Hafiye had used to such devastating effect was firmly at the top of the former camp.

Back in the time they'd come from, Kamal had little doubt that he and Nisreen would have most likely already been captured. Even if they'd made it out of the inn, the Hafiye would have had the area locked down with heavy surveillance; street cameras, perhaps even an aerial drone, would have tracked their every move, the entire digital cordon monitored on all kinds of screens by a crack team that would have coordinated men on foot and in chase vehicles and tightened the noose around them until they had nowhere to run.

But here and now, there were no mobile phones, no handheld radios, no GPS trackers. Any agents pursuing Kamal and Nisreen would have been reduced to individual pawns, foot soldiers directed by verbal commands that weren't based on any kind of live surveillance data, let loose to rely on their wits to try and pick up their quarry's trail.

The lack of technology had allowed him and Nisreen to get away.

They kept moving for well over an hour, ducking into narrow streets and passageways, avoiding major roads where agents in passing cars might spot them. It was harrowing and draining, but it had to done. They needed to put as much distance as they could between themselves and Taymoor.

They also needed a place to hole up. They couldn't risk another charitable *waqf* inn; they needed something less obvious and more anonymous, and for that they needed money. On that front, an idea had sprung into Kamal's mind back at the inn, when he'd first looked down at the courtyard of the mosque.

Their circuitous route across Paris would lead them past several other mosques—the city was dotted with them, whether new constructions or converted churches—and it was outside the first of those that he asked Nisreen to wait. He didn't like leaving her, but walking in alone was less likely to arouse suspicion.

The dusk prayers were still a way off, and the mosque's courtyard was deserted. Kamal advanced cautiously and saw what he was after: a *sadaqa tasi*—a charity stone—in the shadows of a corner of the arcade. Keeping a wary eye on his surroundings, he approached it.

The *sadaqa* was a stone pillar slightly taller than he was, and it had a hollow niche near its top. Its purpose was simple: it provided an elegant method of performing one's duty of *sadaqa*—charity. *Sadaqa*, as ordained by Islamic tradition, was deemed essential for the stability and well-being of a community, as well as critical for every devout follower's eternal salvation. The pillar allowed the rich to donate money anonymously: they only needed to reach up and place money in the niche. Those in need would later approach it and take only what they needed, ensuring they left the rest behind for others in need. The system helped save the poor from having to go begging and face humiliation, while it provided the rich with an elegant, unboastful way to perform their religious duty. The pillars were often hard to notice, tucked into quiet corners of mosques or their courtyards to afford discretion to those giving as well as those taking, but they were always there.

Kamal was well aware of the etiquette regarding the taking side of the system, but right now etiquette would have to take a back seat to survival. He felt little shame at cleaning out the pillar's niche, which he also did at four others in mosques that they crossed on their hotfooted and improvised trek to safety. By the end of it, they had enough money to pay for tramway tickets across town to the Christian ghetto tucked into the shadows of the hill of Montmartre.

Montmartre was one of the few areas in the city that had remained mostly Christian. Its religious roots ran deep: a bishop named Saint Denis was decapitated there by the Romans several centuries before the advent of Islam. A small priory still occupied the site where he was believed to have died, while a much larger Benedictine monastery covered the rest of the hill cresting the community that had grown around its base.

Kamal was familiar with the neighbourhood's future incarnation from his investigative work; besides threats from Arab Islamists, the Hafiye of his time had also dealt with Christian terrorists. The grievances that had given rise to their plots weren't present in the Paris he and Nisreen were currently in, which hadn't yet experienced the empire's economic crash after the collapse of the price of oil. The grievances were a reaction to the xenophobic, heavy-handed policies of Abdülhamid III and his incendiary, divisive rhetoric, which reactionary elements in America had exploited and fed with propaganda and funding. Before then, as in the time that Kamal and Nisreen were currently in, the Christian and Jewish minorities across the empire had coexisted comfortably alongside the Muslim majority, even though they were, in many ways, second-class citizens. And, as was common with minorities, they tended to congregate and live in close quarters, as the Christians did in Montmartre.

In the time they'd come from, hiding there would have been a bad move. The Christian community was riddled with informants desperate to ingratiate themselves with the state. In the time they were now in, things were different. The Christians had yet to be stigmatized by the sultan's populist backlash and weren't paranoid about their security. The neighbourhood wasn't hostile to outsiders, and its businesses welcomed Muslims and Jews. Which was why Kamal and Nisreen didn't stick out or feel overly exposed when they walked into a small, simple inn, posing as husband and wife.

There, they could finally rest their weary legs and catch their breath.

But for how long?

52

Dinner was a simple but filling affair of *dane,* which consisted of mutton and rice, followed by *zirbaç,* a sweet pudding made from raisins, plums and almonds. They ate alone at a small family restaurant a stone's throw from the inn, avoiding any unnecessary interaction, barely speaking to each other both out of tiredness and a desire to ensure they weren't overheard. Nisreen barely touched her food, and Kamal, she noted, was kind enough to only mention it once. Even though her body was clearly craving it, she didn't have the energy to eat. She barely had energy to breathe.

The break from the fear and the running had allowed all the horrors of the previous night to come storming back. The sadness that had been pushed aside by the rush for survival had returned, so profound and debilitating that she could barely lift a finger. Her husband and her children were gone for ever. It was impossible to accept. She kept going over it, again and again, her mind refusing to process it and scrambling for some way out of it, something she missed that could bring them back. Perhaps more than the grief that was tearing her apart, it was this crippling sense of helplessness about the cruel finality of it all that was killing her.

They retreated to their room. They needed a wash and a change of clothing, but it would wait. They were both too wiped out to do anything more than just collapse on their beds and stare at the ceiling.

Nisreen was the first to break the silence.

'It's never going to end, is it?' she said. 'They're going to keep coming after us. I mean, you know what they're like; you know how they work. They're never going to give up.'

'No, they're not. Not given what's at stake.'

'So this is how we're going to live from now on? Constantly looking over our shoulders and worrying about who might turn up?'

Kamal shrugged. 'We can go to another time. Try to lose them again. Make sure we don't leave a trail this time.'

'But we can never be sure, can we? There's always a chance that they'll track us down again. There's no limit to how many agents they can send back to all kinds of past times to find us. Which means there'll always be that fear, that doubt.' She rolled on to her side to face him. 'I can't live like that. I won't live like that.'

'We might not have a choice.'

'We always have a choice.'

An idea that had germinated in her head on the barge the night before was back, and it was cawing for attention. Taymoor's appearance had breathed life into it; the anger and the feeling of helplessness were giving it wings.

'What you were saying last night . . . about how maybe you'd want to change things,' she said. 'How you'd want to use what we know to make our world a better place. Maybe this is all much bigger than us. Maybe it's not about figuring out a way to get back to our old lives. Maybe this has all happened to us for some much more important reason.'

'What do you mean?'

'The world we know—whether it's the time we came from or being here now—it's not how it was supposed to be.'

Kamal looked puzzled.

'He changed it. Rasheed changed everything. All this'— she spread her arms—'it's the way it is because of him. The empire, our whole way of life, is still around because of what he did. But it wasn't supposed to be this way.'

'What are you saying, Nisreen?'

'The only reason we're here, whether it's here now or back where we were, our whole lives—none of it would have happened if he hadn't changed history.'

'You're saying we owe our existence to him?'

'I'm saying everything we know about our world wasn't supposed to be that way. It's a perversion, a cheat of history. And I think we need to set that right.'

Kamal's jaw dropped. 'Set it right? It's our world.'

'It's wrong.'

'Nisreen—'

'It's wrong, Kamal,' she insisted forcefully. 'It wasn't supposed to be this way.'

'He saved the empire and allowed it to spread its rule halfway across the world,' Kamal shot back.

'He perverted history.'

'To our advantage. To the advantage of our people.'

'And to the detriment of millions of others. People who would have, who should have, existed. Who should have had wonderful and tragic and happy and miserable lives but never got the chance because of what he did.'

'While millions of others did, including us.'

She scoffed. 'And look how well that turned out.'

Kamal took a breath to calm down, then rubbed his eyes. 'The world he described, the way it was before he changed it—it wasn't exactly paradise, was it?'

'It wasn't—but I don't think any world can be, do you? Ours wasn't any better. With everything you know about human nature—you of all people—surely you don't think a world without conflict is possible?'

He didn't need to reply.

'Look, it doesn't matter if the world that Rasheed knew was good or bad,' she pressed on. 'But from what he said, it seems to me that it was actually a much better place because of one fundamental difference: freedom. People had freedoms we don't even dream of. They could say what they wanted, live how they wanted, go where they wanted. They could even choose their leadership. They had elections. And surely a world that open, a world where people can express their ideas without fear and engage in open debates about the big issues of their time, has got to be a world that wouldn't allow the kinds of lies and manipulation and corruption that we've suffered from. A world where people can't be ruled by thugs and live under an iron fist. These people were free to shape their destinies. And that's something we'll never have, not here and now, not ever.'

'Yes, but—'

'Rasheed's world wasn't a terrible place, Kamal. It's not like he saved us from some nightmarish existence. And even if he had, that's not the point. The point is that he decided for us. One man. A murderer, a violent, vicious killer—one man decided how we would all live. He took away the freedom of millions of people. He took away their lives. And that can't be right.'

It took Kamal a moment to say anything. He seemed to be having a hard time refuting her point and processing the immensity of what she was driving at. 'It wouldn't be the first time one man decided that,' he finally said.

'What are you talking about?'

'We already follow the teachings of one man.'

It was Nisreen's turn to be shocked. 'Tell me you didn't just say that.'

'All I'm saying is—'

'You're not suggesting Rasheed is some kind of holy messenger,' she interjected, 'guided by a divine hand?'

365

'I don't know,' Kamal replied. 'He's certainly got the power of a god.'

'He got it by brute force,' she fired back angrily. 'From a man who was his prisoner. A man he killed. Does that sound divine to you?'

'Of course not, but—'

'And if you're going to think that way, then who's to say we're not the ones being guided by a divine hand?' she pressed on.

'Us?'

'Why not? Maybe it was God's plan for us to come across it. To fix things. That's just as plausible, isn't it?'

Kamal was tongue-tied.

'There's nothing divine about this, Kamal. I mean, there can't be. I don't know where this incantation came from. I don't know why it was carved into the walls of that crypt all those years ago. All I know is that this—everything you see—this isn't the way the world was supposed to be. He changed it. He *stole* history. And that's got to be wrong.'

'How do you know someone else didn't change it before him? How do you know the world he described was the way it should have been? Maybe there was a different world before it that someone else changed. And another one before that. It could be infinite.'

'Maybe. I don't know.' She was frustrated, but she wasn't giving up. It reminded her of the first arguments they'd had when things got bad, when Paris had begun to reel under the new sultan's repression. 'All I know is what he did. And I know—I'm sure—that it's wrong. It's a cheat, a lie, a despicable defilement of the how it was meant to be. And we need to fix that.'

'Fix it?'

'We need to stop him.'

Kamal's eyes shot wide. 'You want to stop Rasheed from what—from making all this happen?'

'Yes.'

'We exist—we're alive because of what he did.'

'I know. But it's wrong. And we can change that.'

'That's . . . nuts.'

'Is it? He did it. Why can't we?'

'Because . . . because it's—'

She gave him room to finish. But he couldn't. There was no because.

'We can stop him, Kamal,' she insisted. 'We can go back in time and prevent him from changing history.'

'Nisreen—'

'Think about it,' she interjected. 'You saw how this all ended up. Maybe you couldn't see it, but we were living in a terrible, terrible time. People were being put away for voicing their thoughts, for challenging a ruler whose men didn't hesitate to murder my husband and my children to protect this—this big lie.' She heard her voice falter, felt the onset of tears, but she pressed on. 'We were ruled by a cretinous brute, and God knows how much worse it's going to get. And stopping him, fixing this abomination—maybe that's the best way to honour the lives of Ramazan and Tarek and Noor. At least, this way, maybe they wouldn't have died for nothing.'

Kamal felt beaten down by the sheer intensity of her delivery.

Still, what she was proposing—it was reckless, if not mad. 'So you don't want revenge any more?' he asked.

'What do you mean?'

'Before we jumped. You said you wanted them all dead. Celaleddin, the ones who sent the men after you—after us. You wanted them dead. We could jump forward and do that. They wouldn't know we were coming after them.'

'I don't have the incantation for going forwards, remember? I just know how to go back in time.'

'Maybe you can figure it out.'

'Maybe. But this feels much more important.'

'You want to honour their lives?' he pressed. 'Why not go back a few years—I don't know, five, ten years, to get away from Taymoor? Why don't we escape from here to a safe time and then work to change the future—our future, this world's future—from there? Why do you want to destroy it all—'cause that's what he said, didn't he? The empire didn't survive in his world.'

'That wouldn't be making things right. Maybe the empire should never have survived. And anyway, it's not an option because they know we're here. They're going to keep looking for us; you know they are. They could send a bunch of men back ten, twenty years; they could have them put out alerts for us across the empire, across time, just to make sure they shut us down permanently. We know the truth, and we can use it. We're a huge danger to them. And anything we try to change, anything we do to warn about the bad times coming, it'll just be a flag announcing where we are. We'd be giving ourselves away. They're never going to leave us alone. No, the only way to fix this, the only way to guarantee that they never find us, the only way to change things permanently so that they can never undo what we do, the only way we'll ever find peace, is to make sure none of this ever happens in the first place—which means going back to its source. Which is Rasheed. We have to stop him before he changes things.'

Kamal had no valid arguments left to challenge her with. 'Even if we wanted to, it would be impossible, surely.'

'He managed it.'

Kamal let out a tense, tight sigh. 'So you want to—'

'I want to go back to the only place we know he was at. The only place we can find him; the place where it all started. The fields outside Vienna in the month of Ramadan of 1094.'*

'You want to go back to 1094?'

'Yes.'

'And do what?'

'I want to make sure the sultan's army doesn't take Vienna. And I want to kill Ayman Rasheed to make sure he doesn't find a way to undo what we do.'

'You want to kill him?'

'Yes. I don't see any other way.'

Despite everything he'd just heard, this was to him the most shocking part. Nisreen—idealistic, righteous, principled Nisreen—was again talking about killing someone in the most casual of tones. Not even casual. This time, she was coldly committed.

The world had truly spun off its axis.

'Besides,' she added, 'don't forget: Rasheed is still out there. He escaped. He's out there somewhere in the past. He could come back. Any time. He could find us. He could show up here tomorrow. And your idea about going back a few years and changing things for our future—he could easily undo anything we do if he doesn't like it.'

'So could Celaleddin and his men,' Kamal noted.

'Not if we go back to the source. Not if we stop Rasheed before he changes things. If we do that, Celaleddin won't be part of the future any more. He won't be around to send anyone back. He will have never existed.'

'Nor will we?'

'We'll be in the past already.'

* September, AD 1683.

'Yes, but we'd have got there from a future that never existed.'

'It did when we were in it. And we'd already be back there. We're not going to suddenly turn to dust or just cease to exist because of it. Rasheed didn't.'

Kamal just studied her for a moment, stunned by what he'd just heard. He had to move her off that path, to rein her in—and not for the sake of the empire, but for her own safety.

'Nisreen, can you hear yourself? You actually want to go back to a war zone and kill the sultan's most valued adviser? You think you can just show up there and make it happen— how? How would you get to him? And how do you think you would kill him? They didn't have guns like ours back then. They had muskets. Do you even know how to use one?'

'No.' Her eyes were still burning fiercely, but they softened up a touch as she added, 'But you can teach me.'

'What makes you think I know? Nisreen, this is insane. It's suicide—and it's not fair to everyone who—'

'I'm doing this, Kamal. It has to be done. My life here has no meaning, no purpose. What are we going to do, start new lives in this time, alone in this world of strangers, with no one apart from each other, no one else who means anything to us? You want me to plod along for the rest of my life as if nothing ever happened? Maybe you could live with such emptiness, but I can't. I wouldn't want to. And I couldn't sit back and do nothing, not knowing what I know. We owe it to history to fix things. Or at least to try. And if you're not going to help me, then we really don't have anything left to say to each other.'

She stormed over to the door and yanked it open, but before she could step out of the room, Kamal had darted across to her and blocked her from opening the door fully.

'Nisreen, please—'

'Get out of my way.' She pulled the door and tried to barge past him.

He pressed back against it and reached out, grabbing her by the shoulders. 'Nisreen, listen to me, this isn't the—'

She batted his hands away. 'Leave me alone.'

He held his ground, his arm outstretched and blocking the door from opening fully. 'No. I'm not going to let you end up dead in some godforsaken past. Let's think things through more carefully.'

She shoved his arm back, her anger now turning ferocious. 'We just did. It has to be done.'

He moved to take hold of her, but she swatted him off. They both went quiet and just stared at each other in loaded silence.

'How can you not see that this is the right thing to do?'

'Nisreen . . .'

He stilled his tongue, taken aback by the gut-wrenching cocktail of anger and disappointment radiating out of her eyes.

She was breathing hard, just glaring at him. Then she shook her head slowly. 'Where did the old Kamal go?' she finally said. 'You used to be so . . . valiant. So headstrong and untamed. When you first joined the Hafiye, I thought, why? You're intelligent; you could have chosen any number of safer, better-paid careers. But you didn't. You said you wanted to make a difference, remember? And you have no idea—no idea—how much I admired you for that. You put your life on the line for us, for this city. For strangers. And when the first bombings happened, I'd stay up late at night, worried about you. Wondering what doors you were knocking down, what dangers were waiting for you.' Her jaw tightened, and she sighed. 'But then things got ugly . . . and you couldn't see it. You couldn't see the path we were on. And, worse, you couldn't see that you were part of it. Part of the horror that was taking over. But even through the worst of it, even when I hated everything you stood for and couldn't bear to hear your name, deep down there was a part of me that for some perverse reason still admired your strength, your commitment, the way that you didn't just sit on the sidelines but fought for something you believed in, even if it was something that was gone, something that no longer existed, something that had turned into the exact opposite of what you had always defended.'

Kamal felt an invisible vice tighten up around his ribcage so hard he could barely breathe. 'I know I've made mistakes. But this . . .'

'This needs to be done, Kamal. Maybe you can't see it now, but you will. It's the right thing to do. If we do nothing . . . we'll be on the wrong side of history.'

He drew a long breath and studied her intently, feeling her gaze burn into him. 'I can't talk you out of this, can I?'

'Not a chance.' The steely commitment locked into her face was indisputable. 'I'm doing this.'

The question remained unasked. But it was there, looming over him. With crushing force.

And there was only one possible answer he could give her.

She was right. Their past was never going to leave them alone, whether that was Taymoor or others coming after them or the memory of what had happened to Ramazan and the children.

The latter he couldn't do anything about, but the former— there was a chance to end it. A slim one, but a chance.

'I can't let you do it alone.'

'I can't have you doing anything for my sake,' she said.

'I'm not.'

And maybe that was true. Maybe he saw sense in what she was saying. Or maybe he was just too worn out and depleted to think straight. Or maybe he was just too damn in love with her to have ever had a chance of replying in any other way.

'You're right,' he finally told her, his tone soft and even. 'We should do this. For Ramazan. For Tarek. For Noor. For everyone.'

She looked at him, and, for the first time in as long as he could remember, he saw a flicker of warmth light up her eyes and detected a hint of genuine affection and—far more crucially—respect.

And that alone was enough to pulverize any doubts about any other way he might have responded to her crazy, reckless and radical plan.

53

'Can I interest you in a little something about the siege of Vienna?'

Nisreen came back to the reading table loaded with books—a dozen of them, all dealing with one of two subjects: the conquest of Vienna and the life of Ayman Rasheed Pasha.

Kamal took the books from her hands and set them down on the table, perusing their covers. 'I travelled back in time to get stuck with a mountain of homework?'

'I'm afraid so,' she said as she took a seat next to him. 'I hope you're a fast reader. We need to learn everything we can about this and we need to do it quickly.'

He looked at the books sceptically. 'History was never my forte.'

Nisreen shrugged her shoulders and gave him a sheepish grimace. 'Well, now's your chance to change that.'

They were on the left bank, directly across the river from the Louvre, in the main reading room of the Sultan Majid Imperial Library. The magnificent domed building was the largest public library in France and had been a temple of learning for centuries, ever since Louis XIII's infamous cardinal, Mazarin, had founded it to house his enormous collection of books. Under the Ottomans, the Bibliothèque Mazarine had expanded to take over most of the adjacent buildings of the old Institut de France, among which it had pride of place, until even those weren't big enough to house its collections. The new public library, the one Nisreen had spent countless hours in as a student and lawyer, was still decades away from being built, but she'd visited this old building a few times after it had been converted into a museum.

They had to move fast. Taymoor was still out there looking for them. They'd debated jumping back to a safer time, when Taymoor wouldn't be around. It seemed like the obvious safe move. If they left no trace, no record of how many moons they'd jumped back, he wouldn't be able to follow them. Even a hop as short as a week back would do it, assuming that was long enough for them to complete their research. But they weighed that against the risks of making another jump back in time. If they did so, they would be landing there in unknown circumstances, with no clothes and no money again, and there were no guarantees that their arrival wouldn't be noticed and have some record of it kept, a record that Taymoor might find in the time they were currently in and use to follow them back.

There were too many unknowns, and they finally decided that, on balance, they were probably safe enough staying put, provided they kept a low profile. Which was why they chose to travel separately to the library and back to the inn. They couldn't check out any books, since they lacked the ID required to fill out the registration forms, which was just as well: they wouldn't leave any written trace of their presence or what they were looking into.

And so they dived into their research. They read, made notes, discussed their findings, and then read some more. It was long, tiring work to which they were wholly committed, their attention laser-focused on the most minute detail. Their lives, to say nothing of their world-altering objective, depended on it.

By the end of the first day, they'd read enough for their plans to begin to take shape. But the way they were shaping up wasn't ideal.

Kamal closed the book he'd been reading, a recent

biography of Rasheed. 'It's amazing,' he said as he pushed it away with a huff of frustration. 'There's so much about what he did after they took Vienna—the march across Europe, taking Rome, Paris, all that. His inventions, his weapons and his tactics; his ideas about society and politics and technology; his visions for the future—'

'A future he'd come from,' Nisreen added. 'He didn't foresee or invent any of them. He was a fraud.'

'Agreed . . . but, regardless, there's hardly anything about him before Vienna.'

'Because there was no him before Vienna. And whatever there is about that is unreliable,' Nisreen commented. 'We can't use any of it. He made it all up. A past that never existed.'

'We've got to keep digging. We have to find a way to get to him before the army leaves Istanbul.'

'But how? We don't have reliable information of how to get to him.'

'Yes, but after they set off, it'll be much harder to stop him. He'll be at the head of the biggest army in history.'

'We might not have a choice.'

Kamal frowned. 'We have to keep looking. It would be a hell of a lot safer for us to find a way to get to him before the siege. We know he was in Istanbul before the army began its march to Vienna. That's where he first appeared. Maybe we should just go there and wait to hear about his appearance.'

'We won't hear about it. It's not something that will be publicized in any way. And the sultan would have kept him close, so he was probably staying inside the palace, under some kind of watch. I'm sure the palace was as heavily guarded then as is it now. Not exactly an easy target.'

Kamal's frown deepened.

'Short of knowing exactly where to find him, and on what specific day or night,' Nisreen added, 'we'd more than likely get caught. I don't see it as any less risky than Vienna. Plus we'd have to get to Istanbul now, in this time, before jumping back. Without papers, without money . . . and with slower transportation.' Which was true. They'd travelled back to an era of rail travel. The jet engine had yet to be invented. Planes were still propeller-driven, slow and rickety. The concept of passenger air travel was in its infancy.

'Vienna will be easier to reach, for sure. But we'd be diving headfirst into a war zone. That's what I'm trying to avoid.'

'I'm not exactly thrilled by it either,' Nisreen countered. 'But that's where we know we'll definitely find him. I don't think we have any choice.' She shrugged, mirroring his discomfort. 'Look, we won't be diving blind. We have stacks of information about it.' Which was also true. The siege was a pivotal moment in Ottoman history, and historians had dissected it in countless tomes. 'Reliable information. Which means we'll be well prepared.' She picked up one of the books from the unread pile, spun it playfully in front of Kamal, and then arched an eyebrow at him. 'And which is why it's time you got back to reading.'

'We need to find another way.'

'I'm not holding my breath. I think the die's been cast on that one. And it's not one of your legendary *du sheshs,*' she joked, using the Turkish word for double six, a powerful throw of the dice in backgammon.

Kamal considered her for a moment. It felt good to see her looking relaxed and lighthearted for a change, even briefly. Beyond being necessary for their plans, the research was also providing a welcome, if temporary, distraction from the darkness that engulfed her.

He grudgingly pulled the book closer and glanced at its cover. 'Seriously,' he said with a grin as he tapped the book. 'Reliving the least favourite part of my youth, right here.'

'With a much harsher grading curve,' Nisreen replied, her expression taking on a serious tinge. 'A failing mark is definitely not an option.'

'No argument there,' he said before opening the book and ploughing through it.

It didn't take long for them to reach the conclusion they'd been dreading.

The best option available to them, the clearest line of attack, the only one that they could base on reliable information, was also the most dangerous one.

The key event, the decisive intervention of Rasheed that had changed the outcome of the siege and delivered Vienna to the Ottomans, was the suicide bombing that had taken place at the ceremonial review of the Christian army at Tulln, twenty miles west of Vienna.

That's what they needed to change.

Rasheed had bragged about it to Ramazan, who had then told Nisreen about it that night at their apartment. It had been Rasheed's master stroke, and he hadn't held back in describing it.

The history books and biographies covered it painstakingly. The epic, illustrious military victory for the Ottomans was a bold, cunning move that harked back to the exploits of one of the most notorious tacticians in Islamic history, the Old Man of the Mountain, leader of the infamous Order of Assassins.

On that fateful day, Rasheed's explosive-laden envoys had taken out the entire leadership of the pope's army. The various contingents of Christian troops had massed on the north bank of the Danube and had spent the previous few days waiting to cross the river. Their engineers had built pontoon bridges across it, but days of heavy autumn rain had raised the level and flow of the river, causing damage and delays. The bridges had needed rebuilding several times. Two days before the review, however, the rain stopped, and the troops were finally able to cross. Once on the southern bank, they had massed before the town of Tulln, behind a defensive timber palisade that would shield them from roaming Ottoman Ghazi warriors and their Tartar allies. That was where the review would take place before the final push east, to the plains around Vienna, where the Ottoman army was camped out and where the battle for the city would take place.

The best military commanders in Christendom, battle-hardened legends like John III Sobieski, King of Poland and Charles, Duke of Lorraine, had been wiped out in one devilish strike. The Ottoman army that charged in right after the bombing had taken their men by surprise. Forty thousand infidels had been wiped out that day, leaving the besieged and starving people of Vienna at the mercy of the invaders and exposing the rest of western Europe to their remorseless advance.

It was clear that this bombing had to be stopped and the army saved. Sobieski and the others had to be warned, and the ambush had to be turned to their advantage.

But that wouldn't be enough.

Rasheed had to be killed so that he couldn't simply travel back in time and try again.

Kamal and Nisreen needed to make sure both things happened. One on its own wouldn't suffice. And they both had to happen more or less simultaneously, before Rasheed realized he'd failed and made a time jump back to reset the clock and try again.

Killing Rasheed was likely to be the more difficult part of the plan. Kamal insisted that the task was his and his alone. There was no way he would risk letting Nisreen accompany him while trying to infiltrate the Ottoman camp. Which meant that, at some point, they would have to be separated, something that didn't appeal to either of them. But there didn't seem to be a way around that. Getting to Rasheed and killing him in time would be tricky enough for Kamal to pull off without having Nisreen to worry about.

With that strategy in place, their research became more focused. They had a wealth of sources to draw on, and, over the course of a week, they were able to gather enough information to map out what felt like a coherent, reasonable plan.

Kamal and Nisreen knew the many risks and tried to minimize them and stack the odds in their favour by educating themselves about every foreseeable complication. They also read about life at that time, notably from the collected writings of a famous Ottoman traveller of the period, Evliya Çelebi, who had been to Vienna a few years before the siege. But at some point the amount of reading became overwhelming.

The time to bite that bullet and make the jump was rushing in at them.

By the end of it, two things remained.

One was to calculate the exact number of moons they would jump back and translate it into Palmyrene, the language of the incantation.

Choosing when to jump back to was a balancing act: too long before the suicide bombing, and they risked opening up too much room for the unexpected. Too soon, and they might not have enough time to get it done. After much deliberation, they decided to jump back two days before the ceremonial review outside Tulln. This would give them forty-eight hours to get to the Christian army's commanders and warn them of the fate that awaited them and to give Kamal time to kill Rasheed in the Ottoman encampment.

The other issue required a leap of faith.

Ramazan hadn't been able to ask Rasheed for the rest of the incantation—the version for travelling into the future. Kamal and Nisreen had discussed how important it was to have it, and, although using it was not crucial to their plan, they had agreed that they'd be better off knowing it. If things went wrong, they might need it.

Hoping that it was simply a matter of substituting a word in the incantation and not needing an entirely different one to jump forward in time, Nisreen spent an entire afternoon studying it. She analysed the words, comparing them to the Palmyrene source material she could find, translating them one by one, but there was no evident solution. Palmyrene was an obscure, ancient language that hadn't been extensively studied; few ancient texts written in it had survived, and from what she could make out, none of the words in the incantation were Palmyrene for 'past' or 'future' or for 'backwards' or 'forwards'.

One of its words, however, did intrigue her. According to the documentation she had access to, it was the Palmyrene word for 'light.' She considered it and wondered if she hadn't misinterpreted it. The word came after the number of moons one wanted to travel across was specified and seemed out of place. This was the incantation for travelling back in time, and it seemed counter-intuitive to Nisreen that travelling back across a number of moons would be associated with light; she would have expected it to be related to darkness.

But then she considered it some more and decided that perhaps it did make sense.

Travelling into the past was travelling to a time that was known, a time that wasn't mysterious: hence, into the light. And following that logic, perhaps travelling forward in time, which would be going to an uncertain future, might be associated with darkness, the darkness of the unknown.

She studied the incantation again and again and couldn't see any other possibility for what the variant for past or future might be. It had to be that word: 'light'. With no better option, she looked up the Palmyrene words for 'dark' and 'darkness', and from what she could see, both words gave the same result, the same word. She decided that was all she could do. Substituting that word was her best guess for travelling forward in time. Then there was the question of how to get the pronunciation right. It was a lot of guesswork, but at least it was educated guesswork. But perhaps they wouldn't need the guesswork. If all went well, they'd get the forward-travel incantation from Rasheed before getting caught in a tricky situation where they would need to put her guesswork to the test.

Before they could go, they needed to have something else done. They needed to make sure they didn't lose the incantation or the possible reverse spell. They'd try to memorize them, of course. But memory wasn't totally reliable. The obvious solution was to have them tattooed on their bodies, but tattoos weren't common in Ottoman society at that time. The only Muslim Ottomans to have any were men who were part of the military or law enforcement and who, like Kamal, had their unit's symbol and their individual identifying number tattooed on their right arm and leg. Muslim women were never tattooed. Women who had markings were usually from conquered Christian communities. They put tattoos of crosses and ancient cultural symbols on themselves and on their children as a defence against forced conversion or as a form of passive resistance to it, a practice more common in the Balkans than in France.

Hiding out deep in the Christian ghetto of Montmartre, they managed to find an old cobbler who was also a tattoo artist. The man knew better than to ask too many questions; having a tattoo was not something one discussed openly. And so he kept his questions to himself as he got to work on

Nisreen's forearm. She had him mark it with the words to the incantation, with a phonetic version of the Palmyrene number of moons they would need to jump back to find Rasheed, calculated from the day the train they planned to be on arrived in Vienna. She also had the forward-jump word and some other Palmyrene numbers tattooed on as well, in case they needed them—one, ten and a hundred.

Nisreen told Kamal she thought he should also have them tattooed on his arm.

He demurred. 'I don't need it.'

'Why the hell not?'

'I'm not going anywhere without you.'

'Don't be silly,' she insisted. 'You might need to. For both our sakes.'

'I've memorized it.'

'You're absolutely sure of that? With all the extra words for changing the number of days?'

Kamal's face scrunched inward sheepishly. 'Kind of.'

'Kind of isn't good enough. You're not scared of a little needle, are you?'

Needless to say, he got the tattoos.

They were the same as hers, to add to the Hafiye markings he already had on his arm and leg. He didn't need the cobbler to see those, and he made sure to present his other arm for the tattoo of the incantation.

They were finally ready to go.

They spent their last night before leaving Paris in a small restaurant they hadn't been to before, maintaining their practice of not returning to the same place twice. Dinner was subdued, with both of them trying to ignore the nervous anticipation and fear of what they were about to do.

They finished the meal with calming cups of anise tea and a long bout of silence.

'The moment of truth,' Kamal finally said. 'You're still sure of this?'

Nisreen finished her sip, set her cup down and cast her eyes on it. After a brief, pensive pause, she looked up at Kamal. 'I won't lie to you and say I'm not scared. I'm actually terrified. It's so far from anything I've ever done. But I'm still absolutely convinced that it needs to be done.'

Kamal nodded solemnly. 'If it's any consolation, it's way beyond anything I've ever done. Maybe anyone's done.'

'Apart from Rasheed.'

'Apart from him, yes.'

Nisreen nodded. 'So we can be terrified together?'

Kamal gave a brief chortle. 'We'll shiver and rattle our teeth in unison.'

She smiled at that—a melancholy, sad smile. The memory of the horrors was never far from her eyes.

Kamal drank in the moment, unsettled by thoughts of the journey they were about to embark on. He joked about it, but wasn't immune to feeling anxious or fearful. Simply put, he did not look forward to it, but believed in it and was committed to getting it done. And if there was an upside, it was that preparing for the journey, spending all those days consumed by research and planning, being completely focused on the momentous task ahead, had steered Nisreen's thoughts away from the tragedy that had befallen her. She was a different woman from the one he'd jumped across time with. He never doubted that the pain was still there. He still felt it, too. He had heard her light sobs late in the night, when she should have been mentally drained and fast asleep. But during the days, the darkness in her eyes had gradually lifted, replaced by an animated sparkle. She was brought back to life, however temporarily.

Maybe, he thought, she might find happiness again. Maybe in that unwritten, uncharted future, she might meet someone who could give her a new beginning and, eventually, replace the pain of her past with a better present.

Maybe.

If we survive this.

His expression shifted, turning more serious. 'Once we do it, if we manage to change things . . . there's no going back to the life we knew. It'll all be wiped out.'

'I know.'

'Everyone we knew, everything about our old lives . . . it'll all be gone for ever.'

'That doesn't scare me. I wouldn't ever want to go back. There's nothing there for me.' She paused, then asked, 'What about you? You still want to do this with me?'

He let it sit for a moment. 'Are you kidding?' he then said. 'I'd never hear the end of it if I didn't.'

He caught her by surprise. Her face relaxed, and she flicked him a dubious raised eyebrow, which he deflected with an appeasing open hand. 'I mean . . . yes. Absolutely.'

A delicate warmth suffused her face. 'Thank you.' Then she reached across the table and cupped his hands with hers.

54

To the other passengers on the Kostantiniyye Express, they didn't seem out of place.

A married couple, sharing a two-berth cabin, taking the overnight train from Paris to Vienna. A trip to visit relatives, a romantic holiday perhaps, maybe an anniversary. No one would really know which, since the couple spent almost the entire trip in their compartment and kept to themselves when dining.

The fact that they had presented themselves on the track that morning with only one small piece of luggage between them was unusual, but it wouldn't necessarily raise eyebrows. No one needed to know that it was a used bag that they had hastily bought, along with the slightly more fashionable clothes they were wearing, from a second-hand shop in Montmartre, nor that all it contained were the clothes they had stolen from the madrasah at Fontainebleau, which was also the sum total of their belongings.

Kamal only began to relax once the train pulled out of Paris's grand Osman Sofu Pasha Station and began its journey eastward to Istanbul. Even then, he was still on his guard. They'd done their best to pass unnoticed on their journey from the inn early that morning to the grandiose rail station and across its towering halls to the platform where their train waited, with Kamal's stern expression projecting a silent barrier to any approach and Nisreen's face hidden behind a headscarf that was more opaque than anything she'd ever worn. They hadn't attracted any attention, nor had they been approached by any policemen, which was a better outcome than Kamal had expected. After all, they'd been in Paris for a little over a week, and even given the technological limitations of the period, there had been plenty of time for Taymoor to have the authorities set up an all-points bulletin for them. Perhaps Kamal had overestimated Taymoor's influence with the Zaptiye. There were no routine identity checks either, since the train wouldn't be crossing any borders. The entire journey was within the territory of the empire, which offered unhindered travel to its citizens.

The conductor punched their tickets and they were settled into their compartment by the time the train rolled out. It was early morning, and the weather had turned again, with a chill in the air and angry clouds threatening a downpour, but as open country replaced the dense urban sprawl of the French capital, Kamal felt a sense of calmness break through his defences. He welcomed the feeling, knowing it was only a temporary respite. It would lessen once they got off the train and vaporize along with them once they did their jump.

It would take the express twenty-five hours to reach Vienna, so they'd arrive the next morning after brief stops in Strasbourg and Munich. The train would carry on after they disembarked, taking an additional two days to reach its terminus, the Müsir Ahmet Pasha Station in Istanbul.

To pay for the tickets, Kamal had resorted to something he would previously have considered unthinkable. Having exhausted the charity stones within reach, his only option was to steal. This was a risky undertaking, mostly in terms of his identity being discovered. Although the penal law of the *shari'a* had fixed punishments for most crimes, it didn't cover more modern situations such as forgery and blackmail, and its stringent rules and procedures made prosecution overly complicated. To counter that, Murad had introduced a secular legal system, the *kanun,* which made prosecution easier and more effective. During Murad's reign, under that system ordinary robbers who were caught, even those who had killed their victims, didn't always receive the severe corporal punishments of Islamic law. Instead, they were often only forced to return the money or the stolen merchandise to the victim's relatives, along with compensation that would be agreed on by both parties.

Kamal wasn't overly worried. He could always use the incantation if he were captured, provided he wouldn't be leaving Nisreen behind. Still, he was placing himself and Nisreen at risk, but he had no choice.

When it came to matters of crime, his significant experience and skills mitigated the risk. And so he'd walked hours that day, far from the inn, sizing up various potential targets, even considering a post office before deciding it was too dangerous. He'd eventually settled on a merchant of luxurious woollen textiles from Carcassonne, a choice that was cemented after he'd been rudely patronized by the gruff, haughty merchant on his exploratory foray into the store.

The gold coins he'd taken from him had allowed him to pay for the clothes, the suitcase and two tickets in a small sleeping compartment. It was a B-class cabin, which was more than suitable. It had wooden panelling, a large window, a couch that converted to two bunk beds, and a small vanity unit with a washbasin. Each sleeper carriage, of which there were twelve, had two separate toilets for its passengers' use, but there were no baths or showers on board, not even in the A-class coach. Two restaurant cars and three brake vans, all finished in the same imperial red livery, completed the train.

By mid-morning, the train had left the French province in its wake. The ride was smooth, the newly introduced sprung undercarriages dampening the powerful coal-powered engine's rumble and any irregularities in the tracks. Flat terrain soon gave way to a more rugged landscape, and, as the train began its climb into the lush wooded hills of the Vosges Mountains, an accompanying sense of trepidation rose within Kamal and Nisreen, one that grew with each advancing mile, even if it remained unspoken.

They spent the day in their compartment going over their plans time and again to make sure they hadn't missed anything that might prove disastrous, only emerging for meals in the dining car.

They needed to reach the Christian leadership before the suicide bombing at the ceremonial review outside the wooden palisade at Tulln. To do that, they couldn't do their time jump in Vienna, which was surrounded by the largest army the Ottomans had ever assembled. Under constant attack for two months, it was on the brink of collapse. Those who had stayed behind and the thousands of refugees from the countryside were trapped inside the city's crumbling walls, barely surviving in desperate conditions. Given that the city's stout-hearted governor, Count Starhemberg, had refused the Ottoman leader's demand to surrender and convert to Islam, they faced slaughter or slavery if the city fell.

Kamal and Nisreen didn't want to be trapped with them. They wouldn't be able to get out to warn the commanders of the pope's army about the suicide bombers. So their plan was to get off the train in Vienna and take a car or a horse-drawn carriage out of the city, to a place far from the siege, where they could do their time jump and connect with the Christian leaders safely.

Their research showed that the Polish king and the rest of the military leaders had gathered at Stetteldorf Castle before the move across the river to Tulln. The castle, an elegant two-storey structure with a Renaissance façade, sat on a commanding hilltop that overlooked the Danube meadows and the town of Stockerau. Kamal and Nisreen would make their time jump somewhere inside the castle, choosing a date when the commanders were there and warning them about the suicide bombers and Ottoman onslaught. The commanders would then need to think up and execute a counter-plan, which, if successful, could decimate the Ottoman advance and put an end to Rasheed's conquest.

But that wouldn't be enough. Kamal also needed to kill him while all this was happening. He had an idea about how to achieve that, but he didn't share it with Nisreen. She wouldn't like it. He wasn't enamoured by it either but couldn't think of a better option to make sure he got to Rasheed. The history books told them where Rasheed was during the suicide bombing and where he witnessed the massacre that ensued: on a hilltop, where Kamal would get to him.

If all went well.

Shortly before lunch, the train made its first scheduled stop at Strasbourg. Kamal and Nisreen didn't join the passengers who stepped out to stretch their legs. They preferred the safety of the cabin and took in the view of the great mosque of Strasbourg from there. It had been a cathedral before the conquest, its second spire never having been completed. The Ottomans had finished the construction in their own style. Both spires, in keeping with those of other converted churches, were now capped by domes and surrounded by even taller minarets.

The stop was only for ten minutes. Just before they left, another train pulled up on the track alongside them. It was a slower, local train, heading in the opposite direction. Kamal glanced through one of its windows. It was a bare carriage without seats. A few peasants sat on the floor, huddled around bundles of farm produce, smoking long gilt pipes.

One of the women looked out and saw Kamal. She held his gaze, staring back at him through impassive eyes.

The sight stirred something inside him. These people, these simple folk, would soon be eradicated if he and Nisreen succeeded. He wondered about that. Was that fair? And what did that mean? Would they simply vanish? Would they have never existed? It was both troubling and perplexing, and he was glad the express started moving again, distracting him.

As the day progressed, the woods of vivid spring greens that cosseted the winding tracks became engulfed by the shadows of the falling sun. By the end of the day, they'd be crossing the Danube, rolling into Munich a couple hours later. Again, Kamal and Nisreen elected to stay on the train for the brief stop. The train then headed back the way it came, reversing out of the main station before looping around the south of the city and resuming its eastward journey. Vienna, the next stop, would be waiting for them after breakfast.

Before long, the express had left Munich and its spires in its wake and was straining on its long climb through alpine country. The air grew colder as the train snaked around the foothills of the snow-capped mountains that straddled the Bavarian states and their Austrian brethren, the whole majestic edifice backlit by a flaming sunset that had somehow managed to elbow its way through the oppressive cloud cover. It was on that slow climb, and shortly after leaving Munich, that the conductor sounded the bell for dinner.

Kamal and Nisreen left their cabin again and crossed to the dining car, where the meal was an even more subdued affair. The moment of truth was almost upon them, and it was weighing heavily on them. The air around them was thick with the intoxicating mix of honey-and apple-flavoured tobacco from the multitude of water pipes, which only added to their heavy-headedness. By the time their waiter offered them coffees and rosewater infusions, they were mentally drained, their spirits as sombre as the sepulchral darkness outside the dining car's windows.

'We should get some sleep,' Kamal said. 'Might be the last comfortable night we have for a while.'

Nisreen's face was tightly drawn, her eyes lost in a faraway stare.

'You okay?' he asked.

'Yes. It's just . . . there are so many unknowns. The language. The war. What they'll make of us there . . . the food, the diseases, all kinds of things our bodies aren't used to. We're taking a huge leap into darkness.'

Kamal shrugged. 'True. But we're not going in blind.'

'Still . . . I don't know what to feel. I keep trying to think of it like we're early pioneers off on some exciting adventure, explorers heading into uncharted waters . . . but I can't stop feeling terrified.'

'It can only be a mix of the two.'

'We're going to be okay, right?'

'Absolutely. Just promise you won't leave me behind and go off to another time without telling me where you're jumping.'

'You mean, when.'

'That too.'

The tightness across her face loosened marginally. She picked her napkin off her lap, set in on the table, and pushed her chair back. 'Give me a few minutes to wash, would you? I'm feeling sticky.'

'Take your time,' he told her. 'No rush.'

He watched Nisreen rise from the table. She gave him a weak smile, one that was miles from reaching her eyes, then headed down the aisle of the dining car before stepping out through the door at its far end.

*

Nisreen's mind was still swamped by questions that had no answers as she walked away.

She navigated the narrow corridor, past a steward and an elderly couple, before stepping across the interconnecting gangways between the dining car and their sleeper carriage.

She inserted the key into the lock of their compartment, opened the door and stepped inside. She had barely started to undress when a couple of gentle taps at the door interrupted her. She let out a light snicker and stepped over to the door.

'I thought you said no rush,' she said as she unlocked the door.

It flew open, pushed in with brute force by strong, unseen hands. She faltered back, narrowly avoiding getting hit on the head by it, and in that confusing instant she realized what was happening.

It wasn't Kamal charging in.

It was Taymoor.

He was moving fast, shutting and locking the door before spinning around and coming right at her, clasping his hand around her mouth before she could even scream.

55

Kamal turned to stone as he saw Taymoor enter the far end of the dining car. He was looking his way, and their eyes met instantly, Taymoor's expression neutral, his face an impassive mask as he ambled down the aisle towards him.

'No hysterics, please,' Taymoor said with open palms before he pulled Nisreen's chair back and settled into it. 'It's just me, all right. Just me.'

Kamal was alternating glares at him with alert scans of the dining carriage, both behind Taymoor and around them, looking for Nisreen, looking to see who else Taymoor had with him, looking to gauge any alarming reactions from other diners.

He saw none of it.

Kamal felt a sudden dread constrict his chest. 'Nisreen. Where is she?'

'She's fine,' Taymoor replied. 'She's absolutely fine. I just bought her some snooze time. Figured it would be more productive to talk alone. One to one.'

Kamal glared at him, on the boil, all coiled up to lash out, but Taymoor raised his hands again in a calming gesture.

'Take it easy. I told you she's fine,' he repeated.

'Where is she?'

'Safe. And sound asleep. So do us all a favour and get a grip and settle down. I just want to talk.'

Kamal sucked in a deep, frustrated breath. He was on the edge of yanking Taymoor out of his seat. 'How'd you find us? How'd you even get here?'

Taymoor shrugged, looked around to assess who might be within earshot, then settled back. 'Celaleddin sent me.'

'To do what? Kill us?'

Taymoor held Kamal's burning gaze, then shrugged again, leaned in, and lowered his voice. 'He told me what Nisreen and Ramazan discovered. He gave me the incantation and told me to use it to find you.'

'And kill us.'

'Brother, if I wanted you dead, you'd both be worm food already. I'm not here for that.'

Kamal sat back and said nothing. All kinds of questions were pelting him. 'How'd you know where to—' Then it hit him. 'My phone. You found my phone.'

Taymoor nodded. 'We knew how far back you'd gone. The thinking was that it was a random, spur-of-the-moment escape, a date chosen purely for ease of translation. Correct?'

It was Kamal's turn to nod.

'But how'd you find us? We had a big head start.'

'You had zero head start.'

'What are you talking about?'

Taymoor let out a little snort of derision. 'You're still even more of an amateur at this than I am, brother.'

Kamal just stared at him, confused.

'I got here before you,' Taymoor said. 'We added an extra day to the incantation. To give me time to get here and prepare. I was here before you. I was out by the lake, waiting for you. I saw you and Nisreen appear. It was freaky. One second, there was nothing there. Then, poof—you're both there. In the flesh. Literally. I watched you both run off into the woods. Not an unpleasant sight, I might add,' he said with a wry grin. 'At least where she's concerned.'

Kamal shot him a fierce look that cut short that avenue

for banter. Taymoor was still keeping up the pretence. Even here, now . . . after all that had happened.

'I followed you all the way to the *han*,' Taymoor continued. 'But when I decided it was time to talk to you, you went ballistic and jumped out of the window.'

'How'd you convince them to work with you?'

'Who?'

'The Zaptiye. How'd you get them to believe you?'

Taymoor's expression clouded. 'What Zaptiye?'

'At the *han*. You had men with you. Local cops.'

'I was alone, brother. There were cops there, yes. I saw a few. But they were nothing to do with me. I was as wary of them as you were, especially after you punched your way out of that courtyard.' He eyed him curiously. 'You really thought I had a whole crew with me? A local one?'

Kamal didn't reply. He felt like a fool. Had he known it was only Taymoor, he wouldn't have felt as vulnerable. He wouldn't have bolted.

'You had a gun,' Kamal said.

Taymoor glanced around the wagon before easing his coat back a little to expose the holster he still had on his belt. 'Have,' he corrected Kamal. 'Let's just say I requisitioned it. Same with the clothes and some extras. And the money to buy this train ticket.'

'So you then followed us to Montmartre? Why didn't you approach me there?'

'I didn't, actually. I lost you outside the *han*. I've been looking for you all week.'

'How'd you find us?'

'The library. I got lucky.'

'The library?'

'Celaleddin asked me to let him know once it was done. He came up with a way to do it from here—from this time.

I was to go to the Sultan Majid Imperial Library, which we knew was around back then—well, back now—and leave him a message on the specific page of a book that was around in this time, one that's rarely taken out. Some obscure, dusty old tome that he got his people to identify. Three of them, actually, to be safe. So after losing you and coming up blank all week, I figured I ought to go there to see if the books were there, thinking I should scribble the message before he decided to send someone else back, maybe even a whole team.' He then added pointedly, 'I was going to tell him it's done.'

Which intrigued Kamal. 'Done? As in, we're dead.'

'Yes.'

'Why?'

'All week, I've been thinking about things, a lot, since it sank in that I was really trapped here—I mean, we *are* trapped here, right? You don't know how to travel forward in time?'

Kamal felt a prickle of alarm at the question, but masked it and just shook his head. 'No. Ramazan was going to ask Rasheed about it when the Z guys showed up and the shooting started.'

'So that's why you were researching Rasheed and Vienna? You want to go back and find him to get the rest of the incantation from him?'

The prickle grew into a stab. Taymoor hadn't just seen them at the library—he'd looked into what they were doing there. But he'd given Kamal the perfect out, the perfect excuse to deflect attention from what their real purpose was.

'Yes,' Kamal told him, his tone as even as he could manage. 'It's the only way. He's the only one who knows it. We have to go back and get it from him.'

'See, that's what I thought. But then, I thought, why Vienna? And why all the research about the battle for the city?' He paused, as if gauging Kamal's reaction, then pressed on. 'You could go back to a more recent time than that. To Paris, after he became governor. It would be much easier—you wouldn't have had to take a train anywhere—and it would have been a hell of a lot safer.'

Kamal felt skewered. Taymoor had been baiting him with his earlier suggestion regarding Vienna. He tried to back-track without appearing flustered in any way. 'Vienna after the invasion is also safe. But, of course, we considered Paris, too.'

'But you chose Vienna. That's what's on your tickets and that's why you didn't get off at Strasbourg or Munich.'

Kamal leaned forward. Taymoor had done his homework. 'We know he was definitely there, we know the times and the places. It's all well documented. The rest, Paris . . . we don't have specific information.'

'How hard could it be? He was the governor. And he was sick. He couldn't have been that hard to find or to approach. And yet you chose to go back to a war zone?'

Kamal tried to mask any semblance of feeling cornered, which he was. 'Things might have changed after he went back. We don't know how far back he went after he disappeared from the hospital after the shooting. But we know it can't have been before Vienna. So we thought we'd go there to make sure we find him. Besides, after I saw you at the *han* and assumed you had the backing of the Hafiye and the police, Paris didn't seem safe any more, in any time. You could have gone back decades earlier and set up a whole load of wanted notices about us.'

Taymoor looked dubious. 'That seems rather extreme.'

'Maybe. But you guys are obviously desperate to find us, so maybe extreme isn't unreasonable. I just wanted us to get the hell out of there.' Kamal realized there were holes in his argument as it tumbled out, but Taymoor just sat back, stone-faced, and nodded. There seemed to be something else on his mind.

'Maybe . . . or maybe there's something you're not telling me.'

'I'm levelling with you, brother.'

Taymoor eyed him calmly for a beat, then shrugged. 'Either way, let me ask you this. Why do you want to go back to our time?'

The question surprised Kamal. 'Why?'

'Yes, why? You're both wanted there. I can't imagine Nisreen will be happy there, given what happened. And yet you're taking this huge risk to get hold of the rest of the incantation. For what?'

Kamal ran with it. 'It's home. Like you said—it's our time.'

'Yes, but what about here, now?' Taymoor's face was animated now—and markedly less antagonistic. 'We could stay here. All of us.'

'You want to stay here?'

'I thought about it all week after I lost you. Maybe it's not a bad thing to be stuck here. Maybe it's actually a great thing. Think about it. Things are good here. They've got a good sultan. It's peaceful. No terror threat, no enemies of the state. Oil is starting to bring in piles of cash, and people are enjoying good times. And it's not so backward that it's uncomfortable . . . I mean, there's electricity and cars and hot showers. And no one knows anything about us. And with everything we know about the future . . . we could live like kings. Right? We could get rich. Absurdly rich. Rich like we never dreamed.' His face tightened. 'But I can't have you and Nisreen jeopardize that for me. No way. Do you understand me, brother?'

Kamal let out a small chuckle. They weren't partners for

nothing. He'd had the same daydream, and it had appealed to him, a lot, but that was before Nisreen had changed his mind. And his mind was changed, even if Taymoor's suggestion did stir a powerful questioning within him, a questioning he needed to make visible, because he couldn't let Taymoor find out about their plan.

Taymoor's ambition made perfect sense to Kamal. He wanted to reinvent himself, to carve out a life of comfort and wealth in this time and place—a time and place where, Kamal also knew, Taymoor wouldn't need to hide his sexual preference as he did in their old life, where he wouldn't have to keep up the charade of being a ladies' man, where he wouldn't fear the severe consequences that would befall him if the truth ever came out.

Kamal and Nisreen's plan, on the other hand, would destroy that ambition. The present they were now in would no longer exist. An altered version would have replaced it, and Taymoor would get wiped out in the mix.

Kamal decided now might be the right time to use what he'd long known about Taymoor. 'I know it might suit you more to live here. It would be . . . safer for you.' He looked at him pointedly. 'You wouldn't have to live a lie.'

A flash of surprise lit up Taymoor's face; then he relaxed and shrugged. 'We've all been living a lie, haven't we?'

Kamal held his questioning gaze but decided to duck Taymoor's point and move on. 'The life you describe . . . I thought about it, too,' he offered, not having to lie to sound convincing. 'It doesn't sound half-bad.'

'And . . . ?'

'Nisreen doesn't want to stay. She wants to get the reverse incantation and go back to get justice for Ramazan and her kids.'

'Justice? That's crazy. You know she doesn't stand a chance. Surely you told her that?'

'I did. She won't change her mind. Given what happened, can you blame her?'

'No, but . . . you know what will happen. She'll wind up dead, too.'

'She won't hear of it. She wants to make them pay. But look, either way—it doesn't affect what you want to do. We'll go back and find a way to get the forward version from Rasheed. You stay here and live your life the way you want. If we get it, we'll go back to our world, and I'll do what I can to help Nisreen get the closure she needs. It won't matter to you. It's decades from now; you'll be long dead by then.'

A sceptical expression clouded Taymoor's face. 'You could change things inadvertently when you go back. Mess up the timeline. Change the future. My future—this future. What happens to me then? What happens to this world?'

Kamal frowned. He felt the sides of the dining car close in on him. 'She needs to try. Maybe we won't even get near them. Maybe they'll see these two naked people appear and think we're *djinn* and just kill us on the spot.'

Taymoor's expression grew darker. 'I can't take that risk, brother. I can't live with that uncertainty hanging over me. Like my whole life could get wiped out just like that.' He snapped his fingers.

They faced off in silence for a moment.

Taymoor was the one to break it. 'Help me out here. We need to find a solution, but I'm not seeing one. Not when all it takes is a few words for you to both disappear.'

Kamal was having a hard time thinking of ways to defuse him. 'I can try talking to her again.'

'Sure, you could, but even if you did get her to change her mind now . . . how can I be sure that it's going to last?'

'You'll just have to trust me on that.'

Taymoor gave him a slow, regretful shake of the head.

'Any other girl, I'd take that gamble on you, brother. But not with her. I know how headstrong she is. And I know what she means to you.'

'They took away her whole life,' Kamal told him, a familiar rage unfurling inside him.

'So you can understand why I can't risk having you take mine away.'

Kamal just stared back at him, coolly, but said nothing.

Taymoor edged his coat open again, enough to expose the gun in its holster. He gave Kamal a sideways nod, aimed away from the table. 'I wish there was another way, brother.'

'Me too.'

Kamal got up, slowly, his senses now operating at hyper-alert.

He started walking down the aisle, passing the few remaining travellers who, unsuspecting, were enjoying the close of their evening, and headed towards the sleeper car, Taymoor inches behind.

56

As he walked down the centre of the dining car, Kamal felt a familiar electric charge radiate across his entire body.

It was a sensation he knew well. He felt it every time he was about to launch into a dangerous situation, a frequent occurrence over the last few years. It was a state of heightened mental and physical alertness. Every sensor in his body was spinning at full capacity, fast-tracking and processing the onslaught of physical and mental inputs charging in while continuously adjusting the optimal response and making sure his body was fully primed to execute it.

Not just his life but Nisreen's hung in the balance. And he wasn't about to let her down. Not now, not here, not after everything she'd gone through.

With Taymoor right behind him, he reached the end of the carriage and stepped through the narrow doorway into a small vestibule. It had a number of small wash rooms followed by an exit to the passageway that linked the dining car to the next carriage, the one Kamal and Nisreen's cabin was in.

Kamal was quickly processing his options when the door to one of the wash rooms opened. A morbidly obese, sweaty-faced man came out to find himself facing them, blocking the tight passage. Kamal considered the moves he could make, but the man would loom large in all of them, and that wouldn't do. He needed to find an out that didn't put innocent civilians at risk. After an awkward pause, Kamal squeezed by him, then turned to watch Taymoor do the same, the man looking sheepish before he waddled off.

Kamal opened the door and stepped out. The two gangways of the carriages were nestled inside an accordion wall that protected passengers and crew from the soot that the engine belched out and any rain or snow. Although the ride was smooth, the gangways were doing a jittery dance with each other, and it took a reasonable amount of care and a careful grip to step from one carriage to the other.

The door into the next carriage opened just as Kamal reached it. A steward was about to walk out, but he held back when he saw Kamal and waved him through.

'Please, after you, *khawaja*.'

Kamal accepted with a courteous nod and squeezed past him.

The steward made a move to go through; then he saw Taymoor following. He pulled back again and waved Taymoor through, wishing him a good evening.

Kamal turned to see Taymoor glance over at the man as the steward ducked into the air behind him and headed out, pulling the door shut. A split second of distraction, eyes flickering away from their target for the briefest of moments—that was often all it took, and he had it now. Maybe the last time it would happen before they got to wherever Taymoor was keeping Nisreen.

His ex-partner also didn't have his weapon drawn.

He lashed out.

He lunged at Taymoor in the narrow vestibule, rotating at the waist to generate power before launching a hammer strike that caught him squarely on the side of his neck and snapped his head sideways. He'd rendered other opponents unconscious with that move before, but Taymoor was still standing, a rabid scowl now aimed at his ex-partner as he turned back to face him. Kamal wasn't waiting—he followed with a quick, thudding hook punch to his ribs, but

Taymoor knew the moves, and he'd taken a punch or two in his time, which meant he recovered faster than Kamal would have liked, having managed to deflect most of the impact. Still, Kamal was on a rampage, using fists, elbows and knees to subdue his opponent, the picture of Nisreen as a prisoner more than overwhelming any latent temperance brought on by the fact that Taymoor had been his partner. He also knew that he had to end it fast, before any of the crew or another passenger saw what was happening and rang the alarm.

Taymoor certainly wasn't holding back. Kamal kept up the onslaught, and although Taymoor had well-honed fighting reflexes, that first strike had put him at a disadvantage. Kamal kept chipping away at him with strikes until landing a solid punch to the solar plexus again. Then Kamal leapt at Taymoor, put him in a headlock, and started to choke him. Kamal's body was in full fighting mode and his mind was racing ahead, reeling through potential outcomes. If he could render Taymoor unconscious, then pull him into one of the wash rooms and tie him up—but then what? Vienna was still far away, and either the crew would be alerted to a wash room that was continuously locked or Taymoor would regain consciousness. There was no way he'd get Taymoor to their cabin, not on his own.

The tangle of thoughts was ripped apart when Taymoor surprised him with a savage backward head-butt, catching him in the jaw. The blow rattled his skull, and his hold over Taymoor loosened momentarily, an opening that his ex-partner was quick to exploit. They traded more ferocious, frenzied blows, Kamal now forced into the deflecting role, Taymoor crowding him against the exit door when a shout, the scream of a woman, interrupted them both. A quick glance identified its source: an elderly woman at the far end of the carriage had spotted them. She stood rooted in place with a clenched hand against her mouth before disappearing back out of the carriage.

Kamal had seconds to end this.

Taymoor had also fallen for the distraction, and this gave Kamal the gift of an unprotected target and a nanosecond to enjoy it. Kamal pooled all the energy remaining in his battered body and channelled it through his right shoulder, down his arm, and into his fist, unleashing it into the side of Taymoor's face, his skin and bones turned into an anvil of anger and survival. The blow was immense. Blood, spit and air streaked out of Taymoor's mouth, and his eyes rolled back as he wobbled in place, his knees weakened by the crushing blow. Moving quickly, Kamal gave him a monster thumb strike to the throat, grabbed him and spun him around so he was facing out, and shoved him against the small return that housed the exit.

'I'm sorry, brother,' he hissed into his ex-partner's ear as he reached out and pulled the door of the carriage open. A biting cold air rushed in, along with the loud clatter of the train's advance.

He shoved Taymoor out of the carriage.

His ex-partner fell from view instantly, swallowed up by the darkness. Kamal leaned out to see where he landed. It was too dark to see much, but the train was still climbing into the mountains, and the landscape slipping by was thick with trees.

He quickly closed the door again and, pushing back the pain that was throbbing across his face from the repeated blows he'd suffered, he sprinted down the corridor to their cabin. He needed to disappear before the conductor or any train security personnel rushed to investigate what the old woman had seen. He also thought he had a fifty-fifty chance of finding Nisreen there. There were two places Taymoor could have sequestered her: their cabin or his. Of the two, theirs was the easier option. To use his, Taymoor would have had to lead her there at gunpoint: in the case of foul play, their bodies would end up there, which could cause Taymoor some serious complications if and when they were uncovered.

His pulse quickened as he found the door to their cabin unlocked, a quickening that came to a dead stop when he saw her inside, lying on the ground with her eyes closed. He dived down and checked her pulse, then put an ear to her mouth.

She was breathing.

'Nisreen,' he whispered as he kissed her on the forehead while cupping her cheeks. 'Nisreen?'

She didn't reply.

He tried to awaken her, gently, but she wasn't responding. He checked her eyes, tried pinching her, but he knew the signs. He'd encountered them before. She was drugged.

He didn't know what Taymoor had given her. He looked around but couldn't find a trace of anything, no clue as to what it might be. He knew from experience it could be one of any number of compounds, although he didn't know what was around back then. Pills, gases and potions to deal with insomnia or to put surgical patients to sleep were plentiful in his time, but here, eight decades earlier, the science of soporific drugs and sedatives had to be much more primitive. The drug had to be something Taymoor could get hold of without much difficulty, and something that he could administer easily. He could have forced her to drink it or to swallow it if it was pill form, but Kamal suspected it was more likely that he had injected it. He looked for signs of a needle puncture on her arms but couldn't find any.

Whatever it was, it was critical to know how long Nisreen would be under its influence. The next stop was Vienna.

He tried waking her up again, to no avail. He put a pillow under her head, then sat down on the floor beside her—then he heard some commotion outside the cabin.

He got to his feet and put his ear to the door to listen. He could hear the voice of the conductor knocking on the door of another sleeping compartment, announcing apologetically that they were just checking if the passengers were all right. The woman who had seen him fighting with Taymoor must have reported it, just as he'd feared.

He didn't have time to lose.

He pulled back the bedding on Nisreen's bed, lifted her off the floor, and set her down on the bed. He then tucked her in, making sure enough of her face was showing so there was no question that she was a woman. Then he stripped down to his long white tunic and ruffled up his bed. He turned off the lights just as the knock came.

He left the conductor to knock again and then, in a tone of feigned grogginess, cleared his throat and said, 'One moment,' before cracking open the door slightly.

Light broke into the room, illuminating the beds and Nisreen's face. In the narrow corridor outside, the conductor was standing close to the door, looking in. A security guard was behind him and, further back, Kamal could make out the curious face of the elderly woman.

He inched back to avoid giving her a clear look at his face in case she could identify him. He also didn't want to give the conductor too close a look at any swelling and bruising he could feel on his face.

'What's going on?' he asked, raising a hand to shield his eyes and narrowing them as if he was bothered by the brightness, and speaking in a low tone as if he didn't want to wake Nisreen up.

'Profuse apologies, *effendi,*' the conductor said, 'but a passenger reported seeing a fight in this carriage, and we're just making sure everyone is safe.'

'We didn't hear anything,' he half whispered, edging back

into the darkness to give the conductor a clear view of Nisreen. 'My wife felt a bit unwell during dinner—I think it might be the winding climb up the mountain, she's not used to it—so we turned in early.'

The conductor peered in, giving the scene a quick study. Kamal's body language and his facial expression was tense. To further move him along, Kamal said, 'I appreciate your diligence. I'm sure you have everything well in hand.'

He moved sideways, as if preparing to close the door. The conductor hesitated, then demurred and gave him a polite nod. 'I'm sorry to have bothered you, *effendi*. May you both wake up in good health.'

'A pleasant night to you too.'

Kamal shut the door quietly, then locked it. He stood with his ear to the door, trying to hear what was being said. He held his breath as he heard murmurs of deliberation between the conductor and the old woman, but then she said that she didn't get a clear enough look to know if he was one of the men involved in the fight. She added that it had been so quick and so intense that she hadn't really had a good look at either one of them.

He heard them shuffle away from his cabin and then knock on the next door.

He breathed out.

He'd dodged that bullet—for now. But he knew how these things played out. The conductor would be thorough. And at some point, most likely before they reached Vienna, they would find Taymoor's cabin empty. And that would lead to all kinds of questions. Questions that might lead to a second sweep of the train—one they might not be able to dodge as easily—or a security cordon once they rolled into Vienna.

He needed Nisreen to wake up soon.

57

There were no further knocks on the door that night, but Nisreen hadn't woken up either. Whatever Taymoor had given her was evidently potent and long-lasting. She was breathing regularly and yet completely unresponsive. Kamal stayed up throughout the night, by her side, checking on her, sporadically trying to wake her, then sitting back and watching with rising trepidation as first light crept out of the darkness and the sky turned gradually brighter.

Vienna was close. They were scheduled to reach the city at nine fifteen that morning, after breakfast. Nisreen was still out when he heard the bell announcing the meal and other passengers shuffling outside their cabin. He began to fret about what he would do if she were still unconscious when they reached the station.

The train glided across the broad plains that suckled on the Danube before following a deep mountainous pass through the snow-capped limestone peaks of the easternmost edge of the Alps. Kamal sat there in silent contemplation as the dramatic scenery unfolded before him, his mind springing back to what he and Nisreen had read about what had taken place there in 1683. As the train powered through the lush highlands of the Vienna Woods, he imagined the thick forests teeming with Ottoman troops, Polish hussars and all kinds of fighting men on foot and horseback, moving around like chess pieces before launching themselves into the massive bloodletting that would turn the ground red, and he felt a disturbing shiver. He'd soon be throwing himself right in the thick of it.

The temperature warmed up with the rising sun and the drop in altitude as the train snaked its way down to the edge of the foothills and approached Vienna. Kamal's trepidation grew with each advancing mile, spiking once the train broke into the suburban sprawl of the big city. His imagination conjured visions of what the city endured during the siege.

The Habsburgs had turned their capital into the most modern fortress city in Europe. It already enjoyed a favourable geographic setting, with the River Danube providing a natural barrier to the north and east. By 1683, it was surrounded by a ring of twelve bastions linked by fifty-foot walls. A sixty-foot-wide ditch fronted the walls; beyond the ditch, triangular advanced gun emplacements called ravelins provided the first line of defence and kept the attackers at bay long before they could threaten the city's walls.

To face the Ottoman attack, the Viennese had mounted over three hundred cannon on the ravelins and bastions. From there, they had a clear field of fire over any approaching Ottoman troops. It would be next to impossible for a conventional assault to breach the walls. The invaders' cannonballs wouldn't be able to bring them down. But the Ottomans were no fools. And they had also learned a few lessons from their earlier attempt, in 1529.

This time, they left their bases much earlier in the year. The invading force—well over a hundred thousand men— was camped outside Vienna by mid-July. And even though they rained cannon fire on the city daily, they weren't relying on their artillery. Instead, they had brought along a small army of sappers. Five thousand of them, many of them Christian slaves, were quickly put to work digging a veritable maze of trenches and tunnels to the defensive walls of the city. Using underground mines, the Ottomans began to chip away at the fortifications with the intention of creating a large breach and using the collapsed wall as a ramp through which to storm the city.

Rasheed's suicide bombers would ensure their success and pave the way for the slaughter or enslavement of all those trapped inside.

A low moan brought Kamal out of his reverie, and he felt a stirring next to him. He sprang across the small cabin to Nisreen's bedside and laid a gentle hand on the back of her head.

'Nisreen?'

She moaned again and took in a deep breath, then turned her head slightly, the pained expression on her face giving the impression that it was as difficult as moving a ball of lead. Then her eyes cracked open, barely at first, then squinting groggily, clearly disturbed by the onslaught of light.

'What did . . . Kamal?' she mumbled.

'I'm right here, *hayatim,*' he said, stroking her hair softly. 'I'm right here.'

Clarity slowly seeped into her face; then the numbed tranquility was swatted away by a sudden burst of dread. 'Taymoor. What's going on? Where is he?'

'He's gone,' he told her. 'He's no longer a problem.'

'What did you do? What happened?'

He ran through what happened before moving on to the more pressing matter of what might be awaiting them at the train station. He helped her straighten up and gave her some water. She said she felt foggy-brained and stiff and wanted to understand what Taymoor had done to her to knock her out. She thought she remembered him pressing something against her mouth and nose, and some kind of nutty smell. Kamal knew it had to be an earlier, perhaps more potent form of an anaesthetic that they'd used in the Hafiye on occasions when they'd needed to grab a suspect.

There didn't seem to be any lasting damage, and Nisreen was regaining her focus, which was all that mattered. The train was now moving slowly through the city, and Kamal saw the old defensive walls that had kept the Ottomans at bay all those years ago slip past their window. They were inside the old city now, and he needed Nisreen to be sharp if there was trouble waiting for them at the terminus.

His fears were confirmed as the train pulled into Sultan Majid Central Station and took its pride of place on a central platform in the cavernous hall. Kamal edged up to the side of their cabin's window and leaned right up against the glass. The scene on the platform was busy and chaotic. A throng of people were waiting to greet the arrivals, including the swarm of porters and small merchants jostling for position. Among them, Kamal spotted the conductor conferring with a clutch of uniformed Zaptiye officers.

One of the officers sent the others trotting off up and down the platform. They were shouting out commands and using their whistles to round up other policemen.

'*Bok,*' Kamal cursed. 'They must have discovered that Taymoor is missing.'

Kamal knew how precisely the Ottomans ran their rail networks. The conductor would have questioned the empty cabin and sounded the alarm after being unable to find its occupant on board.

'What does it have to do with us? Can't we just walk away like it has nothing to do with us?'

Kamal's frown deepened. 'He sat with me at the dinner table after you left. We were there for a while talking. The stewards and other passengers would have seen us. The moment they stop us, we'll be suspects. We don't even have any identifying papers.'

'So we let them arrest us, and then we use the incantation

to jump back a month, a year—back to a safe time. We're in Vienna now; that's what matters.'

'They'll most probably separate us,' Kamal said, 'and we don't know this city. We don't know what was here a month or a year ago. If we jump, we run twice the risk of landing somewhere fatal. Besides, I don't want to risk us doing it apart or ending up in two different places. I don't want to lose you.' There was little choice. 'We have to go,' he added. 'Fast. Before they can set up.'

He grabbed their small suitcase and waited by the door, listening to ascertain if the coast was clear, while she slipped on her shoes and adjusted her kaftan and her scarf. When she was ready, he cracked the door open and peered out. A clutch of passengers were at the end of the carriage, making their way off the train.

'Come on,' he told her.

'Wait,' she said as she grabbed his arm before he could open the door. 'What if we do get separated? We need to have a plan. Just in case.'

Kamal's mind hurtled ahead. 'We'd have to jump back and meet there.'

'How far back?' She pulled her sleeve up to expose the tattoos on her forearm and pointed at the Palmyrene words for the various numbers they'd chosen. 'All the way?'

'No. We'd land during the siege. We'd be trapped inside the city.'

'Then how far back?'

'I don't know. A week. Ten days. Doesn't matter.'

'Ten days then.'

'Okay.' He was feeling the urgency to move. 'Let's just not get separated, okay? Come on. We have to go.'

They slipped down the corridor and joined the other passengers.

At the narrow corridor by the exit door, Kamal spotted two policemen on the platform, by the steps of the carriage. They were checking the papers of those disembarking and questioning them, causing a small backup.

He stepped back to get out of their line of sight, then looked around for another exit.

He glanced through the window of the opposite exit door. There was no train on the tracks alongside the ones they were on. He stepped across to it and tried the handle, but it was locked.

He muttered a curse.

'What?' Nisreen asked.

'It's too late. We're boxed in.'

58

Kamal led Nisreen back to the other end of the carriage, moving at a fast clip.

Shielded from view by the accordion wall, they crossed the interconnecting gangways and stepped into the dining car. It was empty, and the tables had been cleared after breakfast. Kamal sped up, cutting through its central aisle, Nisreen right behind him. They were almost through when a steward appeared from the far doorway, carrying a tray of cutlery.

He paused when he saw them heading towards him, an uncertain expression on his face. Kamal tried to defuse it with a placid smile.

'The dining car is closed, sir—' Then his eyes noted the suitcase in Kamal's hand. 'Ah, you must be looking for the exit. It's back there.'

He was holding the tray with one hand and gesturing towards the other end of the carriage, behind them.

Kamal slowed down but didn't stop moving. 'Is it? Well, I'm sure we can get off from here, too. We've come all this way.'

The steward hesitated, an unnerved tightness overcoming his face. 'I'm afraid you can't leave this way, *khawaja*,' he stammered. 'It's only for staff and—'

Kamal hadn't stopped moving forward, with Nisreen right behind him. The steward inched backwards, intimidated by his pushiness. Then something lit up in his eyes. Kamal's body language, the edge in his tone, the anxiousness across Nisreen's face.

He understood.

'*Khawaja,* please,' he said as he faltered back, 'I don't mean any offence.'

Kamal pushed forward. 'None taken.'

The waiter edged sideways between the backs of two chairs to let them through.

They burst through the doorway and into the small kitchen, where a chef was busy marshalling a young man bringing in a carton of aubergines.

'Excuse me, *ustaz,*' he said—but Kamal had no intention to pause. He ignored him and kept moving, leading Nisreen past the delivery boy, who squeezed aside and almost dropped the carton.

They reached the exit door. Another chef, a large man with meaty arms, was standing at the foot of the steps, supervising two other young men who were offloading more produce from a simple uncovered horse-drawn cart pulled up alongside the train. Kamal peeked out the doorway. They were at the front of the train, with only one service carriage between them and the engine. A bearded grey-haired man, probably the food trader, stood by the front of the cart, paperwork in hand.

'Hey!' the first chef called out from behind. His call alerted his colleague below, who turned and spotted Kamal and Nisreen huddling by the doorway. The beefy chef's expression skipped from cordial to curious to suspicious, his stance tightening up in anticipation of a confrontation.

Kamal knew he must have seen the Zaptiye officers trotting up and down the tracks. Any chance of slipping away unnoticed was pretty much gone.

'Stay close,' he said as he bolted off the train.

The chef moved to block his path, but Kamal shoved him back before blowing past him. The older bearded man by the cart tensed up to face him, but he was too lethargic and slow for Kamal, who grabbed him by the lapels of his coat and flung him aside before leaping on to the reach plate and clambering up to the wagon's seat.

'Come on,' he called to Nisreen, extending his hand.

He pulled her up just as a whistle rang out behind them. Kamal didn't turn. He just released the brake handle, grabbed the reins, and gave the single horse a smack and a loud 'Ha' to spur it forward.

The horse flicked its ears back, leaned into its harness and launched itself. With police shouts and whistles echoing around them, the cart hurtled down the platform, sending passengers, porters and traders scurrying out of its path. By the front of the engine, Kamal spotted two officers rushing over and pulling their handguns out of their holsters. He steered the horse away, and the cart cleared the front end of the train just as the first shots rang out.

'Get down,' he shouted to Nisreen as he flicked the reins and yelled out to energize the horse further. The cart hurtled along the service road, past a number of stalls and into the main concourse, sending people and goods flying out of its path. Policemen were converging from all corners and chasing after the wagon. Kamal kept spurring the horse forward while scanning the large hall frantically, looking for a way out.

The main entrance to the station was up ahead, backlit by the low sun outside. Kamal gave the horse another flick of the reins and steered it there. The entrance consisted of two side passages on either side of a bigger opening that seemed high and wide enough to fit the cart.

They charged through it at full speed, only to emerge on to a colonnaded portico at the top of a monumental flight of stairs.

'Hang on!' Kamal yelled as the horse burst through two

columns and bounded down the stairs, the cart clattering down behind it, cartons of produce flying off it while a trail of shouts and whistles chased it out.

The street outside the station was chaotic and crowded with cars, taxis and horse-drawn carts ferrying all kinds of goods. The cart hit the ground unscathed and charged towards the traffic. Kamal spotted an opening between two cars that looked wide enough. He guided the horse towards it, but, just as it was cutting through, another car came up on the inside lane behind them. Kamal pulled back hard on the reins just as the car's driver slammed on the brakes, but neither of them was fast enough to avoid the collision. The cart almost cleared the car, but the hub of its rear left wheel slammed heavily into the car's front bumper, tearing through it with a loud metal crunch. A loud snap followed a second later as the axle broke, and the cart immediately began to wobble wildly.

Kamal spurred the horse forward, but it was a losing proposition. With people converging and shouting angrily from all corners and police whistles now coming from outside the station, it only managed to charge ahead a few more car lengths before the rear axle gave up completely and snapped in two. The rear left wheel went berserk for a few seconds before shearing off, and the cart listed precariously before the right rear wheel snapped off, too. With both rear wheels gone, its tail-end hit the ground, scraping along the asphalted road.

Kamal and Nisreen hung on to the back of the seat as the horse strained to pull it forward, but Kamal knew it was time to bail. He pulled hard on the reins, and as soon as the horse stopped moving, he jumped off.

'Come on,' he urged Nisreen.

They ran down the street, chased by several policemen. Cars and onlookers, alerted by the shouts and the whistles, stopped to see what was happening, some of them blocking their way. They crossed a side street and carried on down a row of old buildings that housed several shops, Kamal steam-rolling ahead relentlessly, Nisreen in his wake. They needed a solution and they needed it fast. It became all the more urgent when Kamal saw an armed officer down the pavement coming at them. He had his gun out and screamed at them to halt as he ground to a stop and crouched into a firing stance.

Kamal pulled Nisreen to one side and ducked into the door closest to them. It was the entrance to a bakery. Women were standing at a wide counter waiting to be served while stacks of breads and pastries lined the shelves and display cases. Kamal charged through, past a cacophony of screams and protests, and barged into the kitchen, thinking there had to be a rear service entrance through which they could slip out.

There was—but it gave on to a narrow alleyway that was walled in on one end and led back to the main road by the station on the other.

A couple of old doors, other rear entrances, faced them on the opposite side of the alleyway. Kamal rushed across and tried to open the first one, but it was locked. The second was also. He pounded on it and yelled for help, but to no avail.

Kamal knew they were trapped. Reinforcing this was the policeman who appeared at the mouth of the alley and spotted them.

'Don't move!' he hollered before blowing his whistle repeatedly and pulling out his gun.

Kamal turned to Nisreen and grabbed her by the shoulders. 'We have to jump. Now.'

Her eyes were wide as saucers, and she was nodding frantically. 'Okay, but . . . how far back? Ten days?'

She pulled up her sleeves and stared at the markings, her eyes doing a jumbled dance across them.

Kamal could see the confusion whirling around her. 'Whatever. Yes. Do it.'

Nisreen looked frazzled. 'Wait. I have to put in the word for "ten" instead of—'

Kamal snapped his gaze back at the cop, who was walking towards them cautiously, his gun levelled at them. 'There's no time. We have to go.'

'But I'm not yet—give me a sec to—'

'Use what we know!' he yelled out as he rolled up his own sleeve and pointed at the whole incantation. The one that had the full number of moons in it.

The one that would take them back to the siege.

'We have to do it,' he said. 'Now.'

She looked at him with wild eyes and nodded.

He took her face in his hands and kissed her, powerfully, on the mouth, his lips fusing on to hers, never wanting to pull back. But he had to, and he did, and he held her face there, his eyes burning into hers, and nodded. 'I'll see you there.'

The moment barely gave them a second to breathe, the shock lighting up her face for no more than a heartbeat before they started mouthing the incantation again, only faster this time, even more urgently.

Nisreen first, Kamal repeating her words without taking his eyes off her.

Police officers creeping towards them, arms drawn, mystified by what they were seeing.

A man and a woman, facing each other, locked into each other, oblivious to the warnings and orders being shouted at them, lost in some kind of silent, mesmeric ritual.

And then they were gone.

59

Vienna
Ramadan, AH 1094 (September, AD 1683)

They landed in hell.

They made the jump successfully and landed together, facing each other, exactly in the same position they'd been in when they uttered the last word an instant ago. But that instant, that blink of an eye in which the very fabric of their bodies seemed to explode limitlessly before reassembling with infinite brutality, was 252 years away.

They were in a very different Vienna now.

The noise was the first sensation that assaulted them, and it was deafening. Cannonballs and mortar bombs were hurtling through the air before crashing down in bone-shaking explosions and kicking up geysers of fire and stone. Flights of poison-tipped arrows escorted them over the city walls, arcing across the smoke-filled sky before lunging downwards in whistling death dives. Musket detonations crackled in the distance. And screams, all kinds of them, echoing out of the mayhem, coming at them from all corners: the battle cries of the city's surviving defenders fighting on the walls, the howls of the wounded and the dying, the moans of the sick and the starving. Strongest of all, though, was the smell: a rancid, nauseating stench that weighed down the air around them and seeped into their naked pores like a malevolent rising tide. It was unlike anything they'd ever smelled before, but, given what they'd read, its cause was no mystery. It was the smell of rotting flesh combined with the stink of faeces, the 'bloody flux' from the dysentery that was decimating even more of the city's frail occupants than the Ottoman's cannon and blades had.

It was the smell of death.

The onslaught of sensations pummelled them, pounding clarity into their groggy, thrumming heads, and their eyes fell into focus to find each other, naked as before, in the narrow alleyway between the two rows of old buildings.

Kamal cupped Nisreen's face with his hands, as if to make sure it really was her, to confirm to himself that they had made it alive.

'Are you all right?' he asked.

She nodded, her eyelids batting nervously.

Then his eyes swung away, taking in their surroundings with urgency. The roof of one of the buildings backing up to the alley was caved in, and the wall of another was missing a large chunk that had been eaten away by a projectile. The alleyway itself was littered with rubble and debris.

He turned to Nisreen just as a cannonball slammed into a nearby building. The ground shook under them, but Nisreen didn't flinch. Instead, she was fixated on something behind Kamal, at the far end of the alleyway.

'Kamal,' she said, her voice crisp and urgent, her lips quivering, her finger pointing behind him.

Kamal turned. He saw what was making her tremble: between mounds of rotting trash, bodies, a couple dozen of them or more, were piled against the wall at the far end of the alley. A cloud of insects was feasting on them, as were some rats. Through eyes that were still sizzling from the jump, Kamal realized there was something else, too. People— live ones, or barely so, three scrawny, dishevelled figures—were using the pile of bodies as bait to catch anything edible.

Kamal knew the survivors had, by then, almost run out of

food supplies. They had eaten all the dogs and cats in the city and had been reduced to hunting rats.

The figures were so skinny, so filthy, their clothes so tattered that it was hard to tell if they were men or women. Not even when one of them spotted Kamal and Nisreen, alerted the others, and all three started moving towards them, rasping something incomprehensible in what they assumed was Viennese German, the language of Vienna at the time.

'Let's get out of here.' He grabbed her hand and started running.

They emerged from the alleyway into a slightly wider street, their shocking appearance—naked, their bodies clean and healthy, as if they'd just stepped out of a royal bathhouse—attracting more startled attention and drawing in more frenzied locals, who somehow found the energy to start rushing towards them.

Despite the imminent threat of capture, the sheer power of what Kamal and Nisreen saw was too stunning to ignore and just froze them in place.

Most of the buildings up and down the narrow street were heavily scarred by the war. Rubble was everywhere, as were more dead bodies, some piled up against the walls, other, fresher victims still lying where they fell. A couple of bone-thin, filth-covered survivors pulled a two-wheeled cart on which more bodies were stacked. Dust and smoke hung in the air, soaked in that oppressive, omnipresent stench.

The city had endured weeks of the most savage shelling and fighting Europe had ever seen. Even without the apocalyptic mutation, this Vienna was very different from the city they'd glimpsed before the jump. Its scale was much smaller. Despite being the fourth most populated city in Europe at that time, being enclosed by the massive fortifications meant that it couldn't spread outward. It was a tight warren of medieval streets crowded with stone houses that were three or four floors high, most of which were topped by sharply slanted tiled roofs, some of which had dormer windows. Scattered among them, the tall spires of several churches jutted up into the smoke-tainted sky. St Stephen's Cathedral and its soaring south tower dwarfed them all, looming over the crippled city from its central position. Miraculously, it was still standing, and right now it was acting as a beacon and drawing Kamal towards it.

'This way,' he hissed as he pulled Nisreen away from the growing posse, but moving barefoot over debris-strewn ground wasn't easy. Shards of stone and tile were cutting the soles of their feet, hobbling them and causing them to falter. More locals, drawn in by the shouts that neither Kamal nor Nisreen understood, converged on them.

Kamal led Nisreen around a corner, but more men appeared, this time half a dozen scraggy Austrian soldiers in grimy uniforms who froze at the sight of them. He pushed her behind him as he backed up against a wall, the soldiers and more locals rushing at them. He slammed away at the outstretched arms that reached for him and tried to punch and kick his way free, but he was easily overwhelmed by their number. One of them pointed angrily at his tattoos, particularly the one on his right shoulder—the one marking him out as a member of an Ottoman detachment—and he was thrown to the ground, where the battering worsened. He could hear Nisreen's screams of 'No!' and 'Stop!' from behind him, and tried to turn to see what state she was in, but the blows were coming in too hard and furious to allow it.

Bloodied, out of breath, and crippled by pain, he was pulled to his feet. He twisted round, searching for Nisreen, and saw her there, by the wall, held in place by several leering men, a look of sheer terror gripping her face.

'We're here to help you,' he wheezed, 'we're friends.'

But using Ottoman words to plead with the rabid Viennese mob only made things worse and triggered more shouts, slaps and punches. He tried to make out the faces of his tormentors, tried to see if there was a leader among them, someone he could focus on and try to connect with, but they all blended into each other, a sea of desperate survivors who could only see a tiny, unexpected opportunity to vent their rage.

They pulled and prodded Kamal and Nisreen, kicking and screaming, through the wrecked city, the mob growing with every step. They were soon at the fortified walls, where the prisoners were shoved and dragged up endless steps until they reached the wall-walk on top of the rampart. The noise was now deafening, and Kamal could barely think straight, but the few thoughts that did coalesce were ones of tortured regret and anger at the state of Nisreen, at what she was being subjected to with him. Reaching the firing step that overlooked the ditch between the inner and outer fortifications only made things worse.

The sight was surreal.

Savage close-quarters fighting was taking place on the mountains of rocks and rubble from the partly collapsed walls. Swarms of Ottoman soldiers and Viennese defenders were using muskets, swords, halberds and pikes to slaughter each other, even resorting to rocks and bare fists. There were dead bodies lying scattered everywhere—on the rubble, in the pitted and cratered ditch at the base of the ruins—some of them whole, some of them missing a limb or a head. The ferocity and the gore were staggering. He'd read about the battles, he'd imagined what it must have been like, but there was a major difference between seeing it in his mind's eye when reading about it and actually being there, in the thick of it, and witnessing it first hand.

A quick glance at Nisreen told him she was at least as shocked and horrified as he was.

Beyond the walls, the ground outside the city's defences

was a maze of trenches, lines of them, a testament to the blood and sweat of the five thousand sappers who had been ripping out the ground for weeks. The trenches, which sheltered elite janissaries poised for assault and light siege batteries to support them, ran parallel to the walls as far as the eye could see. They were intersected by trenches that led back to the Ottoman camp: tens of thousands of multicoloured tents, a fifteen-mile-wide veritable city laid out in a crescent formation, home to all the warriors who had answered their sultan's call and made the long pilgrimage to subdue the infidel. They were also home to the more than thirty thousand villagers— men, women and children—prisoners from the small towns ravaged by the Ottomans on their march to Vienna. Some of them would be chosen for slaughter in full view of the city's defenders as a demoralizing spectacle, while the rest would be carted off to a life of slavery in imperial territory. The entire spectacle of horrors was playing itself out to the deafening blare of the Ottomans' *mehter* military bands, their kettledrums, cymbals and horns echoing across the killing fields and propelling their men forward.

To his immediate left, on the *plongée* at the top of the parapet, he saw something that didn't register at first, not until the full horror of it sank in: shrivelled, deformed severed heads impaled on pikes. And, if it were even possible, something even more ghastly: flayed skins of men nailed to the wooden posts. Inhumanly gory displays intended to taunt and demoralize their besiegers.

He had read about that, about what the Viennese avenging mobs did to captured soldiers and to those they suspected of being spies or saboteurs in their midst. The Ottomans' savagery was being repaid at every possible opportunity.

A repayment that now awaited Kamal and Nisreen.

60

They were shoved past huddled marksmen and grenadiers, around the front of a cannon, and on to an embrasure cut into the curtain-wall top and held there, in full sight of the city's besiegers. The man to the immediate left of Kamal was a reed-thin soldier with angry red blotches on his face, who stank and seemed to be the leader of the mob. He took cover behind Kamal to avoid the snipers and started yelling something in a fiery tone, his words aimed at the unseen troops huddled in the trenches below and the fighters converging on the mounds of rubble to join the mêlée.

The man's tirade caused the musket fire, sword clangs and janissary war cries to die down, as did the clamour from the nearby military bands. Kamal couldn't understand what he was saying, but given that the man was pulling him up by the hair and jabbing a finger at him and Nisreen, the man was clearly talking about them. His spittle flew into Kamal's face as he continued his rant to raucous cheers and jeers from all sides. He was evidently taunting the Ottoman besiegers about the barbaric display that was about to take place.

The soldier pulled out a large knife from his belt and, with his grip still clamped on Kamal's hair, yanked Kamal closer and pressed the blade against his neck, all while shouting out more angry words. A mad panic shot through Kamal, and he fought to wrest himself free, but he was too well restrained by too many of them. The effort only got him a driving punch to the kidneys and an elbow to the jaw.

Half dazed, he heard Nisreen scream out, 'Stop, please, stop! We're here to help you. We're here to save you.'

A sharp slap silenced her, which sent Kamal into a fit of rage.

'Listen to her, you bastards,' he roared. 'Sobieski and Lorraine are here—they're close—but they're going to die if you don't listen to—'

More incensed shouts and a couple of solid punches cut him short.

Groggy from all the battering, he found Nisreen and his gaze locked on to her. Her pained expression reflected the despair that had hollowed him out, but in that desperate instant, an unspoken message of appreciation and love passed between them, a moment of profound closeness that transcended the utter wretchedness of their state and cleared all the horror and misery from around them for a blissful few breaths—until it was interrupted by the blotchy-faced soldier, who raised his knife into the air and hollered something that seemed to announce the start of the bloodletting ritual.

Kamal saw Nisreen's eyes flare out. Overcome with terror, she started shouting again for them to stop, but Kamal was too focused on the barbaric glint in his executioner's eyes to make out her words—until other words broke through, not hers but a man's, words that electrified the air and shifted the dynamic around them, causing the soldier to hesitate.

The man kept repeating his sharp, forceful missive, his tone powerful and defiantly unbending before the angry jeers fired back at him by the mob. Then Kamal saw him, a lone figure shoving his way through the crowd towards him.

The man was around Kamal's age. He had dark olive skin and a thick black beard, but what was most striking about him was that he was in visibly better condition than the men he was pushing aside. He wasn't a walking skeleton like the rest of them. His face was clear; his clothes weren't tattered or covered in grime. He also wore a broad felt hat that sat low and covered his entire forehead, casting a dark shadow that shielded his face in a way that felt intentional.

A fierce argument broke out between him and the others. They shoved him back and jabbed angry fingers in his face and at Kamal and Nisreen, but the man held his ground and shouted them down before yanking the executioner's arm away from Kamal. Ignoring the outcry and breathless from the strain of the confrontation, he pushed in closer to Kamal and, speaking in Ottoman Turkish, said, 'Answer me quickly. What about Sobieski? What were you saying about him?'

'He's near,' Kamal replied. 'The relief army is near. But they're going to get blown to bits before they reach you if you don't listen to us.'

The man considered Kamal's words for a charged moment, then turned to Nisreen, scrutinizing her.

'We're telling you the truth,' she added. 'We're here to help you. The city's close to falling as we speak. Why else would we be here?'

Suspicion and curiosity crossed the man's features as he kept his gaze on her; then he spun back to Kamal, his eyes darting around nervously, his tone urgent. 'How do you know this? And how did you get inside the city? Why are you naked?'

Without warning, the air sizzled with a volley of arrows. Some streaked overhead while two of them found flesh and blood among the mob gathered on the rampart.

Urgent shouts rang out as musket fire now rained down on the wall and the men surrounding Kamal and Nisreen scrambled for cover. The bearded man in the felt hat rattled off some orders and repeated them more forcefully. They generated a grudging acceptance in the mob as the men dragged Kamal and Nisreen away from the embrasure and across the wall-walk in panic.

They all rushed back down the long flight of stairs, the bearded man leading and four men escorting them from behind. With mortar bombs now chasing the arrows and raining down more suffering on the ravaged city, the small group hurried through its narrow streets. A couple of houses were on fire, the water shortage making it impossible for their owners to put them out. The bell tower of a church a block to their left took a direct hit as they sprinted past. The street below was showered with chunks of stone before its bell crashed down in a deep, eerie thud.

Hugging the walls, they turned two more corners and reached the main square outside the cathedral. Several carts sat outside its main doors, and men were carrying in dead bodies. As they got closer, Kamal and Nisreen were overcome by an ungodly smell coming from the cathedral. It was far worse than what they'd smelled before and made the air almost unbreathable. From their reading, they knew its source: the city's main cemetery was outside the fortified walls, and so the dead were being dumped in a huge vaulted space deep under the cathedral. The Ottomans had discovered thousands of skeletons and decomposing corpses in it after they'd taken over the city. Then Kamal remembered something else and, to steer his senses away, glanced at the cathedral's bell tower, straining to see all the way up its four hundred and fifty *kadems* to the observers he'd read about, the ones who manned it. The tower was a crucial part of the city's defence, and it had survived the siege and fall of the city, before the cathedral had been turned into a mosque. But the sun was strong and his eyes didn't have time to focus before he was prodded away, hustled up the stairs of an imposing stone building that also fronted the main square, to the side of the cathedral.

Whatever grandeur the building once had was long gone. A

cannonball had punched a large hole through its façade, and the chunks of stone and debris inside its entrance hall hadn't been cleared up. Broken furniture was strewn around, with fresh traces of a bonfire in one corner. It was as grimy as the men leading them through it, with traces of blood and filth smearing its marble floors.

They marched past the monumental central staircase and through a low doorway that squatted in the shadows next to it. The men grabbed a couple of torches from their wall mounts and used them to light the way down a narrow circular stairwell that led to a basement. There, Kamal and Nisreen were led down a dank corridor and shoved into a dark, windowless chamber.

They were ordered to sit on the floor. Nisreen looked uncertainly at Kamal. He tried to comfort her with a confident, patience-signalling nod, and they did as they were told. The stone floor was cool under their bare skin, and the room was damp, dusty and littered with empty crates marked with names and dates. Kamal realized the space must have been a wine cellar, now long depleted.

The bearded man loomed over them, studying them intently. He pulled off his hat, ran a hand through his thick, matted hair, then asked, 'Who are you?'

Kamal scowled at him, then glanced across at Nisreen. She was curled up and doing her best to cover herself, but her expression turned defiant when she looked back.

'Where are your manners?' Kamal asked the bearded man. 'Give the lady some clothes, and then we can speak.'

The bearded man seemed affronted by Kamal's outburst, but Kamal stared him down. After a short moment, the man relented and said something to the others. They hesitated; then he repeated his order, more firmly this time. One of them nodded and rushed out, returning with a couple of long military coats that looked like they hadn't had a wash in a while. He handed one to Nisreen and gave Kamal the other.

As he stood up to pull on his coat, Kamal heard the bearded man issue another order to the others, who all turned away to give Nisreen some privacy. Surprised, Kamal looked a question at his inquisitor.

'We lost the luxury of manners many weeks ago,' the man told him. 'But some of it survives.'

'Thank you,' Kamal replied. This time, he stayed on his feet. Nisreen did the same.

'So . . . who are you?' the man asked.

Kamal looked uncertainly at Nisreen. Answering that question was something they'd thought about, of course. It would be asked if and when they made it to Sobieski, and they had hoped to face that scrutiny in less extreme circumstances—dressed, for one thing. Giving a convincing answer was crucial. But thinking about it and actually living it were very different things.

'My name is Kamal Arslan Agha. I am—I was—a senior officer in the sultan's *Tashkeelat-i Hafiye*.'

He and Nisreen had agreed that the best approach to any questioning was to stick as closely as possible to the truth. It was something he'd learned from his experience as an undercover agent. Nothing came across more credibly than a legend that was based on truth.

The bearded man looked confused. 'I've never heard of it.' Which wasn't surprising. The Hafiye hadn't yet been created. It was Rasheed's brainchild, part of his legacy, one of his timeless contributions to his adopted motherland.

'With good reason. We're a secret detachment who serve the sultan. Our job is to uncover and stop any plots against him.'

The bearded man gave him a non-committal grimace, as if

433

he thought it could be plausible but he had his doubts. 'And her?' he asked, pointing at Nisreen.

'Nisreen Hatun is my sister-in-law. Her husband was my brother.'

'Was?'

'He was killed recently.' He paused just slightly, then added, 'The sultan's men killed him.'

'Along with our two young children,' Nisreen added, her voice cracking at the memory.

The bearded man's expression softened immediately. Visibly troubled by the revelation, he said, 'My condolences, *hatun*.'

'Thank you.'

Kamal watched Nisreen. He hated that they had to use the tragedy in this way and could see how much it pained her to be doing it, but it was the truth and it was important to use it to seed everything else.

One of the men stepped in with a question, his tone gruff, his stance confrontational. He obviously couldn't under-stand the language Kamal and the bearded man were using and was losing patience. As he spoke, he was eyeing Kamal suspiciously, clearly itching to get back to the flaying. The bearded man hit back with some hard words, which led to a quick, heated argument before the man grudgingly fell silent and took a step back.

The bearded man turned to Kamal. 'And what is it that you want to tell us that's so important you would risk having my friend Franz here peel your skin off?'

Kamal felt a tinge of confidence. Perhaps they wouldn't be flayed after all. 'Sobieski, Charles of Lorraine and their armies—they're close. They've got Bavarian forces with them, too. The king and all the commanders are at Stettel-dorf Castle as we speak.'

434

As he mentioned the castle's name, he noted a ripple of curiosity among his captors. It was the one word they understood, apart from the names of the two commanders that he'd blurted before, up on the rampart. But the castle wasn't a major landmark; it was an unremarkable local aristocratic residence, and it was on the north bank of the Danube, at the edge of any Ottoman or Tartar raiding ground. For him to throw out its name definitely got their attention.

'They're going to hold a military review of all their forces in two days' time, outside Tulln,' he pressed on. 'But what they don't know is that they're going to be killed there. The king, Lorraine—all of them. They're going to be blown up. And then their army is going to be ambushed. And after that . . . Vienna will fall.'

This elicited a grave scowl from his interrogator and shuffles of discomfort among the others. The same man as earlier grumbled aloud angrily, clearly demanding to know what Kamal was saying. The bearded man shut him down with a few crisp words and turned back to Kamal.

'How are they going to be killed?'

Kamal cleared his throat. 'In two days, on Wednesday. Three couriers will arrive at the review on horseback. They will be trailing camels loaded with sacks of gunpowder. They will claim to be carrying a message and gifts from the sultan. The gifts are a massive explosion that will wipe them all out.'

The bearded man shifted uncomfortably. His men saw this and two of them spoke up this time, but he silenced them harshly. He was visibly perturbed by what he was hearing.

He asked Kamal, 'And you know this how?'

'As a senior officer of the Hafiye, I was privy to all the planning for this campaign. And this was planned from the start. They knew the relief army would be coming. They knew it would be there, waiting. A perfect target. Why do you think they haven't blown up a big charge under the Löbl bastion and stormed in already?'

This evidently troubled the bearded man. Since the beginning of the siege, the Ottoman sappers' work had been concentrated on the two strongest bastions, the Löbl and the Burg—the Lion and the Castle—and the ravelin that sat between them. Of the twelve arrowhead-shaped bastions ringing the city, the ones by the Danube were the weakest, but the river was too near and too deep, which meant digging tunnels to explode mines under them wasn't feasible. The Löbl and the Burg were chosen because the fields facing them were suitable for trenches, the ditch in front of them was dry, the wall between them was long, and their geometry was imperfect. The grand vizier's tent compound was erected in the part of the Ottoman camp that faced them. The ravelin—the massive, thirty-foot-high triangular firing platform—that stuck out from the wall halfway between them had already been destroyed by mines, and the two bastions had also suffered heavy damage from underground explosives. They were hanging by a thread.

'The sultan wants Sobieski, Lorraine and the others here, near Vienna, coming to its rescue, thinking they can save you,' Kamal continued. 'He wants all of Christendom's military pillars in one place. He wants to wipe them all out with one blow.' Kamal let it settle in, then added, 'He wants to leave Christian Europe without its champions.'

The bearded man was visibly unsettled—but he also looked doubtful.

'We've been firing signal rockets into the sky every night for the past week, but so far we've had no reply. And yet you say the army is out there?'

'They're there,' Kamal insisted. 'Maybe they're too far to

see your rockets. Or they're not answering you because they're hoping to surprise Kara Mustafa. I don't know. I just know they're the ones who are going to be surprised. In the worst possible way.'

The bearded man pondered his words, nodding slowly to himself. 'Assuming what you say is true ... Why are you here? Why are you telling us this?'

'My brother was brutally murdered by the sultan's men because they questioned his loyalty. He was just a doctor. A man who devoted his life to saving others. They didn't hesitate to kill his children, too. They were all innocent.' He shook his head with genuine, heartfelt anger. 'My sister-in-law managed to escape, as did I when they came after me. We had to run, and here we are.'

'Betraying your sultan, your people?'

Kamal shrugged. 'Getting revenge for our loved ones. We are marked for death there anyway.'

'That's a pretty extreme kind of revenge.'

'What they did was an extreme kind of evil. We have no life there any more. Our hope is that if we help you save the city, you would allow us to start new lives here.'

The bearded man gave it a slow, pensive nod.

It was imperative that their motivation be convincing. Kamal and Nisreen had devoted a lot of time to honing it, and this was the moment of truth.

Nisreen took it as her cue to speak up. 'They took what I cherished the most in life. I want to do the same to the sultan.'

The bearded man studied her for a long moment, then nodded, seemingly satisfied. 'So the pasha knows the commanders are at Stetteldorf?'

Kamal nodded. 'He has bands of Tartars and bashi-bazouks roaming the land and reporting back to him. Very little escapes them.'

The Tartars were nomads from the Turkish steppes who had settled in Crimea three centuries earlier and converted to Islam. Their leader, the khan, was allied to the Ottomans. Exceptional horsemen and archers, they lived for plunder, and their khan's mission was to lead them into war zones where they could enrich themselves. They were notoriously brutal raiders, which was why the Ottomans deployed them as a force not just of reconnaissance but of psychological warfare. They ploughed ahead of the Ottoman army, pillaging towns and farms before setting them ablaze. Those they didn't kill would be ransomed off or taken away and sold into slavery.

The unruly bashi-bazouks performed much the same task. They were irregular Ottoman soldiers—unsalaried mercenaries who served the sultan in return for the spoils of war, whatever slaves and booty they could grab. They were equally undisciplined and barbaric—their name literally meant 'damaged head'—all of which were qualities that served Kamal and Nisreen's current predicament well.

'I'm still missing something . . . how did you get into the city? And why were you naked?'

Kamal kept his tone casual, to underplay the question's importance. 'We shadowed the army, intent on making a difference. After I found out about the meeting in Stetteldorf, we were making our way there when we were captured by a band of bashi-bazouks. They decided to have some fun and ripped my sister-in-law's clothes off before . . .' He left the rest unsaid.

Judging by the bearded man's expression, he didn't seem surprised. 'And you?'

Kamal let the question hang for a second and gave him a leading look, as if waiting for him to come to the obvious conclusion. 'They weren't all partial to women.'

The man gave a small wince. 'But you managed to get away?'

'She's my sister-in-law,' Kamal said, his tone dead even. 'I wasn't going to stand back. And we got lucky. They got into a brawl about who gets to go first. I made use of it.'

The bearded man looked at Nisreen, as if picturing the scene in his mind's eye and assessing how much of a trophy she might have been for a gang of unruly bandits.

'But why come into the city?'

'We were naked, with no food or horses and with the rest of them on our tail. We had to move fast and find safety. Fortunately, it was under cover of darkness; otherwise we wouldn't be here.'

'How did you get into the city?'

'We swam across the river and climbed over the east wall. It's the least protected side of the walls. We knew that right from the first days of planning for the siege. Two people in the dead of night, your exhausted defenders who can barely stay awake . . . perhaps we also got a bit lucky.'

'But coming here . . . if you wanted to warn Sobieski, this isn't the place to do it. We're surrounded.'

'Like I said, we didn't have a choice. But we managed to get in. Which means we can get out. Can't we?'

The bearded man didn't reply. He was deep in thought, as he'd been since Kamal answered his first question. It was clear that he was still brooding over whether he believed what he was hearing. It was a lot to process—a barrage of shocking, disturbing statements.

'Your accent,' he finally said. 'It's . . . unusual.'

Kamal decided not to give it air. 'No one's ever had trouble understanding me. You certainly don't.'

'Perhaps not.' He pondered it for a moment, then moved in closer and, keeping his eyes on Kamal, took his arm and pulled up his sleeve, exposing the incantation. Kamal didn't resist.

The bearded man pointed at it. 'And this? What is it?'

The incantation was tattooed in Arabic letters, but it meant nothing to anyone who didn't understand Palmyrene. Kamal and Nisreen had discussed it. They knew it would likely come up and be hard to explain, so they had decided on the most plausible answer they could think of.

Kamal said, 'It's personal.' It was a blunt gambit, designed to goad his interrogator.

'I don't think anything of yours is personal any more.'

Kamal glanced across at Nisreen, then shrugged. 'It's our mutual pact.'

'Your pact?'

'Our revenge pact.'

'It's not in your language.'

'No, it's in Croatian. We hid out in the *balkan*,' Kamal said, using the Ottoman word for 'mountain' that had ended up giving the whole region south of the Danube its name. 'After escaping from Istanbul, in a small village near Sisak, the townspeople took pity on us and sheltered us. Their women and children had all these markings on them. They explained the significance of it, their belief that it could provide a spiritual defence from the Ottomans . . . and given what we were planning, I thought we could make use of it, too. They were happy to oblige us.'

The bearded man fell silent. He seemed overwhelmed by all the information, while his men looked like they had reached the end of their tether at being kept in the dark.

Kamal broke the uneasy silence by asking him, 'How is it that you speak our language so well?'

The question elicited an even more stumped look from the bearded man, but before he could reply, a series of explosions rocked the room. They were deep growls that rumbled in from somewhere near and were much bigger than anything they'd felt since they'd landed in the city.

The blasts shook the ground under them, cracking the walls and ceiling and showering them with dust and debris. Kamal grabbed Nisreen and pulled her close to shield her from danger. And although he didn't know what had caused it, a crippling worry instantly seared through him: that the Ottomans' plans had changed, that he and Nisreen were too late, and that the city was about to fall.

61

Kamal hugged Nisreen protectively as the bearded man and his men exchanged panicked outbursts in their foreign tongue.

'What was that?' Kamal asked him.

He ignored the question and just jabbed a finger back at him. 'Don't move.'

'What was that?' Kamal insisted.

The man's jawline tightened; then he relented and said, 'Mines. Big ones.'

For those trapped in the city, the constant, and greatest, psychological terror they faced was not knowing where under the city's defences the Ottoman sappers were burrowing or when the next explosion would happen—the one that could open the floodgates to the invaders.

A man ran into the room, his emaciated face riveted with fear. He was breathless and waved his arms as he fired off his words.

Whatever it was he was saying did not sound encouraging.

The bearded man gave him a short reply, nodded to his men, then rushed out of the room. Two of the others barked orders to Kamal and Nisreen and shoved them to the ground, positioned so they had their backs turned to each other. They then proceeded to tie their hands behind their backs with a length of rope. Once they were done, they rushed out of the room, locking it from the outside and leaving them in darkness.

'Are you all right?' Kamal asked her.

'I'm fine.' She was tugging at the rope, but it wasn't loosening. 'Can you untie us? I can't find the knot.'

Kamal's fingers were already working at it, but without success. 'It's too tight. It won't give.'

'We can't stay here. We need to make another jump.'

'We can't read the tattoos like this. Do you remember the whole thing?'

Nisreen went silent for a moment. 'I can't be sure. I didn't have time to work out the adjustment to fewer days before we had to jump.'

'*Bok,*' Kamal cursed, then grunted under the strain, but he still couldn't loosen the rope. 'It's too tight,' he told her. 'Try raising and twisting your arm. Maybe I'll be able to read it.'

Nisreen adjusted her position to bring her arm out. 'That's as far as I can go. Can you see it?'

Kamal twisted around, then leaned out, contorting his body to try to read the incantation off Nisreen's forearm, but, no matter what he tried, he couldn't make it out. 'I can't. You try.'

Nisreen leaned to her right.

'Other side,' Kamal told her. 'It's on my right arm.'

She bent the other way and craned her neck as far as it would go.

'I can't see it either,' she hissed. 'It's too dark anyway. I can hardly see anything.' The only light in the storeroom was a faint glow from a torch that was filtering in from under the door. 'This is ridiculous. As soon as we can, we need to find the time to memorize this bloody incantation once and for all. We need to be able to jump without having to read it each time we're in a jam.'

'You planning on doing this often then?'

'Ideally, no. But I'm not too crazy about hanging out here any longer than we have to.'

They settled back and took in deep breaths.

Kamal could feel the pounding of her heart through his

back. He was still processing something he'd sensed earlier. 'Maybe there's no point in jumping off again,' he told her.

'Are you nuts? They were about to flay us. I mean, my God . . . these people—they're all savages, on both sides. Did you see what was going on out there?'

'I know. It's . . . it's just insane. But—'

'It's one big slaughterhouse. What were we thinking?'

'We knew what we were getting into.'

'And these people,' Nisreen said. 'These poor people, reduced to living like animals, scrounging for rats . . . It's beyond horrific. It's . . . inhuman.'

'It's war.'

'I know. I just didn't imagine it would be this barbaric. I mean, I knew it, but . . .' She sighed and rested her head back on his shoulder.

'No one should be subjected to this,' Kamal agreed. 'We have to help them.'

'We've got to get out of here first.'

'Well, I'm thinking maybe we've got a chance. I think I got through to that guy.'

'The one who brought us here?'

'Yes. I think he believes us. Which means maybe we shouldn't jump. We need him. It would make it a hell of a lot easier to convince Sobieski that we're telling the truth. If we jump, we'll be on our own. We'll be starting from scratch.'

'But at least we'll know what to expect.'

'Maybe. Maybe not. There's still a lot we don't understand about how this works. We jump back a day, what happens the day after, when we first arrived? Would there be two of us? Do we just disappear?'

'I don't know.' She frowned. 'I don't think one day or ten would be any different from now anyway. We'd still be in the thick of it.'

'So it would have to be longer. A hundred days,' Kamal said, recalling the third of the safety numbers that Nisreen had translated into Palmyrene and tattooed alongside the full incantation.

'Which would take us back to early summer, well before the siege. It would give us plenty of time to prepare.'

'But we talked about this,' he told her. 'It's dangerous. We have to cause as little disruption as possible, come in as late in the game as we can. We could inadvertently change things, which could cause Rasheed to change his plans. Then we wouldn't know how to stop him. Plus, we'd have to actually live out those hundred days here, in this time, since we don't know if you've figured out the forward travel incantation correctly.' He grinded over it some more. 'No, I think we're better off staying. We have a chance to make it work.'

'What if this guy doesn't come back? What if he dies out there and the others take us back to the wall?'

'Then we'll have to find a way to read the spell and say it very, very quickly,' he replied.

She frowned. 'I don't like it.'

'I'm telling you, I think we have a chance with this guy,' he insisted. 'Which is half the battle. There's no point risking everything again. A hundred days is a long time to survive out here with no history. We don't even speak the language.'

Nisreen didn't reply.

'Do I at least get a "maybe"?'

She let out a small, mocking breath. 'Maybe.' Then she nodded as his words sank in. 'No, you're right. But if they take us up the wall again, I'm not letting them do it to me. I'm jumping off.'

'No one's going to hurt you, *hayatim*,' he told her.

This time, there was no snort of derision. She just slumped

445

down, leaned back and rested her head on the back of his shoulder again.

'I wish I could be as certain of that as you are, *canim*.'

A few hours must have passed before they finally heard the rattle of a key in the lock.

The bearded man appeared, this time with two different escorts. His face was pulled tight with anger and anxiety, and he was sweaty and breathing hard. His outfit was also heavily splattered with blood. He looked as if he'd been dragged through the pits of hell.

'What happened?' Kamal asked him.

He didn't reply at first. He was just studying Kamal through hooded, suspicious eyes. 'They sprung several mines under the Löbl,' he finally said. 'Then they charged.'

Kamal felt his blood go hot. 'Are they in?'

'No, which is a miracle. They had waves of fighters hurling themselves at the breach, but the ruins of the collapsed wall were very difficult to climb, which is why we were able to hold them back.' His eyes took on a haunted air. 'But only at a huge cost.'

'What happens now?'

He pulled off his hat and ran a filthy hand through his hair. 'They'll try again. We're reinforcing the curtain wall. It's our last line of defence. After that, it'll be house-to-house street fighting.'

A somber silence smothered the room. The bearded man bent down to a squat so he could face them properly. He was studying them intently, his expression locked in an irritated scowl. He seemed both weary and conflicted about something.

He eyed Kamal and said, 'I speak Croatian.'

It took Kamal a couple of seconds to get it, and his eyes flared with understanding when he did. But before he could react, the man grabbed hold of his arm brusquely and pulled up his sleeve, exposing the tattoos. He pointed at them angrily. 'That's not Croatian.'

Kamal's pulse rocketed, but he didn't reply. He was cornered and just sat there as the bearded man's glare burned into him.

'You think you can make a fool of me with your fantastical stories?' the bearded man raged.

'Sobieski and his men are near,' Kamal fired back. 'They can save you. But if you do nothing, they *are* going to be killed. We came here to try to stop that from happening. That's all that matters.'

'They're nowhere near here,' the bearded man growled.

'How do you know that?'

'I know because I've been out there looking for them,' he roared. 'I was even out there last night. There's no sign of them'—then regret flooded his face, and his jaw tightened, and he held back from saying anything more.

Kamal's eyes widened with surprise. He had read about how the Ottomans and their Tartar allies had captured several scouts and couriers disguised as Ottomans who were carrying coded messages about the siege to the emperor.

His captor was one of them. Only he'd managed to make it back safely. 'You've been out? You've been outside the walls and back?'

The bearded man didn't reply. He was inches from Kamal's face, his eyes twin cauldrons of rage and frustration. Then he pushed himself to his feet, towering over them. 'Who the devil are you?' he rasped. 'Tell me the truth.'

'We've told you why we're here,' Kamal countered. 'Why would we lie about that? What possible advantage would it give your enemies?'

'It might distract us. And if Sobieski was really out there, it might divert his focus from the battle that needs to take place.'

447

'Then we'd have gone straight to him, as you said,' Kamal replied, his tone firm and steady. 'Why would we be here, in his hellish place? Stripped naked and about to be skinned alive?'

'I don't know. Maybe you're here to kill the count or blow up the arsenal. It could be anything. But I'll get to the truth. Count on it.'

The man made a move to leave the room, but Kamal called out to him. 'Wait. Listen to me.'

The man hesitated, then turned.

Kamal mustered a final surge of conviction. 'Torture us if you like. Do what you need to do, but you're only going to get the same answers. And we're running out of time. More lives than you can imagine depend on what happens next. Not just here and now, but in the months and years to come. I could tell you the whole truth about us, but one of two things would happen. You wouldn't believe us, but even if you did, everyone else would think you were either crazy or in league with us. And either one would be disastrous, because it would mean the end of this city and of Europe as you know it. So I implore you instead to focus on one thing and one thing only, which is the conclusion you need to draw from all this: we're here to help save you and save this city and save the rest of Europe, which means saving Sobieski and Lorraine and their army. If we move fast, we just might be able to pull it off. But it all depends on what you do. It's your decision. I just hope you make the right one.'

An eternity of loaded seconds passed between them, the bearded man visibly struggling to divine whether to trust his two prisoners, and Kamal willing him to do so. Then the man fired off another blunt command to his men and stormed out of the storeroom.

His men followed him out, leaving Kamal and Nisreen locked in and alone once more.

'Still think you convinced him?' Nisreen asked.

A couple more hours passed before someone came for them.

By then, they were aching from being tied together and weakened by hunger and thirst, but anxiety and adrenaline were fuelling them. Both sensed the moment of truth galloping towards them, and its heralds appeared through the doorway and pulled them to their feet.

The bearded man wasn't among them, which didn't bode well. Nor did the brusque manner with which they were untied from each other and jostled out of the cellar, their wrists still bound behind their backs.

'Where are we going?' Kamal asked, but he got no reply. And although he didn't think the men spoke his language, he asked again, and still got no response.

They were escorted up the stairs and on to the ground floor. The light filtering in from outside was a blazing orange, and Kamal couldn't tell if it was coming from the setting sun or the flames of a raging fire. He felt a rising dread and glanced at Nisreen as they neared the entrance hall. Her eyes were alight with fear, even as they were clinging to defiance.

As they were being marched off, ghastly images of being back on the rampart and what was in store for them rushed his mind. But just as quickly, the fear gave way to relief as they were ushered not out of the building but up the monumental curved staircase that led to the first floor.

They were led through a set of tall doors to reach a large room at the back of the building. It was lit by a couple of oil lamps and still had traces of lost elegance—mouldings and cornices on the walls, a huge, elaborate ceiling rose—and had probably been the setting for some elegant gatherings in better days. Currently, it was as decrepit as the rest of the city, with dust and debris littering its floor and planks boarding up its windows.

What it did still have was a large carved wooden table with a winged chair behind it and four armchairs facing it. The table was strewn with maps and other documents.

The bearded man was standing next to one of the chairs, facing them.

Straining to get up from the winged chair behind the desk was a tall wiry man with a long aquiline nose and a small upturned moustache. Kamal was quick to recognize him from his readings about the siege: Count Ernst Rüdiger von Starhemberg, the military commander of the city and the man the emperor had charged with defending it.

Neither of the two men looked pleased to see them.

62

Starhemberg didn't look well.

The only images Kamal had seen of him were portraits that had been done before the siege, engravings and oil paintings that showed the count at the peak of his glory. The siege had taken a heavy toll on the forty-six-year-old count. He had been wounded in battle early on and was, by now, also suffering from repeated bouts of dysentery. He was barely mobile and had to be carried to the walls to oversee the battles. Yet despite his condition and the scruffy wig he wore now that he wasn't in the thick of battle, not to mention the battered jackboots that hadn't seen polish for months, Starhemberg still possessed an air of unmistakable authority. He was an aristocrat and a military man through and through, and a mere battle injury or a life-threatening illness weren't going to undermine his dignity or his stature.

Starhemberg nodded to the bearded man, who turned to his prisoners.

'Sit,' he ordered them.

Kamal and Nisreen each took a seat facing the large table.

Still standing, Starhemberg scrutinized them. He had the fierce gaze of a fighting man, and Kamal felt uncomfortable under it. He had read all about how brilliantly the count had defended the imperial capital, and he felt intimidated by him. He also felt unsettled by something else: the realization that he was sitting there, face-to-face with this brilliant general, all while knowing that, as things stood, the man would soon be dead. He would be captured when the city fell and put to the blade, and his head would be gifted to the sultan—all things he knew but couldn't share aloud.

Starhemberg had been appointed by Charles of Lorraine to lead the defence of the city. He arrived in Vienna one day after the emperor and the rest of the city's wealthy residents had fled and had only one week to shore up the city's defences and prepare for the Ottoman onslaught.

Once the siege began, his tactics were highly effective at frustrating the enemy and repelling them. Displaying great skill and leading counter-attacks himself, he earned the full respect of those trapped there with him, but it was a losing battle. Weeks of relentless attacks had sapped their morale, and the overwhelming forces facing him, starvation and dysentery had decimated his ranks. Out of an initial force of eleven thousand men, already outnumbered fifteen to one at the onset of the siege, only four thousand Austrian soldiers were still standing. Lesser men would have long since surrendered, but Starhemberg knew there was no point, not when the result would be certain death. Fighting it out and dying defending the city were far preferable to suffering the Ottomans' infamously inventive ways of inflicting a long, slow death.

The count asked something of the bearded man, who turned to them and introduced his leader. Kamal and Nisreen both responded with courteous bows, and then Kamal asked him, 'What about you? What is your name?'

The bearded man hesitated, then said, 'My name is Georg Kolschitzky.'

Which somewhat surprised Kamal. 'You're not Austrian?'

'I'm Polish.'

Kamal felt puzzled. 'But your Ottoman is flawless.'

'I spent many years in Constantinople. I was a translator for the Austrian Oriental Company. When they started making our lives miserable and I tired of being a guest at the sultan's delightful jail, the charm wore off.'

Realization spread across Kamal's face. 'That's how you've been able to get out and back safely. You can pass for one of them.'

Kolschitzky gave Kamal a faint, world-weary smile. 'I can pass for many things. Especially a humble merchant from Belgrade plying his trade.'

The count grew impatient and interrupted them, prodding Kolschitzky along.

'I told his excellency what you told me,' he told them. Pointedly, he added, 'the relevant parts.'

Nisreen asked, 'So you do believe us?'

'I don't think I have a choice. If what you say is true, we can't afford to ignore it. We have to act on it to save them . . . and to save ourselves.' He made a nod at Starhemberg. 'But the count wanted to see you for himself. He usually has good instincts in these matters.'

Kamal felt a surge of relief, daring to imagine that their plan might just work. He looked at the count, who began to speak. Judging by his tone, his words seemed ominous.

'His Excellency says your arrival is auspicious. Until you showed up, we had given up hope of relief. We knew death was coming and were prepared to die here, in the knowledge that God is with us. You have changed this, which could be merciful—or savagely cruel. He wants you to know that if this does turn out to be a ruse, he will allow his men to do whatever they please to you both for as long as they please.'

Something about his words didn't sit well with Kamal. 'Wait, what does that mean? How do you intend to warn Sobieski?'

'We're going to send out some couriers tonight.'

'What about us?'

'You stay here. If the city is saved, you will be fêted as heroes. If your words turn out to be lies, then you die here with us. Or before us, I should say.'

'No,' Kamal said. 'We have to go, too. We need to warn them ourselves.'

This took Kolschitzky by surprise. The count also seemed curious about Kamal's outburst and asked Kolschitzky something. A brief exchange followed, then the Pole turned to them.

'His Excellency doesn't see the need for you to be there when the message is delivered. He also thinks it would be unwise to allow it. He wants to keep you here in case this turns out to be a ruse.'

Kamal felt the walls of the room tightening around him. Staying in Vienna, even if the couriers made it through, meant Rasheed might not be killed. Which could make all their efforts pointless.

'We have to go,' he insisted. 'Look, I can be useful beyond the warning. I know a lot about how Kara Mustafa and his commanders think, how the army operates. Even the smallest insight could prove invaluable, and there's no way of telling beforehand what they might be.' He turned and addressed Starhemberg directly, even though he knew the count couldn't understand him. 'Excellency, I beseech you— let us accompany them. We could be useful should they encounter enemy troops. Let us see this through successfully, right to the end. And if all goes well, we'll be back here to celebrate the city's survival together.'

The count studied Kamal, then muttered something to Kolschitzky, who relayed Kamal's words to him. He considered them for a moment, then gave the Pole his reply, never taking his eyes off their prisoner.

Kolschitzky told Kamal, 'Very well. The count says you can go. But the lady stays.'

Kamal and Nisreen were simultaneously outraged. 'What?'

'You can go. She stays.'

'No,' Nisreen insisted. 'I'm not staying behind. You can't separate us like that.'

'I'm afraid it's not your choice,' Kolschitzky said.

Duelling thoughts were vying for attention inside Kamal's mind. On the one hand, perhaps it was safer for her to stay behind. On the other, he didn't want to leave her. Not when there was a real risk that the city would be captured and that horrors awaited her if she were there when it happened. Then again, there were horrors outside the walls, too.

But before that, a bigger worry swept in.

'There's something else. You can't send out several couriers,' he said. 'That would be a mistake. What if even one of them gets captured? They'd soon know what his message was, they'd know that you know what they're planning and would simply change their plans. Then you would lose any benefit of taking them by surprise.'

'But at least we'll have saved King John and the others,' the count replied after Kolschitzky translated Kamal's reasoning.

'Well, if you just want to do that, just send out one volunteer, a messenger who will let himself get captured,' Kamal countered, 'he can tell them what we know and say there are many other couriers on their way to Stetteldorf, too. They won't know he's lying. They'll assume the king will be warned and they'll cancel the bombing. But then they'll come up with something else, and you won't know what that is. They might decide to just go ahead and blow up the Löbl and take the city.'

Kolschitzky and Starhemberg murmured as they debated his troubling words.

'Look,' Kamal interjected, 'you have a historic opportunity here: to catch Kara Mustafa and his whole army with their pants down. You can deal them a massive, crippling blow and maybe wipe out that threat once and for all. But that means making the right move here, and the right move is sending one, and only one, committed and capable team to Stetteldorf.' He fixed Kolschitzky squarely. 'And that's you and me, sir. You know it as well as I do.'

Nisreen spun around to face him, mouth agape. 'What? You'd go without me?'

'Nisreen, please,' he told her. 'It'll be dangerous out there. And we'll move faster. Two are less likely to be spotted than three.'

She was speechless—but Kolschitzky stepped in before she could voice her disagreement further.

'We'd be gambling a lot on our success,' he said before translating for the count.

'Yes, but if it works,' Kamal replied, 'the Ottomans will probably never threaten Vienna again.'

'I'm not staying behind,' Nisreen insisted.

Kamal turned to her but didn't reply, preferring to remain focused on the two men and their deliberations.

'It's going to be dark soon. And whatever we decide has to happen tonight,' Kolschitzky finally said. He nodded to his men and mouthed a brief order. They stepped up to Kamal and Nisreen and put their hands on their shoulders, ready to usher them out. 'I'll let you know.'

Nisreen stormed ahead without looking back at Kamal.

They were locked back inside the same storeroom, still with their hands tied behind their backs. Only this time, they weren't tied to each other. Which was what Kamal was counting on.

Nisreen was livid. 'I can't believe you'd go without me and leave me as a hostage to rot here alone,' she blurted. 'What happened to us doing this together and you never leaving me behind?'

Kamal said nothing. He just looked at her with a half-smile, a perverse side of him somewhat enjoying the sight.

Which made her even angrier. 'You don't have anything to say? And what's with the weird look?'

He stepped closer to her and lowered his voice. 'They out-played us. I wasn't counting on that. And if they send out several couriers and one of them is caught, everything falls apart. We can't let that happen. We have to move before they do.' He lowered his voice right down to a whisper. 'I'm not leaving you behind. We're going to go find Sobieski together.'

'How?'

'You're missing something.' He turned around and twisted his arms up so she could see them. 'We're not tied to each other any more. We can read the incantation.'

It took her a split second to process it. 'You want to jump?'

'Yes. One day. We go back one day. That's all we need. We sneak out of this room, which shouldn't be locked—it's just an empty storeroom. Then we sneak out of the city and we find Sobieski, just like we originally planned. Kolschitzky and the rest of them wouldn't even know we exist. They wouldn't have met us yet.'

Nisreen's eyes went wide, then relief washed over her. 'When?'

'Right now.'

63

They were in the same cellar, only two things had changed.

They were naked.

And the door wasn't locked, just as Kamal had expected.

They were in total darkness, with no light from a torch creeping in under the door. But they were untied, and they could get out.

Their first priority was to find some clothes. They listened in silence, then cracked open the door slightly, keeping a watchful eye on the corridor outside, gauging the feeble amount of daylight filtering in from the top of the stairwell. Given that they were in almost complete darkness and that their eyes had adjusted to it, even the faintest light was registering on their retinas. It wasn't long before the last vestiges of day were swept away by nightfall. Which meant that it was time for them to make their move.

Kamal slipped out first, keeping Nisreen close behind. There was no awkwardness about being naked any more. After everything they'd been through, it was second nature.

They scurried down the corridor, checking each door they passed. The doors gave on to various storerooms that were all empty. Anything even remotely useful had been used up over the weeks of the siege.

They crept up the narrow stairwell to the ground floor and paused when they reached its doorway. Kamal pulled it open carefully. Some faint light slinked in around them. The thunder of cannon, mortar pieces, and small shot echoed in the distance. Closer, Kamal could hear voices—men's voices.

He gestured for Nisreen to stay quiet, then inched forward for a closer look. He could see the silhouettes of two men standing just inside the entrance of the building. They seemed to be backlit by a torch somewhere in the hall and looked as haggard as everyone else they'd encountered in the ravaged city. On closer look, they were musketeers. Their guns were next to them, leaning against a wall. There didn't seem to be anyone else around.

Kamal turned to Nisreen. 'I'm going to need you to do something.'

His words were greeted with a raised eyebrow. She could read him well. 'What?'

'Lure them over.'

Her jaw dropped and she mouthed a silent, 'What?'

'We need their clothes and their boots,' he told her. 'Unless you feel like running around the city like this again.'

She gave him a peeved look; then she nodded her grudging consent. She took in a couple of deep breaths to steel herself, and then she casually stepped past him and out into the open hallway outside the stairwell, in full view of the two men.

At first, they didn't notice her. Which made her give them a giggle. A playful, cheeky one. One of the men turned and saw her, and the sight hit him like an electric charge. He flinched and his eyes shot wide. His friend noticed, looked her way, and was equally floored. Then she held her finger up and curled it inwards, slowly, teasingly, beckoning them over, deploying a beguiling smile to seal the deal. She watched as her mind-boggling request pulverized the logic barriers in their frazzled brains and made them walk, then run, towards her.

She ducked through the doorway, past Kamal, who waited for them to reach it before stepping out to face them.

It was an unfair fight. He had expert training, and they were only half alive. An upward palm strike to the chin took

459

care of the first. The man's neck kinked back heavily and he instantly rag-dolled, unconscious. A punch to the temple with a closed fist and a middle finger's knuckle sticking out had a similar result on the second.

Moving quickly, Kamal and Nisreen dragged them into an alcove behind the stairwell. They stripped them of their clothes—over-the-shoulder bandoliers, scarves, surcoats, tunics, doublets, hose and breeches—and pulled them on.

Nisreen winced. 'These are disgusting.'

Kamal shrugged. 'We'd better get used to it. Deodorants haven't yet been invented.'

'Now there's something else we could help them with.'

One of the men had shoes; the other, knee-high jackboots, both pairs tattered beyond repair. They were all too big for Nisreen, but she opted for the shoes, strapping them in with a length of cloth to keep them from falling off. Kamal took their daggers—one was a janissary *yataghan,* no doubt taken from a fallen enemy—and tucked them in under his belt. They then each slipped on a wide-brimmed felt hat to complete the look, Nisreen bunching her hair up under hers to hide it.

Kamal looked at Nisreen and crinkled his nose. 'Not your finest moment.'

'You don't look particularly dashing either.'

They emerged from the alcove and headed towards the entrance. There was no one around, but when they stepped outside, Kamal spotted a man walking towards the building—and straight at them.

The sight momentarily puzzled Kamal. The man was wearing a cloak, but under it Kamal spied something unexpected: baggy trousers, a long tunic, belt and Yemeni shoes that were distinctly and unmistakably Ottoman, ancestors of the civilian clothing Kamal was accustomed to seeing back in his world. The man was also carrying his *bashlyk* hat in his hand, and, as he drew nearer, Kamal realized that it was Kolschitzky.

The Pole's heavy-footed gait clearly telegraphed his weariness.

'Watch out,' Kamal whispered to Nisreen, nudging her elbow discreetly to alert her. As they crossed paths, Kamal turned to Kolschitzky and gave him a courteous, mute nod of the head, which the Pole didn't bother to return. They each kept moving without further interaction. Kamal breathed out with relief, but he quickly realized his fear had been unfounded. After all, Kolschitzky didn't know who he was. They hadn't yet met, and if all went well, perhaps they never would. Still, he and Nisreen didn't speak the language and would have been discovered if Kolschitzky had initiated conversation.

They needed to avoid any interaction.

Except that a sudden realization ambushed Kamal—the fact that, if they got to Sobieski, they'd have as much trouble convincing him as they had with Starhemberg and Kolschitzky. Trouble that would be neutralized if Kolschitzky were with them.

It was an instinctive, reckless reaction. But he couldn't stop himself.

His entire body lit up with nerves as he turned and called out, 'Herr Kolschitzky.'

Nisreen hissed, 'What are you doing?' She was looking on in shock—but it was too late. Kolschitzky had heard him, stopped walking, and turned.

'*Ja?*' he replied curiously, straining through the darkness to see who was calling out to him, but Kamal had already closed the space between them and pounced, lightning-quick. He grabbed Kolschitzky and spun him around, holding him from behind while pressing the *yataghan*'s blade against his neck and pushing him against the wall.

Speaking in Ottoman Turkish, he said, 'You've just been outside the walls looking for the relief army, which is why you're dressed like this. But you've found no sign of them. Am I correct?'

Kolschitzky stiffened defensively. 'Who are you?' he asked in the enemy language.

'We're friends,' Kamal told him, keeping his grip tight. 'We're here to help you. But we don't have much time. Sobieski and Lorraine and the others—they're out there. You just didn't go far enough. We can take you to them—but we have to move quickly. Kara Mustafa is preparing an ambush for them that will wipe them out and devastate their army.' He let his words sink in for a second, then released his hold enough to turn Kolschitzky around and reposition the blade under his chin. 'Listen to me, Georg,' he pressed on. 'I know you want to help these people. I know you've made this city your home ever since your days as a translator for the Austrian Oriental Company and your time in jail in Constantinople. I know that the misery they brought to your life back there has followed you here tenfold.'

Kolschitzky's eyes widened. 'How do you know all this?'

'It doesn't matter. What matters is that the relief army is here. But you've made several sorties looking for it, and you don't believe me. You want to know who we are and how we know this. You want to call for your men so you can have us locked up and questioned thoroughly. And even if you believe us, you'll want to discuss it with Count Starhemberg and his council. But there's no time for any of that. If you want to save this city, you need to decide right here, right now. Decide if you're ready to believe me and help us. Alone. Just you—and us. Right now.'

It was the biggest gamble of his life, but somehow it didn't feel like one. He was still charging ahead on pure instinct and adrenaline. Caution didn't even get a chance to show its face.

Kamal kept his gaze locked on the confused Pole; then he watched Kolschitzky's face flood with surprise as he pulled back, turned the dagger in his hand and held it out to Kolschitzky.

'It's your choice,' Kamal told him, offering him the *yataghan*. 'Take us in as your prisoners—or come with us and help save your people.'

Kolschitzky took the dagger, slowly, then raised it so its tip was nudging Kamal's neck. 'That was a mistake,' he hissed. 'We'll soon get to the bottom of this.'

Kamal didn't flinch. 'Fine. It won't change what you hear from us. But it'll seal our deaths. Yours, and ours. We'll all die here together.'

They glared at each other in stiff silence as explosions and gunfire rocked the night around them.

'Well?' Kamal pressed.

Kolschitzky's lips were quivering. He was visibly struggling with his decision. 'Come with you—where?'

'To warn Sobieski.'

His eyes narrowed, sizing up Kamal. 'Where is he?'

Kamal hesitated—then Nisreen stepped in, adding her voice to take one last gamble. 'Stetteldorf. They're all there, at the castle, preparing their battle plan. You can help us get there. And they'll listen to you more than they'll listen to us.'

Kolschitzky's hand was shaking, his eyes darting back and forth nervously between them. Furious battles, as intense as those on the walls, were clearly being waged inside his head.

'We don't have time for this,' Kamal blurted. 'Do you want to save this city or not?'

Kolschitzky demurred. 'I'd be crazy to trust you.'

'You'd be condemning everyone around us to a terrible fate if you don't.'

The bearded Pole stood there, tense as a steel rod, breathing hard. 'This is madness.'

'You'll be dead in a day or two if you don't come with us. Or you can save yourself and everyone else in this city—and beyond. Because don't think the sultan's plans end in Vienna. They go a lot further. And stopping him is going to be a hell of a lot harder once Sobieski and Lorraine are dead.'

Kolschitzky's eyes were blazing with indecision and frustration—then he lowered the knife and nodded his acceptance. 'You're either a godsend or a demon.'

Kamal clapped him on the shoulder. 'Perhaps I'm a bit of both. But you won't regret this. We should go. Now.'

Nisreen asked, 'Which way?'

Kolschitzky glanced around, thinking, visibly still tortured by his decision, then said, 'The east walls. That's our best option. Follow me.'

64

They passed the cathedral, which was lit up by torches and thronged with people, more of whom were arriving from all directions—haggard, bone-thin survivors, shuffling along slowly, hanging on to each other, flinching with each new explosion that shattered the night around them.

'All the churches are full, every night. They all come to pray for salvation,' Kolschitzky told them. 'So far, their prayers haven't been answered.'

'Let's help change that,' Kamal told him.

Kolschitzky nodded grudgingly and they kept going, staying close to the walls, moving with purpose to detract attention.

They reached a recessed doorway, where the Pole gestured for them to take a pause. Kamal scanned his surroundings to get his bearings. He drew on what he'd read about the siege and tried to visualize the maps he'd studied.

The weakest points in the city's perimeter were the two areas where the river ran close to the walls. One was the eastern flank, the area around Vienna's port and the Leopoldstadt island, where a small channel of the Danube ran parallel to the walls and led to quays. The other was the southwestern edge of the city, where the River Wien snaked down from the highlands of the Vienna Woods to join the Danube. Both areas had weaker, older fortifications that were also less heavily defended, since they were harder to attack given the presence of water, which made tunnelling impossible and carried a risk of flash floods and entrapment.

Kolschitzky seemed to have made the right choice. They

were moving east, and, given that their objective was to get to Stetteldorf Castle, which was northwest of the city, the eastern walls made sense. The bulk of the Ottoman camp and the crescent of densely forested hills of the Vienna Woods beyond it ringed the west side of the city. Going out from the east would be safer, even if it did mean a slightly longer route, but Stetteldorf wasn't that far, anyway. Besides, having just jumped back a day, they had gained more time to get there. Avoiding the massive camp didn't mean they would be clear of enemy troops: Ottoman irregular troops, their Hungarian allies and hordes of Tartar raiders all roamed the forests and meadows on the north bank of the river.

Kolschitzky explained his logic to them; then he bent down and rubbed his hand in the grime that lay on the threshold of the doorway.

'What are you doing?' Kamal asked.

'Do as I do.' He smeared his face with the grime, making it unrecognizable.

Kamal and Nisreen did as he directed. Then they all set off, moving on at a fast trot through the dark, narrow canyons that made up the old city.

A plump moon hung overhead, occasionally hindered by some passing clouds. It smiled down on them when it flared up to light their way before shrinking back to turn the landscape into a desolate, dark netherworld. They crossed a few more of the city's worn-out survivors, and their pace and air of purpose allowed them to get away with no more than a passing nod or salutary wave. As they neared the eastern edge of the city, the sound of battle and bombardment further west receded slightly, and it wasn't long before they saw the silhouette of the walls looming up ahead.

They sheltered in the shadows across from the walls and watched.

'Why are we hiding?' Nisreen asked. 'Surely they know you?'

'Fewer people than you think. The fewer people who know what I'm doing, the better.'

That side of the city was defended by two smaller bastions, the Gonzaga and the Little Gonzaga, which was also known as the Spike. Between the two was an old fortified wall with a new palisade fronting it. Huddles of armed men, some in uniform and others in civilian clothing, were scattered around the base of the walls. Some were asleep, while others were just sitting there, waiting for the next assault. A few men were up on the ramparts, a skeleton crew of marksmen, gunnery crews and musketeers on watch.

They needed the moon that had helped them navigate the city to cloak itself. When it was out from behind the clouds, the stairs going up to the walls were too visible to allow them to sneak up unnoticed. The light did help them locate one thing they desperately needed, however: rope. Kolschitzky saw a bundle of it lying on the ground in front of one of the buildings that faced the wall, dumped with a mess of crates and other rubbish. The mound would also serve as cover to get closer to the base of the stairs.

They waited until the moon slid back behind a cloud. Then they hurried across the open ground and ducked behind the crates. The moon peeked out again, and Kolschitzky checked the rope. He found a length long enough and rolled it over his shoulder, fastening it behind his belt. Then they waited again.

The moon was being stubbornly exhibitionist, but then a loud scream cut through the air, startling Kamal and Nisreen. They huddled closer to the crates and looked up at the sky, where the sound was coming from. A signal rocket streaked up into the night from the tower of the cathedral, rising high above the city before exploding in bright white flashes. Two

467

more followed. The Viennese were firing their nightly distress signals, desperately hoping a relief army was out there, praying they'd get a signal back.

Kamal and Nisreen looked at Kolschitzky. He hadn't been surprised—he knew the flares would be fired. Kamal and Nisreen knew that no response would be coming, but the rockets helped in another way. The men flanking the fortifications and up on the walls all stood up, waving their hats and yelling, their attention riveted on the flares.

'There's never an answer,' Kolschitzky said, his tone and eyes heavy with suspicion.

'They're still too far,' Kamal replied. 'But we're going to make sure they get here.'

Kolschitzky studied him for a beat; then he said, 'Let's go.'

They scurried across the open ground. Kolschitzky joined in the gestures and whoops all around him, which Kamal mimicked as they reached the stairs. A couple of men were climbing up ahead of them, rushing to get a front-row seat for the hoped-for response. The three followed them up, Nisreen making sure that she kept her hat well down to cover her face.

They reached the top of the rampart and slipped away from the others, making their way furtively along the wall-walk until they were on a stretch of wall that was unmanned. Moving fast, Kolschitzky climbed on to the firing step and peered out, then waved them over.

Through the wall of tree trunks that made up the palisade, they could see the curved contour of the Danube below, now almost completely dried out after a particularly hot summer. Beyond that was a forbidding darkness, only broken up by the faint glow of scattered campfires from the Ottoman batteries and platoons of janissaries lurking behind large earth emplacements, waiting for an order to attack.

Right now, all was calm. And the moon was about to pull another disappearing act.

Kolschitzky unfurled the rope. He tied one end to a brass spike embedded in the face of the parapet, then, making sure no one was watching, he flung the bundle over the edge of the wall.

One last check of the moon and the watch confirmed they were good to go.

'Stay close,' he told them.

He was about to clamber up on to the merlon when a sharp yell rang out from the darkness to their left, from the opposite side to where they'd come.

Kolschitzky crouched down and spun around defensively. Three men appeared out of the darkness, trotting towards them. They had their muskets levelled at them.

'Don't say a word,' Kolschitzky said to Kamal and Nisreen in a low voice, taking a step forward to keep them behind him. 'I'll handle this.'

The men halted a few paces away from them.

The leader of the Viennese musketeers fired off a couple of questions at Kolschitzky while eyeing the three of them suspiciously and gesturing with the barrel of his musket. The Pole replied calmly, but his tone was clearly firm. Another heated exchange followed, and although Kamal and Nisreen couldn't understand that either, it was clear from the body language all round that it wasn't friendly.

Their tones rose; then the leader of the patrol turned his attention to Nisreen and asked more questions. Kolschitzky's reply didn't seem to satisfy him, and the man stepped forward for a closer look at her. Which was when Kolschitzky sprang into action, pulling out his *yataghan* while grabbing the man in an unexpected lightning-fast move.

He held his blade against the man's throat and spoke in a

sharp, cutting rasp, giving them what was clearly an enraged dressing-down. Kamal heard him say 'Starhemberg' a couple of times; then Kolschitzky ended with some final words that sounded like a firm question, which he repeated twice.

The other two musketeers hesitated, then nodded their acceptance grudgingly.

Kolschitzky muttered a few words, then he flung his prisoner off him. The Pole tucked his blade away and shooed them off with a dismissive gesture. The men gave him a short bow, then receded back into the darkness, their leader giving Kolschitzky one last resentful glance before turning away.

'What was that all about?' Kamal asked.

'Desperation,' Kolschitzky said. 'Never mind. Let's get going.'

He looked up at the sky, made sure the moon was cooperating, and led them on to the merlon.

They used the rope to clamber down the scarp to the ditch. At the bottom, they crouched defensively, scanning their surroundings, making sure they hadn't been spotted. Everything was calm. Kolschitzky gestured for them to follow him. Then he sprinted across the open ground, skirting the deep craters of the Austrian grenadiers' bombs to reach the opposite wall—the counter-scarp.

It looked like a forbidding climb, but two things helped. It wasn't vertical, and it was made of brick, which gave them toeholds and handholds. At the top, they darted over the covered way to reach the palisade. Only the thick, sharpened tree trunks hammered deep into the ground now stood between them and Ottoman-controlled territory.

'I hope this isn't a monumental mistake on my part,' Kolschitzky said, the doubt still clouding his expression.

'Let's save Vienna first,' Kamal replied. 'Then you can decide if it was a mistake or not.' He held out his hand to

Kolschitzky. The Pole hesitated for a moment, then took it and shook it firmly.

Kamal turned to Nisreen. 'Ready?'

'Would it change anything if I said no?' Nisreen replied.

Kolschitzky managed a smile—then he took one last look through the gap, saw nothing to cause him alarm, and moved ahead.

The palisade was no obstacle. It wasn't a solid, continuous wall. The trunks were spaced apart widely enough to allow one person to slip through sideways, but they were tight enough to block an attacking horde from storming through. Once across, there was nothing but open ground leading to the canal, which they quickly reached.

The canal had been reduced to a stream that was probably no more than waist-deep at most.

'We'll follow the canal bed up to the main stream of the river,' he told them.

Staying crouched, they scuttled along the bed of the canal, staying clear of the water to avoid making any splashing noise. The ground under them was muddy, which made their progress a bit slower, but they were safer there than on open ground. When the moon emerged, they hugged the bank and waited, wary of the Ottoman positions close by. Small campfires were dotted across the charred ruins of the grand villas and orchards of Leopoldstadt, the wealthy suburb that Starhemberg had ordered destroyed before the siege to prevent the enemy from using it for cover.

It was still night when they reached the main body of the Danube. The river ran north, then it dog-legged left and ran west, toward Tulln and Stetteldorf. They would need to cross it at some point, since the castle was on its north bank. Kolschitzky felt it would be wiser to get the crossing out of the way here, since the water was low enough to wade across. Any rain far away upstream could change things unexpectedly.

And so they waded across, slowly, close to each other. The muddy water felt strangely invigorating and uplifting to Kamal and Nisreen after the ordeal of being trapped in the besieged city. Once across, they lay down on the bank, soaked, their breaths coming in short and fast as they stared up at the night sky.

After a long silence, a slow growl unfurled itself from Nisreen's stomach.

'Someone's hungry,' Kamal said.

'When was the last time we ate?' she asked.

'A couple hundred years ago?' he replied.

Nisreen let out a small chortle and glanced over at Kolschitzky, who looked puzzled by Kamal's answer.

'I'm afraid it might be a while before you eat again,' he told her. 'The castle is a day's walk away.'

'I'll manage,' Nisreen said.

Kamal turned to Kolschitzky. 'How many times have you done this?'

'Too many,' the Pole replied.

Kamal took in a deep breath. 'Hopefully, this will be the last time.'

He noticed Kolschitzky studying him; then the Pole asked, 'I think you owe me an explanation about what brought us here.'

Kamal pondered his question, debating what to say.

The Pole had led them out of the city safely. They were on their way to Stetteldorf. They did owe him an explanation. Or at least a semblance of one. And even though he was exhausted and wary of the dangers still lurking around them, Kamal had to oblige.

He gave him the answers he needed to hear, the same

ones he'd given him before—or rather, the ones he gave him when he and Nisreen were tied to each other in the basement storeroom, in a different tomorrow, one that now wouldn't happen. A short version about his being part of the sultan's secret detachment, out for revenge over his brother's killing. It wasn't the whole truth, but, as before, Kamal hoped that it was enough to convince him that they were on the same side.

By the end of it, not even the pale glow of the moon could disguise the fact that Kolschitzky didn't look entirely convinced.

'Why do I sense there's a lot more to your story?' he asked.

'Let's see this through,' Kamal replied in an even tone. 'We'll have more time to talk later.'

Kolschitzky studied Kamal, then nodded and stared up again.

Kamal glanced at Nisreen. She was on her back beside him, lost in her own thoughts.

He decided not to intrude.

Instead, all three of them took a moment to themselves and allowed the silence back in, even though it was a breeding ground for their fears about what lay ahead.

They knew they had to keep moving. Before daylight came, they needed to put as much distance as they could between themselves and the Ottoman camp that ringed the city.

Stetteldorf Castle, and the commanders of the army of Christendom, were only twenty miles away. And their appointment with death was ticking closer with every passing second.

65

By dawn, they had made decent progress.

Led by Kolschitzky, they had followed the bank of the river north, moving with extreme caution, their senses alert to any sound or any flicker of movement.

Travelling at night had been slower and more exhausting than it would have been during the day, but it was safer. The strain of the low visibility and the uncertain terrain, coupled with the hunger they all felt, had drained them and slowed them down. And without horses or weapons, Kolschitzky, Kamal and Nisreen were no match for any threat, so it was crucial that they remain unseen.

With the light breaking through the horizon to their right, they took advantage of a carved cleft in the riverbank to rest and drink water before pressing on. An hour's walk later, the river turned left, heading west, toward Stetteldorf and Tulln. The terrain under their feet had risen into a small hillock, and, as they reached its crest, they saw the thick forests up ahead, the dense carpet of oak and beech that hugged the north bank of the river and would take over from the exposed meadows they were on.

The sun would soon sweep away their cover, and they needed to get to safer ground before that happened.

They were making their way down the hill when Kolschitzky saw movement in the distance. He froze and trained his eyes on the edge of the forest. Some horsemen emerged from behind a thicket of trees and were riding into the plain ahead of them, less than three *berids*—the equivalent of half a mile—away.

'Down,' he said.

The three of them dived to the ground and flattened themselves in the tall grass and wildflowers, raising their heads just enough to track the danger.

More riders appeared, a pack that grew to well over fifty horses. The ground thundered under their hooves as an angry cloud of churned earth swirled around them.

Kolschitzky squinted, studying them. 'Tartars,' he muttered through clenched teeth.

The Tartars were headed their way.

Kamal and Nisreen had never seen anything like them. Even at that distance, the menace they projected was nerve-racking.

They rode in a short-stirrup fashion, their advance fluid and yet forceful. Each horseman trailed two or three spare ponies, which they were known to rotate to always ensure a fresh mount. The horses themselves were huge and powerfully built, specially bred to cross vast distances at speed. The riders wore no armour and carried no firearms; instead, they relied on their distinctive recurved bows, whose forward-curved tips stored more energy while allowing a short, fast and smooth pull. Trained archers and horsemen from a young age, Tartar raiders could unleash a fusillade of heavy arrows with deadly accuracy at full gallop. After centuries of raiding and pillaging, they had fully earned the nickname 'the devil's horsemen'.

Devil's horsemen who were coming straight at them.

Kolschitzky scanned right, then left, beyond Kamal and Nisreen. 'Roll,' he blurted, jabbing his finger at the air behind them. 'Roll away, down the hill.'

The hillock sloped gently down from where they were, back to the water, the tall grass only interrupted by scattered clusters of hornbeams and rocky outcroppings.

'Go, go, go,' he hissed, gesturing insistently.

They rolled sideways, one after the other, moving frantically, hugging the ground, tumbling as quickly as they could. The sensation was dizzying, the spinning amplified by the lightheadedness caused by their hunger, but they kept going, while in the background, with each rotation, their ears picked up the growing rage of the approaching horses.

'There,' Kamal said, pointing at an outcropping that, while low, spread out enough to provide some cover.

Still hugging the ground, they clawed their way towards it, one after the other, the mounted storm getting ever closer. They took cover behind it just as the clamour from the horses felt like it was right on top of them, but the raiders stormed past, bypassing the outcropping and sticking to the clear grassland.

Kamal hazarded a peek as the last of them thundered by. The men looked different from the Ottomans and Austrians he'd seen; their features were more Asian, and they sported pointed beards and wispy moustaches. Their dress was also different: flared caps folded upwards, leather cuirasses, thick belts holding jacketed scimitars, and the unique bows, slung across their backs along with quivers brimming with arrows.

They waited there, breathing hard, muscles taut, until the convoy receded into the distance.

'That was close,' Kamal grumbled.

'They're everywhere,' Kolschitzky told them. 'These barbarians, and the bashi-bazouks. I don't know who's worse.'

Kamal's mind went back uncomfortably to the explanation he'd given Kolschitzky the first time they'd met, about why he and Nisreen had appeared in Vienna with no clothes on. It was too close for comfort.

'We need to get to the forest,' Kolschitzky added.

'And after that?' Nisreen asked.

'We're almost halfway to the castle,' Kolschitzky told them. 'Once we get to the forest, we'll follow the river until we reach the bank across from Tulln. From there, Stetteldorf is directly north. But it's an open trail.'

'Open, meaning exposed,' Kamal said.

'Yes, but not for long. We should be able to cross the open ground in no more than two hours. And if what you say about the relief army being close is true, I should think there'll be less risk of running into more of these savages.'

'Better get moving then,' Nisreen said.

Kolschitzky nodded and took the lead.

Kamal brought up the rear, and they trudged forward, his unease growing with every step. On foot, they were easy prey for the hordes of raiders. Ideally, he would have much rather that they waited another night, but it was not an option. It was Monday. The suicide bombers would strike on Wednesday, at midday. Waiting until Tuesday would barely give Sobieski and his allies twenty-four hours to devise a plan to thwart the bombers and ambush the Ottoman army that would follow. And Kamal needed enough time to carry out his own part of the plan.

He also needed to discuss what he had read about what had happened with Nisreen and Kolschitzky. That part of the homework—the forensic accounts of what had happened on that infamous Wednesday—had gripped him. The great Ottoman victory had been pored over by many a historian, but the work that intrigued Kamal most was Rasheed's own account of it. The time traveller had allowed his ego to run rampant while writing about his ingenious master stroke, which gave Kamal all the information he needed. Kamal had come up with his own counterplan, and he now needed to share it with his companions in case something happened to him on the way to Stetteldorf. They were still exposed and would remain at risk until they were behind the castle's gates.

He also needed to inform them of his plan to deal with Rasheed. He couldn't delay it much longer. He didn't like the idea of leaving Nisreen at the castle, but there was no other way. He knew it would be an impossibly difficult moment for them both, but it had to be done.

As they moved on, he shared what he knew with them about the timing and the specifics of the suicide bombing and the army's onslaught that would follow, the question of what would happen once they reached Stetteldorf festering in his mind.

Once he'd finished, and as if she had been reading his thoughts, Nisreen soon forced the issue.

The question had reared its unwelcome head each time Nisreen had a quiet moment of reflection, which, perhaps mercifully, hadn't happened too often since they'd made their last jump.

Listening to Kamal talk them through his plan, she felt that they had the first part of what they needed to do—warn Sobieski—reasonably well covered. But what about the second? How would they make sure Rasheed wouldn't be able to jump back in time and try again?

Back at the library, in Paris—it now felt like years ago to her, a brief interlude that was more dream than reality—Kamal had told her that he would need to do it alone, and she had grudgingly agreed. But as that moment drew nearer, the dread of confronting it had spread through her like knotweed.

She decided to raise it once Kamal was finished, which coincided with their reaching the relative cover of the forest and cutting through it to get to the water's edge.

Kolschitzky walked around, foraging for food; then he bent down and picked something. He turned and waved them over. 'Over here, my friends,' he told them. 'Let the feasting begin.'

Kamal and Nisreen joined him. Small, light-brown mushrooms littered the ground between the trees.

'Yummy,' Nisreen groaned.

'These ones aren't poisonous,' Kolschitzky said as he chewed on one. 'And there'll be berries about.'

'Too bad we don't have time to hunt for boar,' Kamal said. 'I believe these woods are part of the emperor's hunting grounds?'

'They were. But we're the hunted ones now,' Kolschitzky said. 'Here's hoping for that to change very soon.' Then, wryly, he added, *'Inshallah'*—if God wills it.

Nisreen watched as Kamal gave him a slight, tacit bow of the head.

The dread was still festering in her mind while they collected enough mushrooms, bilberries and primrose flowers to fuel them on. They were eating gratefully by the water's edge when she finally decided to bring it up.

'Kamal,' she asked, her tone hesitant. 'What about Rasheed?'

Kamal stopped drinking the water he'd cupped in the palm of his hand and watched it run off. He just stared at the rippled surface of the river, then inhaled deeply before turning to face her.

'I'm going to have to go. Soon.'

Even though she'd been expecting it, his confirmation still unsettled her deeply.

Kolschitzky stepped in, asking, 'You have to go? Where?'

Kamal took a breath, seeming to need to formulate his response. 'There's a man advising the grand vizier and the sultan. He's the key to all this. I need to make sure he doesn't survive this.'

Kolschitzky looked baffled. 'If we're successful . . . if we stop their assassins and turn their ambush against them, the sultan's army will be defeated. Isn't that enough?'

'No,' Kamal said. 'We need to make sure he dies.'

'Who? I don't understand,' Kolschitzky pressed.

'His name is Ayman Rasheed.'

'I've never heard of him.'

'He's behind all this. He's the mastermind. And his abilities are limitless, believe me. The only way to ensure any lasting effect of anything we achieve here is to make sure he doesn't survive.' He could see Kolschitzky was having trouble processing this. 'I was there with them,' Kamal added. 'I know what I'm talking about—trust me. I need to seek him out and kill him.'

'Where?' Nisreen asked.

'At the camp. His tent is next to the grand vizier's compound.'

It was what Nisreen had been expecting him to say, but hearing him say it still cut through her like a blade.

Kolschitzky looked dumbfounded. 'You're talking about not just infiltrating the enemy camp, but killing a man, someone important, in its most heavily guarded part?' He looked like he was still processing the implications. 'This is madness.'

'Worse than madness,' Nisreen added. 'It's a suicide mission.'

'It doesn't need to be,' Kamal said, 'and there's no other option. It's the one place we know he'll be. He watched the battle with the grand vizier from a position up in the hills, but I don't know exactly where that is. The only place I know he'll be at is at the camp, right until they start moving towards Tulln tomorrow afternoon.'

'Wait, what?' Kolschitzky interjected. 'What do you mean, he watched it? It hasn't happened yet.'

Kamal glanced furtively at Nisreen. She felt as caught off guard as he looked.

'I mean that's their plan,' Kamal backtracked quickly. 'I misspoke.' He turned to Nisreen. '*Hayatim,* I've thought of this long and hard. It's the only way. But I can do it. I've worked undercover before. I can handle these situations. And believe me, I have no intention of leaving you here without me.' He said the last part pointedly, and she understood that he was emphasizing what was unsaid, what couldn't be said in front of the Pole.

He stepped closer and took her hands. 'It's going to be fine, *hayatim.* It'll be easier for me knowing that you're safe at the castle. And when it's done, I'll come back for you there. I promise.'

She held his gaze, even though her insides felt as if they were being shredded.

Reading her, Kamal added, 'Besides, we have our ways of getting out of tight spots, right?'

Her mind still in turmoil, she found herself nodding, even though she was too perturbed to process the implications of what he was suggesting. 'When do you have to go?'

'Once we reach the castle, I'll set out as quickly as I can to make best use of the light. I won't be able to make much progress during the night. That'll leave tomorrow to reach the camp and find him. Which should be enough. Killing him needs to be done as late as possible, just as the army's setting off. I don't want to disrupt anything too early and risk having them change their plans.'

A sombre silence shrouded them until Kolschitzky spoke up. 'All that sounds easy enough,' he said with obvious sarcasm. 'But how do you expect to get through the Wienerwald?' He was using the local name for the Vienna Woods. 'Do you know the area?'

'I've studied maps.'

'Maps? You think you'll be fine because you studied maps?

You don't just cross the Wienerwald with a map. If you get off the high road, it's a veritable maze of narrow trails. One can easily get lost in the paths that snake up and down those mountains. No, you wouldn't have a hope in hell alone. I'll go with you.'

Kamal was taken aback. He couldn't tell Kolschitzky that the maps he'd looked at were far, far more detailed and precise than the primitive ones that were around back then, the only ones Kolschitzky would have known. But the Pole had a point. Crossing the mountains was a daunting challenge, and he didn't have the luxury of time. He couldn't afford any delays and he knew that having Kolschitzky guide him to the Ottoman camp was, in fact, crucial.

Kamal gave him a respectful, small bow of the head. 'My gratitude knows no words, Herr Kolschitzky.'

'Call me Georg,' he said, waving Kamal's words away. 'I think we've been through enough to dispense with formality.'

Kamal smiled, and bowed again.

Kolschitzky studied him, a curious glint in his eye. 'I can't wait for this to all be over so we can finally sit down and have us a proper chat,' he said. 'I intend to get you so drunk you won't be able to control your tongue.'

'I look forward to it,' Kamal smiled, turning to Nisreen and letting his gaze linger on her. 'Agreed?' he asked her.

She studied him for a moment, and couldn't help but feel uplifted by his infectious fortitude. 'I'm going to hold you to it.'

'It's a date then.' Kamal beamed back.

Then they set off.

66

The undergrowth in the forest was heavy and slowed them down, but at least they had more cover than on open ground, from both enemy eyes and from the high sun that was blasting the landscape with its omnipotence, its power.

The woods were eerily, oppressively quiet. No hum from a distant motorway, no occasional planes streaking overhead and breaking the silence, however faintly. The silence was absolute, which only increased their fear of what infected the wood's dark corners.

Still, they were moving with renewed vigour, the fruits of their foraging and the sense of drawing nearer to the castle all helping to spur them on.

'Tulln is close, perhaps half an hour from us,' Kolschitzky announced. 'With a bit of luck, we'll be at Stetteldorf within two hours.'

'We can't spend too long at the castle,' Kamal told him. 'I hope you'll be able to convince Sobieski quickly.'

'Don't worry, I know what to say,' Kolschitzky assured him. 'I've been Starhemberg's messenger since this whole disaster began. He'll believe me.'

Kamal nodded and walked on.

Nisreen edged closer and moved beside him. He glanced at her and gave her a smile that didn't quite disguise the anxiety simmering behind his eyes.

'It's going to be tight,' he told her. 'You'll need to answer whatever other questions Sobieski might have after I leave.'

'I was paying attention—don't worry,' she told him. Her

tone turned more morose. 'It's the moment I've been dreading.'

Without stopping, he reached out and took her hand.

'We're going to be fine,' he told her. 'You'll see.'

She tightened her grip around his, but didn't reply, then she let it go.

For a long moment, they didn't say anything. They just weaved their way through the trees, in silence, their feet crunching down on the thick carpet of twigs and leaves, their glances meeting occasionally.

Kolschitzky was several paces ahead of them, and they were dropping back.

'It's so . . . weird,' she told Kamal, speaking low enough that the Pole wouldn't hear. 'Being here. All this. Isn't it?'

'It does feel very, very strange,' Kamal said. 'I mean, we're here, now, walking through this forest, and it feels . . . normal somehow.'

'Ramazan, Tarek, Noor . . . so much is happening, it's crowding out my mind. It's putting more distance between us and the past. And I don't want it to.' She paused, then added, 'It feels like a lifetime ago. And in a way, I suppose it is. But I don't ever want my life before all this to drift away. Even if it's painful. I don't want to ever let go of it. But if you're not around, I'm worried their memories will eventually drift away. And that would be awful.' She stopped, signalling him to look at her. 'Promise me you'll come back so they'll always be with me, too.'

'I don't want to forget them either. And we won't. Ever. No matter what happens.'

'On the train . . . you promised you'd never jump without me. What happens if you need to, if you get in trouble in the camp? How will we find each other?'

He stopped walking and turned to face her. 'I'm not going

to lose you, *hayatim*. Not in this life or in any other. You can count on that.'

She focused on his eyes, as if willing herself to never forget them. 'What about after? What happens if we manage to pull this off? What are we going to do? Where do we go?'

'I don't know. Let's get it done first. Then . . . who knows?'

'I don't want to stay in this time,' she declared. 'It's too . . . savage.'

'Then we won't.'

'If we're going to go back to a more civilized time, you'll need to get the forward incantation from him.' She pulled back the sleeve on her shirt to present him the tattoo on her forearm. 'We still don't know if I got it right.'

'I'd better get it then,' he said with a faint grin. Then he glanced up ahead.

Kolschitzky hadn't noticed that they'd fallen behind and had kept on walking.

'Come on,' Kamal told her. 'Let's stick together.'

They caught up with Kolschitzky and followed him down a heavily wooded incline. The air felt palpably cooler, given the proximity of water.

'We'll be able to start cutting inland up ahead,' he told them. 'But we should drink before we set off. On open ground and under that sun, we'll be glad we did.'

They marched on in single file across the virgin wilderness.

Before long, the babble of a stream came into earshot, and they headed in its direction.

Kamal was walking just behind Kolschitzky when the Pole slowed down just enough to allow Kamal to come up right behind him.

Without turning back, he told Kamal, in a low voice, 'We're being watched.'

Kamal tensed up. 'What? Where?'

'Up ahead, to the right. I saw one. But there'll be more.'

'Who?' Kamal asked.

'I couldn't tell.'

'What do we do?'

'We keep walking as if nothing's happened. If they're out there, there's no point hiding or putting up a fight. They rarely travel in small packs.'

As if to emphasize his words, an arrow whizzed in and implanted itself into a tree a few feet away.

A man appeared in the pathway up ahead. Then another. Then more of them emerged from behind the trees.

Kolschitzky stopped walking, as did Kamal and Nisreen.

'Bashi-bazouks,' Kolschitzky murmured to them.

Beware of what you wish for, Kamal thought, ruefully remembering what he had told Kolschitzky under questioning the first time they'd met: that the 'damaged head' mercenaries were the reason that he and Nisreen were naked when caught in Vienna.

'Stay calm and let me do the talking,' Kolschitzky added. Then he raised his arm to the men in greeting. 'Easy, brothers,' he called out. 'We're on the same side.'

The men stepped closer.

There were six of them. They weren't dressed in uniform. Instead, they had a ragtag look, from the loosely wrapped scarves around their heads to their flowing capes and robes. Some wore hoops through their ears, and a couple had very dark skin and African features. What they all had in common, however, was that they were armed to the teeth. Most had two flintlock pistols strapped to their waist in leather holsters, bandoliers, and several daggers and sabres.

One of the marauders, a man with an unusual black moustache that speared outwards and eyes with all the warmth of a coal mine, stepped closer and flicked the tip of his sabre at

Kolschitzky and his friends, gesturing for them to make themselves shown more openly.

Kamal and Nisreen understood and stepped out from behind Kolschitzky, standing on either side of him.

The man eyed them suspiciously.

'You say we're on the same side,' he bellowed. 'Then why are they wearing the uniforms of the infidel?'

'They're our spies from inside Vienna. They just managed to escape after they were discovered,' Kolschitzky yelled back.

The man stepped closer, still studying them curiously.

Kamal eyed him, scrutinizing him. Years of training and work had honed his instincts in how to read people, and he didn't like what they were telling him about where this interrogation was heading.

'Whose spies?'

This wasn't going well. Kamal could see it escalating badly very, very quickly. Then an idea blasted its way into his head. A desperate wild card.

'Ayman Rasheed Pasha!' he called out, his tone forceful and challenging.

The bashi-bazouk scowled at him doubtfully. 'Who? I've never heard of him.'

'He's the special adviser to the grand vizier,' Kamal replied.

'I know of no special adviser by that name.'

'You wouldn't,' Kamal replied. 'But he's the reason Vienna is about to fall into our hands, and we answer only to him.'

The raider's face darkened further, visibly affronted by Kamal's insolence. 'You speak with a strange accent.'

'Years of living among the infidel will do that to you,' Kamal said. 'We've been spies for a long time.'

The man frowned, clearly processing what he was hearing. 'You say you work for this special adviser?'

'Ayman Rasheed Pasha, yes,' Kamal told him.

'Let's go and meet him together then,' the man said, 'and we'll soon find out if what you say is true.' He took a few steps closer and raised the blade of his sabre so that it hovered right under Kamal's chin. 'Which I sincerely hope it isn't.'

67

Kamal felt relieved that they hadn't attempted to put up a fight. The gang of bashi-bazouks turned out to number more than twenty men: rough, unruly adventurers who were just itching to spill blood.

They were placed on horses, each of their rides tethered to one of the Ottoman raiders' mounts. Kamal wasn't given a chance to talk to Kolschitzky or Nisreen. All they could do was exchange looks that telegraphed their alarm at what was to come.

On horseback now, they were made to retrace the route they'd taken, riding out of the forest and back down the bank of the Danube towards Vienna.

Kamal was riding ahead, followed by Nisreen, then Kolschitzky, with a raider between each of them. He turned to check on her. She was looking at him pointedly, her expression loaded with a silent message before she gazed down expressively at her arm and tugged her sleeve back discreetly, exposing the tattoo.

Kamal understood her question.

Her look was asking, *Do we jump?*

He shot her back a small, but emphatic, shake of the head.

He hadn't planned it this way, but they didn't have a choice, not any more. And being taken by the Ottoman raiders to Rasheed could be their best, and perhaps their only, opportunity to find him, get close to him, and kill him, even if it happened before they were able to warn Sobieski and the others. If they failed, Rasheed would inevitably use his time-travelling knowledge to hunt them down throughout time.

Disappearing now also meant that Rasheed would most likely hear about it and know that something was afoot. It would also mean certain death for their Polish companion, and Kamal didn't want that either. Besides, even if they managed to communicate enough to agree on how many days to jump back, a limited menu of options in itself, they couldn't be sure that they would both be able to recite the full incantation before one of them was interrupted by their captors. Which would mean abandonment for the one who left and certain death for the one left behind.

There was no question in his mind. They had to make this attempt work.

He gave her a gesture with his hand held flat and his fingers slightly splayed, as if to say, *Calm down, we don't need to do anything rash.*

She nodded her understanding, all the while keeping a fearful eye on their captors.

By sundown, the city's walls were in sight, although there was no fighting on that side of the city, at its northwestern edge. They crossed the Danube again and trotted through the ruins of the suburbs that had been destroyed under Starhemberg's orders in the days before the sultan's army arrived. The first defensive mounds appeared, and they were soon riding past the frontline troops who guarded the dead zone between the trenches and the walls, venturing deep into the heart of the huge Ottoman encampment.

Its scale was mind-boggling. Kamal had only glimpsed it when he and Nisreen had been dragged on to the wall in those frenzied moments after their first arrival in Vienna, but his mind had been too frazzled to register it. There were rows of tents spreading out as far as the eye could see, tens of thousands of them laid out in an arc fifteen miles long—enough tents to house an army of well over a hundred thousand men who had marched all the way there from their homeland.

There were tents for everything: for the troops, for weapons, for latrines, for baths and ritual ablutions. There were even tents for ceremonial executions.

But the sprawling encampment was far from what it must have been in those first few days of the siege.

As they advanced deeper into the camp, their steps tracked listlessly by the deadened eyes of idle Ottoman troops, the dire condition of the sultan's men became more and more evident.

After months of combat and under the blazing summer sun, the camp had become a festering pit of filth and disease. Wounds were left to rot openly, with too many injured to treat. The dead were too numerous to bury and were often left for days before they could be carted away. Those who were buried were barely hidden under a thin cover of loose soil, which their bloated, decomposing bodies soon pushed back. Dead animals also wasted away openly. The camp's cesspools were overflowing. The stench of putrefaction was everywhere, as were the swarms of flies.

Despite that, troops all around them were getting ready for the next day's march. Janissaries and *spahi* cavalrymen were cleaning their boots and getting their weapons ready. They would be setting out in the morning, on Tuesday, for their advance across the Vienna Woods to get into position before attacking the relief army in the fields outside Tulln the following day, on Wednesday. Even in their worn-out state, they would be victorious.

The sight only served to remind Kamal of the urgency of what they needed to accomplish.

The endless rows of tents circled the city from north to south, with the royal enclosure in the middle, where the ground facing the city walls rose up. It was there that the grand vizier's tent came into view. It was much taller and bigger than the others, a mammoth edifice that towered over its neighbours.

Kamal could also now see and hear the steady rise of fighting. The two bastions under attack were to his left, and, even before they appeared, musket fire and the explosions of grenades were tearing through the air. Cannon from both sides were belching death at each other, intercut by shouts of 'Jesus, Maria!' and 'Allah!' from the opposing warriors who, he could now see, were slaughtering each other on the walls.

Seeing it from this angle was unnerving. He'd been on those walls, he'd seen the battle from the opposite side, he'd had a front-row seat to what was happening on those walls. For a brief moment, he wondered about the men who had dragged him and Nisreen up there, wondered how many of them were still alive and how many had already perished in the grinding mill of battle.

They soon reached the part of the camp that surrounded the command enclosure. It sat on higher ground, with Kara Mustafa's tent at its highest point, directly across from the two bastions that were the focal point of his attack. Kamal had read how the grand vizier had been able to observe the progress of his men in the trenches and on the walls right from the comfort of his silk-covered quarters.

The royal enclosure was very different from the rest of the camp. Most striking was how markedly cleaner it was. Kara Mustafa's tent was palatial in size and resplendent in its rich fabrics, a marvel of green silk ornamented with gold embroidery and precious stones. As they trotted past, Kamal looked through the guard posts and saw some of what he had read about in the Paris library: the splendid gardens with fountains and peacocks, the tents housing the grand vizier's favourite horses, the black eunuchs guarding the sprawling tent where he kept his harem. There was even an ostrich roaming the grounds.

The head of the bashi-bazouks stopped to ask one of the royal guards something. Upon hearing the answer, he turned around, scowled at Kamal, then grudgingly waved his men on. The troop moved on and trotted past the grand vizier's compound until they reached an adjacent enclosure that, while smaller, looked just as luxurious.

Kamal's senses were tingling.

They had reached their target destination.

A *boluk bashi,* a captain of the janissary guards, stepped up to greet them. The leader of the raiders dismounted and conversed with him. Then the captain led him past a couple of guards, and they disappeared into the enclosure.

After a few minutes, they reappeared, and, with a nudge of his head and some hand signs, the captain instructed the guards to take in the prisoners.

They dismounted and were led into the enclosure, one guard escorting each of them, leaving the raiders and their visibly displeased leader outside.

Another huge tent sat at the centre of the enclosure, its fabric rich with appliqués and embroidery of floral patterns laid out in a series of arches.

They went through the outer curtain, through the small vestibule area, and then through another curtain and into the main body of the tent.

It was huge, larger than the living room of any Parisian home Kamal had ever visited. The ceiling and walls, which were supported by thick, polished mahogany poles, were draped with luxuriant patterned fabrics, and the floor was covered by several layers of rich carpets. A bed-like divan, studded with precious stones and arrayed with fluffy cushions, occupied pride of place at the far end of the room, while an ornate table littered with notebooks and maps sat off to one side. Oil lamps diffused a warm, soft glow across its cavernous space, while candles of jasmine and lavender infused the air with their balmy scents.

And standing before them at the centre of it all was the man whose machinations had caused them to risk everything and travel back in time.

The tall, imposing figure was bedecked in a panoply of opulence, from the bulbous, elaborate turban that topped his head and the magnificent robes he wore right down to the fine slippers that covered his feet, layer upon layer of the finest silks tailored to perfection and elaborately embroidered with threads of gold. Across his waist, a wide belt held a janissary *yataghan* whose pommel was adorned by a constellation of precious stones that rivalled those on the rings on his fingers.

Clearly, Ayman Rasheed had come a long way since his days as a prisoner of war at Camp Bucca.

He said nothing at first. He just stood there and gazed upon his prisoners, giving each of them a brief but intent study with eyes that radiated shrewdness and guile. He didn't recognize them, of course. He hadn't yet travelled forward in time to when they would meet in Paris. That was still decades away.

His evaluation seemingly complete and his brow furrowed with curiosity, he sucked in a deep breath and spoke.

'What have we here?'

The man standing before Nisreen looked very different from the ailing man who had riveted her with his story from his hospital bed in Paris.

It was Ayman Rasheed, of course. Of that she had no doubt. But this Ayman Rasheed was a younger, slimmer, fitter version of the man she'd met. It wasn't just his appearance that was dramatically different. This man was in the full prime of his life. Contrary to the drugged, vulnerable patient she'd met, he exuded a chilling sense of power and confidence.

A power that, she fully realized, would allow him to take away her life with a snap of his fingers.

She tried to remain calm and keep her fear in check, despite the fact that everything about the scene was deeply intimidating. Kamal was to her immediate right, then Kolschitzky. Behind each of them stood one of the guards, beefy men standing at full attention and coiled to strike at an instant's notice. Rasheed had the janissary captain by his side.

His question hung in the air for a moment; then Rasheed pressed on. 'You told those men you were my spies. You claimed to be working for me, inside Vienna. We both know that's not true. So I ask you . . . who are you?'

Nisreen hesitated, then glanced across at Kamal just as he spoke.

Kamal had never met Rasheed before in person. All he had to go on were the portraits of him he'd seen in the books at the library, images of lavish oil paintings capturing a hero of the empire at his peak.

The Rasheed facing him was very much that man. And he required answers.

During the ride over to the camp, Kamal had fretted over what was to come. He'd used the time to think about what he might do and how things might play out, running the various scenarios through his mental grinder.

Now was the time to go with the gambit he'd cooked up on that ride. He knew it wasn't perfect, but it was the best he could come up with.

'Please forgive the deception, pasha,' he responded in a respectful, calm tone, 'but we had to say it to be brought to you.'

'And here you are,' Rasheed replied. 'It still doesn't answer my question.'

'My name is Kamal Arslan Agha, and these are my companions. We're travellers. Just like you.'

The reply caused Rasheed's face to crease with curiosity. 'Oh?'

'Yes. What you discovered in Palmyra, the words that were carved into a wall? They're what brought us here, too.'

The curiosity gave way to surprise. Rasheed obviously hadn't expected such an answer, and yet he seemed to be controlling his outward reaction expertly. He glanced across at the captain standing beside him, then spoke.

'Interesting,' he said. 'So you must have made quite a journey to get here. A risky one, at that.'

'Indeed.'

'And what made you take that risk? What did you need to see me about?'

Kamal drew on his experience to keep his breathing level and his eyes unruffled. 'We came here to warn you, pasha. Others know about the secret, too. And they're going to use it to come here to try to kill you.'

Kolschitzky had been watching silently, and his expression morphed from confusion to anger. 'What?' he roared. 'You lying son of a bitch. You tricked me—'

The guard next to him flicked his hand up and gave him a hard slap to the side of his head, cutting short his outburst.

'Do behave,' Rasheed told the Pole. 'I'm struggling to find a reason to keep you alive as it is.' He paused for a breath, waiting to make sure his point and his glare sank in, then turned to Kamal. 'These travellers . . . why would they want to kill me?'

Kamal focused on maintaining his composure and avoided looking at Kolschitzky. 'To stop you from doing what you've set out to do. To stop you from changing history.'

He couldn't resist glancing at the Pole. Kolschitzky was seething with rage.

'That's odd,' Rasheed replied calmly. 'Because that's exactly what he claimed, too.'

It was Kamal's turn to feel bewildered. He gave Nisreen a quick sideways glance. Her expression was still inscrutable, but Kamal detected a crack of concern she couldn't conceal.

Before he could ask him whom he was talking about, Rasheed nodded to the captain standing beside him. 'Bring him in,' he ordered.

Kamal felt his pulse rocket as the janissary left the tent, then came back in with another prisoner, with a fourth guard escorting him as well.

It was Taymoor.

His mouth was gagged, his beard was unkempt, and he looked haggard and dishevelled. He'd evidently been there for quite a while, and not as a pampered guest. He was also missing his left leg from the knee, and was using a long stick as a makeshift crutch.

Taymoor's eyes flared wide as he spotted his old partner and Nisreen.

'Leave us,' Rasheed told the captain in a matter-of-fact tone. The janissary gave the prisoners a once-over, then left the tent. Rasheed turned to Taymoor's guard and flicked him a hand signal. The guard pulled out a *yataghan* and held its blade right up against Taymoor's throat while using his other hand to loosen and pull down the piece of cloth that had been preventing Taymoor from speaking.

Rasheed gave Taymoor a stern warning finger. 'You know the drill. Be very careful.' He waited until Taymoor returned a reluctant nod; then he turned to Kamal and Nisreen. 'The same applies to you both,' he announced before issuing a clipped, terse nod at the men who were guarding Kamal, Nisreen and Kolschitzky. The guards pulled out their *yataghans* and held them against their prisoners' throats. 'We can speak freely now. These eunuchs are *dilsiz*,' he said, referring to the deaf mutes that were frequently used by sultans in their palaces. Their usefulness wasn't limited to not being able to hear or betray secrets; as executioners, they also couldn't hear the condemned's final pleas.

'They will be watching me like hawks,' he added. 'Should one of you even begin to utter the incantation, I only need to raise a finger and they'll slit your throat instantly.' He smiled. 'I just think it would be excessively rude for one of you to leave in the middle of our chat, don't you agree?'

Rasheed paused for a moment, then moved in closer. He ran his eyes over them, checking them out, first Kolschitzky, then Kamal, then Nisreen. He hovered in front of her, then, calmly, he reached down and took her arm. Keeping his gaze locked on hers, he pulled up her sleeve, revealing her tattoos.

He studied the markings, then looked up at Nisreen. 'My

men did say you had curious markings on your arms.' Then he smiled at her. 'It looks like you did learn a lot from me—or, rather, that you will.'

The comment threw Kamal, then he realized that Taymoor must have told Rasheed about everything that had happened. He glared at his partner, who held his gaze defiantly.

Looking at Nisreen, Rasheed asked, 'So . . . when is it you come from?'

Nisreen said, '1438.'

Rasheed nodded, like the date impressed him somehow. 'Over three hundred years. And you're speaking our language, so clearly our empire is still around.'

Kamal decided to step in. 'It is.'

Rasheed swivelled his head to address Taymoor. 'So you weren't lying about that.' He shrugged, his scepticism clear. He turned back to Kamal and Nisreen. 'He told me my grand design worked, you see. He told me that more than three centuries later, the empire is still around, bigger and more powerful than ever.'

Kamal nodded. 'It is.'

Rasheed looked pensive. 'So why are you really here? Is it really to warn me? You see, Taymoor Agha and I have had plenty of time to chat since he arrived. He told me this incredible story about, well, *me*—the future me. Not just me, but us, all of us. How we all met, how it played itself out, right up to the moment you pushed him off the train, a fall that damaged your partner's leg so badly that it couldn't be saved.' He paused, studying Kamal, as if to read his reaction. 'He said that on that train, you told him you were coming here to get the forward version of the gift from Palmyra. But I can see that you already have it.' He gestured dismissively at Nisreen's arm. 'So it's clear you were hiding your true intentions from him. You're here for something else. And given what he's told me about your research, and your wanting revenge on the empire that you blame for the deaths of your family, I can only imagine you really are here to do what you claim to be warning me about. You're here to kill me; that much is clear. The question is . . . why?'

No one replied, leaving the question hanging heavily in the air.

Rasheed eyed Nisreen, then Kamal, and then he swung his gaze back at her. 'This silence is so tiresome. Perhaps you'll be more talkative if we start chopping off some fingers . . . for a start?' He gave the guard behind Kamal a crude hand signal that didn't require a trained mind to understand.

The guard grabbed Kamal's hand and brought the blade of his *yataghan* down so that its tip rested between Kamal's thumb and index finger.

Rasheed stared at Nisreen calmly; then, just as he flicked a nod to the guard, she blurted, 'No, stop. Don't. Please . . . don't.'

Rasheed gave the guard a halting gesture, then turned to Nisreen expectantly.

She dropped her head grudgingly. 'It's true. That's why we're here.'

'To kill me?'

She nodded.

'Why?'

'To stop you from succeeding. To put an end to all this,' she replied, clearly trying to repress the quiver in her voice.

'To end the siege?'

'To stop the conquest of Europe.'

Rasheed looked bewildered. He took a few steps, a pensive frown creasing his forehead. 'You want to stop me from achieving this great victory—the victory you owe your entire existence to?' he hissed, a quiet anger unmistakably unfurling itself. 'Why? You blame me for the deaths of your family—is that it? You blame the empire? They were nothing. They weren't even a footnote in history.'

Nisreen stiffened at his mention of her family, at his dismissal of them. She stood taller, as if he had unleashed a fount of strength inside her. 'No one is a footnote in history. That's the problem with you, with everything you stand for.'

'Oh, please,' he scoffed, brushing her off with a dismissive gesture.

He turned away, but Nisreen wasn't done.

'You cheated history,' she declared forcefully.

Rasheed let out a mocking laugh. 'I cheated? That's your problem?' He looked genuinely bemused. 'I gave you an empire that outlived all others in human history. I don't know what it's like in your time: I can't go there yet to see for myself; I haven't changed it yet, but from what he's told me'—he nodded towards Taymoor contemptuously—'it sounds like it was well worth the cheat. And yet you want to do away with it? You want to bring back the world I came from, a world you know nothing about, a world you never lived in?'

'I know enough to know that it was a world where men and women were free to choose how they wanted to live.' Her face was like a hurricane. 'You took that liberty away, and instead you imposed on them, on *us*, one ruler. A tyrant. One man who gets to dictate his terms to us for life.'

'You need tyrants,' Rasheed shot back. 'People love tyrants. They were voting them in back where I came from.'

'I don't believe you.'

'Why would I lie?' He smiled benignly. 'It's the truth. You see, *hanum,* you give people too much credit. You seem to have this romantic delusion about democracy,' he chortled. 'But democracy is just another word for mob rule. A wise man from my world, a man who didn't exist in yours, once said, "Democracy is two wolves and a lamb voting on what to have for lunch." How do you think that turned out?'

Nisreen was stunned, her mouth having difficulty forming words.

'Democracy is a delusion,' Rasheed continued. 'A fallacy. It's the tyranny of the majority. And it doesn't work. Democracies always commit suicide. It happened in ancient Greece, and the same thing was happening around the world in my time, too. They tried it out for a couple of hundred years, and by the time I left, it was on its way out. You know why? They die when they become too democratic. Because if you let ordinary people choose their rulers, they're ultimately going to choose badly. They'll make a terrible, terrible choice for the simple reason that they'll choose someone like them, someone who's a reflection of who they really are. And, let's face it, we're not exactly the noblest of species. We're actually pretty awful. We're selfish, greedy, cruel and racist.

Did I forget something? Oh, yes, ignorant. For the most part. You see, people don't want to be talked down to by some high-minded, brainy statesman. They don't want someone who makes them feel inferior or ashamed. They want to be ruled by someone like them. And at some point, these mobs of gullible fools will end up choosing a crafty manipulator who makes them feel like he's one of them, who tells them they're the only ones who matter, who amplifies their blaming of outsiders for whatever they think is wrong with their lives. Someone who celebrates the worst of humanity and is just in it for himself, for power and money and nothing else. No great vision of their nation's place in history, no burning desire to make lives better. It's just greed and ego. And these power-hungry narcissists will lead their nations down a road to ruin. That's where your great ideal of democracy has reached in many, many countries back in my world. That's where it always ends.'

'Maybe things were as you say in your world,' she countered. 'But at least the people made their choice. And I can't believe that they won't choose a better way once they see their mistake.'

'You're assuming that luxury won't be taken away from them. It always is.'

'So you made that choice for us? For all of us?' Nisreen said. 'And we're supposed to be grateful? I'm supposed to feel grateful that you stole our history?' Rage was blazing through her. 'That your glorious empire killed my family?'

'No, *hanum*. In your case, I know that'll never be possible. Which is a shame, really. I'm sure there are plenty of fascinating things you could have told me about. But then again'—he smiled—'I suppose it'll be more interesting to see what happens without, as you so quaintly put it, cheating.'

And with that, he angled his gaze off her and gave the guards a couple of quick, disdainful hand signals.

Their meaning was alarmingly clear.

The first meant, 'Take them away.'

The second: 'Bring me back their heads.'

69

Rasheed felt reassured.

The unexpected appearance of the first visitor had startled him. It had happened weeks earlier, in the first few days of the siege, soon after the sultan's army had set up camp around Vienna. A man claiming to be a special envoy had found his way to his enclosure and asked to be brought to him. Taymoor Agha had then introduced himself and told him what he knew. He said he'd come to warn him, and all he asked in return was for the rest of the incantation so that he could go back to the time he'd come from and remain a loyal servant of the empire.

The request had surprised Rasheed, especially coming from a man whose career—if he was telling the truth—had been based on manipulation and guile. And yet perhaps it wasn't so surprising, after all. It was evident that the man was desperate to get back to a world he was more accustomed to. And he hadn't been mistaken in coming back, given that these new visitors—the man and the woman now standing before him—had in fact shown up, just as Taymoor had warned.

Rasheed could relax. The crisis had been averted. All indications were that this was an isolated incident. If Taymoor had been truthful, these visitors were lone wolves who hadn't shared their knowledge with others. He felt confident that, once they were dealt with, he wouldn't have to face other uninvited guests any time soon. He'd be free to sail into the future without looking over his shoulder.

Ever since he'd arrived and convinced the sultan of his merit, Rasheed had been careful to cause as little disruption as possible. He needed the siege of Vienna to end differently, but he had to be careful not to change things too much so that events he didn't foresee—events he hadn't read about, ones that hadn't actually taken place—didn't take him by surprise.

His efforts were about to bear fruit.

The army of Christendom and its leaders would soon be wiped out. Vienna would soon fall.

And once that was achieved, he wouldn't need to hold back.

From that point on, everything would change. History would swerve off its path and head into uncharted territory. He'd have free rein to do whatever he wanted, without worrying about disrupting anything he was counting on, since there would be nothing to disrupt. It would all be virgin ground. He'd be able to unleash the full force of his strategy— the new weapons, the wide-ranging onslaught, the targeted assassinations—at will. He would be drafting the future in his own unique vision, forging ahead on an alternative timeline, creating a new world from a clean slate.

A clean slate that had no room for interlopers who knew his secret and could use it to unravel everything he'd achieved.

He'd heard enough. It was time to end this amusing distraction and get ready for the big day ahead.

The new world was waiting.

Taymoor's heart sank as he watched Rasheed berate Nisreen.

Yes, of course they'd brought this on themselves. They'd even caused him to lose a leg. But seeing them there brought a whole history rushing back, a history that was hard to erase.

He'd had a lot of time to think about it all, to think about them, about what they'd done and why. And right now, watching them about to die, he felt a sudden tightening in the pit of his stomach. It was he who'd warned Rasheed about them. If his old friends were going to die, it was in large part because of him.

He hadn't wanted it to be that way, but they hadn't left him much choice.

He'd tried.

After Kamal had pushed him off the train, a couple of days had passed before he'd been found by a passing trades-man who took him to Vienna to be looked after. Medicine back then wasn't as advanced as in Taymoor's time, and they hadn't been able to save his leg. He'd spent many weeks there, first recovering, then finding his place in that new city. He had liked it there. It was smaller than Paris, less hurried. Refreshing. He had wanted to convince himself he could perhaps set up his new life there instead of in Paris. It was a smaller pond for him to swim in. But the dread simply wouldn't let him go.

No matter how well things were going—and they were going well, quickly, for Taymoor was no fool when it came to navigating human nature and creating opportunities—he couldn't shake off the fear that Kamal and Nisreen could cause it all to come to a sudden end. He'd wake up at night in a cold sweat, wondering if he was still there, if the world he had gone to bed in was the same one he would wake up to.

Even though he couldn't quite understand it, the fear had pervaded his every moment. How would it happen? Would he just *cease to be*? Would he even know it, feel it, or be aware of it? The more he thought about it, the more lost and fearful he felt. It became unbearable, this existential terror of sitting helplessly and hoping his life didn't get wiped out.

Only he wasn't helpless.

He could stop them.

The problem was, he only knew how to travel back in time. Which gave rise to a competing terror: that of getting stuck in the past. Almost two centuries earlier. In a much more primitive, savage time.

He didn't have a choice. He couldn't continue like that, living with a worry that was constantly souring his days and nights. He had to do something about it.

Which was why he'd come back here, choosing to arrive in the first few days of the siege to make sure he got there before them. Rasheed had listened to him, but instead of treating him as a valued guest, he'd kept him locked away with his mouth gagged to ensure he didn't escape.

And now he could only watch as his partner and Nisreen were taken to their deaths.

Only it wasn't to be just their deaths, he realized with a sudden panic, as the man guarding him nudged him as well.

'What?' he asked, but his shocked look was answered with a harsher nudge in the kidneys and a command to move. Taymoor resisted, calling out to Rasheed. 'Your Eminence, my pasha . . . ?'

Everyone paused as Rasheed turned, his brow crinkled with mild curiosity.

'My bey, surely your man here has misunderstood your command?'

Rasheed let his question hang for a moment; then his mouth just twisted with apathy. 'Not at all,' he replied casually before nodding to the deaf-mute eunuch to carry on.

'Wait, wait,' Taymoor blurted, pushing back to hold his ground. 'Your eminence, surely . . . I did you a service,' he pleaded. 'I came here to save you and to keep our holy empire safe. I did my duty as a loyal subject of the sultan.'

'And you have performed your duty admirably, Taymoor Agha. I am indebted to you, the sultan is indebted to you, the whole empire is in your debt.'

Taymoor looked mystified. 'I don't understand?'

'Well, for someone with your training and your experience,' Rasheed said, 'I was rather surprised that you could make a major, major miscalculation about something so fundamental. It's actually rather troubling.'

Taymoor's face sank.

Rasheed wasn't done. 'You were hoping for the rest of the incantation? So you could hop off to a time of your choosing and live happily ever after?'

'We had a deal, Your Eminence.'

'A deal? Do you really think I would allow anyone—*anyone*,' Rasheed hissed, 'to be out there, roaming around, armed with this knowledge?'

'But—'

Rasheed flicked his hand curtly again.

Taymoor's pulse rocketed.

He shot a regretful glance at Kamal and Nisreen, who were watching with mounting alarm—then he lashed out.

He whipped his hand up and took the janissary by surprise, grabbing the hand that held the dagger and pushing it away while ramming an elbow up into the man's face and triggering an eruption of chaos around him as Kamal and Kolschitzky followed suit and snapped into action.

Kamal knew what Taymoor was about to do the instant he saw the look on his face. He'd seen that look before—the untamed burn in his eyes, the recklessness to tackle threats head-on. He was ready when, a split second later, Taymoor made his move.

Kamal's focus was on two fronts: the blade no longer under his chin but still hovering close enough to inflict fatal damage to him in the blink of an eye. And the blade that could do the same to Nisreen.

He needed to neutralize both threats simultaneously.

He quickly sized up the geography—Nisreen had been standing close to him, which proved critical as he coiled up and unleashed a rapid-fire sequence of moves on both fronts, grabbing the knife hand of the man guarding him while unleashing a savage kick that caught the knee of the man beside Nisreen sideways and snapped it backward in a loud, sickening crunch.

The guard yelped with pain and fell back, allowing Nisreen to slip away.

Kamal grabbed his guard's arm with both hands and used all his strength to swing him around on to his fallen comrade, sending him slamming into the injured man. Only the guard wasn't that easily dispatched, and he righted himself with unexpected resilience, using his elbow to pound Kamal in the chest and push him back.

Kamal staggered back, stubbornly hanging on to the man's hand and fighting to keep the deadly blade out of reach. From the corner of his eye, he glimpsed Taymoor and Kolschitzky locked in battle with the two other men, with Rasheed still standing in place, frozen by the sudden outburst of savagery.

He deflected an attempted jab from his adversary and countered it with a punch to the man's neck that didn't completely connect. As he did, he saw Nisreen standing by one of the large poles, watching in terror.

But not just watching.

Her lips were moving.

She was reciting something.

70

While Kamal had used the long ride to the camp to run various scenarios of what might happen once they were facing Rasheed, Nisreen had used the time differently.

She'd spent it sneaking furtive glances at her forearm, plugging in the right wording for ten days and committing it to memory as much as possible.

She knew she wouldn't have more than a few seconds to act. On pure instinct, and throwing caution to the wind, she decided to use it.

Ten days in the past.

Her lips mouthing the words as fast as they could.

The last things she saw were Rasheed, still riveted in place, stunned by Taymoor's move—and Kamal's eyes, wide with shock as he realized what she was doing.

Then the familiar rush, the same sensation of cataclysmic tearing apart and searing reassembly that she'd experienced before, and she was in the tent, in the same spot, naked, frozen with terror—and alone.

Rasheed wasn't there.

Her mind raced to decide what to do and quickly settled on the only thing she could do.

Save Kamal.

Hoping he was still alive

Hoping the man he was fighting was too stupefied by her disappearance to react, hoping she might have bought Kamal a crucial few seconds that could make the difference between life and death.

She took a few quick steps across the tent, to where she'd last seen Rasheed standing, then positioned herself a couple of steps behind it and did the one thing she thought they wouldn't expect.

She hadn't just memorized the version for travelling into the past. She'd also memorized the variant she'd come up with, the one Rasheed had now confirmed she'd got right, the one that would allow travel into the future.

The same future she'd just come from, only a few seconds later.

Which was right now.

She raced through the words, the fierce jolt ripping her apart again, and she was back.

In the tent.

Still naked.

With a fusillade of images scoring direct hits in her frazzled brain.

Taymoor's face crunching with pain as his opponent's blade cut into his side.

Kolschitzky, locked in a ferocious tussle with his guard.

Kamal, on the ground, looking dazed, edging back from the janissary who held his blade up and clearly had the upper hand but seemed momentarily stunned and frozen in place by Nisreen's disappearance.

And Rasheed.

Not where she last saw him, not where she expected him to be.

Instead, he had his sabre out and was also circling Kamal, looming over him.

Going in for the kill.

'No!' she screamed.

All heads turned—and for the briefest of moments, the

inside of the tent just froze in place, a still-life study in unbound ferocity.

It was just long enough to buy Kamal a reprieve.

Kamal heard the scream before he saw Nisreen.

She was blocked out by Rasheed, who spun around when he heard it, as did the soldier.

Besides grabbing their attention, her scream did something else. It sent a blast of adrenaline through Kamal, one that was potent enough to cut through the daze, obliterate the pain from the pounding he'd just suffered, and set his battered senses on fire.

But it was all happening too quickly.

He sprang up and launched himself at his stunned and distracted opponent, just as Rasheed began moving towards Nisreen.

His limbs jumped into overdrive, along with his fear.

He caught the guard by surprise with a savage blow to the ear and followed with a knee to the man's groin that sent him crashing to the carpet. Kamal's eyes were locked on the *yataghan*'s blade, but they still registered Nisreen edging backwards, deeper into the darker recesses of the tent, with Rasheed rushing towards her.

Everything became a rush of frenzied imagery, a nightmare unfolding at lightning speed.

Wrenching the dagger out of the fallen eunuch's grip and slitting his throat in the same move.

The jarred image of Rasheed skulking deeper into the tent, his bulk blocking Nisreen from view.

Hurdling over the fallen guard and charging towards Rasheed.

Rasheed's arm swinging back and lunging as his back rushed closer into view.

Hearing Nisreen's high-pitched, pained grunt just as he reached Rasheed and tackled him.

Driving his big blade deep into Rasheed's side.

Hearing him roar with agony as he twisted it upwards ferociously before shoving him off Nisreen.

Nisreen staring at him, her face twisted with shock and pain, her hands clutching her belly.

The blood seeping through her fingers.

The look of terror in her eyes as her legs gave way and she tumbled to the ground.

71

Kamal dived to the carpet and scooped her up in his arms.

His hands trembling, he caressed her face; then he moved his gaze downwards, to the mess of blood spreading across her midsection. Gently, he moved her fingers away to take a look at her wound.

He had enough experience to know that it was bad.

Very bad.

'Stay with me, *hayatim*,' he told her, pressing down on the gushing blood, trying to clear a path through the onslaught of emotions crashing through him. 'I'm going to take care of this, *hayatim*. We're going to fix this.'

Nisreen didn't reply. Her eyes were moist as she shook her head slowly, ruefully, her eyes alternating between staring into his and shutting tight to block out the waves of pain and dread.

Kamal held back tears as he shot a quick look behind him. Rasheed wasn't moving. His eyes were locked in a dead upward stare, his torso a mess of blood and guts. Further back, he glimpsed a bloodied Taymoor drawing on every ounce of strength left in him to choke the life out of the guard he'd been fighting before letting him drop, scooping up his crutch, and stumbling across the tent to help Kolschitzky, who was locked in a knife fight of his own.

Kamal spun his attention right back to Nisreen, his mind racing for a solution, something, anything that might save her.

He could only see one possibility.

'We have to jump, *hayatim*. Jump forwards. Go back to our time.'

'No—'

'I'll get you to a hospital,' he insisted. 'Vienna will be bigger than now. We'll be in the city. There are ambulances. People have phones. We'll get you fixed but we have to do it now.'

Her fingers curled into his. 'No,' she muttered. 'There's no time.'

'Of course there is,' he pleaded. 'Come on. Say the words. I'll be right behind you.'

Her fingers clasped his tighter, and her face tightened with resolve. 'No, *canim*. You have to stay. You need to finish this. You have to warn Sobieski.'

'I'll go with you. We'll get you looked after; then I'll come back.'

She shook her head. 'No. You're so close . . . And there are too many unknowns. And you know how this works. We could land in the middle of a highway. Or on a wall.'

'I'll wait with you,' he managed, fighting his own tears, trying hard to give off an appearance of confidence. 'We'll get you taken care of—we'll take our time to plan it better. Then I'll come back and get it done. I promise.'

She shook her head more forcefully. 'I'd have to come back with you. Otherwise, I'll be gone . . . . after you change everything.'

'So we'll come back together.'

Her expression softened, as if she was finding some kind of inner peace, some stoic acceptance. '*Canim*,' she said in between soft coughs, her voice soft, her eyes warm, her hand straining to rise enough to caress his cheek. 'We came here for a purpose, and you can make it happen. I know you can. Go. Get it done. Get it done for me, for your brother, for our family . . . for everything we talked about. I have nothing left to live for.'

'Of course you do—'

Her fingers slipped across to cover his lips as she coughed again before continuing in a faint, faltering voice. 'No. It's too painful. It's all too painful. I'll never get over what happened. And I don't want to live with that pain. Doing this . . . it's the only thing that kept me going.' She coughed up some blood, squeezing her eyes shut as she did, clearly ravaged by pain now. Her voice was weakening. 'This . . . and you. You've been wonderful . . . the true Kamal, the one I always kept in my heart.'

'Say the words, *hayatim,* please . . . say them. Say them.'

Her touch went lighter. 'Go, *canim* . . . finish it.'

He couldn't hold back his tears, and he leaned in, closed his eyes, and kissed her, melding his lips into hers, wishing she wouldn't die if he stayed that way, if he kept her tethered to him as he breathed life into her.

But he couldn't save her. He just held her there as her last breath slid into him. He felt her very soul curl deep into him and root itself inside him, and he didn't want to move, ever, didn't want to sever that connection, didn't want to risk having her break free and evaporate into the savage, bloodstained air of that malevolent tent.

But she was gone, and, after a long moment, it sank in.

He pulled back slightly, stared at her resting face. Her eyes were mercifully closed, and her expression was one of peace, not pain.

Perhaps he had somehow managed to help her escape to a warm and safe resting place.

He heard movement behind him and twisted around, his body coiled up defensively.

It was Kolschitzky. He was standing over the dead guard he'd been battling, his back hunched with exhaustion, his arms dangling limply by his side, his right hand holding a bloodied *yataghan.*

Taymoor lay beside him, but he wasn't moving.

Kolschitzky looked at Kamal. The Pole was breathing hard, his face animated by the exhaustion, the resolve, and, above all, the bewilderment at what he had just witnessed.

As Kamal held his gaze, all he could think about were two words.

The last words the love of his life had uttered just before she took her final breath.

Finish it.

72

No one else came in.

It was unlikely anything had been overheard, not through the twin sets of thick curtains that blocked the tent's interior from the outside world, not given the noisy battle raging on the city walls and the preparations for the next day's long march. Even if the fight had been heard, it was clear that Rasheed's men took his instructions not to be disturbed with utmost seriousness.

Inside, after Kamal was able to tear himself away from Nisreen's body, he went around the fallen bodies, checking them quickly while Kolschitzky, armed with two sabres, kept watch by the entrance curtains to the tent.

They were all dead—Rasheed, Taymoor and the four guards.

And Nisreen.

Kamal lingered for a moment over Taymoor's body, mixed feelings of anger and regret swamping him. Then he pulled himself away and joined Kolschitzky.

'Doesn't look like anyone heard anything,' the Pole told him. 'The camp's busy tonight; they're preparing for the big march tomorrow.'

Kamal nodded, though his mind was already elsewhere. He seemed oblivious to the fact that Kolschitzky was eyeing him quizzically and expectantly.

'You want to explain what I saw?' the Pole finally asked.

Kamal let out a weary breath. 'There'll be time for that later.'

'Everything they said ... about the future. About what happened. It's true?'

'Yes.'

Kolschitzky looked bewildered. 'And that thing she did ... can you do it too?'

Kamal gave him a reluctant nod.

'What are you ...? *Zauberers*?' His scrambled mind had plucked the German term for sorcerer before remembering to revert to Ottoman Turkish. 'You're a *Büyücü*?'

The question wasn't that easy to dismiss.

Kamal shrugged. 'Only in this respect,' he replied. 'Look, we can talk about it later. Right now, we need to figure out what to do.'

He reconsidered the timeline and ordered his thoughts.

'Tomorrow's Tuesday,' he told Kolschitzky. 'Kara Mustafa's army will leave the camp at dawn to get into position for the attack on Wednesday morning, after the bombing. We need to warn Sobieski before then.' He tried to visualize the map of the region and the various players' positions. 'Sobieski and most of the others should have crossed the Danube and arrived at Tulln today. The rest of the armies will arrive tomorrow; then they'll all be in place for the cere- monial review on Wednesday.'

'Which is when the suicide bombers will strike.'

'Exactly.' Kamal nodded. 'How long a ride is it from here to Tulln?'

Kolschitzky thought quickly. 'It's around five *fersahs* from where we are. But there's the Wienerwald standing between us. The most direct way is to take the high road that snakes up the hills and back down to the plains outside Tulln.'

'That's the road Kara Mustafa's men will take tomorrow to cross to the other side.'

'It has to be,' the Pole said. 'It's the only passage across.

The rest are just small trails and pathways through the valleys and forests.'

'We need to make sure Sobieski and his men are in control of the peak before the Ottoman army gets there,' Kamal said. 'We have to get to him and convince him to make a push for it at first light. If he takes command of the higher ground, the sultan's men will be walking into a trap. They'll get bogged down on the way up and the hussars will be able to cut them down at will. Then this whole camp will be at his mercy.'

'But it'll be dangerous for us to take the high road. Kara Mustafa is bound to have dispatched advance patrols to secure it.'

'How else can we get to Tulln?'

'We can go around the hills. Either from the east—the way they brought us here. Or from the west, along the River Wien. We'd be much less likely to run into patrols that way, but it'll be longer.'

'How much longer?'

The Pole mulled his answer. 'During the day, given the terrain . . . we could do it in three hours.'

'What about right now, in the dead of night? Can you get us there?'

'It might take twice as long, but . . . yes, I think I can.'

Kamal nodded. 'Then that's what we'll do. Right now. We need to get going.'

Kolschitzky glanced around the room. 'We can cut through the tent covers and sneak out the back. In the dark, we should be able to slip away unseen.'

'We can't leave like this. If they find the dead bodies, it might change things. It could affect their plans.'

The Pole looked at him quizzically. 'What does it matter? Better that they do, no?'

'No. I don't want to give them any reason to think something's wrong. We need to keep up the appearance that things are proceeding as planned.'

'But Rasheed is dead.'

Kamal nodded. 'They don't need to know that.' He took in the grim scene. Then his eyes settled on Rasheed's body. He formulated a quick plan and turned to Kolschitzky. 'You said before you can pass for anyone?'

'Within reason.'

Kamal pointed at Rasheed. 'You'll need to pass for him.'

Kolschitzky's brow furrowed. Then he shrugged with acceptance. 'In the dark . . . It's doable.'

Kamal crossed the room and knelt before Nisreen's body. He knew he couldn't just leave her lying there like that either. He stared at her solemnly as he laid his hand on her cheek; then he ran his fingers gently up her forehead and through her hair. She was still warm to his touch.

He turned to the Pole. 'We'll start with her.'

73

Kolschitzky made for a surprisingly passable version of Rasheed.

Both men were of around the same height and build. They were both dark-skinned and wore their beards in a similar fashion, and Rasheed's layers of dress—the richly textured robes, the elaborate turban—left very little of Kolschitzky actually visible.

In the dark of night and only illuminated by the flicker of camp torches, Kolschitzky could easily pass for Rasheed. He'd also heard enough of the man's voice and manner of speech to be able to mimic him, should he need to speak. Passing himself for others was, after all, a talent he'd put to good use already.

For his part, Kamal slipped on the outfit of the guard that Taymoor had strangled. It was the only one that wasn't drenched in blood. He and Kolschitzky got dressed after dragging the bodies into a far corner of the huge tent, pulling back the layers of thick Persian carpets that covered the ground there, positioning the bodies flat and next to each other, digging up just enough soil to lower them and flatten the edges around them before covering them up with the carpets.

He didn't want to leave Nisreen next to them. Instead, they half buried her under the carpets across the tent from the others. Before covering her, he gave her one last kiss on the forehead, holding his lips there for a long moment.

'I'll finish it for you, *hayatim*,' he murmured. 'And once it's done, I'll come back and give you a proper burial.'

He took one last glance at her forearms. He had misgivings about leaving her there, given the tattoos. If she were found, the incantation would be vulnerable to discovery, even if whoever came across it wouldn't understand what it was without trying it. But Kamal couldn't face dealing with it now. It was all too raw in his mind, and time was pressing. He'd deal with it when they returned, after it was all done.

They pulled the carpets back over her, too. Once they were done, the slight rises in either corner of the tent were barely discernible.

The two men crept up to the entrance curtains of the tent.

'Ready?' Kamal asked Kolschitzky.

The Pole took a reassuring feel of his scabbarded, jewel-encrusted *yataghan,* then his expression morphed into a powerful imitation of Rasheed's intense frown, and he barked, *'Gidelim.'*

Let's go.

Kamal nodded his approval, sucked in a deep breath, and stepped through the curtains.

He emerged outside the tent. It was pitch-black, save for the faint light coming from a few torches set up around the edges of the enclosure's perimeter. The captain wasn't around, but three janissaries stood guard by its gate, at ease and talking. They were far enough away that it would be hard for them to be able to make out the specific features of Kamal's face.

'The pasha's horse. Saddle it up and bring it here, with another for me. Quickly!' he yelled out to them, using the precise diction that Kolschitzky had taught him.

The men looked over, taken aback by the late-night order. Rasheed wasn't known to ride off in the night. In fact, Kamal had read in accounts of the siege that he rarely left the camp.

'Move,' Kamal ordered insistently.

The men scurried away and soon came back with two horses. The first of them, evidently Rasheed's, was a magnificent animal—slender, long-backed, with sloping quarters and long, muscular legs. Its black coat had a metallic sheen that shimmered in the light of the torches; on its back was an opulent velvet saddle adorned with precious stones and gilded embroidery and linked to gold-plated stirrups.

The attendant janissaries quickly positioned Rasheed's horse outside the tent's entrance and placed a small stepped platform alongside it. Turning away from the men, Kamal disappeared back into the tent, then reappeared holding open the tent flap from which Kolschitzky stepped out. The janissaries dropped their heads in respectful bows. Wearing a scowl and walking with purpose, the Pole said nothing. Instead, he let Kamal help him step up the platform and climb on to the horse. Kamal then mounted his own, only giving the man holding its reins a stern nod. Then they both trotted out of the enclosure without uttering a word.

None was needed. Rasheed was the sultan's valued adviser, his philosopher-royal. To the janissaries, he was royalty. They were there to serve, not to question—especially not when it came to a man who had an aura of mystique and a reputation for unconventional methods.

Rasheed's enclosure was at the centre of the camp, next to the grand vizier's compound. Both sat on high ground, from which Kara Mustafa and Rasheed could observe the progress on the bastions, safely out of reach of the defenders' cannon. Being at the rear of the camp meant Kamal and Kolschitzky didn't have long to travel before they had left the long rows of tents behind and were galloping away into the darkness.

Once the camp was well behind them, Kolschitzky slowed

his horse to a trot and got his bearings. Even in the pale light of the moon, the narrow River Wien had a clearly discernible glow that snaked away into the woodlands.

'We'll follow the river to Purkersdorf; then we'll veer north and follow the Gablitzbach up into the hills. As long as the moon doesn't act shy on us, it shouldn't be too hard to stay on course.'

'Just get us there,' Kamal told the Pole. 'I've lost too much to fail here.'

Kolschitzky held his gaze. 'I'll get you there, and we'll see this through. If only so you'll have no excuse but to explain what the hell is going on.'

Kamal nodded. 'It's a deal.' Then he gave his mount a squeeze with his calves and set off.

They rode through the night.

They crossed the scrubland before climbing up the unin-habited, heavily wooded hills, skirting the valleys that cut across them and snaking through forests of beech and oak criss-crossed by streams. They were always on the alert in case they came across Ottoman irregulars like the ones that had captured them, but knew that those raiders tended to lie still at night. They hoped to steer clear of advance Christian forces, too—dressed as they were, they couldn't risk wasting time proving their intentions to any of their reconnaissance patrols.

Dawn was still hours away by the time they navigated the ridges that topped the hills and began descending the gen-tler slopes towards Tulln. The further down they rode, the safer they felt, but they were still advancing cautiously, their eyes scanning the night for any sign of life. Then they were on the plains, riding faster now, a soft yellow glint backlight-ing the contours of the hills they'd left behind.

The flicker of distant bonfires acted as beacons to draw them in during the final hour of their journey. They knew it could only be the army of Christendom, and it wasn't long before they were intercepted by a patrol of Bavarian horsemen. Kolschitzky stunned them by pulling off his turban and speaking to them in perfect German while Kamal watched in silence. The Pole knew what to say. After being relieved of their sabres and having their hands tied behind their backs as a precaution, they were escorted back to the Christian encampment.

Even with darkness still trouncing the encroaching light, the epic scale of the army the pope had assembled was unmistakable. An endless swarm of troops—Austrians, Bavarians, Saxons, Franconians and Poles—was massed outside the small town, a sea of tents arrayed across the wide plains that stretched back to the banks of the Danube. And at the centre of it all stood the grand compound of its leader, the king of Poland.

The man Kamal had come all this way to see.

The easier part was done.

The battle that followed would decide the fate of the world.

74

The day that again changed history began as unremarkably as any other.

The sun broke cover and overwhelmed the darkness, spreading its munificent light across the land, while life, it all its manifestations, unfurled itself from protective sleep and ventured out to seek sustenance.

On that particular day, however, something else was taking place. In this pastoral corner of the world, on either side of the glorious foothills of the Wienerwald, two massive legions of men, armed and trained for maximal bloodletting, were marching into battle.

And as had happened before, in a stolen history none of the battle's participants were aware of, the army of Christendom prevailed once again.

Sobieski had listened.

And acted.

Charles, Duke of Lorraine, was instrumental in convincing the king to believe the visitors. The emperor had put Charles, his brother-in-law, in command of the imperial army before the siege had begun. The duke was Viennese and knew Starhemberg well, and Kolschitzky's detailed report about the count's heroic efforts and the desperate situation inside the besieged city were too convincing to ignore. But what probably clinched it was that Sobieski was able to listen to Kamal's arguments first-hand, without the need for an interpreter: before becoming king, Sobieski had spent years in Istanbul as a diplomatic envoy to the sultan's court.

He had learned to speak the language there, and Kamal's commitment and his thorough knowledge of Kara Mustafa's plans for the next day were, like Kolschitzky's grim update, too compelling to brush off.

The commanders quickly drew up their new battle plans.

The ceremonial review was shelved. Instead, the army was roused from sleep and marched off at speed towards the high road that climbed into the Vienna Woods.

The suicide bombers never made it to the ceremonial review that never happened. Instead, they were ambushed by Habsburg marksmen, who were utterly perplexed by the enormous firebomb their musket balls triggered.

The Ottoman army that was to follow the bombing never made it to the empty encampment in the plains of Tulln. It was taken by complete surprise on the slopes outside Vienna, with the Ottoman camp still in sight on the plain behind it. Sobieski had also used his time as an envoy in Istanbul to study Ottoman military traditions, and it was a body of knowledge he would now put to good use.

His army—the mounted hussars and dragoons charging ahead of the infantry—seized the ridges and spread out across the hilltops of the Vienna Woods several hours before the Ottoman troops had planned to reach them. The advance wasn't easy, with steep slopes and narrow passages of loose ground to contend with. Bringing the light artillery was left until last, so as not to delay the movement of the troops. The cavalry found the climb hardest. In many places, the hussars had to dismount and lead their heavy horses up the pock-marked landscape on foot. Still, the pope's men had pressed on, committed to their sacred mission.

And then they attacked.

On the hills that overlooked Vienna, in full view of the Ottoman encampment and the walls of the besieged city, the

Polish musketeers and their allies rained fire on the advancing Ottomans, taking them by surprise before the cavalry—almost ten thousand horsemen—stormed down and cut them to pieces.

Kara Mustafa's men, by now drained and demoralized by the months of siege, just ran.

The Polish hussars, who led the charges, were a terrifying sight: fierce warriors whose deadly reputation preceded them, they wore burnished steel armour, carried over-long lances and rode massive horses. They also had tall wooden frames of eagle and ostrich wings strapped to their backs that gave off an eerie whistle as they galloped into battle. Surging as one in long, tightly packed lines, with wheeled field guns spewing fire from above, they looked like avenging angels of death as they impaled the fleeing Ottoman troops on the tips of their lances or cut them down with the long, triangular swords strapped to their wrists.

There was slaughter everywhere: on the high road that snaked up the mountain, on the pathways that veered off from it, in the forest, on the scrubland approaches to the foothills, and in the vineyards farther down the slopes that led back to the camp. Wave after wave of Christian fighters swept down from high ground, a rampaging army of liberation delivering death under a white flag emblazoned with a scarlet red cross.

The retreating Ottomans found their progress stymied by the steep slopes, the rocky terrain and the fields of densely entangled grapevines. The camp itself didn't have any defences set up facing the attackers coming from the Vienna Woods. All of its fortifications faced the other way, directed at the city walls. There was no shelter behind which to regroup, and those that did reach the camp didn't stop there: they just kept running, abandoning everything and making for the road to Buda, mostly on foot, with only a lucky few on horseback.

Kara Mustafa also fled. After hastily grabbing his treasure chest and the green Standard of the Prophet, the holy banner that the sultan had presented him with at the outset of his campaign, he barely managed to escape on horseback with a few of his bodyguards.

The encampment was now ripe for the taking.

The massacre didn't take long.

In a few hours, the entire camp was reduced to a mass graveyard. For miles around, the ground was littered with corpses and soaked with blood. In between the killing, the liberators also freed the thirty thousand men, women, and children that the Ottomans had rounded up from towns and villages close to Vienna. Kara Mustafa had ordered them killed before he'd fled the camp, but his men hadn't had enough time to carry out his orders.

The relief army's victory was complete, with Sobieski and his allies having suffered an astoundingly low number of casualties.

Vienna was saved.

But it was much more than that.

The Ottoman Empire had suffered a devastating defeat, the worst in its illustrious history. It was a defeat that would trigger a series of wars that would last a century and usher in the beginning of its long decline. The reconquest of territory seized by Islam over hundreds of years would now begin, with the victors' minds awash with heady dreams of even liberating Constantinople itself.

Kamal and Kolschitzky weren't far from Sobieski when he led his victorious troops through Vienna's Scottish Gate.

Everyone turned out to greet him. To a rousing clamour of trumpets and kettledrums, Starhemberg and the rest of the city's officials welcomed him with resounding cheers, while a huge crowd of grateful survivors showered their saviour with cries of gratitude and rushed up to kiss his hands and feet.

Leading one of the grand vizier's prized horses and trailing the captured Ottoman banners, the Polish king acknowledged the crowd's screams of 'Long live the king!' with gracious waves before proclaiming, '*Venimus, vidimus, deus vicit*' ('We came, we saw, God conquered').

It was evident, though, that the city's scars would take a long time to heal. So many had died. Almost every building had been disfigured by war. Disease was still rampant, so much so that its tentacles would soon ensnare the liberators.

But before the rebuilding, the townspeople and the refugees could console themselves with the great pillaging that was to be had, for the Ottoman ghost city was a trove of riches. Tens of thousands of tents had been left behind, along with a sea of horses and over a hundred thousand heads of cattle that included Anatolian buffalo, camels, cattle, sheep and goats. There was more artillery, gunpowder and ammunition than they'd ever seen, with muskets and gold-mounted sabres aplenty and endless stockpiles of grain.

The Polish cavalry went in that same night, the spoils of victory being theirs to savour first.

Kamal and Kolschitzky accompanied them. But Kamal wasn't there for the booty. Accompanied by his Polish companion, he rushed straight for Rasheed's tent, reaching it before the hussars stripped it. Under the carpets, he found Nisreen's body just where he'd left it the night before.

She looked pale, and her skin had a green hue to it, but mercifully the bloating and smell of decomposition hadn't progressed.

At first, Kamal could barely reach out to touch her. He just sat there and stared, crushed by a profound sadness.

Kolschitzky stood back and waited, giving his new friend time to process it. Then, softly, he stepped forward and said, 'We should move her now.'

Kamal nodded.

She was rigid and cold to the touch as they wrapped her in one of the smaller carpets. They took her to the city's cemetery, on the north side of the city, outside the fortifications. But before he could bury her, Kamal needed to do one last thing. A cripplingly painful task, but one he felt had to be done. And he needed to do it away from Kolschitzky's eyes.

Asking him for a moment of privacy, he pulled out a dagger. Then, with trembling fingers, he cut lines across the tattooed words on her forearms, making sure they became illegible, each stroke of the blade simultaneously slicing a deep gash through his heart.

He'd felt no such pain when he'd taken care of the markings on Rasheed's body back in the tent.

After washing her, he performed the burial ritual on his own. He'd managed to scrounge a white sheet, which he wrapped her in, and some rope to fasten it around her. With Kolschitzky standing in silence beside him, he recited the funeral prayer. Then they laid her down to rest under a plain stone marker, on which he had inscribed one simple word: *hayatim*.

My life.

Kara Mustafa's end was equally solemn. But when it came, it was swift and merciless.

He made it to Belgrade. Although he suffered several more military humiliations on the way, it was news of the failure outside the walls of Vienna that spurred the sultan to take the action that would surprise no one, least of all the grand vizier himself.

After noon prayers on that fateful day, he took off his robes and his turban and knelt on the ground. Two imperial executioners then placed a silk cord around his neck and, standing on either side of him, pulled. He died quickly and without resistance. The skin was then stripped off his head, stuffed with dry straw, and placed in a velvet bag that was sent back to the sultan, along with the Holy Standard of the Prophet that the sultan had entrusted to him.

As this was happening, church bells across Europe were ringing, in a curiously serendipitous moment of rejoicing.

It was 25 December 1683.

75

Under a balmy late-summer sky, Kamal and Kolschitzky spent the rest of the night watching the pillaging from the security of one of the bastions that overlooked the encampment.

Below, the camp was a frenzy of activity, an anthill of torch-carrying looters feasting on anything they could carry.

'What about you?' Kamal asked Kolschitzky. 'Don't you want your share? They're picking it clean.'

Kolschitzky chuckled. 'I already told Starhemberg what I wanted. He was a bit puzzled, but he agreed.'

'What did you ask for?'

'The Turks left behind a huge stockpile of coffee beans. Thousands of sacks.'

'And he gave them all to you?'

'No one else wants them. They have a sour taste. They're disgusting to eat.'

'So why do you want them?'

'They don't know what they are, but I do.' Kolschitzky smiled.

Kamal laughed. The Viennese didn't know coffee. At least not yet. Kolschitzky, after years spent in Istanbul, did.

The city could look forward to a long tradition of coffee houses.

'What I really want, though,' Kolschitzky added, 'is for you to keep your promise. I need to understand what I saw.'

Kamal had been waiting for the Pole to bring it up. He'd wondered about how to deal with it, but his thoughts had migrated to a much more difficult question: what to do now.

He and Nisreen had vaguely talked about it, but it wasn't something he thought he'd be considering on his own.

He'd done what they'd set out to do. He'd set history back on its course. There was nothing more he needed to do. From here on, what would happen would happen of its own accord. He'd leave the world to evolve as it once had, without his or anyone else's meddling.

Which was why he couldn't tell Kolschitzky the truth. At least, not the whole truth.

He knew he could get away with saying nothing. Or he could feed the Pole a lie. All Kolschitzky had seen, after all, was that Nisreen had vanished and reappeared in a slightly different location, in the nude. He also knew that Kamal and Nisreen knew a lot, but he couldn't possibly suspect how they'd gained that knowledge. But Kamal felt he owed him more than that. The man had entrusted Kamal and Nisreen with his life; he'd taken the ultimate risk based on nothing but their word.

And so Kamal gave him an abridged version of his story. He and Nisreen had stumbled across the ability to travel through time. They'd discovered Rasheed's meddling with history, which turned them into enemies of the state. The sultan's men had come after them, her family had been killed and they had travelled back to make things right.

He kept things deliberately vague and made sure he didn't give Kolschitzky any specifics that could help the Pole discover more than Kamal wanted him to know. He didn't want anyone else meddling with history, no matter how highly he thought of them. But his words only served to ignite fevered curiosity in the Pole's mind, and Kolschitzky swamped him with questions.

Kamal deflected and demurred as best he could. It didn't take long before it was clear that Kolschitzky understood his quandary. The questions petered out, and the Pole finally asked, 'What happens from here on?'

'Your guess is as good as mine,' Kamal replied. 'This is as much of a clean slate to me as it is for everyone else.'

Kolschitzky nodded thoughtfully. 'And you? What are you going to do?'

Kamal shrugged.

Talking to Kolschitzky had made two things clearer to him. One was that he couldn't stay there. Not in Vienna, not in that time. As an Ottoman, he would be living on the wrong side of the conflict. Sure, he was a hero. Sobieski and the rest of them would make sure he was celebrated as one and well looked after. But it would still be a difficult society to fit into, in all kinds of ways.

Beyond that, though, he realized he needed to know how it all turned out. There was no escaping that. He needed to see it for himself.

There was nothing there for him, anyway. But then again, there was nothing for him anywhere else. But at least there was hope. Hope for a better world, hope for a new beginning in a better place.

76

Vienna
July, AD 2017

Kamal was in a state of constant wonder.

Everything—absolutely *everything*—was different.

He hadn't visited Vienna back in his time, so he could only compare it to the Paris of 1438—now referred to as 2017, he quickly discovered. Of course, back in his Paris, there had also been cars, and buses, and airliners crisscrossing the skies overhead. Even if they weren't of the same design, they were broadly similar.

This was different.

Somehow, it was all brighter. Colour was everywhere: most strikingly in the clothing, which was light and startlingly coloured—and rather minimal, he was shocked to notice—but also on cars, trams and bicycles and in wild, eye-catching shopfronts and on billboards that displayed all kinds of attention-grabbing imagery. Even the light of day seemed brighter, as did the eyes and faces of the people he encountered as he wandered the big city.

It was all more visceral, more vivid.

More alive.

Everywhere he looked, something he saw startled him, but not in a bad way. Most of the men were clean-shaven. Many were dressed curiously in dark jackets and trousers and had a colourful piece of material, like a very thin scarf, hanging from their collars. More than anything, though, it was the women that caught his eye. They were everywhere. Walking alone or in the company or others, men and women. Not just with faces uncovered but with swathes of skin exposed, sauntering breezily in short dresses and skirts, their bare legs teetering on fragile-looking high-heeled shoes, their hair flowing as they moved through the city with purpose and freedom.

As far as his life experience went, it was extraordinary.

He saw couples walking around holding hands; others kissing openly. He even saw men holding hands casually for all to see, strolling past police officers in white caps, who were oblivious to their choice of lifestyle and whose presence didn't seem to instil a feeling of foreboding in the people who crossed their path.

Pavement cafés offering a bewildering assortment of food and drink were bustling with people, men and women of all ages eating, laughing, smoking, many enjoying cups of coffee—clearly, Kolschitzky had left his mark on Viennese history in more ways than one—or openly drinking what he discovered were alcoholic beverages.

The sense of freedom was intoxicating.

There was also a palpable sense of calmness, which took a while for him to grasp. The people of the city didn't seem to be ruled by fear, and yet it wasn't a chaotic free-for-all. There was none of the anarchy he'd been taught about, none of the ruin Rasheed had spoken of. There was order—more of it than he remembered back home. It was clean and tidy, and free of litter. Traffic ebbed and flowed in an organized manner, car horns weren't blaring incessantly, people waited for light signals to cross roads, pedestrians seemed respectful of one another, and none of it seemed due to fear of punishment. And the city was obviously thriving: clothing shopfronts were packed with vivid displays, pastry-shop display cases were overflowing with all kinds of cakes, and crowds of people were strolling around—tourists much like him, he gathered, taking in the sights, chatting, laughing, using their phones to take pictures. It was unquestionably a happier, more relaxed time and place than any world he'd seen. Musicians performed openly in the streets, relying on the generosity of strangers. Even the pedestrian signals at traffic lights flashed a green symbol of two people holding hands with a small blinking heart above them.

He just wandered and wandered, his eyes feasting on the new world, his mind drunk with awe while it processed the torrent of fresh imagery. And all the time, he couldn't help but think of Nisreen, about how she would have reacted to all this, too, to the freedom and equality she'd fought for all those years.

How she would have loved it.

His starting point had been in St Stephen's Cathedral. He'd correctly assumed the cathedral would still be there all those years later, and he'd been proved right.

He arrived during the night, when it was closed to visitors, and the difference had immediately struck him: the hordes of sick and dying were no longer there; the stench of death was long gone. Instead, the cathedral's glorious interior had been restored to its full grandeur: a gleaming beacon for living, breathing worshippers, as its builders had intended.

He felt filthy and craved a wash, which he was able to do in a small cloakroom, taking huge delight in the clean, warm running water. After drying himself with paper tissues, he was lucky to find a bundle of used clothes and shoes in a small room by the lower vestry. He couldn't know they were donations for the needy collected by the Church, and they weren't like any clothes he was used to, but he still helped himself to what seemed like a reasonable male outfit. He also found some coins in a desk drawer, which he pocketed. Then he waited until daylight rose and the church doors opened before venturing out.

The shock was instantaneous. He'd left a heavily destroyed city that was drowning with death and suffering. The visual contrast was tough to process at first, especially since the first building he saw was the one he and Nisreen had been held in, next to the cathedral. It, too, was now in pristine condition. There was no trace of the damage from Kara Mustafa's cannonballs; its arcaded ground floor now housed a collection of restaurants and cafés.

Dazed and bewildered, he roamed the city, marvelling at everything he saw, heard, smelled, breathed, noticing every innocuous detail and trying not to attract attention while doing it. He tried to find his bearings by replicating the path he'd taken with Kolschitzky and Nisreen to get to the walls, but he quickly lost his way. He couldn't find the fortifications or the bastions. Only the occasional church jarred his memory.

He tried to find the cemetery where he had buried Nisreen but failed. The city was now much bigger. It had expanded wildly in the almost three and a half centuries since the time of the siege, way beyond its old fortifications. With mixed emotions, he kept on walking, but, before long, a sense of unease started to seep into him.

He couldn't speak the language. Being familiar with Latin script, he could read the words, but it only told him what they sounded like, not what they meant. He had no friends, no contacts, no one who knew him. He had little money and no papers.

He felt utterly, completely alone.

His meandering eventually led him past the Hofburg Palace and its magnificent gardens and into the Naschmarkt, a sprawling market with stalls that sold all kinds of foods and bric-a-brac. He felt a stir of hope at the sight of a stall that had a familiar feature from his old life: a large, rotating spit of döner meat, a kebab shop, the likes of which peppered his Paris. The lettering on its awning spelled out 'Bosphorus'.

Hesitantly, he approached one of the men who worked there, the older of the two. The man was in his sixties, had a burgeoning white moustache, and wore a white apron and a matching cap.

In Ottoman Turkish, Kamal pointed at the grill and asked, 'How much for one of those?'

The man looked at him curiously, then replied, 'Where are you from, brother?' He spoke Turkish, but his accent was different from what Kamal was used to, softer somehow, easier on the ear. And clearly he found Kamal's accent unusual.

Kamal felt a stab of discomfort. He half smiled sheepishly and began to step away when the man called out after him. 'Hey, wait. I'm sorry. I didn't mean to pry. We're all brothers here.' He came round from behind the counter and put out a welcoming hand to coax Kamal back. 'Come, please. You look like you could do with something to eat. Let me offer you a sandwich.'

Kamal hesitated; then, at the man's insistence, he relented and accepted his offer. They sat at a small raised table in front of the stall, where Kamal greedily wolfed down the sandwich and a carton of *ayran* yogurt.

He was a bit guarded at first, but he soon understood what the kebab chef, who said his name was Orhan, had assumed: that he was a Turk like him, Turkey being—Kamal surmised—the surviving part of the empire. He learned that there were a lot of illegal Turkish immigrants in Vienna, and Orhan took him for one of them. Kamal found it useful to let the assumption run. Kamal told Orhan that he was from the east of the country, near Diyarbakir, despite feeling uncomfortable about dredging up information he remembered about a Turkish terror suspect who was once on his radar.

The chef was familiar with and sympathetic to the plight of his desperate countrymen. He gave Kamal some useful insights into what to do now that he was there: how to find shelter and food, how to apply for asylum. Kamal wondered if that was what he'd need to do, at least as a temporary measure, before he understood the place better and figured out how to navigate this new world.

'Amazing that the people of this city can now welcome us,' Kamal commented, 'after everything we did to them.'

Orhan's face clouded. He hadn't understood the reference.

'Kara Mustafa's siege,' Kamal explained, his tone quizzical. 'All those years ago.'

'Ah.' The chef brushed it off. 'It's such a long time ago. I doubt anyone even thinks about it. Are you a history buff?'

'You could say that.'

'Then you'll love the museums here. They're outstanding.'

The chef told Kamal more about them, but one thing he mentioned sunk its claws into Kamal and wouldn't let go.

He felt an urge to get going, and, after promising Orhan he'd come back soon, got up and walked away.

Less than an hour later, he was outside the gates of the Heeresgeschichtliches Museum.

The Austrian Military History Museum.

77

Kamal stood outside the museum, unable to move. The beauty of the building was doing nothing to calm his nervousness about the emotions that entering might stir.

The kebab chef had told him that the museum held large displays devoted to the wars against the Ottomans. Of those, the siege of 1683 was the most renowned. He even said that there was so much on display that viewing it almost felt like being there, a comment Kamal had to resist rebutting, even if he could have summoned up the detachment to do it playfully.

The memories had nothing playful about them.

He watched as throngs of tourists stepped off buses and made their way to the entrance. Taking a deep breath, he finally pushed ahead and strode through the open gates.

The museum was a nineteenth-century building, built in a grand, neo-Byzantine style with a distinctly oriental flavour. Its two-tone brick façade was decorated with geometric terracotta ornaments and was topped by a crown of stone crenellations peppered with turrets. Three majestic arches led inside.

He had difficulty understanding what the cashier was saying. She eventually pointed at the price on a pamphlet, and he paid for an entrance ticket with six of the euro coins he had taken from the cathedral. She asked where he was from, to which he replied, 'Turkey.' The cashier pointed him to an adjacent counter and said something to the woman looking after it. He stepped across, and the woman handed him a curious kit comprised of a small electronic box with a lanyard clipped on to it and a cable that led to a set of earphones. After a bit of give-and-take, Kamal finally understood what she was giving him: it was an audio guide to the museum, and she had selected Turkish on it.

He put the earphones on and pressed the play button.

Curiously, it seemed to come alive at specific times, referring to whatever exhibit he was standing in front of, the first of which was the Feldherrnhalle—the Hall of Fame.

The space was magnificent, a forest of gloriously decorated columns arrayed in clusters of four that soared to a series of gilded rib vaults. Four life-size marble statues nestled around each set of columns, fifty-six in all, depicting almost a millennium's worth of Austria's most famous warlords and military heroes, their names carved into plates mounted above each statue.

It was there that Kamal got his first jolt.

For there, perched on his podium and staring down at him, was Count Ernst Rüdiger von Starhemberg.

The statue was remarkably lifelike. Better than lifelike, for it depicted a healthy Starhemberg, not the dysentery-racked and injured survivor Kamal had met during the siege.

Kamal stood there, unable to look away as a horde of images and sensations stampeded through him. He edged right up to the statue, hesitantly, as if scared that he might somehow wake Starhemberg up. Seeing the statue took him right back to that fraught meeting in the debris-strewn room. It also reignited painful memories of Nisreen, not alive and vibrant, but dead in Rasheed's wretched tent.

When he was finally able to tear himself away, he recognized another of the men immortalized in marble. The man, then much younger, had been at the meeting with Sobieski outside Tulln. The audio guide told him in was Prince Eugene of Savoy, who, after playing a supporting role in liberating

Vienna, Kamal learned, had gone on to become one of Austria's most celebrated war heroes.

Kamal left the Hall of Fame and ventured deeper into the museum. As the chef had told him, the halls devoted to the Ottoman campaigns were substantial. Huge arrays of weapons were on display, from recurve bows to all kinds of swords to muskets, cannon and mortars. One hall contained a vast collection of suits of armour and helmets alongside statues of musketeers and pikemen that were eerily lifelike. There was even a great tent on show, one of the Ottoman dignitaries', given its richly detailed fabric; next to it, a display case housed the captured horsetails of the enemy's commanders.

Walking through the halls, Kamal learned that there had been many further wars against the Ottomans after the rescue of Vienna: Zenta in 1697, Peterwardein in 1716, Belgrade in 1717. The Turks had been pushed all the way back to Constantinople, but the great Byzantine capital had never even come close to being liberated.

The scale of it all, however, was unsettling. There were still many halls to explore, but he'd finished walking through the ones devoted to the Ottoman wars. What else was there?

A feeling of deep unease rose inside him.

The first jolt happened when he stopped in front of a curious exhibit, one that seemed out of place in a museum of military history. It was a classic car, a huge black convertible limo, very old, even older than the cars he'd seen in Paris during that first fateful jump he did with Nisreen.

He stepped closer to allow the audio guide to explain.

He learned that it was a Gräf & Stift motorcar that Archduke Franz Ferdinand had been travelling in when he was assassinated in Sarajevo in 1914.

The guide then went on to explain that this was the event that triggered the outbreak of the First World War.

A bolt of dread shot through him.

World war?

The *first* world war?

Meaning there were others?

His veins throbbing, he sat patiently through the guide's entire presentation, his heart sinking with each word. When it was over, he staggered into the next room, which only made things worse. It chronicled, in unflinching, gory detail, the fall of the Habsburg monarchy and the First World War.

The next hall was even worse.

It was an entire wing dedicated to the Anschluss and the rise of the Nazis.

It wasn't the displays of weapons that shocked him, not the huge siege howitzers or the tanks from different nations displayed in the Panzergarten outside the museum. It was the unending collection of dizzying films and photographs displayed on flat screens.

Kamal felt as if he'd been pummelled.

He left the museum in a daze and walked around, unsure about what to do. All he knew was that he needed to know more.

Once he did, he regretted it.

He managed to find an Internet café and began catching up on what had happened in the intervening centuries—no easy task, since he discovered that the Turkish language was no longer written using the Turko-Persian script he had always used. It was now written in Latin script. But once he found the right website, the information was debilitating.

There had been many, many wars in the years since Vienna had been saved. Wars that hadn't happened in his world, after the Ottoman conquest of Europe.

There had been countless conflicts pitting one European

nation against another. There had been bloody revolutions in many countries, notably in France, America and, most disastrously, Russia. The subsequent rise of communism had brought on a whole new onslaught of death and suffering. In Ukraine alone, four million people had died in the early 1930s as a result of Stalin's campaign to crush its people's nationalist aspirations. Deaths under communism were even higher in China and Cambodia.

The Great Terror and the purges. Two world wars. The Holocaust. The Armenian genocide. Vietnam. Nuclear bombs—he had to look up what they were—in Japan.

He felt numb as the number of deaths just kept rising. How many had died since he buried Nisreen? Fifty million? A hundred million? More?

It was staggering, and it left Kamal almost unable to breathe.

He reeled with regret and a hollowness that wanted to suck him into it and wipe him off the face of the earth.

One question battered him repeatedly: Had he made a gargantuan and unspeakably tragic mistake?

He knew the Ottoman campaign to conquer Europe hadn't been without bloodshed. Many had died as the sultan's army had swept across the continent. The war with Russia decades later had also been bloody, and everyone knew that a war with the Americans, especially given the sparring over energy, was certainly a possibility. But it didn't lessen the sense of horror Kamal felt at what had befallen the planet in this timeline, after the Ottomans had failed to take Vienna.

And it was all his fault.

78

He spent the night wandering the city aimlessly, unable to sleep, stopping occasionally to rest before moving on, not really registering anything, just lost inside his own thoughts, haunted by a crushing sense of guilt.

At one point, as if guided by some cruel, twisted hand, he found himself waiting to cross the street at a corner, and his tired eyes latched on to a word on a street sign affixed on to the side of a building: KOLSCHITZKYGASSE.

Kolschitzky Street.

He stood there, foggy-brained, as the word sunk in. Then his eyes floated upward to find something else: a large statue, at first-floor level, mounted on a plinth that projected from the corner of the building.

It was Kolschitzky. He was dressed in Ottoman garb and held a coffee pot in one hand and a tray in the other. The pose depicted him standing tall while pouring coffee into a small cup with an assortment of swords, battle-axes and shields by his feet, presumably in commemoration of his heroic role in saving the city.

The sight only served to deepen his anguish.

As he drifted through the city, he began to wonder whether he should fix his mistake by going back and trying to undo what he did. His thoughts accelerated, running through different scenarios, desperately playing out the ramifications of each.

He could go back, of course. But to what date? He couldn't go back to any time that he and Nisreen had already gone to. Would he go back to the early days of the siege? To when

Taymoor had arrived, perhaps even get there before him? Or go to Istanbul even earlier and find Rasheed there? What would he do there? Warn him? Tell him that he and Nisreen were coming for him in the future? Could he even think of doing that, of betraying her that way? Or would it change everything if he did? Would Rasheed alter his plans in some way and change the future timeline so that Kamal and Nisreen never met or even never existed?

It was all too mind-boggling to think about, and, in his exhausted state, it sent him deeper and deeper into despair. He found it impossible to escape the dark thoughts he was drowning in.

Thoughts of suicide even crept into his mind.

It was many hours before he found himself in familiar territory again.

The Naschmarkt was busy, but the crowd was thinning in tandem with the sun's imminent curtain call. There were a couple of customers at the kebab stall, but as soon as Orhan saw him, his jovial expression faded and turned to concern. He still managed a warm smile and waved him over.

Orhan offered Kamal another meal and joined him at a small table while the stall enjoyed a lull before the evening rush. Alternating sips from a cup of coffee with pulls from a cigarette, he watched Kamal curiously as his new friend picked at the food.

'What's wrong, brother?' he asked him. 'You look like the sky's fallen on top of you.'

Kamal shrugged. 'It feels that way.'

Orhan looked at him pensively. 'It'll get better; you'll see. Life is good here. Much better than back home. You'll be glad you came here.'

Kamal appreciated the sentiment, but he knew that Orhan obviously had no idea what was really going through his mind. 'I thought I would,' he said, his voice feeble. 'I'm not so sure any more. Maybe my world, for all its faults, was . . . better.'

'No,' Orhan said. 'It wasn't. Believe me.'

Kamal looked away, taking in the expansive rows of stalls spreading out in all directions, but didn't reply.

Orhan leaned in and pressed on. 'Listen to me, Kamal. Our world . . . it's still got a long way to go. And that's if it ever gets there.'

'Gets where?'

'Here.' He indicated the world around him with his arms. 'To everything you see around you.'

He took a deep drag of his cigarette, then squashed it into a tin ashtray. 'This part of the world,' he told Kamal, 'they've had their wars. They've had their revolutions. They've fought to abolish monarchy and slavery, to separate government from religion. They've fought for their freedom. And they've paid heavily for it. Millions have died fighting for freedom. Which is why they know its value. Life here has a value.' His tone was insistent. 'A person has rights. We have rights. All of us. Me, him, her,' he said, pointing at random people wandering through the market. 'We're all equal. Rich or poor—it doesn't matter. Whether your great-grandfather was born here or you're fresh off the boat like me . . . everyone's freedom and dignity is respected—and defended. Maybe not always. Maybe not by everyone. It's not perfect . . . but it's much better than anything we have. That's why I'm here. Where we come from . . . our part of the world . . . they're still way behind. They're still going through their wars and their revolutions, and right now life there is worthless. A soldier can drag you out of your bed and make you disappear, and no one can do anything about it. A thousand people can be gassed to death in a village, and no one can stop it. And who knows? Maybe they'll never get there. Maybe they'll stick to their tribal ways for ever. Either way, it doesn't matter to me. I'll be long gone by then.' He chuckled. His eyes took on a faraway look. 'I had a good business in Istanbul, you know. I had a restaurant and a small shop. We were doing okay. But the country was changing. So I left. But even with nothing but this little stall, it's still a much better life here. You'll see.'

'How was it changing?' Kamal asked.

'Years ago, we were different from our Arab neighbours. Right? We were. We were a democracy. A real one. We had a free press. Religion and government were kept well apart. We were the modern, civilized bridge between the West and the Middle East; we were on our way to joining the European Union. Then we elected a man who thought the country was his personal empire and locked up anyone who dared to disagree. That's when I left. When it got ugly.'

Rasheed's dismissive tirade in the tent outside Vienna reverberated inside him. 'He was elected?' Kamal caught himself halfway through the question and adjusted his tone so that it didn't sound as much as a question as it did a statement.

Orhan snorted. 'Of course. It was just a means to an end. Have you forgotten that famous speech of his many years ago? "Democracy is like a train. You get off once you've reached your destination". But no one paid attention. People never do until it's too late.' He sighed. 'Elections aren't perfect. Far from it. And as we see more and more—even in America, right?— they can be manipulated. Even before social media. That monster in Russia, he's been elected—"elected"'—he clarified, using air quotes—'president how many times now? In Syria, the president officially wins elections with ninety-seven per cent of the vote. They actually announce that on their local news. Not an ounce of shame . . .' He shook his head. 'But real elections—fair, open elections, with many parties and real opposition and a real exchange of ideas, a real debate about how to live . . . what could possibly be better?'

'But the cost of this freedom . . . all those wars,' Kamal said, gauging his words carefully, Rasheed's mocking words still echoing in his ears. 'What if they could have been avoided somehow?'

'How?'

'What if one empire had conquered—I don't know, all of Europe—centuries ago. The Ottomans even. Imagine if they had been able to.'

'They came close,' Orhan mused. 'They almost took this city.'

'Well, imagine they had,' Kamal countered. 'Imagine they'd gone on and conquered all of Europe. Maybe if they had, there wouldn't have been all those revolutions and world wars. Maybe it would have been better.'

Orhan laughed. 'What have you been putting in your *shisha*, brother?' He waved it off dismissively. 'Better? Not a chance.'

'Why not?'

'Who knows how history would have evolved. But listen to me, brother. Living under a dictator—because the sultan was a dictator, make no mistake about that—can never be better than living in a free society. Never. And I can assure you of two things. A dictator, whether it's a sultan or a president who only believes in democracy as a train ride, a way to grab power—they'll never give up power on their own. Never. Which means that sooner or later, no matter how strongly a dictator controls his people . . . sooner or later, they will rise up. They will be fed up with corruption, they will want freedom, they will want to be heard, and they will

552

inevitably have to die for it. It's human nature. It's happened all around the world. It would happen in your glorious Ottoman Empire too—you can be sure of it.'

Kamal nodded sombrely. It all seemed like a hopeless, endless cycle of pain and suffering. Orhan's words had resuscitated all the turmoil of his life in Paris and brought it rushing back into his mind with frightening clarity. All the upheavals, all the arguments and debates he'd had over his last few years there with Ramazan and Nisreen. All the hurt.

Orhan was right. The fuse had undoubtedly been lit. A big war had been brewing. And when it happened, when the people rose up for freedom, there was no telling how bloody it would have been, or how it would have ended.

Or how it would have affected Nisreen, Ramazan and the children, or him.

Kamal thought back to Nisreen, to the passion that had been driving her, and to the freedom she had always championed. It was an ongoing struggle, he realized. And, he was starting to understand, he was now in a time and a place where a lot of that struggle had already played itself out.

In that moment, he wondered how Nisreen would feel if she had been there with him, sitting next to him outside Orhan's stall, and couldn't help but feel that she would be profoundly pleased with what she saw.

The thought brought a bittersweet warmth to his face.

'Someone—I think it was Winston Churchill,' Orhan continued, 'once said, "Democracy is the worst form of government, except for all the others." Which I totally agree with. But the people in our part of the world, and in many others . . . they're not there yet. They love living under their tyrants. A lot of them believe it brings stability. Like in Iraq and Syria and Libya, before the mess. Maybe it did. But that's backward thinking. It was never going to last. People can now see how other nations live, and want it for themselves,' he said as he indicated the city around him, 'while others still don't want to live this way. And until they all get there, there will be bloodshed. Which is why I'm here. I know what life I want.' He spread his hands out at the city around him. 'Isn't that also why you left?'

'I suppose so,' Kamal said.

'You'll see,' Orhan told him, a comforting smile suffusing his face. 'I'm not saying it's going to be easy. You'll have to work hard. And some of it will be a struggle. There are dark forces at play. Racism is rising. Xenophobes are gaining power. But, for now at least, life here is still better. Because despite everything that's happening, your dignity and your rights as a human being will be more respected than back home. And believe me, once you taste that, you won't be able to believe you ever lived without it.'

Kamal smiled back at his host.

Perhaps he was right. Perhaps Nisreen had been right all long.

This was a better world.

And right then, right at that moment, a stunning realization breezed through him, a spectacular, unexpected thought that lit up every cell in his body.

It was a better world, yes.

But perhaps he could make it even better.

Epilogue

Palmyra
November, AD 2010

Kamal had an open book when it came to deciding when to make his visit to the ancient city.

As with everything he did, he chose to go back to a time as reasonably close to the relevant event as possible, to minimize any unintended disruptions that his jump might create.

In this case, he knew the uprising's first stirrings were the protests that began in early 2011. The day that was considered the beginning of the Syrian civil war was 15 March, the 'Day of Rage'. It had followed the torture and murder of a thirteen-year-old boy who had scribbled some anti-government graffiti on a wall. Furious protesters in Damascus had thronged the streets, demanding political reforms and the release of thousands of political prisoners. The fuse had been lit.

Before then, however, Syria was a relatively safe place—provided one didn't anger its tyrant president or his gang of crony-thugs. And when Kamal landed at the Damascus airport, the government was in the thick of a major PR campaign promoting Syria across the world as a charming tourist destination. One of their core messages was about how it was the cradle of Christianity, how welcoming it was, how visitors could actually follow in the footsteps of St Paul and walk the fabled road to Damascus.

Kamal had already had his epiphany.

He was more interested in the road to Palmyra.

He'd only be spending one night in the capital. He had already booked a car to drive him to Palmyra early the next morning. It would be a long drive—three hours, he'd been told, as the road was narrow, a single lane in each direction.

Which it turned out to be.

The desert soon bowed to man's ingenuity, pushed back by olive and palm tree orchards and cotton and grain plantations. Then the glorious ruins of the ancient city appeared in the distance. And by the time his chauffeured Mercedes pulled up outside the city's museum of antiquities, Kamal could see that the government's message was working.

Palmyra was throbbing with visitors. All around him, tour buses were disgorging groups of excited visitors who'd made the journey from around the world, with good reason. The 'Bride of the Desert' was breathtakingly epic. Famous for its majestic architecture, colonnaded streets and distinctive tower tombs, it had been inhabited for over four millennia. Romans, Greeks, Parthians and Sassanids all had their day in shaping it, building temples and palaces, the ruins of which still stood at the time Kamal was visiting. Palmyra was now a World Heritage site, its history as a melting pot of Western and Eastern cultures as important a symbol of historical harmony as it was of Syrian diversity.

If only they knew what was coming, Kamal thought as he stepped out of the car. The ancient city would soon become more of a testament to the fragility—and savagery—of civilization.

He'd booked an appointment with the museum's director of antiquities, claiming to represent a wealthy German patron who wished to help fund the ongoing archaeological work.

The director, Kamal discovered, had been looking after the city and its heritage for more than fifty years. Now in his early seventies, he was a one-man powerhouse, managing the museum, presiding over excavations and restorations, raising funds and assisting scholars who journeyed there from around the world. He was more than the pre-eminent expert on the ancient metropolis's rich history. He was its protector.

And he would soon be dead, Kamal knew. Shot in the face by an ISIS commander of Iraqi origin called Ayman Rasheed.

But not if he could help it.

He was received graciously by the director, who offered him freshly made mint lemonade before giving him a tour of the museum. The man had an amiable, gentle air about him, a scholar who worshipped at the altar of knowledge and history and adored his city.

Which meant that what Kamal was about to tell him would be even more painful to hear.

They were a couple of hours into their encounter and walking around the remains of the Temple of Nabo when Kamal decided that it was time to say what he had travelled across time to say.

'Forgive me, director, but . . . I need to talk to you about why I am really here.'

The director's face clouded. 'Why you're really here?'

Kamal nodded, then, in as casual a tone as he could muster, he said, 'I know about what you found. In the crypt, carved on to a wall.'

He waited to give his words time to sink in, then, seeing hesitation and fear in the director's eyes, he pulled up the sleeve of his shirt, exposing the tattooed incantation.

The director sucked in a shocked breath, and his eyes shot wide. He studied the words on Kamal's arm, then looked up at him.

'How do you know this?' he stammered. 'Who are you?'

'It's a long story, and I think it's best I don't burden you with it.'

'But you've used it? You've been . . . *travelling*?'

Kamal nodded. 'Yes. A lot.'

Travelling. And learning. Kamal had spent hours upon hours studying the strange new world he had helped create—or, rather, re-create. Trying to understand it.

Deciding what he would do next.

Throughout, he thought of Nisreen. Her words, about how no man should decide for all others, ricocheted in his mind continuously. The idea was, after all, what had pushed them to reset the clock of history, to put the world back on to its natural course. But she didn't know the full story. She didn't know about all the horrors the world had endured in the centuries that followed Vienna and the extreme evil it had suffered.

If she had, he was sure that she would have changed her mind.

No decent man or woman could sit back and allow it to happen.

The director's mouth fell open again. He was having trouble formulating his words.

'Into the past? The future?' he asked.

'Both.'

'My God!' the director gasped. His legs went weak, and he took a few steps to a fallen column and sat down on it.

'I take it you haven't?' Kamal asked him.

'I used it once, after I first discovered it. I went back. It terrified me too much to try it again. So I never did.'

Kamal shrugged. 'A wise choice, I would say.'

'But you've been using it?'

'Not by choice,' Kamal told him.

'Is that why you're here?'

'Yes. There's something you need to know,' Kamal said, his tone even. 'I need you to listen to me very carefully.'

The director nodded.

'There's a war coming. It's coming here, to your country, and to your beloved Palmyra. And it's going to be bad. Very, very bad.'

'When?' the director asked.

'Soon. Within months. You'll think it's hopeful at first. You'll think it'll lead to better things. It won't.'

'The Arab Spring . . . it's coming here, too?'

Mass uprisings had already happened in Tunisia, Libya and Egypt. Syria would be next, only the uprising there would turn into a massive civil war that would suck in foreign powers and cause hundreds of thousands of deaths and millions of dispossessed refugees.

'Think of it more like an Arab winter. It's going to be a disaster.'

'Why are you telling me this?'

'A man is going to come here. A brutal man. He's going to make you tell him what you know about this,' he said, pointing at the tattoos on his arm. 'Then he's going to kill you and do terrible things with the knowledge you give him.'

The director's eyes receded into themselves, sucked into black holes of gloom. 'What should I do?'

'As soon as the troubles start, you must do two things. Destroy the crypt where you found this. And leave.'

'Leave?'

'Leave Palmyra. Take whatever treasures you want—hide them, bury them—then leave. If you stay, you will be killed. I can assure you of that. The men coming here are not fans of history. Not this history,' he added, gesturing at the glorious ruins around them.

The director just sat there, shaking his head slowly, lamenting the stranger's news.

'Can I count on you to do that?' Kamal asked.

It was a question that had weighed heavily on his mind. Could he, in fact, trust the man to do as he asked? Could he risk leaving someone else in the world who knew what he knew, who could use that knowledge to change things himself?

Or should he use a more permanent way to neutralize that risk?

The idea had been swiftly strangled before it even caught its first breath. The director was an innocent, decent, well-meaning man, and Kamal was no cold-blooded killer. And now, after meeting him, Kamal felt confident that he could, indeed, count on him to do as he asked.

The director, as if reading Kamal's internal deliberations, nodded. 'I don't really have a choice, do I?'

'Not if you want to live. And not if you want what's best for the world.'

He nodded again. 'I'll do as you ask.'

'Thank you,' Kamal said, and held out his hand.

The director stood up and shook it.

Kamal held his gaze. 'Good luck.'

He began to walk away when the director called out after him. 'What about you? What are you going to do?'

Kamal stopped, then turned, remembering the exact moment the realization had struck him at Orhan's stall in Vienna, the realization that would guide the rest of his life from that moment onward.

'I've got work to do,' he told the director.

He gave him a small, pensive nod, then he turned and walked away.

End Note and Acknowledgements

For as long as I can remember, I've been drawn to time travel in books, movies and TV. It wasn't long before this interest was joined by my love of alternate reality stories. So you can imagine my delight when the idea for a book that combined both ambushed me late one summer's night. Researching and writing it was going to be a lot of fun; that much was obvious from the start. But what made it irresistible to me was that it would be—it *had* to be—an unusual mirror to the times we live in—unsettling, troubled times. Because these last few years, no matter where I look, it feels like we're spiralling down an ever-darkening episode of *Black Mirror*.

A lot of the disturbing stuff that's happening in Kamal's world is happening in our world. Truth and freedom of speech are under threat across the globe. The Social Credit System is a reality in China. Article 275 of the criminal code, which deals with treason, is a reality in Russia, as was the Z Directorate, now part of the post-KGB SVR. The Comprehensive National—not Imperial—Cybersecurity Initiative Data Centre is a huge NSA data storage facility located in Utah. The Insider Threat Program, which deals with whistleblowers, is up and running in the US. Other winks at our world and at our history are peppered throughout the book, in names of characters, places and organizations, and in events—but I'll leave it to you to have fun digging them up if you're so inclined.

Most of the history you'll read here is true. The horrendous siege of Vienna, and all the names and events associated with it (apart from my time travellers' interference), is faithfully depicted. The statue of Kolschitzky, commemorating the debatable story of his bringing coffee to Vienna, hangs there above the street that bears his name. ISIS was indeed born in the prison camps of Iraq, after the 2003 invasion. Its raiders did capture Palmyra and execute the director of the ancient city's museum. Kara Mustafa was executed under the Sultan's orders on Christmas Day, 1683.

Researching this book was truly a blast, but the most challenging part was trying to picture what the Ottoman Empire might look like in the 21st century. It was difficult because I couldn't simply extrapolate forward from its last days, when it collapsed at the end of the First World War. I had to start much further back—in 1683—and project forward from there. This was simply because the failure in Vienna was the beginning of the Ottoman Empire's decline, and although it did last another two and a half centuries before it finally died out, its evolution over those centuries was very much informed by the Ottomans' efforts to catch up with a Europe that was charging ahead with the Enlightenment and the Industrial Revolution, not to mention a major revolution or two. In Kamal's world, none of these took place, which meant I needed to imagine how 300 years of history might have evolved in a vacuum with none of those seismic events to shape it. I hope you find it to be a credible take on how that might have unfolded.

The other challenge in the research was figuring out how Ayman Rasheed could plausibly lead the Ottomans to not just conquer the rest of Europe, but hold it—and hang on to it for more than two centuries. Again, I hope I managed to do a convincing job. I would have loved to include all the fruit of my research on all those fronts, but that might have undermined the page-turning experience I was aiming for.

A lot of people helped me along this journey—friends,

experts, and colleagues who helped me through brainstorming or sharing their knowledge of all things Ottoman with me. I'm grateful to them all, but, specifically, I'd like to single out my agents Mitch Hoffman and Eugenie Furniss, the high priest and priestess of perseverance; my editors and friends at Michael Joseph in London: Rowland White, Ariel Pakier, and Sarah Kennedy; and their equally stellar counterparts at Tor/Forge in NYC: Bess Cozby, Devi Pillai, Linda Quinton, and Lucille Rettino.

Last, but far from least, I'd like to thank everyone who worked on this book in sales, marketing and publicity at Michael Joseph and at Tor/Forge for all their hard work in getting this book on the shelves and on your attention radar. I'd also like to thank all the booksellers who welcomed it into their stores and championed it with their customers. In our Facebook/Instagram/Netflix/Fortnite-consumed times, neither one sounds like an easy task. My thanks again to you all.

He just wanted a decent book to read ...

Not too much to ask, is it? It was in 1935 when Allen Lane, Managing Director of Bodley Head Publishers, stood on a platform at Exeter railway station looking for something good to read on his journey back to London. His choice was limited to popular magazines and poor-quality paperbacks – the same choice faced every day by the vast majority of readers, few of whom could afford hardbacks. Lane's disappointment and subsequent anger at the range of books generally available led him to found a company – and change the world.

'We believed in the existence in this country of a vast reading public for intelligent books at a low price, and staked everything on it'
Sir Allen Lane, 1902–1970, founder of Penguin Books

The quality paperback had arrived – and not just in bookshops. Lane was adamant that his Penguins should appear in chain stores and tobacconists, and should cost no more than a packet of cigarettes.

Reading habits (and cigarette prices) have changed since 1935, but Penguin still believes in publishing the best books for everybody to enjoy. We still believe that good design costs no more than bad design, and we still believe that quality books published passionately and responsibly make the world a better place.

So wherever you see the little bird – whether it's on a piece of prize-winning literary fiction or a celebrity autobiography, political tour de force or historical masterpiece, a serial-killer thriller, reference book, world classic or a piece of pure escapism – you can bet that it represents the very best that the genre has to offer.

Whatever you like to read – trust Penguin.